Family
~
First

Sbrina xoxo

Authored by Sbrina

©glenese facey2020

Cover Design: Marcia M Publishing House
Edited by Marcia M Publishing House Editorial Team, D Spence-
Lewis, Aisha Otiti & Susan Brookes.

Published by Marcia M Spence of Marcia M Publishing House,
West Bromwich, West Midlands the UNITED KINGDOM B71 1JB

All rights reserved 2020 Marcia M Publishing House.

FICTION

The author asserts the moral right to be identified as the author of this work of fiction. The
names and characters are created by the author any similarity to real life events are
coincidental.

MARCIA M
PUBLISHING HOUSE

www.marciampublishing.com

Acknowledgements

Thanks to my family for your patience, unconditional support and love you've shown me over the years, even when I didn't deserve it.

Thanks to both my son's Jayden and Jerimiah and my nieces you have no idea how much you have changed my life, you can count on me to be there whenever you need me, remember you can be anything you want to be.

To Sharlene, my cousin, thank you for bringing books back into my life, giving me that book back when was the start of rekindling my love of reading bringing me to this point in my life, for that, I thank you this once for you. Ex-factor still my favourite book, no clue who the author is whoever you are; I appreciate you also.

To my sister Tiffeny, I want to thank you most of all; you have no idea how much love I have for you and what I feel for you. Girl words can't express the love I have for you. I want to thank you for putting up with me and having my back all these years and never leaving me behind no matter what, one day I'm going to repay you for everything you have done for me tenfold. I love you, sis.

Mr Hussein Thomas, you saw me through my worst and now you're getting the best of me. Thank you for always being there for me and encouraging me in the best way possible. Love you unconditionally always thank you, keep being you and we will be the true example of love.

To the team at Marcia M Publishing House, I thank you for helping me bring my craft to life.

To the ladies of H.M.P keep your head up, freedom is a must.

Your imagination is your greatest weapon, use it.

"A successful multi-millionaire, a third of triplets, leader of a community, good looks and a big, never you mind. With a knack for business and an keen sense for the stock market. What more can a brother want! You'd think a man who has everything and gets anything would be living larger than life. You would think a man with so much money would be happy but... No, I have to have two sisters with my face trying to kill each other whilst on vacation, no less. And a motor mouth grandmother, from Jamaica is all I'm saying, so you already know what I'm dealing with. The drama I'm facing right now, I'm going to need another vacation."

Storm

Prologue
The Love of Catherine

Catherine

When I got pregnant, I felt blessed. Even though it was not part of the plan, I just knew things were going to be perfect. God had answered my prayer in some way. I had asked him to always make Jacob a part of my life and continue blessing me like he had. I was in love; I'd just moved into my new two-bedroomed apartment; everything was perfect. Then in one great swoop, everything came crashing down on me. Unknown to me at the time, Jacob was already married with a family. So, what was supposed to be good news, became the worst possible news of the century. He told me to get rid of it. Told me, I couldn't keep my baby; our baby, because he already has a family. His wife wouldn't approve, and she'd think I was trying to break up their family. Their family! What about my family?

He gave me the money for the abortion, and no matter how much I begged and pleaded with this man that I loved, his mind was made up. This was not what he wanted; he loved his family. He'd made a lot of promises to me, that he had no intention of keeping.

When I told him, I was pregnant; he started confessing all his sins. I cried and cried, but forgave him; he was my world, my joy, my everything. I believed if I forgave him and gave him time, he would come around, but he didn't. He just left. He left me with my tears and the cash for an abortion. I cried for what seemed like forever. I just couldn't imagine life without Jacob. We'd spent the past three years together. I'd never suspected him of cheating on me, never mind him hiding an entire family. What was I going to do now? After weeks of unanswered phone calls, begging, crying, and leaving pleading voice messages, I began to lose faith. At three months pregnant, I was beginning to show. Mostly I told people I was bloated, in the hope that he would change his mind.

I woke up one Thursday morning with my mind made up; ready to start again, start life without Jacob. So, I booked the appointment with the abortion clinic. However, my growing offspring had other plans. There seemed to be more movement in my tummy that day than any other day of my entire pregnancy. It felt like a million and one butterflies were having a party inside my stomach. When I got to the clinic gate, the butterflies sped up. So, I turned around and headed back home with a new outlook on life.

Instead, I booked my appointment with the antenatal clinic. When I saw the life growing inside me on the scan monitor, I was overwhelmed with joy because I could see that God had blessed me with twins. It was like the little ones were sending me a message begging for their tiny lives. In the early hours of the night, February 14, not only did I get the shock of my life, but the doctor's got a surprise too. The heart monitor had only shown two hearts beating for the past nine months. My breath became shallow; I felt like I was suffocating.

"Push Catherine," Dr Jeff said as he looked up at my blood-stained thighs. "Ok here comes another contraction, now push," he said sternly. I gave it my all and out came what looked like a tiny pink blob. The baby wasn't making a sound. The nurse took the baby and carried it off to God knows where.

"What's wrong with my baby?" I asked anxiously, but no one spoke up, and the pain started all over again.

"Ok Catherine, you did well, you have a few seconds before the next contraction starts. Now! One more time, let's meet your other baby. Ready?" the doctor asked.,

"No, I can't, I'm tired!" I said, I was exhausted and wanted to find out about my first baby.

"Yes, you can, Catherine, you can do this. Now just like before, push," he urged.

I screamed in agony, as I looked to the ceiling, I fell into a disturbing daze. I had never felt so much pain before.

"Push Catherine!" I heard the doctor scream at me.

"I am pushing!" I yelled at him through gritted teeth.

Let's see him try to push two human beings through his ass and see how he likes it. One last push and out came the other one. I was so relieved. The nurse took the baby away again after the umbilical cord was severed from me. All the monitors around me started blaring, and the babies weren't making a sound, I was worried. When both my babies were born, and the pressure and pain returned, I knew something was wrong. My blood pressure dropped, and my heart rate sped up dramatically, I went into shock. More contractions were coming on.

"Dr! I don't feel so good, it's happening again," I told them in panic. Doctors and nurses flooded the room to ensure my survival. All the while, I had no idea what was wrong with my babies. They were all frantically trying to monitor my vitals.

The doctor started examining me and to his shock and according to him, a medical mystery he told me:

"Miss Valentine, you're going to have to push again, it seems we've made a mistake."

"What?" the machines started going off again, uncontrollably.

They had discovered another baby in the breech position. The baby's heartbeat was faint, so faint that the monitor couldn't even pick it up, so I was rushed into surgery for a C-section. By this time, I had passed out from exhaustion, I was unaware of the surprise that was awaiting me. The children were born on the morning of love; Valentine's Day. As each child was born, the weather outside was going crazy, as if shifting from one season to the next. It was phenomenal, even for British weather. You could feel the crisp cool breeze in the air, and there was snow still lingering on the ground covering the trees like a warm blanket. It was like God was speaking. When I woke and saw the three most beautiful babies next to me in their cribs, my heart was filled with joy and peace, along with confusion.

"Excuse me! Excuse me! Nurse! Can someone hand me, my babies?" I asked.

The nurse came over and rolled the crib closer to me with a bright smile.

"It was touch and go there for a while, I'm glad you made it. Here you go," she said with glee in her voice. She handed me the two baby girls wrapped up in pink, I was overcome with happiness and love for my babies. I felt so much joy. As the nurse reached for the other baby wrapped up in blue, I instantly asked,

"Nurse whose baby is that?"

"Yours ma'am! And isn't he wonderful?" she looked confused at the question I had just asked.

"I don't understand. I gave birth to twins." I was so filled with drugs; I'd forgotten what had happened before I passed out.

"No! Unfortunately, there were some complications. I'll let the Doctor explain," she said.

"Can I see him?"

"Sure," she handed the baby to me and went to fetch the doctor.

Looking at the beautiful baby boy with sea bluish-green eyes, I fell in love. I knew he was mine for life; I knew that he would never forsake me or leave me like his father did.

The doctor came after an hour and apologised for the confusion and explained that the beautiful baby boy I now held in my arms, was indeed mine. He was a miracle. He explained that the baby was in a difficult position and how he'd had to perform an emergency caesarean to save both mine and the baby boys life. He explained the surprise and the uniqueness of my babies. How they all started crying once the third baby came along. All three cried in unison and that it appeared they were waiting for him to arrive. I barely heard what he was saying. I was in awe of this baby. He apologised for the confusion I must be feeling since I was only prepared for twins and got triplets. They couldn't explain why the monitor didn't pick up the third heartbeat but assured me that everything would be fine and answered all my generic questions about the baby.

The doctor placed the twin girls in my hands, positioning them so I could hold all three, they were so tiny. I, the new mother, was left to be alone with my children. As I gazed down on my sweet innocent bundles of joy, I vowed to never let anyone, or anything make my children feel alone in this world. I couldn't help but remember the past couple of months and how I had got to this day.

It was 1989, and it had been shaping up to be the greatest year thus far. It had been a little over two years since Professor Edwards and I had started dating. Our secret affair was an exciting one, and now that I was graduating, we could finally be together in public. There'd be no more hiding, no more late-night rendezvous; no more stolen glances and secret meetings. I was happy. We could put our lives on track and be a real couple. I could be the lady he was proud to call his own. Finally, I could shout it from the rooftops without a care in the world because I no longer attended the university. I was free; we were free to be together at last. Things were finally looking up; I got my degree with honours in Event Management and Promotions. I got the promotion at work that I wanted and was now the catering events manager of Dine in Style agency and I was in love.

I had saved all my money from my job and lived in near squalor until I had enough to put a down payment on my first mortgage. Jacob had volunteered to help me search for apartments. We must have visited all the estate agents in the surrounding area until we found one that fitted my budget. We found a cute two-bedroomed apartment that suited me perfectly, close to the city centre.

Everything was going perfectly. Everything was going to plan. Until I found out I was pregnant. I was scared yet excited because I'd just started my new life and had no space for distraction, but with Jacob by my side, I was sure we could make it work, I was sure I was going to become Mrs Jacob Edwards, but I had to be certain of the pregnancy first. I bought at least five different tests before I booked the appointment with the doctor. I'd missed taking the pill once a couple of weeks before when I was sick and running a high temperature. Jacob came over to take care of me; he was so sweet, kind, and gentle, simply perfect. I couldn't have asked for a more perfect gentleman. He made love to me; he attended to my every need.

I was in heaven, sickly heaven, but heaven, nonetheless. So, when I missed my period, I wasn't surprised. I just needed to confirm it before revealing it all to my beloved.

One June morning, I was up bright and early, ready to take on the world and headed to my appointment. Even though I'd taken five tests, I wanted professional confirmation. So, when the doctor confirmed my belief, I simply smiled and thanked her and walked out with the biggest grin on my face, that could be seen from the moon. I was so happy. The nerves kept on building up to the point of me telling Jacob.

I wanted to wait until my six-week check so he could attend with me. I wanted to enjoy my secret bundle of joy just a bit longer, plus I had a few things to figure out. Even though things seemed great, I still had to make sure this was something I wanted and was ready for. The more I thought about it, the more I became nervous and terrified. Over the next couple of weeks, I felt out Jacob to see where his head was at. What were his thoughts about children? How did he envision our future, did he even see a future with me?

Jacob was a tall, well-educated white man with salt and pepper hair, deep blue eyes that washed over me and took me to another place. He always looks sharp in his suits and captures everyone's attention when he walks into a room. The day I told Jacob was supposed to be another great day, one that marked a turning point in my life. I was ready to go the distance for life with this man and our unborn child. So, when I told him, and I saw the blood drain from his entire face and the look of disgust that he gave me; my world began to unravel.

Then came the words I never thought I would ever hear come out of the love of my life's mouth. So, I did what any self-respecting strong independent woman in love does. I begged and cried and became a powerless pathetic pool of a mess.

So now my babies are here, I will never subject them to ever feel like that, because God, Buddha, Allah or whoever, whatever God was out there was smiling down or up, whichever way, blessing me. They not only blessed me with twin girls, but they blessed me with a beautiful handsome son. I was highly blessed. I will never need a man again because now I had one of my own and I know he will never forsake me the way his father has.

And It Begins
Winter's Coming

Winter

"**F**uck!"

I'm purring like a kitten, getting her stomach stroked, as I lay bare with my legs spread wide like an eagle on the store's reception desk, with a beautiful bald head between my thighs devouring me. Lapping up every drop of sweet nectar from my honeysuckle. My head tilts back as I reach the climax I had waited for. The evening is turning out to be wonderful considering the awful day I'd been having. Since this afternoon, my mood had just shifted like something awful was coming my way, a sort of sadness that I just can't explain. Since I don't have anything to feel some type of way or depressed about, I know it has something to do with one of my siblings.

I can always tell when something is wrong with my brother or sister. I get this gut feeling and boy, today is one of those days. Already having checked in with them, I know that someone is lying.

"Suck it harder," I moan, trying to concentrate on what is happening to me and distract myself from the gut-wrenching sadness coursing through me.

I'm about to blow a hard gasket when the loud annoying ringing of my phone distracts me.

"Ignore it," the voice from between my thighs moans.

So, I do as I'm told. But goddamn they're persistent! I can't ignore the phone any longer. I glance over and peek at the screen to see a familiar face. It's my older sister, she's only older by a few minutes, but she never lets me forget it.

"Keep going, don't stop," I tell the stranger between my thighs, still trying to please me. I grab the annoyance that is ringing; I put it to my ears and yell,

"What? I'm busy!" through gritted teeth.

"Girl please, I will slap the taste out of your mouth. Whatever you're doing, stop! Storm needs us,." says the voice on the other end of the phone.

Only my sister can take such a tone with me and get away with it, because of the womb we shared, with anyone else it would have been a different conversation.

Rolling my eyes and trying to get the most out of this sexy piece of meat between my legs, I say: "Whatever, gimme two mins."

"No! Now! I'm heading downstairs. Bitch fucked up, that is why we have been feeling like shit all day. So, whatever you're doing STOP! You're making me sick." she commanded in disgust.

"Ahhh! I'm coming!" I scream as I reach the point of no return. Even though I'm speaking to the gentle giant between my legs, the words are fitting for both parties.

"I'll be out front in two minutes, be ready," she says.

Ending the call with my sister to pay attention to whatever his name is. I push his head away before he can start the delightful assault on my pink goodness again. I thank him sweetly while stuffing my underwear down his back pocket. "I got to go!"

"Meaning?" he asks.

He's handsome, muscular built with perfect broad shoulders, looking like a tall drink of hot chocolate. A darker version of Vin Diesel, bald head, and all.

"Get dressed," I tell him laughing.

He smiles with a hint of confusion at my instruction. He has a hard-on, thicker than an oak tree, between his legs.

"Why do we have to leave so soon, we just got started?" he protests.

"And now I'm finishing, like I said, I've got to go now." I snap at him with finality in my voice. I exude confidence and grace in anyone's presence, but I don't like to repeat myself.

"Listen, it was fun, you were great; I was going to be even greater, but I don't care where you are going or staying, but it's not here. Now Bye," is all I say as I push him out the front door as he's getting dressed.

I can hear Autumn's car horn outside honking away. As I pull the shutters down on the storefront, I spot the sex bomb a few feet away, looking baffled about what just happened. I shake my head and think about how amazing I was going to be. He'd come in for an outfit for some relative or other and ended up with more than he could've hoped for. I was about to close the shop when he walked in, and I just had to give him more than customer service, and since I needed a service, I thought, why not? He was six foot, five, built like a Greek God, dark, with sexy chocolate skin and bright eyes; wearing a grey jumper and blue jeans; gold necklace and Cartier watch with the matching ring. He just had sexiness written all over him; I mean, clearly God sent him to cheer me the hell up. I take my blessings; however, they are delivered, God has never failed me yet.

"I'm coming!" I had to scream as I turned the key on the shutters.

Autumn's car horn blows again alerting me, damn this girl is impatient. I punch in the security code to the store and pull down the shutters to our shop. I'm so proud of us and what we have built together. My sister is the most beautiful woman alive, we maybe triplets but there's none like her. Her beauty shines both in and out, but her temper is like no other either. That said, she's still my queen, my heartbeat.

"Let's go, it's freezing out here," she says to me as soon as I open the car door.

"Chile, you need to learn patience," I tell her once I get in the front seat, chuckling at my sister's intolerance.

I guess that's why she was born first because she couldn't wait to see the world.

"You never let me have any fun," I grumble.

"And you're a whore; he is sexy though, so I can't even blame you at all," she smirks.

"Slut," I say while poking my tongue out at my sister exposing my tongue ring.

Shaking her head in laughter, she puts the car in motion and speeds off down the road honking at poor stiff dick Clinton. Yes, that's his name. Clinton.

"So, what's so urgent you need to be making so much noise out here?" I ask her.

"He needs us, that bitch left him," she says like it is her who got dumped.

Me, on the other hand, I'm happy about it, but I can still feel the anguish that she feels. Storm should have left that girl's ass a long time ago; she was never any good for him.

"So why are you so mad isn't that what we wanted anyway?" I ask her with confusion and slight happiness.

"No, we wanted him to let her go, so he wouldn't be feeling so damn miserable," she explains.

I know my brother, he's just miserable over the love of his so-called life and the fact that she still doesn't want him like that, not this one month ago chick.

"Hmmm, he's going to be feeling miserable regardless. He thought he was using this bitch to get over something that he can't get rid of, why I don't know, but nonetheless, he's feeling it." I tell her trying to calm her mood.

"Oh, please what the hell has love got to do with it? We warned his dumbass but no, just wait till I get my hands on her skinny-ass she'll have no more pussy to go around. Does she not know who the fucks brother she's been messing with, and what the repercussions are? Well, she's going to find out soon!" she says all in one breath.

I can't get a word in. I shake my head at my angry sister. See everyone knows my temper because I walk around with a permanent don't fuck with me look planted on my face, but they are always surprised by my sister.

"Ah, no you won't, Autumn Valentine you will leave that slack-ass pussy, good for nothing bitch, germs of a whore alone, she's out of his life, and that's all that matters," I warn her.

"Whatever but I still want to push her into oncoming traffic," she says laughing, my sister has a sick sense of humour.

As part of a set of triplets, we have a bond so strong it seems almost magical and surreal. We can always feel when one of us is in trouble or any other emotion known to man; we have a sort of psychic connection to each other. Autumn, Winter, and Storm, we're a force to be admired and reckoned with.

"She was a waste of oxygen," I say, referring to Storms ex-girlfriend.

"I know. I mean, what he sees in these women," she says, exasperated. "My brother's tastes are the worst, I think. I swear after Peppa, things just went from bad to worse with these bobblehead bitches," she reminds me.

"What happened to her anyway? Is she out of prison yet?" I ask curious about how our old friend is doing.

"No! I need to book a visit to go see her, remind me to call her mom to get the details. I should send her some money as well, that also reminds me I gotta go see my God-baby." she tells me.

Peppa was my sister's best friend and brother's girlfriend in high school.

"I miss her. Now she was real. A bad bitch at that. Too bad her and Storm didn't work out. Every bitch hated her back in the day, and every bitch was happy as hell when they broke up. Especially Alicia, remember her?" I remind my sister.

"Oh yeah! Alicia. I remember her. Peppa and I beat the daylights of her," she says, laughing at the memory of her and her once best friend.

"Wait! What, When?" I'm shocked at this piece of information.

"Because! She had a thing for Storm and Peppa wanted to beat her into the next millennium. She didn't because you know how Storm is about women fighting," she explains, rolling her eyes at the thought of our brother's rules.

"So, what happened?" I enquire.

"Well when he turned her down, she went after my Darius, and you know how I felt about my Darius, back in the day," she states.

"You mean how you still feel." I correct her.

"Anyway, wasn't he in love with Peppa for the longest?" I ask and immediately regret my question to my sister. For as long as I've known this dude, he couldn't keep his eyes off Peppa.

"Yeah! That was the reason we didn't work out, but I do miss me some Dee," she says, smirking at me.

"And you call me a whore!" I shake my head in condemnation at her.

"You are, and did you know Trouble liked you?" she declares.

With a puzzled look on my face, I stare at her dumbfounded.

"Why am I just learning this? He was the perfect mix of dorky and sexy." I'm stunned by this news.

Shaking her head and being mindful of the road she replies, "You were with that idiot from St. John's Academy, what's his name? Jordan."

"Oh Yeah! He's doing twenty five to life now," I say remembering.

"Wow! You and Storm sure can pick 'em!" she exclaims. Like she's any better at picking decent partners.

"You know Storm had to knock him out," I tell her,

"Really?" she gasps,

"Yeah! Idiot put his hand in my face, so I slapped him; that's when he went psycho on me, and someone must have told Storm; he came to the rescue and whooped that ass. I mean I get in there and help fuck him up. You remember I came home with that black eye that one time. But I can't believe it, you could have told me that Trouble had a thing for me. I would have definitely worked on him." I tell her.

She rolls her eyes at me and says, "See, whore."

"I'm not a whore or playa, I just crush a lot," I tell her

"Pisssh! Bye." is her only reply.

We pull up outside our home, and I can automatically feel the sadness pouring out of my brother. We've always had that psychic sibling syndrome type of communication shit going for us, we can always tell when one of us is hurting or in danger. The Valentine siblings have always been close, so when one of us calls or is in distress, we always come running, no matter what. I also know he isn't upset about no skinny bitch; he's upset over Sunshine as usual.

We own the building we live in and several around the inner city and various others. We invested our money well. With these two knuckleheads' minds for business, we turned the little money mom left us into a profitable cooperation that only we can profit from. Only family members are on our board of directors. I mean we have our hands in everything from property development, nightclubs, clothing lines, several stores, stocks and bonds. But our everyday run is in the store and Autumn dance studios.

Being part of a set of triplets for us is one of the greatest things God ever did for us, which comes in handy since we never met our father and never wanted to.

Catherine La'Trisha Valentine brought up her children to never need or want for anyone, more than they needed each other. She taught us to be dependent, only on each other; more than we can care and love her. Our mother never wanted her children to feel the sadness and loneliness of this world, to feel abandoned or alone throughout our lives. So, she made sure that we had each other no matter what. When our mother died, we were only thirteen. We found out the hard way, what our mother meant when she kept singing the importance and value of us needing each other and how we should never let anything, or anyone come between us. We know that as long as we have each other we need no-one.

We don't need anyone we got us!

Autumn + Winter =
The Perfect Storm
~

Winter

Taking the elevator to the fifth floor of our apartment complex, Autumn and I continue catching up on our daily rundown of the store. We occupy the largest apartment in the building. The apartment has a very homely feel to it with soft furnishings and huge family portraits over the fireplace. With an open plan dining and kitchen area, with an island separating the two. A glass grand piano is stationed by the floor to ceiling windows. Decorated in nothing but white, copper steel material and a hint of mint green, it is the perfect home for us. We enter the apartment to see our brother in his dark blue Hugo Boss jogging bottoms and a white vest top and sadness in his deep green eyes which have a hint of blue. His jet-black hair is a loose afro curl, wild like a lion's mane, which complements his caramel skin tone. When he has his hair loose like this, he always looks like a girl.

"It's going to be ok, you've always got me," I speak up first and then Autumn chipped in with,

"And me."

"So, forget about her lying, cheating, good for nothing, don't know a good dick when she sucked it, can't fuck broke ass..."

Autumn joined in on the end of my rant "BITCH", and we both laugh trying to lighten the mood. A faint smile breaks through, all the frustration and headache that is plastered on him.

We triplets, aren't just family, we are best friends and identical down to having the exact same freckle in our greenish-blue eyes. We never needed anyone but each other. We are the envy of everyone in the neighbourhood, at school, college. Wherever we go, people stare or whisper. We are either loved or envied instantly; it is both a blessing and a curse, and we love it.

"This bitch had the nerve to think she could cheat on my brother," Autumn speaks up, "She must be crazy, she better not let me see her. I swear I'm going to tear her a new hole. She'll regret the day she crossed a Valentine." Autumn rants on.

Autumn is exactly like her weather, sweet, cool and chilly. She is a gentle soul full of compassion. She's disciplined, honest, dependable, nimble, and intelligent with a whole lot of attitude, all the things you'd hope your daughter would be. She's the quietest of the bunch except for when you mess with one of her own, then she becomes your worst nightmare.

I, on the other hand, am literally the opposite to both my siblings. I am the loudest, sassy yet classy and the most abrupt one of the bunch. I live life without any restrictions or apologies. I never take any shit from anyone. I don't care what anyone thinks about my family or me. I give as good as I get.

"I told you, baby boy, play these girls and don't let them play you," I remind him pointing at him.

"Yeah! Yeah! I hear yah! But I can't just keep fucking like a duck with no end results, Wint, I feel like it's time to really settle down." Storm replies. Wint is what my siblings call me.

We sit on the plush silver and white custom-made velvet bathtub shaped sofa; drinking Remy Martins while venting and trying to help Storm get over the bitch formally known as Rachel. Even though we all know he's pining over Sunshine, but let's all pretend.

"Well here's to the trash we don't need, to the bitch that thinks she could and the bitch that wished she would. Cheers." Autumn states, raising her glass.

Autumn hated calling a woman outside her name. Still, one who hurt her brother deserves to be called whatever comes to mind.

"I mean baby boy; do you know how handsome you are? I do! Cause you look like me and I'm beautiful, cute and fabulous and all the above, so trust me, you're all that. Because of you, I know what I would look like as a man without shaving off Auto's head," I say laughing while a little bit tipsy from the alcohol coursing through my veins. Auto is what we call Autumn.

"Why do you gotta shave my head?" Autumn says, whining, interrupting me mid-sentence.

"I'm great, and I would fuck me and dip me in chocolate," I tell my brother.

"Yeah! Pretty boy, I mean we are the dynamic trio. We are Autumn and Winter, and together we create the perfect Storm, remember? We are the crème de la crème baby; the cherry on top." Autumn reassures him.

"You're the strongest of us all, no whore named Rachel is going to be the calm after you. Especially after I'm done with her," I say encouraging my brother to be proud of who we are. Of whom he is. "Stupid bitch won't know what hit her when I'm done."

"Leave it Wint; don't need you getting arrested. Plus, I don't want her to have the satisfaction of knowing that she even had the chance, just leave her be. Karma's twice the bitch she is," he says.

Rolling my eyes at my brother because we are going to have the last laugh one way or the other "Well, all I'm saying is, she made the biggest mistake when she decided to whore it out," I say with confidence.

"Leave the whore alone, it's just us again the way it's supposed to be. I have been thinking, we should go somewhere, do something. No more sitting around singing sad love songs like we are Toni Braxton or Mary J!'

We all laugh at Storm's analogy and burst out singing Toni Braxton s, 'Just Another Sad Love Song.' We drink, eat and dance while telling stories of exes. We make fun of each other's stupid mistakes and poor judgment on life. Somehow, we end up on the floor, all wrapped up in each other with a large zebra print blanket, like we used to as kids.

"So, where are we going then baby Storm?" I ask

"We could take a Euro Tour or Australia," he offers.

"Oh yes, I can get some of those down under boys to go down under," I suggest, suggestively.

Shaking his head, Storm replies "I swear, sometimes you forget I'm your brother. I don't want to hear that nastiness."

"Then develop selective hearing, besides you just as nasty as me," I say laughing at my brother.

"So no to Australia. We want Wint to still have a vagina when we get back," he says while rolling his eyes at me. Autumn laughs so hard that she snorts.

"Well, I could always use yours," I suggest.

"Wint! Do you even still have a vagina?"

This chick is serious.

I say, "Well someone has to use it since you two seems to want to hide yours away. I gotta use it for all of us. I mean, look at us, even as a man I'm still fucking gorgeous. When God made you Autumn, he thought Damn I'm good! I'm good. I want another one, so he made me. He called Jesus over and was like a son, look at these beauties. He just couldn't get enough. Then he thought to himself fuck it I'm going to make another one, but this time, it's going to be a boy and then Boom. Here comes Mr good-looking Mutha-fucka himself."

We all laugh at my explanation for their existence.

"I mean just think when the dickhead of a father abandoned mom and us. Who knew God would punish his stupid ass and make three seeds instead of one?" I say, laughing. "Then again Storm you kind of look like him, you're lighter than us," I tell him.

"Ha! Ha! Very funny. If I do so do you, dummy. Identical triplets – jackass!" he retorts. Teasing my brother is always fun; he was always the sensitive one.

"Nope! We look like mama, but you look like ..."

"You!" he says, cutting me off mid-sentence. Jacob is always a sensitive subject in this house.

"I wonder what the others look like," Autumn says from out of nowhere.

"Other what?" I ask with a confused look on my face.

"Well I saw our sister; she has a little boy." Storm interjects like we are supposed to be entertaining this type of thinking from her. I look back and forth at both of them even more confused.

"What! When?" now I am alert and curious.

"A couple weeks back, they came into the store, the little boy was around four or five and looked like us but white with blond hair and bright blue eyes. For a hot second, I thought I fathered a son, and no one told me, then I saw the mother and knew, I didn't because I have never met her," he explains.

"What was she like?" Autumn asks with a little too much enthusiasm.

"Short and stocky, but with Wint's attitude," he explains.

"Shut up and anyway who cares. I don't want to know them. And stop calling them our sister. I have one sister, and she already gets on my last nerve." I tell them.

Kissing her teeth, Autumn continues questioning Storm about the sibling with no name. "So, what did she say?" she enquires.

"Nothing. I gave her the family discount and told her thanks for coming. She even tried flirting. Ewe. But I never mentioned anything to her. I like our family the way it is just the three of us. I don't need anyone else; the two of you are enough," he explains.

I smile at my brother with nothing but love and admiration in my heart for him. "Damn straight. I love it this way. They didn't want us, and we don't need them now. He didn't help when mama died, and we survived.

"Speak for yourself," Autumn says boldly.

"Hold on, after everything we've been through. Mom dying, Storms kidney failure, being homeless, being separated. We survived it on our own with the help of our grandmother, yes, but alone nonetheless and we survived it all. So now we're not good enough for you?" I ask her, fed up with this conversation already.

"I never said that," she replies.

"I don't want anything to do with them, and neither should you. I gave them a chance, and they didn't want to know, so fuck them." I tell her with irritation in my voice. I hate speaking about his dumb white ass.

"Wait? What do you mean you gave them a chance?" Autumn questions.

I swear this girl doesn't miss a beat. "Just before mom died, she told me where to go to find him and told me to let him know what was happening and how much we needed him, so I did. I went to look for him, to ask for help and the son of – a bitch just told me to go away. He didn't care; he didn't care what happened to us." A small tear falls down my cheek, and Autumn comes by my side and gives me a hug. I hate talking about the only man that broke my heart.

"Wow! Why didn't you tell us?" She asks.

"Why! What difference would it make? He didn't want us then, and he doesn't now. Nothing's changed." I tell them.

"Wow! So, you've met the asshole named, dad? Storm queries.

"Yep and unfortunately we have his stupid petite freckled nose," I say while touching their noses.

"It would have been nice to see him though. I've always wondered what he looked like?" Autumn states.

"Trust! You're not missing out. He's an arrogant prick. Nothing like mom told us about. I mean even when Storm got sick, and the doctor called, you didn't see him come running did you. His son was dying, motherless and he couldn't even be bothered. Thank God for Nana!" I exclaim.

"New topic. So, where we are going. The stores are doing well, and I could do with a holiday." Storm interjects.

"How about America. Land of dreams plus Wint can still lose her vagina there," Autumn says, trying to lighten the mood.

"Hahaha. Very funny. America sounds great. Autumn can finally find her vagina," I tease.

"Cool, I've always wanted to go to Vegas? Storm suggests.

"Yeah, Vegas sounds cool. We just have to keep you out of them chapels. No one's accidentally getting married," we all laugh.

"Then how about Jamaica, we can visit grandma. It could be fun to see all our cousins again. Besides, I'm due for a visit anyway, and it's Nana's birthday soon too." Storm reminds us.

"Beats being cold for the winter, plus Storm can finally get a tan," I state.

"You raise a fair point there girl," Autumn mocks.

"Yeah! And Wint's vagina could return back to normal from the seawater," he chimes in.

"Yeah, and you can grow balls finally," I utter.

"So, Jamaica it is then ladies!" Storm declares.

"No! America then Jamaica. We can make two trips into one if we plan right." Autumn starts trying to take charge. I swear to God; this girl can't do anything without planning first.

"Yes, now we are talking, so it's final, so when can we leave?" I am ready to go now, plus this will give me a chance to see Nana Bird since she's been nagging the life out of me about coming to see her.

"Well, I got to visit our other stores in Bristol and London and someone's gotta go set up and make sure everything goes well for the grand opening of the new branch in Manchester because I'm going to be busy. I---"

Storm interrupts cutting her off because he knows she's just going to ramble on and on about this to-do list she's got going for all of us like we don't pull our own weight in the business.

"I'll get on it, so does that mean we are going after the grand opening?"

"Yep. Road Trip. The dynamic trio taking over." Shaking his head, Storm concludes with "April it is then, great timing because it's time to go see grandma anyway. I'll call the travel agent." he announces.

We drink, dance and talk into the late hours of the night until we all fall asleep.

So, What's The Plan?

Storm

Afaint noise disturbs my sleep, waking me up. Looking around the room, I notice everything is ok, and the early morning sun is just coming up trying to peek through the wall to floor curtains. With my two feelings of pride and joy beside me, I smile knowing that with them, I am always content. Smiling at the sight of my sisters, I feel calm after the storm moving over me. Everything is right with the world if I have them. Whispering to the still of the breathing beauties beside me on the ground. "I promise!"

Before mom passed away, she told me of the love she had for my father and how much he changed her life. She made me promise that I would never leave or forsake my sisters and that I'd always protect them, no matter what. Since then, I have always kept this promise. I even had it tattooed under my left breastbone close to my heart, with no explanation to anyone, not even my sister's just a simple reminder for myself (I Promise). Whenever any of my sisters are in trouble, I come to their rescue, knocking out whoever hurts them, putting them in their place. Being a brother is a huge responsibility, especially when they're your triplet sisters.

Reaching for my cell phone, I get up and send a quick text message to Clive, our store supervisor, letting him know that he needs to open the shop up today and that I won't be in for the rest of the week. As I stand by the large window overlooking the canal; I prepare myself for whatever is to come. I start making mental notes of what needs to be done before our trip abroad and what needs to be in place for us to go ahead..

Winter wakes up and comes to stand next to me and smiles, I can see the love and appreciation she has for me, resting her head on my shoulder. She's wrapped in a blanket. I wrap my arms around her, letting her know that she is safe and that I'm ok.

Looking up at me, she kisses my cheek and tells me, "I got your back." I look down at my sister and thank God for her. Most people don't take to her, most are just simply jealous, but she's the most loyal and straight forward person I know, and I dare anyone to say a bad word about her or fuck with her.

"I know," I reply. We stare out the window in silence for a moment, then we hear Autumn shuffling on the ground; guess she's got morning chills since Wint took the larger blanket.

"I have an idea. What if we both go with Autumn to Bristol and London before heading to Manchester to set up the store? We could go shopping," she suggests, this girl loves clothes more than breathing.

"Sounds like a plan," Autumn walks up from behind, her voice is always raspy in the morning, and she comes to stand on the opposite side of me.

"You guys realise we're going to a tropical island, right?" Wint always likes to state the obvious.

"Yeah so! What's your point?" I ask.

"We live in England, where am I going to find bikinis this time of the year?" She asks. This girl has more bikini's than Victoria's Secret summer collection, and she's complaining.

"I'm sure you'll survive and find a way. Anyway, we're going to America first remember!" I say, shaking my head at my sister's question.

"L.A. then New York, fuck Vegas," I tell them.

"I was thinking more Miami". Wint suggests.

"I like the sound of that, but I still say we do New York." Wint states.

"Sure! What do you think, Auto?" I ask.

"Fun. You two love changing your minds, so I'm up for whatever and wherever," she replies.

She looks at the enormous wall clock surrounded by a dozen other smaller clocks showing the time of different countries, it shows 6:35 a.m. for our time zone.

"I'm going to take a shower and get ready for the day. What are you guys doing today?" she asks.

"Thought we could all take the day off and just chill," I offer.

"Ahhh. Don't think so little brother, we got an empire to run, plus a store opening in a few weeks. You can have the morning off," Auto says with authority while disappearing into her bedroom.

"Yes, ma'am," I reply playfully. She pops her head back out and says, "Wint. I need you with me today."

"What for? I'm taking the day off," she complains.

"No, you're not! We got to fire Trevor's thieving ass and replace him today. I placed the ad last week we got eight candidates coming today; plus, stocktake and some other errands to run," she says.

"Why can't you do it? I was gonna work on my designs today," Wint protests.

"I have to meet with my class for dance rehearsal, and you know the weekend is our busiest time. Stop complaining. I don't have to be at the studio until 4 p.m. and we have interviews from 1 p.m. till 3 p.m. so you two can be late in, but you're not having the day off," she warns.

"So, you don't need me till then?" Wint enquires.

"Yes, I do. I want to go to the distributor, and I don't want to go by myself. I wasn't born by myself, you know," Autumn tells us and Wint just rolls her eyes at Autumn's request.

Wint replies with her own demands and questioning, "Fine! What time is that?"

"Ten this morning," Autumn replies.

"So why do we gotta move now?" Wint asks.

"Because you move slower than a snail. That's why," Auto replies.

"Whatever, but we are going jogging first, so be ready in 10 minutes," Wint tells her.

"I don't think so," Autumn pops her head back in the room and tells her.

"That's my offer. Take it or leave it" Wint says, smiling because she knows how much Autumn hates jogging or any form of exercise. How she became, a dancer is beyond anyone. Mom used to say it was the Jamaican in her, and Wint got the island spirit vibrant and loud. I, on the other hand, got a bit of everything. "10 minutes Auto, I mean it."

"Fine, 10 minutes," Autumn sighs.

"Have fun," I tell them. I already know what I want to do with my day and it damn sure isn't whatever Autumn wants.

"Join us for lunch?" Wint asks.

"Sure," I have some serious thinking to do and phone calls to make. Even though I am feeling better. I know exactly who can make me feel even greater, Sunshine. Just the thought of her makes me smile inside.

At 8:00 a.m. and the ladies head out on their jog on the canal side. Black people seriously have a different internal clock because no matter what, we are late. I clean up the apartment and make myself a hot coffee. I head to the study to figure out our plans, but first I need to call Sunshine.

She's a dark-skinned chick I can always count on when I'm in Bristol, she knows how to get a guy's mind off anything. Thick in all the right places. Unlike me, she isn't ready for a relationship; she wants to concentrate on work rather than a relationship, but she's always up for some fun whenever I call.

Autumn

Closing the building door behind us, we take off. This chick knows I hate running, yet she's got my black ass out here in the cold running.

"Do you think he's going to be ok? I think he really liked her?" I ask Wint.

"Well that's what happens when you fuck with the white devil in heels," she says mindlessly.

"Not all white people are the devil, Wint," I tell her.

"No! Just the ones fucking with our family. The sperm donor, Rachel, Miss Simpson from primary school, Mr Elbridge from high school, the list goes on. That bitch right there trying to run cute," she says matter of factly.

"You need therapy," I tell her.

"And you need Black Jesus or a Black Dick," she points out.

"I don't hate white people, I'm half white and so are you, so get over it."

"Yes, and it's the part I choose to ignore," she says boldly and without regret.

"Like I said, therapy!"

"Whatever. This ass, full lips, and nappy ass hair says I'm more black than white. The woman who brought us into this world and the man who gave her money to abort my BLACK ass made my choices clear. Thank you, mama," she says, throwing up her deuces and jogging off.

"Shut up and run," Winter can be such a dick sometimes. I think shaking my head.

As we run in silence, I can't help but consider what Winter just said, which brings my thoughts to the man that abandoned our mother and us. I have been thinking about him more and more lately, and it's starting to bother me. What is he like, does he think about us? What does he look like today? I'm in such deep thought that I don't even realise we've reached the cute little coffee shop Wint always visits on her jog. I stay outside while Wint goes inside for hot chocolates. I call a taxi because if she thinks I'm jogging back, she is seriously mistaken, it's cold as hell out here, only Winter loves winter.

Winter

"Three mochas to go and an almond croissant please," I ask the teller once it's my turn in line. The barista looks up and stares in amazement at the beauty before him. He must be new because I've never seen him in here before. As he scans my entire body, lingering on my perfectly taut breasts; because it's cold outside, my nipples are protruding through my top.

"Hey! Up here. How much?" I snap

"I'm sorry that will be £11.95 please," he replies.

"Next time pay attention to my order, not my breasts," I say, giving him a little sexy attitude. I love playing with these pathetic simpletons.

"I'm sorry," he says again.

Autumn

I walk up to my sister's side at the counter as the barista finishes apologising I'm assuming.

"Hey what's taking so long? It's freezing out there," I ask.

"Educating the locals on manners," she says.

"Stop giving that poor man a hard time," I tell her. "Hi! Ignore my sister, she's the evil twin," I tell him with a smile. The young man is in awe as we wait in the coffee shop. He must think he's dreaming or that there is a God after all, from the way he's staring and gawking at us, his jaw is practically on the floor.

"Hello!" Wint snaps at him.

"Sorry! Here you go. I was just thanking God for a moment," he says flirtatiously.

"For what?" Wint asks, already knowing the answer.

"Because he made two of you," he said, complimenting us. We laugh at his obvious lame come-on.

"Actually, he made three. Thanks for the drinks," Wint tells him, swaying her ass just a little too much, for his and her own pleasure. As she leaves the coffee shop, she grabs everyone's attention.

"Trust me. You got no chance. Keep trying though, it's good practice," I tell the poor man and leave him a generous £5 tip with a wink.

"Thanks," he says appreciatively.

"No problem cutie," I wave goodbye.

"Hey, wait up," I say, hurrying up to catch her as she exits the door.

"Thought you were cold?" she asks.

"I am. That's why I called a taxi. It's too damn cold."

Seasons!

Autumn

When we arrive at the store, it's pretty quiet. We'll stay a little while and collect a few things before its time to head out to the distributor. The store supervisor updates us on the morning's activities. We sit in the back office and go over the day's plans.

"Hey, why can't you buy things online like the rest of the world, saving us some time?" Wint asks me.

"Sounds good, but I wanna negotiate a new contract; I think they're ripping us off."

"Fine! Ready when you are. I'm going to sit up front do my designs and man the front desk until you are ready," she tells me.

You'd think the store was my baby the way I do things, she's supposed to be head of everything in-store around here. I run my chain of dance studios, and Storm does do a bit of everything, including investing our money in stocks and other shit which I have no clue about. That boy can give Richard Branson a run for his money, the way he's trying to take over everything in the cities.

"K. I'm going to go out back. Let me know when Trevor comes in," I tell her.

"Sure, but you're firing him, not me," Wint states.

"Yeah, whatever. I'll be in here," I say brushing her off.

We have a lot to be thankful for, we run a successful business that keeps expanding, and thanks to a few TV appearances when we were born and again when our mom died, and the dream Storm has of making our mother proud, we have a financial portfolio that means not even our great-grandkids will have to work again.

Winter

I haven't heard a peep out of my sister, so I figure she's changed her mind about the distributor. It's 10:22 when Trevor walks in.

"You're late!" I bark at him.

"I'm sorry. I was stuck-" he tries to explain.

"Save it for someone who cares, head to the back Autumn is waiting," I say, cutting him off mid-sentence.

"Yes, ma'am," he answers.

"Excuse me I'm twenty five not fifty five, I'm not your ma'am. The name is Winter!" I yell at Trevor as he walks towards the back-office.

Autumn

"Good morning Miss Valentine. Sorry, I'm late," Trevor knocks on the office door and enters without permission.

"Come on in. Trevor, take a seat," I say with a smile. "Look at something for me and give me your honest opinion," I say and turn the screen on so he can see clearly.

"Sure, what is it?" he asks.

As he stares at the monitor in front him, I know he has butterflies in his stomach because I can see a large lump form in his throat as he watches himself on screen stealing merchandise from the store.

10 minutes later, Winter watches as Trevor leaves the store with a sorrowful look on his face feeling defeated and deflated.

"Bye, don't come again," she says chuckling.

A few hours later, a young woman no more than thirty in age interrupts Winter's thoughts asking about a product.

"Excuse me. Do you have any more of this, in age 5?" the lady asks.

"I think so". She tells the woman. Recognising the woman with the child instantly. Her skin is fair, dark eyes, with brunette hair, a little bit on the chubby side, nothing a gym membership couldn't fix, along with a new wardrobe. I have to admit, she is on the slightly pretty side.

"We also have other designs in the back, which just came in. I'll bring them out for you if you wait one moment," Winter tells her.

"Ok. Is the manager here? She asks with a bit of excitement in her voice. Knowing that she is talking about Storm, I feel a little sick inside.

"Hey, Jazz. Do they have it," a more boisterous one shouts.

"Gimme a sec this young lady is going to find out for me"? She replies to the other woman. I look at the other woman standing in front of her and for once I am lost for words.

"I'll be right back," Winter says, hurrying to the back of the store to the stock room to grab the pieces of clothing items the ladies want and then running into the office to grab me so that I can see for myself.

"Auto," she gasps, "Guess who's in the store."

"Who?" I say, looking up over her glasses,"

"Your sisters," she tells me.

"My sisters?" I repeat, looking puzzled.

"Yes, two of them," she says, and I get up and poke my head through to the front to see exactly what she is referring to.

"She wants these; I may say something you'll regret. They make me edgy." Winter says shaking her head and urging me towards the reception desk.

"Why is there no one to help in this store?" the larger than life woman asks .

"Because we fired everyone. How can I help?" I snap.

"You can help with what you went for. Do you have any more of these or something similar?" she says with a little more attitude than I would like.

"Lady, the door is that way, if you don't like the service," I tell her, I hate rude ass people.

"Where's your manager. I'd like to speak with him?" she asks.

"At the gym," I say, referring to the woman's size.

"And the supervisor is busy," pointing at Clive at the window dressing a mannequin. "But I'm sure the owner would love to help. How can I help?" I ask dramatically.

"The last time we came in here, the owner assisted us. Where's he?" she enquires.

"He's not in so I guess you're stuck with me," I say leaning on the counter

Interrupting the two of us the other lady chimes in.

"Thank you. May I see the new t-shirt you've got, I'm sorry for my sister Darcy's behaviour. She was born grumpy" she pointed out.

"Don't apologise for me," the one called Darcy says.

"Stop being rude. Perfect, the boys will love these" the slimmer one says.

"Certainly, that will be £45.50," I tell her.

"Whose drawings are these? They are really good" the slim chick asks.

"The owners," I tell her.

"They're his?" she exclaims questioningly.

"No, the other owner. She'll be out in a sec." I hand her the receipt, the store's loyalty card, and her bags as her annoying sister points out it is almost lunchtime.

"I'm Jasmine. It was nice meeting you. Love the shop and again sorry for my sister." Jasmine said.

"Come again soon, " I tell her while rolling my eyes at her too big to fit through the door sister and wave my fingers bye to the pair.

I can hear Jasmine whisper, "Wasn't she wearing a different outfit when we first saw her?"

Winter comes strolling out, with a look of total bewilderment on her face,

"So, what are they like?" she asks all of sudden interested after all the shit she gave me just last night.

"We have two sisters, one's a bitch, and one's not. Nothing like us, they are both cheap and in need of a spa day, could tell she didn't want to pay the £45.50" I explain.

"You didn't give her the family discount?" she asks, and the look on my face speaks volumes.

"Damn and they say I'm the cold one," Winter said, shaking her head.

"Well, I'm having one of those mornings. Guess they weren't that bad. And who names their child Darcy?"

"I know what you mean, PMS is a bitch. Ready for lunch?" Winter asks.

"Yeah since someone only thought about their brother this morning. I'm starving." I tell her, deadpan.

"Ok. Hold up. What are you complaining about? Your skinny ass doesn't eat anyway." she said, defending her actions.

"Whatever. Call your brother; tell him to meet us, where you want to eat. I'm up for whatever." I tell her.

"You need to get laid; clearly whatever you're doing isn't helping". Winter said.

An older woman comes to the till for assistance interrupting or chin wag.

"Excuse me, may I have this in size 18?" she asks politely

"Hold on Miss. I'll get someone to assist you." I call one of our sales reps over to assist the old lady and follow Winter after grabbing the stuff from the counter. As we walk to the front door, I tell Clive we are leaving for lunch and that he should call if he needs anything, we set off into the town centre.

"I texted Storm to tell him, to meet us in McDonald's on the corner," Winter informs me.

"Whatever, let's go," I reply.

Change of Plan

―――――― ❧ ――――――

Winter

I can feel my sister's energy shift and her mind going at a million miles a moment thinking about those two and the father who is not. This child, in her feelings and messing up my food high. Where is Storm? He needs to come and fix this child because I just can't deal with her emotions fogging up my mind with all these thoughts of people I wouldn't even piss on. Why is she wondering what the other piglets are like and what they missed out on?

I mean what more does she want from us. Doesn't she see what she has already? Damn, sometimes I hate our triplet bond because I wouldn't have to be feeling her funk all the time. This child is never happy, always thinking about some fucked up shit. Now she is sitting here wondering about shit that she has no business thinking about. Why does she need to know what the idiot who paid for her death is doing?

Who gives a fuck, personally I wouldn't mind knowing that devil came for his ass personally. SIGH. She is seriously pissing me off. They say misery loves company, and I refuse to be miserable, especially over them.

"Nothing! So, stop it, you're killing my vibe" I shout a little too harsh at Autumn.

"What?!" she asks, astonished.

"Auto we missed out on nothing. We have everything we ever needed. Mom made sure we had everything humanly possible. So, stop thinking about those oversized can't afford a gym membership, even if it is free; can only buy a t-shirt with discount women. They're not your sisters. I am, and you don't need them," I say point-blank.

"I know, I just can't help wondering about dad and mom" she explains.

"Well, stop!"

"Don't you ever think of him, what he's like?" she asks.

"No! I already know. He's an ass," I state.

"Well, I don't know that. Yes, he's an ass for leaving us like that and mom, but I can't help it" she tells her.

12:33pm sent

Storm to Wint: *Be there in 10min I'm at the garage, brought the car in.*

"Bitch you need to get over it. Cause you're starting to piss me off with this, I need my daddy bullshit." I snap. Kissing my teeth at my sister.

"Winter I don't have any daddy issues and who's being a bitch now, Bitch." she says while tilting her head and staring at me I just can't understand how she doesn't feel or understand where I am coming from.

"Stop wondering, stop asking and stop annoying me and let me eat my burger in peace."

"Everything annoys you; I was just thinking. Stay out of my head." she tells me.

"Well don't. It's like Storm, and I aren't good enough for you?" I say with a hurt look in my eyes.

"Now you're being stupid. You know I love you and wouldn't trade our lives for anything. People wish they were us. I was born with extras, who can say they were born with spare parts." she tells me.

Storm

Entering the McDonald's restaurant, I can see the irritation on Winters' face. "Seasons! What are we talking about?" I say as I approach them, rubbing my hands together.

"Here's your burger. For some reason, your sister thinks we are her spare parts" Winter informs me

"Shut up Wint, you know what I meant. We're talking about the dad that wasn't" Autumns tells me.

"Oh! What about him?" I ask, curious.

"Nothing! Just sometimes I think about him, and today, two of our sisters came into the store again. I think they came in for you," Autumn tells me. Winter rolls her eyes at Autumn as if to say the notion is a waste of energy.

"I think about him too, but more in an, I pity him sort of way. I mean he missed out, and that's down to him, he wasn't man enough and -" I try to tell Autumn but get cut off by Winters rude ass.

"And we don't need him. Now let me eat my burger in peace," she argues.

"Don't mind her Auto. She was just born cold-hearted, that's why she's called Winter". I said, trying to soothe my sister.

"And don't you forget it. A man will never break my heart because I don't let them near it, unlike you two. And I ain't trying to find a replacement daddy. I'm happy with you guy's in my life." Winter says.

"I'm happy too. And like I said I don't have daddy issues or a daddy complex. But I know you think about his dumbass too otherwise your stupid-ass wouldn't be so bent out of shape talking about him who should not be named." Autumn says rolling her eyes.

Winter replies with, "His name is Jacob Edwards. Professor Jacob Edwards. He's a middle-class white man with a black pussy agenda." She speaks a little too loud and everyone in the restaurant is staring or peeking over their burgers.

"Winter, stop," I tell her to calm down.

"He only wanted the taste of black pussy, and mom was the right candidate for the job. Plain and simple" she says.

"Winter! I love you. But disrespect the memory or name of my mother again, and I'll show you the definition of a storm. Just SHUT UP." I say through gritted teeth.

"Excuse me! Can you guys keep it down please?" this older woman asks. She looks to be in her sixties.

"We're sorry ma'am. We'll keep it down," I tell her, but Autumn chimes in.

"Sorry, my ass; she needs to mind her own business," these two are heading into dangerous territory now, and I can just see a fight breaking out.

"Just ignore the depressed housewife," Winter says. These two have no damn manners. I shake my head at them. Sometimes I wish Nana never left, because she can deal with their bickering.

"Wint. Don't be rude." I swear these two can get on my damn nerves sometimes.

"I'm not being disrespectful. I'm just honest. In fact, he used her, and I know mom said he was the best thing to happen to her because she got us, but seriously if we think about it; as much as she loved us and did all she could for us, can you imagine how she must have felt to be so in love that she forgot to love herself first. I mean she thought he would leave his wife and white picket fence family for her; I mean come on. I refuse to allow any man to treat me that way or even dream, imagine or consider it." she explains. I feel sad about my sister's view of things.

We shake our heads, listening to her ramble on amazed by what is coming out of her mouth.

"Wint that's sad, you need to let people in," I tell her.

"No, I don't. I leave that up to you two idiots. Can we go? I need a nice hot chocolate, please? Costa is around the corner," she says, getting up from the table, gathering up her things.

"How you keep that shape of yours is beyond me, I mean a double cheeseburger, fries and now hot chocolate" Autumn tells her.

"I got it from my momma; besides, I also had a bottle of water and some fruit. It's called balance," Wint replies proudly. The walk to the coffee shop is short, but the lunch queue's long.

"That reminds me. Autumn, do you need me later for rehearsals?"
I ask.

"Maybe, I'm still working out the kinks to the steps, but the kids
would love to see you," she replies.

"Well, let me know if you change your mind. I'm heading to Bristol
today." Both girls look at each other and say "Sunshine" and laugh
while I blush like an idiot.

"Whatever. I want to redecorate the shop, before the Manchester
opening," I tell them.

"That sounds great. What were you thinking?" Wint asks
excitedly.

"I was thinking you could come down and do some spray
paintwork on the walls. I want to shut up shop from Monday and do
a reopening event on Thursday or the Saturday depending on when we
get done". I tell Winter.

"And when were you going to tell me this? I mean, can we even
afford this with the new store opening in the next couple of months?"
Autumn asks.

"Of course, we can. I wouldn't even try if we couldn't and when
did I need your permission to revamp my store?"

"Big Head. That's our store, not yours and Auto was just looking
out for us. Stop being so defensive!" Winter declares.

"No. She's not. She's being controlling again. Thinking she makes
all the decisions, and I should ask for permission. I don't tell her how
to dance or you how to draw and make clothes." We have more money

than the bank can count and she is complaining about money. Women.

"That's because I do everything around here, including run YOUR business" Autumn states.

"OUR business. Both of you shut up, you are giving me a headache." It is our turn in the everlasting queue.

"Hi! Can I get a large hot chocolate, please? Oooh and half a carrot cake and three slices of that cheesecake, to go, please. You guys want anything?" Winter orders and then asks us.

"Yeah to ask the good lord where the bottom of your stomach is? And a hot chocolate" Autumn adds, and I laugh.

"Make that two-hot chocolates and a blueberry muffin and a larger mocha to go" I chime in with my two cents.

"Lord, please don't let all this fat go to my ass and stomach because I know the devil is working with these two, so please help my black ass out" Autumn prays.

"Oh, now you're black. Besides, as fine as you look and all that exercise you get from dancing, stop complaining," Winter tells her.

While the girls are squabbling about how they look, I tell them I got this, so they go outside to continue their debate. I pay for the hot beverages and cakes and join them outside with hot drinks in one hand, a muffin bag in my mouth and a half of a carrot cake in the other hand.

They take their orders from me, leaving me with mine.

"Anyway, like I was saying. I'm going to Bristol later tonight. Wint, can you drive up tomorrow and do some painting to the store on Monday for me?" I ask my sister, sweetly.

"And what exactly am I painting?" she enquires.

"How about a mural of mom at the reception back wall and redo the changing rooms with the logo, you can choose the colour scheme for that," I suggest to her.

"And the rest of the store?" she asks.

"I was thinking a ballerina jumping over a hurdle in gold soccer boots for all the sports gear. Not sure about the rest, still thinking. I want to go from today so that I can go in tomorrow and brainstorm." I tell them.

"And what exactly will I be doing in the meantime?" Autumn asks.

"What you do best. Complain, moan, bitch and then come join us," I tell her.

"Cool. Sounds like a plan. Not the bitch and moan part, Auto can do that with you. I've had enough for today. I'm heading back to the shop; you're going Bristol, Auto what are you going to be doing?" Winter asks.

"I'm going to head home with him, then come back for rehearsal. I have a headache." Autumn tells her.

"I'm heading to the garage to pick the car up. I've dropped it in for a service and a clean, we can share a cab," I tell her.

"So, I'll see you before I head off, right?" I ask Winter.

"For definite, because with everything, this all seems very rushed, so we all need to sit and brainstorm really quick," Autumn answers for Winter.

"Whatever Auto. Want us to walk you back?" I ask Wint.

"No, I'm good. I may come with you tonight. No way you are leaving me with Madam Miserable all night. But I may join you later for the class to burn off these cakes Aut," Winter says.

Winter

I kiss my sibling's goodbye and head off in the opposite direction. Isn't that some shit after dragging my ass to work Autumn leaves me behind. When I get back to the store, Clive is speaking to a customer at the reception desk. When he is done, I relieve him and tell him to take a break. Before he leaves, he informs me of who else is due for their break. We only employ four people in the store, so they are easily managed. I suddenly remember Autumn set up interviews today. I quickly send her a text reminding her of the shit she organised for today. The damn girl is working my nerves.

I say, *"Just a reminder missy, you forgot about the interviews today. Get your butt back here. Now!"*

She replies, *"To Wint: you're the boss as well remember, as you pointed out early today. It's our store. Do some work? It's not that hard, you've done interviews before. If all fails, ask Clive for help. My head really hurts Wint. Just Handle it."*

The nerve of her. My sister can be a bitch sometimes, and if she wasn't my better half, I would seriously consider doing her some damage.

After all the damn interviews, I am drained. I weed out the riffraff and damn there are so many. I guess even they need to eat, but I need someone who is passionate about fashion. So, I hire the fashion student part-time and a single mom looking for a break. She reminds me of mom. I even come up with some ideas while interviewing some of the potential candidates.

At the end of the day, I really need a workout. I need something to work my aggression out on. So, I lock up the shop and go upstairs to the studio. I check my phone and see two messages.

Storm says, *"left earlier, I'm heading down now. So, jump on the train or drive. I took the Range."*

Auto says, *"I won't make it in for rehearsal either, can you take the class. Just do some warm-up and go over what we learned last week. Send my apologies, please. Let them know I will be in next week. I've already told Eric to take the class if you're not up for it. Love you. Muah!"*

I don't even entertain a reply to either of them, because they are working my damn nerves. I wait till the senior dancer comes in and leave him with shutter keys and head for the gym. I seriously need that work out after the day I've had. When I arrive at the gym, it is packed out, which irritates me even more because that means all the treadmills are occupied.

I change into my workout outfit designed by me ($eason fitn$$) and fill my water bottle and head toward the workout area. Like I thought all the treadmills are taken, so I decide to join the next class. By the time, the class finishes, I am still in need of something. So, I try the stepper, and still, nothing fulfils me. Finally, a treadmill becomes available. I run for over an hour. I get distracted a few times by a couple of brothers over by the weights station playing who had the biggest dicks with the weights. After that, I decide to go for a swim and steam and relax my muscles from the beating I just gave them.

I start to feel much better until this awful hairy beast comes and sits next to me in the steam room with a smile. That does it for me, it's time to go. I get up and take a quick shower and head home. The taxis are pulling up when I go outside, thank God. Once I reach home, Autumn's in her p. j's knocked out in her room and the place in darkness. At least she cooked. I eat, then climb into bed with her and lay there with her until I fall asleep. I can feel the frustration that's taking over her. I know all she needs is a good night's rest. One things for sure though, I will be retiring very soon. I've only stay on this long because of them. With all our business ventures, I can afford to work from home and laze around if I want to.

Autumn Breeze

~

Autumn

I wake up to find Winter next to me, sleeping peacefully. I go to my en-suite bathroom and when I get back, she's awake.

"Hey, beautiful," I greet her sweetly. I really do not want to argue with her anymore.

"Hey. What time is it?" she asks.

"One. How did it go today?" I enquire.

"Fine, I hired two people instead of one and before you start, don't," she says.

"I wasn't going to, we may need the extra hand for what I was thinking," I climb back into bed and get under the covers with her.

"You ate already?" I ask her.

"Yeah. Thanks. This PMS is no joke, huh. I feel your pain and mine," she says, and I laugh because I know exactly what she's talking about this time of the month as a woman and a twin. It always feels like I am carrying the burden for two. The only good thing is: Storm would feel all the pain. Which means he becomes more annoying?

"So, you want to go for some PMS therapy," she asks.

"Phase one or two?" I ask. We developed stages for our PMS. One is ice cream and plenty of it and two is clubbing and pissing off the locals.

"Definitely two," she replies.

"I'm glad you said that because guess who's playing tonight at club Fire," I say with excitement.

"Who?" she asks, perking up.

"Darius. And you know anywhere Darius is Trouble will be there too." I tell her.

"Hmmm yes, please. I haven't seen them in years," she says and jumps up way too excitedly and starts going through my wardrobe.

"What are you doing?" I ask.

"This calls for a Little Black Dress. But I was thinking little white dress for you and black accessories and the opposite for me, we twin flossing tonight." She says, and I laugh because I love playing Winter on a night out. We get dressed in our matching Seasons velvet dresses designed by my sister with tassels along the shoulder and arm, and sheer see-through material along the side; and glass heel stilettos. I wear full white, and she's dressed in the exact same but in black with white accessories. We use each other as mirrors to correct any minor flaws in our make-up. Our make-up's done the exact same. We have smokey eyes. Our lips are naturally pink and perky, so there's no need for lipstick—just a simple liner and gloss.

Turning off the lights in the apartment, we head down to the garage. We jump in my brand new matte White BMW with custom made interior and a cool aquamarine and champagne leather. It's my baby. You would think Storm would have a fetish for cars, but nope, that's my thing, Storm has a fetish for saving pennies and buying buildings and putting our stamp on it.

When we reach the club it's packed out, the queue's all the way around the corner and parking is hard to find. I roll up at the entrance and check for the bouncer, to see who's managing the door. We generally get in anywhere we show up but if it's a woman bouncer, sometimes things can become a task. Damn, we can't catch a break.

Chick blocked. I park in the staff car park behind the club, link arms with my sister and head for what seems like a marathon to get inside. We own practically every building on this strip. Thank God because I don't think I can stand out there for much longer in this shorter than a midget dress.

As usual, eyes start wandering in our direction, and the hatred starts. Still, we're used to the attention, so we bypass it all and go to the bar and open a champagne tab. We dance and enjoy ourselves. Someone taps Wint on the shoulder. It is handsome as ever Darius, he never disappoints. He looks as devilishly gorgeous as the day I met him. Tall, muscular built, with a P. diddy fade and waves. He has sweet berry lips and deep brown come fuck me eyes. His ears are still big like Dumbo's, but he's grown into them. I must admit grown up Darius is definitely something to desire. Fuck a Greek God; he is an African Warrior Hercules.

"Hello ladies," he greets us, and Wint speaks up first because I am gob smacked.

"Hey. How are you doing?" Winter answers.

I can see his poor little brain working overtime, trying to figure out who's who. We haven't seen each other in so long. I guess we've changed because he was always able to tell us apart, so I play along.

"I'm good, and you?" he says with a quizzical look in his eyes.

"We're good," I answer.

There's an awkward silence that fills the air as he tries to figure us out. I know the look oh too well. It has been a long time since we've seen each either but considering our past, he should be able to tell the difference. Any man who can't tell the difference between my sister and me is never worth keeping.

"So what time are you playing?" I ask because I am beginning to get annoyed.

"Any sec now. Can I get you, ladies, a drink?" he offers.

"No, we're good," I say, I am done playing guess who.

"Ok. Well, you want to come and join us?" Daruius asks, ''The family is over there."

Winter replies keenly as I roll my eyes. "Sure, lead the way."

We make our way through the crowd, and all eyes are following us. Once we reach all his little friend's eyes are all gleaming like a child on Christmas morning.

"Hello, ladies," they all say.

"Hi!" Winter quickly holds my hand and turns to Darius and gives him a look that makes him aware of how uncomfortable we feel. He quickly picks up on it.

"Guys these are my friends and off-limits. Ladies, I'll be back. Behave." He walks to the DJ booth to start his set. Trouble strolls over with two buckets filled with ice and Cîroc. "Who do we have here then gents?" Trouble asks.

"Hello, Trouble. Still the same I see," I speak up.

"If it ain't little Summer and Spring. All grown up. And if I do say so myself, you both look marvellous." he states.

"Tell me about it," one of their goons adds.

Trouble always refers to us as Summer and Spring instead of our real names because Winter used to catch an attitude with him, and he loved it.

"Thank you. I see you haven't lost your sense of humour. But you've cleaned up very well, you look as handsome as ever," Winter replies.

Winter and I dance the night away, drinking and having a good time. I am disappointed that Darius can't figure us out. A few hours pass by and I hear my name over the music.

Darius is giving us a shout, "ladies the gents are in the building tonight feel free to show them a good time," he says and makes a few jokes and plays a few songs.

Then I hear him say, "And my girl Autumn's here as well."

Everyone take a look,

''She's in the pretty white dress over there. Yes, the beautiful twin, that's all me. I see you brothers have been eyeing her since she touched up in here, hands off. That's my business."

I start blushing a bit and feel sweet because I guess he finally figured it out.

"Guess you can be mine then lovely lady?" their friend Ricky says to Winter.

"Ahh! No, I don't think so," Winter tells him, and they all laugh.

"So young Winter shall we shake a leg?" Trouble asks her.

I know she'd been waiting for that all night. I smile at my sister, giving her the go ahead nod, and I continue swaying to the music and jam with poor Ricky. Poor guy, I'm giving him a little bit of an ego boost, looks like he needs it. He is fine as hell too, so that is a bonus. His caramel-brown skin with braids is kind of sexy.

One and a half hours later, Darius finishes his set and makes his way over to us.

"My man, which part of my property, didn't you understand," he jokes with his friend. They pound fists, and he takes my hands, leading me off to some corner to dance.

I'm having a great time, forget all my troubles and just chill. He could always make me forget my troubles. We find a table in the VIP area, but it's still a bit noisy, so I suggest we go chill in the car. I tell

Wint, and she says she's fine. We walk to my car with his arms around my waist, and I feel comfortable, and at home in his arms. It's cold, so he offers me his jacket. I can't stop smiling.

"So, I'm your property, now am I?" I ask.

"Did you want to be Ricky's?" he asks grinning.

"I prefer to belong to myself, thank you," I smile at him.

"Well, you'll always belong to me, you know that right," he states.

"No, you belong to Peppa."

He laughs like I've said something funny.

"How's my girl doing? I feel bad I haven't visited," I ask.

"You should feel bad. She's fine and why you say I belong to Peppa?" he asks. Now that's a stupid question, I think.

"Because I know about you and Peppa from way back when."

"What about Peppa and me. You know you shouldn't listen to gossip,' he says.

We sit for what seems like hours and catch up on everything. He's still the gentleman I used to know and love. We talk about work, Peppa, life, love and loss. We even get around to talking about why we broke up back in the day. He confesses the love he had for Peppa was deeper than he even realised. But I still can't help feeling that he didn't love me the same way. I even ask for his advice on the refurbishment. He agrees to play at the stores for the openings. Which gives me a great idea to showcase our product? I receive a message from Wint saying the club's over and she's going to Trouble's place. I shake my head and text back.

"Be careful. Don't hurt him," I say.

"You too," she replies. *"Imma gonna hurt him alright, on purpose. Love you, sis."*

Even though I am feeling a bit jealous of my sister, I can't help but smile. Poor Trouble won't know what's hit him. I drive Darius home, and we sit for a while and talk some more. Time seems to stand still while we talk. I notice foot traffic getting a bit heavier, so we say our goodbyes and he kisses me good morning. I swear this man can always melt my insides, but I know better than to sleep with another woman's man, even if she doesn't know it yet.

I get home to the empty house and get phase 1 out of the fridge. It's well needed. I kick off my shoes at the bedroom door and crawl into bed and start the self-pity party. God knows when I fall asleep.

To-Do-List

～

Winter

I crawl in a little after two Sunday afternoon, well satisfied. Auto's still asleep and has a melted tub of ice cream leaking on the bedsheets. I quickly take it off the bed. Wipe the sheet off and climb in next to her and wrap my arms around her. She seems so sad, so I just hold her. She wakes up slightly and looks up at me, but quickly drifts back once she realises it is me. I kiss her forehead and say a small prayer for my sister. We both fall asleep. It's four when ringing wakes us from our slumber. It's Storm calling on Skype. I click on the TV and answer the call, and his face appears on the TV screen. Since the Apple Mac's connected to the TV, we can talk to him via the television.

"Hey, what are you guys doing?" he asks.

"Sleeping. What do you want?" I ask him.

"It's four in the evening, wake up, what time are you coming down?"

"I don't know. What time is the last train? I'm still frass from last night, and I'm sure Auto is too," I state.

"I'm fine," she says groggily. I give her a wary look, and she stares me down. So, I let it go.

"Have any of you come up with any ideas yet?" he asks.

"Yeah. I was thinking we could refurbish all three shops, do a quick redecoration and reopen. Do a big production," I tell him.

"I was thinking the same thing. We could use my dancers as models in the shop windows, live models, and Darius agreed to play live music for us free of charge. I say we go hard and make history and get some publicity and exposure," Autumn says.

"Can we pull that off? Three revamps and a grand opening?" I ask.

"We start with Bristol, then London then Birmingham and end with the great grand opening of Manchester. We use the others as a warm-up and a build-up to the spectacular showcase of Chester is our largest store. Winter can handle all the designs and merchandising. Storm you can deal with staffing and management of the revamping. I'll deal with entertainment," Autumn explains..

"Wow, you've thought of everything," I state.

"So, what do you think?" she asks.

"Love it... let's get started,'' Storm says.

"By the way, I love the idea of the mural of mom on the back wall of the reception desk. Let's do that on all the walls of the store. Storm I still need you to liaise with the decorator of the Cheshire branch. It's a woman so work your magic," I say.

"You are pimping me out?" he jokes.

"Yes... now get to work," Autumn replies.

"Yes, ma'am," he salutes.

"Wint, you think you can do that?" she asks.

"Already done. Imma be on the last train so pick me up, don't be late Storm."

He raises his eyebrows like I just made a ridiculous comment.

"So, everyone set?" little miss bossy boots asks.

"Listen I was thinking we need to promote Clive to manager. Because while we're away, we need someone to man the stores?" I suggest.

"Whatever you feel is best, go for it. Wint, I just checked the times and the last train is 10:10 tonight, be on it," Storm tells me.

"K. Hi Sunshine," me and Autumn say, and she waves and passes by the camera screen.

"Later bro," I say.

"Yeah. Later Wint," he says.

"Yeah, later." I click off the screen and Autumn gets out the bed, and I follow her because something's up and I want to know. I am tired as hell and this girl has me chasing her for information. But to no avail, she says she's fine, but she's my sister. I know when things are troubling her.

We change our clothes and do our Sunday ritual deep clean of the apartment, while I tell her about my night with Trouble himself. I brag about my night, and she stays in denial about whatever is bothering her. I shower and drag on my jeans, a simple white t-shirt and a jeans jacket to match with my white Air Max. Spring is in the air, but the air is still moist and crispy.

I run down to the local corner co-op. I stock up on female supplies because my stomach is already starting to kill and most importantly, ice cream. I feel bad that I am leaving Autumn alone tonight to go be with Storm for the next couple of days, especially when I know something is bothering her. I hate to see my sister upset, and I know it not just PMS. I change my mind, Storm is going to have to be OK without me, my sister needs me.

So, I have to let him know that there's something up with our sister. Before I head home, I stop outside and call Storm to let him know what's what. I wrap up the conversation with him. He agrees I should stay, and I can always go later. I can work from home, and the spray painting will only take one day anyway. He can handle all the other stuff himself. Plus, he doesn't need me there bossing him about and annoying the hell out of everyone.

"Just take care of my sister. I got this. I'll see you soon. Love you, sis,." he says.

"Love you too. Don't forget to paint the entire shop white, before I come down," I remind him.

"Bye Winter," he says, hanging up.

I head upstairs. I tell Autumn that I am staying because I really don't want to be in a house with Sunshine and Storm, a white lie, but it's necessary. We own an apartment in every city we own a store. The two-bedroomed apartment in Bristol is an open plan complex, small but efficient. Nothing like the apartment we have in Birmingham. The one in London is in a skyscraper. It makes these Essex bitches mouth's water with envy. Autumn seems a little annoyed by my decision. We also own several other homes across Europe and small islands that get rented out until we have a need for them. Something mama used to say to us about 'not having all your eggs in one basket,' made Storm buy properties in various countries.

"You don't have to stay because of me, I'm fine," she says.

"Who said anything about you?" I ask.

"You don't have to," she says sternly.

"Whatever. Grab two spoons. I'm staying. I'm gonna change into something comfy. Be right back."

I change into my shorts and t-shirt and comfy fluffy socks and matching boots. Auto is sitting at the kitchen table on her laptop. She had on her p. j's and kimono nightdress. She closes the lid of the laptop as I enter the room and spins around quickly to face me.

"What you up to?" I ask.

"Not much, ready for some therapy?" she replies.

"Yes," I say.

She walks over to the countertop and grabs the spoons and ice cream and joins me on the couch. We wrap ourselves in the blanket, and I switch on the TV for the NCIS Marathon. I love me some Mark Harmon The one white dude can do no wrong, and he is a silver fox too, yum. After a couple hours of crime drama, it's time to address

Autumn's issue, which she's trying to hide. She knows she can't hide anything from me.

"Got a message from Trouble when I went out earlier," I tell her.

"Hmmm... you hurt him that bad huh?" she asks.

"You know I always leave them wanting more."

"You're something else," she says shaking her head.

"So, come on, spill?"

It's about time she starts telling me what's going on in that brain of hers. I know it has something to do with that son of a bitch father that we never had, or that the sex was disappointing with Darius. It's a shame when your hopes are high for a man, and he disappoints in bed.

"How was it last night with your DJ?" I ask.

"He was a gentleman," she says.

"Ehh boring. What the hell does that mean? He was a gentleman. He didn't hit it, right?" I enquire.

"No, we didn't do anything if you must know. We just talked all night. Caught up on what we've got going on in our lives, and he gave me some advice and I gave him some real truths," she explains.

"And what was that? What advice did he give?" I ask stuffing ice cream in my mouth.

"He just told me he would help out at the store with the music and how I could do a huge production from one end of the centre that leads to the store and put it on social media and YouTube. He has a friend at

ITV, so he's going to contact him for some coverage and is going to try getting us on the This Morning show," she says.

"What! That would be amazing!" Brilliant, Mr Gentleman is useful after all.

"He loves your dresses," she says.

"Tell him if he gets us that gig. He can rip it off you," I tell her.

"You're not funny. I wouldn't sleep with him. The offer is there, and maybe if you didn't make your speech the other day about mom, I would have gone there. I –"

"What speech about mom?" I ask her interrupting whatever she's about to say.

"About Jacob using her," she says.

"Why are we still talking about him? So, what about it? How is Darius using you now?" I ask her curiously.

"He's not. I haven't given him the chance. He's clearly still in love with Peppa. Even though she's in prison and has two kids with two different dads. She's still the apple of his eye. Oh, and get this Peppa is still in the dark about it. Isn't that some bullshit? He defends her no matter what she does, always has, always will. So, he has been slinging his dick here and there just for the release, I guess until, she gets out and falls in love with him." She explains.

"Well if she hasn't fallen in love with him by now what makes him think she will?" I ask.

"Well, he's looking after her son while she inside, visits her every week even though the drive is three hours long and sends her money every week" she informs me.

"If he's doing all that, what's her family doing? I ask.

"They help too of course. Her mom has the kids and the dad's well, I think they chip in here and there. But as for him, he's so far up her ass, he no longer can smell the shit. It's a bit creepy how much he's doing without her knowing. He really looks out for her, so much so I wish he would do the same for me. He's the one that got away," she finally says.

"Huuuh you were sixteen when you broke up. You've dated how many men since then? You should be over that by now," I ask in confusion. I don't even remember most of the idiots' names I was with back in the day, never mind last year. My sister needs to get out more.

"I was, at least I thought I was. But last night just brought back a heap of heartbreak and sadness that I thought I'd got past, that's all," she says.

I give her a hug and squeeze her tight—my poor sister.

"I'm sorry you got your heartbroken Auto. See that's why I refuse to do that love shit," I tell her.

"It wasn't all bad, it was actually great, and like I said he's the perfect gentleman, everything I ever wanted in a man. I just refuse to be second best or runner up for that matter. That's what I would be if I was with him. You know he brought me my first ever ring. Yeah, said it was his promise to me that one day he would change it to an engagement ring. The next week I broke up with him. Thank God, we had finished our exams and it was the last week of school. I knew I wouldn't see him again. I couldn't bear it," she explains.

"Damn that's cold sis. So, you gave back the ring?" I ask.

"No. here it is. I wore it last night because I wanted him to know that I never forgot him," she says.

"Let me see."

It's gold, with a stone, cubic zirconia.

"Ahhh. It's cute. More than a man ever did for me boo. I also see you're into that mind game shit." I tell her.

"What do you mean?"

"I mean you were hoping things would go back to how they were back in the day. Time travelling is impossible," I tell her.

"No, I just wanted to remind him that I still have love for him," she says.

Love my ass. Seems like I'm going to have to school my sister about the affairs of the dick because this playing with your heart business I'm not into. I would hate for someone to take advantage of her and break her heart, and I would have to break some damn necks.

"Look Auto. By putting that ring on, you set yourself up for failure straight away. You wanted him to travel down memory lane and find the love he had for you as a teenager. He's a grown-ass man now. You don't know what he's like as an adult. For all you know he is a complete asshole, singing the perfect tune that speaks to your heart to get to your cookie jar," I explain.

"He's not like that I'm telling you," she says.

"I hear you, I do, but just be careful. I would hate to have to fuck a fool up."

"Like I said he's not like that. He was sweet, the perfect gentleman. We just talked mostly about Peppa, and how he should just finally come clean with her if that's where his heart is. Because he's wasting his time with every other young woman he beds," she says.

"Hmmm. If you say so. So, what's with the ice cream meltdown?" I ask.

"I felt a bit depressed that after all this time he's still hung up on Peppa especially after seeing me. Like you said, God broke the mould when he made us Wint," She says.

That makes me laugh, remembering what I said, sometimes I crack my own self up.

"Don't worry big sis. There's someone out there for you, who meets all my approval," I tell her.

"What about all my approval?" she asks.

"What about it. They have to pass through me before any wedding bells can go off in here," I tell her.

"Who said anything about any wedding bells? As much as I want that man in my bed every day. There's no way I'm playing second fiddle to no other woman," she says, making herself clear.

"Good because we're not about that life."

I'm glad my sister sees sense not go there with Darius because if he ever hurt her Storm would be his worst nightmare. I feel bad for my sister losing out like that to another woman. I guess it's true what they say. The heart wants what the heart wants. I wish I could take away her pain, right now, all I can do is offer more ice cream.

"You want another tub? You could tell me all about this production you and Mr Gentleman talked about," I ask her.

"No. no, I want in-depth details, because you gave it up like that with Trouble himself. I know it must have been better than you said because he hasn't stopped calling since you got in. What did you give him?"

"Nothing, I just left him wanting more. Gave him a bit of finger action and let him please me a little," I tell her.

"When you say please you a little, what does that mean, because earlier you said he was the best, the best what?" she asks. She's a nosy parker this one.

"Let's just say his tongue action is on point, hit every spot there is to hit. After that, I was too tired and drunk to even think. I slept like a baby. I snuck out before he woke up and jumped in a taxi. I wrote my number on his bathroom mirror, like in the movies," I tell her.

"So why are you dodging him. I thought you liked him?" she asks.

"I do, but it's sisterly time. So, he should wait. As a matter of fact, that's exactly what I'm going to tell him."

So, I text him, *"Patience grasshopper. Good things come to those who wait, patiently. Spending quality time with the fam. Later."*

"Winter exactly how many men do you have?" she asks.

"None. And I want to keep it like that. I saw how many times his phone buzzed off the hook while he was with me until he had to turn it off, but I just played like I didn't see because I couldn't care less. I'm not looking for one, or anyone, just my own pleasure," I tell her.

"Girl just be careful and watch yourself, and strap it up at all times," she advises.

"You don't have to tell me. I am twenty five and still never felt the real thing without latex, and I never will," I tell her.

"Really? Even when you lost your V?" she asks, shocked at my revelation.

"Child, I know you guys think I'm throwing it here and there, but no I was still a virgin at twenty,, unlike you guys. Having a guy please me with his fingers or tongue is not sex. I have never sucked a dick in my life either," I say, surprising her.

"What! How the hell have you been pulling that off for so long?" Autumn asks quizzically.

"Simple. I'm a BOSS. I lay down the law beforehand, if they don't like it, I'm out. Most men think they're the one who's going to change my mind and be my first. Plus, I'm picky as hell with a bad attitude," I say, shrugging my shoulders.

"I can't believe it, all this time!" she exclaims.

"Now who's the whore now? I like to flirt, and I'm good-looking, so sometimes I like to make them beg for it."

My brother and sister are always the quiet ones, but they do say those are the ones to watch out for. I kept my virginity for a reason. I just choose to keep it to myself for my own benefit.

"So, miss holier than thou. When do you plan to settle down?" Autumn asks me.

"When I find a man, who can please me and make more money than me, then maybe I'll consider it. I don't see me dating orange Donald Trump. So never." I tell her.

"Lawd, please take the case and gimme the pillow," Autumn blares out, causing me to laugh.

Creating a Storm

Storm

After my conversation with Wint, I brief all the staff at Stormy $easons, which is technically my store, but we are all part owners. I let them know the drill for the rest of the week. I promote the store supervisor and get him an assistant so that they can manage when we leave the country. She has one week to learn all the relevant ins and outs of the store and get them to come in tomorrow and break down the store ready for painting on Tuesday. I can already see my vision coming together. I'm glad the girls are on board with the remodel and I can't wait to see what Autumn has in store for the modelling thing. She always makes a big production of everything. It always turns out great.

From what Winter is saying I'm a little worried about her. If that punk of an ex-did something to her someone is seriously going to get hurt. Why would she put herself back in that situation with him after all I've told her and opened her eyes to? She should know not to ever look back. The past is the past. Women! I will never understand them even if I did share the same umbilical cord with them. Everything seems to be running smoothly.

Now Sunshine, there's another headache I really don't need right now. She's supposed to be my go-to girl for stress release, and now she has another idiot demanding her time. I mean she always picks up when I call no matter what hour I call, which is great, but I guess she ditches the whole career woman thing and got herself a man. I'm not trying to step on another man's toes, but anyone she's dealing with better believe that he's got to share; no ifs or buts about it. Better yet it's time she tells this fool to go. I'm in town now, plus I'm fed up with this game we've been playing for the past eight years.

I still need to book the flights and sort all this business shit out. My house back in Jamaica is almost finished with just a few more interiors needed, and then it will be complete. I love Jamaica, our grandmother took us back there when mom died, and I've gone back every year since. I can afford it, and now my house is almost complete. I'm glad, I'm not too fond of sleeping in the ghetto like that. I like peace and tranquillity. Too much commotion all the damn time. But grandma Bird loves it. She refuses to move, so we had to rebuild her house right smack bang in the middle. Apparently, the place has sentimental value. It's where mom was born and where she chopped grandad allegedly and a whole heap of nonsense. In the end, her refusal to move prompted us to build a steel iron electric gate. Which she got rid of after I paid for it. She got someone to take it down, said she's not a prisoner in her own place, so she doesn't want any damn fence and gate. I swear all the women in my life have been sent here to drive me crazy. I'm only one man with too much responsibility. I make it my point of duty to call her every week and check up on her; make sure she has everything for her comfort. The last time I spoke to her, she didn't sound too good, so I'm glad we are going to see her. Imma makes it a surprise.

I have to contact the contractor for the new store in Manchester and boy is she a piece of work. She can't do this, and she can't do that. I don't know what we're paying her for.

"Hello, Mrs Simpson. I got your new estimate for the shop. This is supposed to be a simple job. Why does it cost so much?" I ask.

"It's late in the evening, business hours are over, why are you calling this late?" she points out.

"At these prices, I can call any damn time I please. I see here you've made some changes. We didn't ask for this. It's simple. If you can't do the job then maybe we should find someone who can do it the way I want and not the way you do," I tell her.

"Sir. I'm more than capable of doing my job but with the short notice and things you and your sisters want, they are going to be expensive. Plus, there's the manpower to pull it off."

"Fine. Please send me a visual of the layout and hire the manpower needed. But before you make any decisions, please contact me beforehand. I'll be in touch. And Mrs Simpson. I know when someone is trying to rip me off, so please don't insult my intelligence. Have a good night."

Shit imma have to go down there tomorrow and check shit out because this bitch is up to something. Every five seconds she changes and charges me for some bullshit. Like I don't have enough shit going on. I got to deal with her stupid ass too. This can work out in my favour though; I can take Sunshine with me and do a bit of shopping. She loves to shop and burn a hole in my credit cards. Her head game seems to always get better after shopping.

So, I text her, *"Sunshine: how about shopping tomorrow in Manchester, then dinner?"*

It'll give us a chance to talk about this new dude she's trying to hide. We have this weird relationship, some would say. Still, I have always treated her with love and respect no matter who is in my life, never threw anything in her face and respected her wishes when she asked me to leave and give her time and space. This chick always seems to want time and space. She lives alone, and when she's short on the rent and has a big credit card bill, I make sure she's taken care of.

When one of my girlfriends finds out about me giving her money or going to see her, they kick up a fuss, but that's their downfall because my Sunshine keeps it sophisticated. She forwards their messages, or adds me in on any phone calls that they try to have behind my back and things never end well for them. Because that means I would be spending the night alone or with Sunshine. They just need to know that Sunshine will always be my best friend, and it's just that simple. So, we fuck occasionally, but they never know that, and I never give them any reason to feel jealous. I never lie to any one of them about who she is. She is and always will be my friend. So, what if we talk nearly every minute of the day and I value her opinion above most people. It's just the way we are. Sure, I was upset with Rachel for cheating, but if I'm truthful to myself, I sabotaged that myself a long time ago. I always seem to do it, because they aren't Sunshine.

Sunshine has her head on her shoulders. She's educated, and it doesn't hurt that she reminds me of a black Nubian princess, with a pair of perfect huge breasts that a guy can get comfortable laying on. Her body is the perfect hourglass shape with a full sexy lip always tasting like peaches. I remember the day I first saw her in a crowded park. I was at Bristol carnival with my friends for the weekend. There she was in one of those beautifully made costumes, grinding her hips to the rhythm of the Calypso beat; it was mesmerising. The ass on her is out of this world. I gave her the name Sunshine because the name she gave me sounded more like a dude "Sonny". That didn't seem to fit the beautiful girl before me.

It was a cloudy day, and I swear when she smiled, the sun came out, so I called her Sunshine because she brings out the sunshine on any cloudy day for me. She is my little ray of sunlight. On that first day, I ditched my boys, followed her around all day and bugged the hell out of her until she gave me her number and the kiss of a lifetime. I told her straight away to ditch that name it just didn't suit her. Sonny was her nickname, so I was relieved to find out that her actual name's Monique Sanchez. One day, one day, I will make her Monique Valentine, but until then, I will just have to keep dreaming. I guess that's why none of my relationships ever last with any of my other women. They just aren't Sunshine; they aren't Valentine material. That's why I decided to open a shop in Bristol to be closer to her.

She texts back, *"Come home to me, I've cooked dinner, and we can talk about your plans for tomorrow."*

I tell her, *"I'll be right there."*

I had to respect her wishes and let her go when she went off to university. She didn't want a relationship, she wanted to focus. That really broke my heart. I didn't even know if I would ever get over her, once we broke up. A year passed, and I had finally fucked her out of my system and moved on. That was until she called in the middle of the night, in distress, crying. I hate to hear her crying, so she got my attention immediately. I jumped in my car instantly without even knowing where or what had happened, to be by her side. When I asked where she was; she told me the hospital, all my alarm bells went off. I said a small prayer and begged God to let her be ok. I kept asking her what happened, but she just kept crying into the damn phone. I just couldn't take it anymore, so I just jumped out of bed forgetting about the young woman I'd left lying there, and drove the two-hour journey to hear the worst possible thing had happened to her. She'd been assaulted, beaten and raped. She had a broken rib; a black eye and bruises all over. I was so furious I punched through a wall; I had to pay for the damage of course, and I bruised my knuckles a bit. She couldn't even speak or open her eyes properly when I first saw her.

I could tell she was self-conscious about the whole thing, so I didn't ask any questions, I just sat and held her hand. She climbed off the bed. I jumped up to help her off the bed. She just wobbled over to me and sat on my lap and rested her head on my shoulder. I couldn't do anything but hold her and cry with her. She fell into a deep sleep. I got up with her in my arms and laid her back down on the bed. The doctors had given her some strong pain relief, she was so exhausted, she looked so helpless hooked up to that IV drip. I couldn't sleep, I was restless, there were so many unanswered questions.

The morning came, and I got her breakfast, helped her wash herself and brush her hair; she was still the most beautiful girl to me. I brought her some flowers and a teddy bear to be by her side when I wasn't. By lunchtime, the doctor came and did his check. The police from the night before, came back to question her. I could see that she was uncomfortable talking in front of me, so I left the room, I couldn't bear to hear the details; anyway. I wanted someone to pay for what they did to her. I hated myself for not being there for her when she needed me the most; instead, I was balls deep inside another woman.

Once the doctor gave us the all-clear, I had to rent a hotel room because she didn't feel like going back to her flat. She no longer felt safe, so I got us a room at the Hilton. She slept for the best part of a week while I watched her and aided her back to full strength. They did find the coward who violated her, and he's in prison now. I'm glad because if I ever see him, that will be the day he takes his last breath. For the moment, prison is keeping him alive. Apparently, he's under protection now because I made it my point of duty to find a friend on the inside to do some damage, for a price of course. Still, it's something I don't mind paying for repeatedly. The day of his release will be his last day on earth. I put out a prison hit on his ass; he's never leaving that hell hole he calls home alive, and I feel no sympathy or remorse about it. He's just lucky I didn't get a hold of him before the police did.

It took six months before her mental state would return to somewhat normal and for her to be intimate again. I got an apartment and opened the store in Bristol the same year to keep myself busy and to keep an eye on her. A strong black woman that's for sure, she passed with a first from the university after all that she had been through. It's what I admire about her the most. She never let anything come between her dreams, no matter how hard she had to work for it. After that eventful year, we are closer than ever before, but she still wants to remain friends with benefits, so to speak.

When I get through the apartment door, a beautiful scent captures my attention. The lights are off, and scented candles are burning all around the apartment. Two dinner place settings are laid out perfectly and there's two candles in the centre of the table. I can see petals leading to the bathroom and hear slow jams playing on the surround sound system. She has prepared dinner, and it looks delicious. I love fish, any type of fish, whether baked, stuffed or battered. Once it's from the sea I love it. I can see her silhouette in the hallway approaching. She appears in a mini champagne coloured Jasper Conrad dressing-gown; her hair freshly done and with minimal makeup. She takes up a place in between the archway and just smiles. Her smile always gives me goosebumps. I rub my chin and take off my jacket and place it on the back of the chair. She gets all my attention now. I ignore the vibration and ringing of my phone. whoever's calling can wait.

"I'm guessing all this is for me?" I ask.

"No, it's all for me," she says seductively. I decide to play along.

"OK! So, if this is for you, why am I here. You could have done this at your house I could have met you there," I tell her.

"I like your tub better. So, which is first a bath or dinner?" she asks as she walks over to me and puts her arms around my neck and licks her lips.

"Your choice. You call the shots," I reply as she places her lips over mine and pecks me on my lips.

I grab her around the waist and hold her in place and swallow her mouth into mine. I need to taste her. To let her, have her way with me, let her satisfy my every need. But she releases me from our kiss and walks over to the kitchen table and beckons for me to come to her. At this point, I would crawl through broken glass if she asked. She pulls out the chair, and I sit down, she joins me, and we eat, while I devour her with my eyes.

"I never get tired of that," she tells me.

"What is that?" I ask.

"The way you look at me. Like I'm the only woman in the world. Like I'm going to break if you take your eyes off me. You never seem to notice anyone else when I'm with you. Don't ever stop looking at me like that," she requests.

"Why would I stop looking at you like that? You know how I feel about you. You'll always have a place in my heart and my tub apparently." I tell her.

"See you always make me smile. I love that."

"Eat, your bath will get cold," she says.

We eat dinner. I continue to admire the beauty I am sharing dinner with. I enjoy the view of her swallowing each bite, how it slides down her throat smoothly, the strand of hair that settles over her brow, the natural tone of her full plump lips. Dinner's delicious, and the wine's perfect. Everything she does, she does perfectly. I wait for her to finish her meal, she eats slower than the average, but it's a pleasure to watch her eat.

Once she finishes, she leads the way to the bathroom where the tub is filled with rose petals and a fresh scent that I can't place. It must be one of those bath bomb things she's forever filling up my bathroom with; drives me mad most of the time but tonight it smells heavenly. She slowly peels off my clothes and tells me to step in, so I do as I am told. She drops her dressing gown, now she's completely naked, and she's a vision.

"See that look right there, that's what I'm talking about. It's like you've never seen me naked before, it's endearing," she says.

"With you, it's like opening my birthday present constantly and still feeling excited," I confess.

She takes the bathing sponge and lathers it up and slowly washes me. When she reaches my dick, it is already hard and dripping from anticipation. She strokes it up and down and gives me a mind-blowing hand job, which leads me to think I am in for a long night. She washes me from head to toe and then tells me to sit down and rest back while she gives me a show so sexy I feel stupefied. I watch as she caresses her body slowly and plays with her clit, and once her juices start flowing, she puts her fingers inside herself, then takes them out and places them on my lips. I love the way she tastes. She takes my hands and places them between her thighs and instructs me on how she wants to be pleased, I do as I am told. I play with her clit until she moves my hands from between her lips. I am starting to get impatient, I want her now, but this is her show, so I'll be her puppet for tonight. She comes in between my legs and kneels down stroking my already hard dick and with one hand letting some of the water out with the other. She kisses the tip of my bad-boy, and it seems to have gotten even harder for her, like she's a maestro, and he's her instrument, he only moves to her beat. She licks and sucks to the rhythm of the music playing in the background and boy that just sends me into a trance like no other. I'm ready to bust another nut after the workout she gives me with her mouth. I ease her off because I'm ready to fly off the handle. I want to be inside her for that. She looks up and smiles and tells me to relax. I am more than relaxed. I am ready to give her everything I got. But she just turns around; sits down between my legs and relaxes against my chest.

"What are we doing, Sunshine?" I ask stupefied.

"We are relaxing in the tub," she states.

"I'm fully relaxed, you've cleaned, polished and shined every inch of me. Why are we just sitting here in the tub waiting to freeze to death?" I enquire.

"You afraid of a little shrinkage?" she snickers.

"No. my daddy may have been a white man but my granddaddy sure as hell Kunta-Kinte, African mandingo. Plus, when I'm around you, I never worry about that because you keep me standing to attention always," I remind her.

"I bet that's what you say to all the girls," she teases.

"No, just you. You know I would never lie to you, and I would never tell you the same thing I tell another woman. I'm not that kind of man," I promise her.

"I'm sorry," she says with sincerity in her voice.

"For what?" I ask curiously as to what she has to be sorry for after the meal and shine and polish she's just given me. Maybe she'd done something I need to forgive her for that's why I'm getting special treatment tonight, but then again, she always likes to do this kind of thing for me, always surprising me with random gifts of pleasure.

"Rachel and your other relationships. I know it's because of me, they all broke up with you." Yes, it was, but I will never admit that to her.

"Is that what tonight is about?" I ask.

"No, I just want a relaxing night with you making love to me. Is that too much to ask?" I sense a bit of insecurity in her voice. Doesn't she know that all she has to do is ask, I will always come to her side. We have been a bit distant for a while, but I would never leave her behind. Doesn't she know that?

"Don't do that to yourself?" I tell her, "Rachel left because she couldn't keep it in her draws; she got jealous and lashed out in the wrong way. And you not picking up my calls the past few months was wrong and so was sending me lame-ass text messages. Don't worry about Rachel, I'm not," I tell her.

"Yeah because I was causing a rift in your relationship, making your life a misery. They were necessary," she proclaims.

"You are necessary. I enjoy you in my life. Like right now."

If I'm honest with myself, I sabotaged that relationship myself. Slowly caressing her beautiful dark-skinned legs and tracing kisses along her neck. I tickle her side to get her to shift to my leg.

"I'm serious. What are we doing?" I ask.

"Now, I want you to pick me up and take me into that bedroom over there and make love to me." she requests.

"That I can do," I get up and do as I am told; step out of the tub and lift her out and dry her off. Pick her up and rest her head on me, she fits perfectly in my arms. She looks so peaceful and sleepy. I chuckle, the sight of her brings me nothing but happiness.

"Don't fall asleep yet pretty lady," I take her to the bedroom and our song plays in the background, so I place her on the ground.

"May I have this dance?" I ask.

"With pleasure," she replies.

As Prince sings, the words seem fitting for her because she is the most 'Beautiful Girl In The World' to me. As it plays, I hold her close dancing with our naked bodies pressing up against each other. I release her grasp and reach for the body oil on top of the dressing table and pour a handful in the middle of my hands and massage her ass first before I cover her body with oil. I caress all over her body. The candlelight hits her body, and she glows more beautifully. I place my lips to hers and devour her mouth with mine; her hands around my neck, I lift her up and place her legs around my waist. She was made for me, our bodies fit perfectly together like the pieces of a puzzle.

I lay her on the bed to kiss every inch of her body. I take my time with every delicate spot that turns her on. I move from one chocolate tipped nipple to the next until they are perfectly erect. I trail kisses down to her navel and make circles with my tongue and then make my way to her pink velvet. I kiss it for her. I lift her legs and trail sweet kisses down them until I reach her spot again and repeat the same movement again on the other leg. I've learnt anticipation alone can get a woman to do anything you want and sing to your name. It's never a good idea to rush into anything with a woman. So, I take my time when it comes to pleasing the woman I love. With every other woman, I'm always in it for my pleasure only. I kiss her sweet spot and use my fingers to explore her, she's purring like a sexy black cat in heat, and I love that I can make her feel this way. I trail my tongue between her slit and stick my tongue deep inside her and write my name, 'Storm King Valentine' she moans and wiggles trying to get away, but my grasp on her won't allow her to move. I want her to feel every stroke I give her. She comes full force on my tongue quenching every thirst I've ever had. I go to work on her again until she screams my name over and over, but I still don't hear what I want to hear. I want her to beg me for this dick, and she does.

"Please, baby, please let me have it," she coos. Laying her feet flat on the bed.

I climb inside and slowly whine my hips inside her wet pussy; it feels just like what the doctor ordered, an ideal fit. I pound with every stroke while nibbling on her ear, whispering,

"Is this what you want?"

"Yes. Give it to me please."

I love hearing her beg for me. I love it when she needs me. I plough so deep inside I swear I lost my balls inside her walls. I want her to feel me inside her tomorrow. I flip her over and massage her sweet little ass, she's positioned just right for me. I slap that pretty pussy with my steel and tease her with just the head, and she squeals with delight. I enter her with great precision and work her inside like my life depends on it. She's come several times already, and I can feel the nut of a lifetime coming, so I pound even harder for my pleasure. Her pussy's just so damn juicy, flowing with the juices of our lovemaking. I come harder than I have ever before and collapse beside her, leaving smiles that could brighten up any room on her face and mine.

Through heavy breathing, she whispers, "I love you."

I cuddle her up in my arms and whisper, "I love you too, Monique."

We fall asleep in each other arms.

I wake up around four in the early hours of the morning. She's still peacefully sleeping, so I cover her up and get up. I clean up our little sexcapade. including in the kitchen, and by the time I finish it's a little over 5 a.m. I lay beside her and cuddle up inhaling her scent, making a memory of the beauty beside me. She wakes up and smiles her beautiful smile, then goes to the bathroom and when she returns we make love all over again until the morning sun tells us to stop. We fall asleep into sweet sexual bliss. I wake up around ten in the morning to the sound of my phone ringing.

I quickly reach for it, it's the thieving Ms Simpson, so I answer with a touch of annoyance in my voice. We speak briefly. The noise is disturbing Sunshine's sleep, so I get up and take the call into the bathroom. Once I hang up, I jump in the shower and make a few more calls. By the time I return to the bedroom, she is gone. I get dressed and go in search of her. She's naked in the kitchen, switching on the kettle. Now that's a sight I could get used to.

"Good morning," she turns and smiles with delight.

"Morning. Leaving already?" she asks me with a bit of disappointment in her voice.

"No. Go get ready I'm taking you to breakfast then our day starts. We are still going shopping, remember. Plus, I have a few errands to run before we head out on the road," I remind her.

"Ok. Imma shower and get dressed."

I watch her walk off towards the bathroom, I slap her on her ass, and she squeals with amusement. I enjoy the way her ass jiggles at the touch of my hands. I make a few more calls to my partners in crime, confirming everything that needs to be done. I tell them about my intended visit to Manchester and call the travel agent about our flight plans.

"Yes, three first-class return flights to Jamaica. With two weeks stopover in New York and Miami, please," I ask the travel agent.

"Ok, and how would you like to plan your journey, Sir? Do you need accommodation?"

"Excuse me?" I ask, not understanding her question.

"What are your dates, Sir?"

After going back and forth with the agent on the phone, we finally conclude, thank God because she is trying my patience, with her small talks.

"Going somewhere?" I hear a voice ask from behind.

I spin around to face her, and she looks radiant.

"Yeah. The girls and I are taking a trip to see grandma Bird. You're welcome to come if you want," I offer.

"No. so when are you going?" she asks.

"Next month," she seems a little disappointed by my answer.

She confuses the hell out of me; sometimes, her words never reflect her true feelings. I can see she wants to come, all she has to do is say yes, and it's a done deal. She knows how I feel about her, but she's on some independent woman bullshit. Ever since the unfortunate night, she's even more determined to prove that she is strong all by herself. Guess I'm just going to have to remind her that she doesn't have to be strong all the time; I can help carry her load.

"Ready?" she asks, dismissing the conversation.

"Yeah. Let's go, I'm starving."

Escorting her out the flat, I lock up. drive into town. We go to Starbucks for breakfast then we head to the shop to check on the contractors for the revamp. The store's new manager was in from early this morning, from eight, to let the rest of the crew in. I get the rundown on everything so far and instruct them on what else needs to be done. Everything is running smoothly. The pop-up clothing stands outside the store are still making us money. Autumn's production in fashion is already in the pipeline and seems to be coming together. I've just got to get the parents of the kids to sign off on the journey, book the coaches, and hotels for the family. Winter will be joining me in two days to spray paint herself silly and dress the store to perfection as she always does. I have faith in everything that girl puts her delicate little hands on.

Now to go deal with this thieving ass contractor in Manchester. I press gas once I hit the motorway and we are there in record time. But I have to ask what the deal is with this new idiot she's hooking up with.

"So, tell me about your new conquest?" I ask plainly.

"What new conquest?" she asks amused.

"Mr too colourful, from the other day."

She sighs heavily like she always does when I annoy her, or she thinks I'm being stubborn.

"He's my friend, and that's all you need to know, and mind your damn business," she replies with a little too much attitude for me. But I'm choosing to ignore the mood that my prying is getting her in.

"Why are you getting so defensive? I only asked a question," I tell her.

"No, you're playing the jealous boyfriend, sneaking, and questioning me for no damn good reason, other than jealousy." There goes that attitude again.

"And why, do I need to be jealous?" I ask.

"You tell me. Every time you see me with someone you get jealous and overprotective" this conversation's getting me nowhere, so I drop it for now.

This contractor really seems to be unable to follow instruction, and it's too late to find a new contractor but fuck it. Today's not the day to piss me off, especially since Sunshine's avoiding my questions and playing mind fucking games. She, I have to tolerate, but not this bitch, so she has to go.

"You're fired. I expect you out in 30 minutes." She must have seen the fire in my eyes because, for the first time, she follows instructions.

I text the girls in our family chat group.

"Fired the contractor and needs a new one like yesterday, asap. We got 4 weeks to get this done."

Wint asks, *"What? Where are we gonna find one now?"*

Autt says, *"Already on it. Told you."*

I tell them, *"I'm locking up and going on the hunt see you later."*

Autumn's Production

～

Autumn

Everything 's running smoothly with just a day to go till our first revamp. The three of us are sitting in the makeup chair getting dolled up for our feature on the 'This Morning' television programme. Darius has come through for me and got us the interview. Storm's wearing something from the men's department. I'm wearing sportswear to showcase our sportswear department, as for Winter she's wearing something she made just last night, looking like she's ready for the club. She's even made the host and hostess something for the red carpet. I've got to say the outfits look amazing.

"CK. Guy's they're ready for you," the dorky looking lady comes into the dressing room and tells us.

Walking on to the set was surreal when we were babies. We appeared once on the news because of Storm and our birthday being Valentine's Day.

The hostess speaks up first, "Hello Valentines. It must be pretty special being triplets."

"Yeah. It's the best thing being part of a God-made team," Storm answers.

"Yeah like having your own spare parts right, Autumn?" Winter says, reminding me of the comment I made the other day.

"I know right," I reply with sarcasm in my voice.

The hostess addresses Storm directly. "What's it like having two twin sisters that look like you?"

"Well, it feels like I was part of God's guilty pleasure. Our father didn't want us so, God gave him three of us, "

We chuckle at the notion because it is something that mama always told us whenever we wanted to know about the man we called dad.

The hostess smiles and asks, "Oh, really. So, tell us about this production of yours."

"Well, it's a showcase of all of our talents. We're doing a production with my dancers, modelling Winter's outfits across all store windows. There will be a dance production in the city-centre dancing from a specific point and leading to the store. We're revamping all three locations that we have up and running now, and that will lead up to the big grand opening of our branch in Manchester." I explain to the women standing across from me.

We wrap up our segment on a positive note. It all goes well; they even offer to send a crew over to the store once it hits Birmingham and London, which would be great. Storm and Wint go back to Bristol to ensure everything is set and ready. I call Darius to ensure that he meets me later so we can go over the song for the production and how I want things running. Darius agrees to come by at around 8 p.m.. I got all the parents of the children who are taking part in the showcase to sign off on the contract and ensure that they know exactly what is expected of their children. I ensure that all participants are paid, just in case they are losing out on a wage. We provide the coach transport too. Now, I've just got to cross all my fingers and toes, that everything will run smoothly for our first open day. The artwork Wint did on the mural for mom is absolutely radiant, she is truly a talented artist. I'm so proud of her, and I know mamma would be too.

It's the night before the show. I finish class and take a shower. "Crap I have no clean underwear! I guess I'm going to have to go commando" I put on a dress that I grab off the rack from downstairs. It's one of Winter's new collection of spring dresses. Her dresses always makes my ass look twice as big and my boobs triple in size, I don't know how she does it. I sit with no underwear on waiting on a cold bench in the dance studio. It gets to 8:30 p.m. and Darius has not turned up or called. So, I decide to call it a night and head home. On my way out, my phone rings and Darius' name spreads across the screen. I am excited and pissed at the same time, so I ignore it. As I walk down the stairs to the main street, I can hear a car beeping loudly. I can't believe it, so I hurry downstairs to shut up whoever it is making so much damn noise. I exit the building without closing the shutter and walking over to the car. Darius is inside but so is someone else.

"SHUT THE HELL UP. Quit making so much damn noise at my place of business." I say, kissing my teeth and turn on my heels, walking back over to the shutters to close up.

I notice the driver smirking and giggling and whispering something to Darius, but I don't care what his opinion is, he's irrelevant. As I turn the keys waiting for the shutters to close all the way I feel someone creep up behind me. I know it's Darius by his Issy Miyake cologne mixed with cocoa butter, something's about him never change. He grabs me by the waist and kisses my neck affectionately. He says sorry for the noise and being late. I turn and give him a stupefied look letting him know that I am still upset with him.

"A call to say you are going to be late would have been just fine, thanks." I state with an attitude.

"Noted, won't happen again, can we go get something to eat while we talk?" he asks with a cocky smile on his face.

Nodding my head, I agree and lead the way to my car since his friend has kindly driven off, beeping his horn and playing his music way too loud, trying to get attention.

"I know a quiet little place that serves the best barbeque rack in town," he tells me.

I follow his directions to the restaurant. When we get there, it is packed out, and I think we will have to wait to get a seat, but instead, we are led to a quiet area with a table for two. The restaurant has a sensual, intimate feel to it. There are no lights, just Yankee candles burning with a sweet vanilla scented aroma. Smooth jazz is playing throughout and there is African tribal paintings along the walls, making it all very romantic. I take in the entire place and admire how the owner has made such a small restaurant seem like the perfect couple's night out. We are surrounded by couples making cute faces at each other, holding hands. There's nothing but love in their eyes for each other, which brings my attention to the man in my company. He's wearing a sexy grin on his face whilst staring at me.

"I've never been here before; the atmosphere is truly romantic," I tell him while locking eyes with him.

"I know," he replies.

The waiter comes over, greets us and asks if we are ready to order. Darius orders while I skim the menu. I order my food and Darius orders us some Magnum Tonic Wine, one of my guilty pleasure drinks. I am not sure how he knows, but so far, he's impressed the hell out of me, I'm starting to forgive his little miss-hap earlier. We talk more about what I expect on the day of the production and about the 'This Morning' show. We eat, laugh, drink and enjoy each other's company. The waiter comes and takes the empty plates away, and I finish my second glass of Magnum.

At the end of the meal, Darius stands up and walks over to the bar area to pay the bill. I send Winter and Storm a text to let them know where I am because, during dinner, I can hear my phone buzzing off the hook. Storm simply says ok have fun, Winter instead makes jokes and tells me to do everything she would do and nothing I'm used to. I smile at my sister and place the mobile phone back in my handbag. Darius beckons for me to come to him. So, I stand up and go over to the bar ready to leave but instead, he pounds the bartender's fist and takes my hands and leads me to the side down to some sort of basement. I feel kind of foolish blindingly following his lead, so I ask where the hell he's taking me, and he simply smiles until we get to a dark red room.

There's a dim red light in the middle to light the entire room; you can barely see anyone in there. The interior is similar to upstairs with the candles. Slow jams and sensual reggae music is playing, and couples are bumping and mostly grinding on each other.

"I own this little joint. I sometimes play here. I guarantee you'll enjoy yourself," he confesses.

He leads me to a quite dark corner where no one can see us and leaves me to go to the bar. He returns with more Magnums and two bottles of water. I take the bottled water from him. He laughs and calls me lightweight, but that doesn't faze me. He pours half the Magnum in a red plastic cup and then takes my bottle of water from me and pours it in with the Magnum and hands it to me and says, "drink lightweight," with a mischievous smile planted on his face.

He takes up residence behind me, and we dance on each other moulding our bodies together to become one. He slowly caresses my body as we dance like my body belongs to him. The basement is so hot we start sweating through our clothes, but we continue grinding on each other like no one else is in the room. The heat and the liquor is becoming intoxicating, making every touch heightened. He puts his hands under my dress, revealing my neatly shaven pussy exploring my most sensitive area. Kissing the nape of my neck, he plays with my inside as I grind on his finger. I can feel the build-up of sweet sensation within my walls and my legs are about to give out from underneath me from the assault he's giving my delicate flower. I guess he can feel my legs trembling because he releases me quickly and for a second, I am pissed. After he has me all hot and bothered, flushed and on the brink, he stops, typical man. I spin around glaring at him. He still has that menacing smile on his stupid face, and before I can speak, he kisses me passionately shutting me up, pulling me into him, I feel his hand go back under my dress. This time he has ice in his hand massaging and melting it on my already soaking wet ass cheek. He places an ice cube on the bridge of my ass crack, allowing it to melt and seep down the crack. It sends a cold but sensual thrill through my body. He uses another ice cube retraces it down my neck, sending more shivers up and down my spine. He's torturing my body with anticipation, and I don't think I can take any more of this torture. Releasing the kiss between us, he places two ice cubes in his mouth tells me to hold on to the walls then knelt down in front of me. I am in total shock, I am aware of my surroundings, our location is dark and out of sight, and I couldn't care less. I place my hands on the walls to brace myself for whatever is about to happen. He puts his head under my dress and parts me, placing the ice cubes inside me with his tongue. I am in shocked pleasure. He kisses my clit and comes back up and tells me that they won't last so we should go now, still, in shock, I am in no mood to walk with ice in my vagina. So, I shake my head.

"Autumn if you're as tight as I remember they won't drop out; they'll melt before that," he tells me.

It's like he's reading my mind because I fear when walking they will just drop out in front of everyone. He grabs my hands and leads the way out of the club up the stairs. I can feel them starting to melt, so I walk faster to the car. He grabs the keys and drives us back to my apartment. The drive home is intense because I can feel the ice melting inside of me and Darius' assault on my pussy with his finger leaves an imprint inside me. I take the Magnum we have leftover and take a huge gulp I need it. My sex drive is well and truly on overdrive, out of control. We park in the designated spot in the apartment complex garage he hops out and comes around to open my door. Blocking my way out the car, he tilts his head to the side and smiles devilishly like he's had a light bulb moment.

I turn in my seat, and he gets down again using the car door to block the vision of passers-by and tells me to rest back and enjoy. Lifting my dress above his head, he goes to work on my lotus flower. He's definitely done this before. I'm not sure why I am being so reckless with this man, but this is the way he always makes me feel like we are the only two people in the world, when we are together. I am in total ecstasy; he's blowing my mind with his tongue as he licks every crevice and corner, my eyes roll in the back of my head. I can't help the euphoria that I am experiencing—definitely the best head game I have ever experienced in my entire life. I come again and again as he laps up every single drop like a dog. His tongue is strong and silky smooth to the touch. I can't believe what I am allowing this man to do to me in the parking lot. When he's finished his assault on my clit with his tongue, I am too weak to move. When he comes up for air I am panting heavily like I just ran a marathon he lifts me up and carries me to my apartment.

I am smiling from ear to ear with what I have just experienced. I hope tonight never ends, but I know it must, so I am going to ride it out till the Lord God brings his sun up again and we have to return to reality. We make love all over the apartment, moving from one room to the next. We have dessert in the kitchen; we lick and suck cake and ice cream off each other's bodies and cuddle up in the living room. Then I ride him like a skilled horseback rider until we somehow end in the bathroom and make sensual love in the shower. We sit up in bed talking the rest of the night, until I finally fall asleep.

Stormy Season
Bristol Branch

~~~

Autumn

The sunlight shines through the curtains bright in my eyes, waking me from my peaceful slumber. I glance at the wall clock, and it states 7:35 a.m.

"Oh shit!" I scream, "Darius wake up, we're late!" I tell him jumping out of bed while he tries to wipe the sleep out of his eyes.

I have no time to watch how delightful he looks in the morning. I search around for my mobile phone but to no avail, I can't find it. It must be in the living room with my clothes and handbag shit. I dash to the bathroom and am ready in record time. Thanking God for my natural beauty because makeup and all that shit I don't have to bother with; just vaseline, a quick shower and brush my teeth and I am ready in 15 minutes.

I exit the bathroom to see Darius sitting at the edge of my bed with a smile.

"No time to be cute, get your ass up and get ready and don't be a girl about it. Hurry up. Or I'm leaving your ass behind. We're late!" I state plain and to the point.

"You know you are cute when you are angry. I'll be ready in a few," he says as he walks over to me and kisses me on the forehead and heads towards the bathroom.

I go in search of my phone to make a few calls. Once I find it, I have so many missed calls from almost everyone. I quickly call Storm to let him know my position and then call my head dancer and tell him I'm on my way, just get everyone on the coach until I arrive.

He tells me that the DJ isn't there yet and is unreachable. I giggle on the inside because I already know his location. I reassure him that everything will be fine and not to worry I will pick up the DJ. I shout in the direction of the bedroom to let Darius know that I am calling the taxi now, so he needs to hurry up. He shouts something back, but I don't quite catch it.

By the time we pull up at the shop, everyone is already on the coach and ready to go. I get out of the taxi, leaving him to pay the driver and hop on the coach and apologise for my tardiness. Darius comes aboard and takes a seat in the second row at the front.

Everyone looks so happy and ready. I thank everyone for turning up and say a small prayer before we start our journey. The driver drives off in the direction of the motorway, heading towards Bristol. For the next four weekends, this will be my crew and family. All the girl's hair is done the same, with ribbons going through. I had a hairdresser come over yesterday to do their hair, and all the boys and men are groomed as well and are looking very debonair. Even the moms all look pleased, they really help out, with the kids and thank God they have agreed to help with the production and the tour for the next month. Some parents cook, while others babysit and do late night pick up and keep me sane. I sometimes admire their strength as black women because they remind me of the strength, my mom, my sister, and I have and what we can accomplish without a male figure in our lives. It also makes me miss my mother, even more, when I see them doing it on their own.

The drive takes an hour and 45 minutes. I address everyone and brief them on what's going to happen today and tomorrow. I reassure everyone that the hotel accommodation is already taken care of. They all exit the bus and I lead them through to the staff room to get changed into their costumes for the day.

Winter's waiting for us to mend any clothing problems and the mothers help her out. We place two of the moms in one of the front windows where the toddlers can play while their parent's shop. There's a play area in the same front window with a table where the children can draw and colour, play dress up and just be kids instead of being dragged around the store. The moms are given uniforms to blend in with the staffing crew. In the other front window, dancers are dancing and having fun in the mirror. Darius is set up outside, thank God for the sunshine today. He quickly gets busy doing his thing. There's going to be a fashion show during the day, and everyone can take part. The dance production is going to be during the lunch hour. Once everyone is posted in position, it's time to open up.

Everyone's running around like headless chickens. Storm quickly takes control of the situation and gets everyone's attention.

"We're ready. This is what we've been working all those late nights for. Remember I'm proud of each and every one of you and don't worry about anything. I got you all. Just do your best. Moms, please watch out for every child in our care and everyone please stick with your partners today, no one is allowed to go anywhere alone. You will all get a break, and there are free refreshments at all times. Plus, I can smell all that food the ladies have cooked up, just save me some chicken. Let's bow our heads."

He says a prayer asking the good Lord to take us where we need to be before this opening.   After the prayer and Storm's little speech, everyone seems more relaxed. The shutters go up, and the doors fly open. Customers come flooding in, and passers-by stop in amazement, taking pictures and videos on their phones. They come in to see what 's going on. We get a lot of positive feedback about Winter's idea of the play area in the front window for customers with children.

The rotating window display of different activities happening, is also a success. There is a change every half hour in the window to give everyone a chance to showcase their talent. The lunchtime production draws more crowds than we thought it would. The crowd follow us from the other end of town to the shop. It's amazing, the kids are all on point, and for once no one misses a beat. I am gleaming like a proud mother. People take pictures and make it into a shop party. Darius and Trouble play their little hearts out.

Everyone's back on the coach at 8 p.m. and drained, but I am proud of them. I accompany them to the Premier Inn and make sure everything is in order. Tomorrow will be the same productions again, but we won't be travelling from the other end of town, just in front of the store.

The weekend ends on a high, there are so many photos from Saturday and Sunday on social media that it is trending on Twitter and Facebook. Stormy $easons is a success. It even makes the local newspaper. We don't take a picture of us though, just of the dancers and mothers who helped make the day a success. Next weekend is London's opening and it will definitely be a hit. I can't wait. Winter owns London. I go on a dance retreat and come back, and they open up a store for her to fully showcase her brand. So, I open Birmingham with the studio above it. Although we all have a stake in all stores, we individually take responsibility for one of the cities. Manchester will be all three of us' responsibility.

Winters' Season
London Branch

~

Winter

London's the same routine, and the same success. I change the display in my window to more of a showcase of changes instead of dancing. I have four partitions on rotation. One of a girl in front of the mirror, with a bunch of clothes thrown down on the floor while getting ready for a night on the town. The next is a man ironing his shirt while dancing. The third, a mom and child in matching outfits. The next is simple, five people dancing in the club enjoying themselves.

London is a huge city and has many different cultures to cater for, so I want it to be tasteful and seductive, for our demographics. It rains a little, but mom always said a little rain is always a blessing. So, I'm still upbeat about the day. People still come out to support us. The local news come out, along with 'Channel 4 Music.' They heard about what we did in Bristol and wanted to check us out for themselves, and we don't disappoint. News of what we are doing gets around really quickly. Darius playing makes everyone come out. If there's one thing I can count on black people to do, it's to turn everything into a block party. We even have the police come out for surveillance. They want to shut us down, but with the controversy that they had with the riots and shooting just last year, they try different tactics. We aren't selling alcohol or breaking any laws, so we have no problem. We simply bring people out for a good time while spending their money and supporting the community.

Even our neighbouring store has to appreciate what we are doing because they are getting exposure too, for free. I can't help but be proud of my siblings for what we're trying to pull off. Twitter is going off again about what is happening, not to mention Facebook. We are being tagged in so many pictures that it brings more people out. It slowly becomes more than we can handle, we surpass our profit goal that weekend and nearly sell out of everything.

People start asking where the after-party is, and I can't answer, so I turn to Storm for an answer. I didn't know there was an after-party after all. I am so busy I don't have time to deal with that type of stress right now. Before I know it, Darius and Storm have organised an after-party with one of the local clubs using their rooftop. These men know how to turn water into wine in the middle of the desert, I swear. My brother has connections for everything. Once the dance crew get dropped back to Birmingham, we regroup and catch up on what has happened. For a dude, my brother can spend like a girl. Just wasteful.

"Storm why the hell did you tell these people we are having an after-party. I'm tired, all I want is my bed. I have been nonstop all week?" I snap at him.

"I just gave the people what they wanted," he says grinning from ear to ear.

"Boy, what about what I want?"

"Oh, come on Winter, stop your moaning, because you know you would have got up and gone out at some point this weekend."

"Whatever. Stop spending our money."

He rolls his eyes at me and is about to say something, but I just cut him off because I have no time for him now I need to get a dress for this after-party bullshit. Trouble is smirking at my ass like I am amusing him or something.

The night actually turns out good because everyone comes out to support us from earlier and is having a good time drinking and partying. My sister's even having a good time. She's been spending a lot of time with Darius; even though she said she wouldn't go there with him, it's clear that she has changed her mind. Everywhere she is, he isn't far behind. It's like everyone's a couple. Sunshine and Storm are the same as always, inseparable, why those two aren't married yet is beyond me. And then there's me and Trouble, I'm simply having fun, but this dude's always making it into something else. As far as the eyes can see we will never work because I swear he's a pimp, a dealer, or a whore because God damn his phone keeps going off more than a normal human being's. Then again if he is a dealer, he isn't very good at it because you never leave a customer hanging for some pussy, no matter how good it is. Whatever it is it's starting to get on my nerves, I'm glad I only got two more weeks left until I can get an overdue break.

The night ends, and for once, we all leave and go in the same direction. Our apartment is a two-bedroomed apartment but thank God for the pull-out sofa. The others claim the bedrooms because I am too tired to get there first. We chill, and chit chat for a bit and then everyone goes their separate ways into the bedrooms, leaving me and Trouble to sleep. I crash out in my outfit with not a care in the world. I know Trouble's upset that he doesnt get any, but I couldn't care less. I'm tired, and nothing comes between me and my beauty treatment. He coses up to me, and the vibration in his pants is starting to annoy the hell out of me even more. So, I roll out from under him in the early hours of the morning and dig it out of his pants and answer. Now I know I'm not his main chick, and I have no right to answer his phone, but damn it's annoying, and it's always the same number. I swipe at the green answer call button and answer with anger.

"What is so damn important at four in the fucking morning that you need to call his phone constantly? You're starting to piss me off," I shout into the phone.

"Who's this?" the person asks from the other end. Trouble wakes up and stares at me, surprisingly. But I just cut my eye at him.

"Tired. That's who I am and you disturbing my damn sleep. He will call you at a decent hour. Bye."

I hang up the phone and turn it off and throw it at him. I lay back down, turning my back to him. I swear these women are something else.

"I dare you to say something, right now, I'm tired, and you and your bitches are getting on my fucking nerves. Learn to turn your phone off when you are next to me."

"Talk about it in the morning, now you're disturbing my sleep!" he says.

Now I know he must be joking because I'm disturbing his sleep! We definitely are going to address this in the morning. He crawls closer to me, hugs me and falls asleep.

I wake at the sound of footsteps. It's Sunshine heading to the kitchen in the shirt Storm was wearing the night before. It looks huge on her petite little frame. I get up, greet her and head to the bathroom for my morning rituals. Once I am fresh and clean, I am ready for anything, so I go back in, ready to take on Trouble and his fuckery. But he's still asleep. So, I head for the kitchen to make lunch for everyone. The smell of food seems to draw everyone out of their rooms, even waking tired ass Trouble up. Sunshine comes and helps out, but she's getting in my way, so I tell her to just set the table and make the hot chocolate. I send Autumn and Darius out for whipped cream and marshmallows, she grumbles, but that don't faze me because she's going whether she likes it or not. Once they return, I place everything in the middle of the table, and everyone helps themselves.

"You guy's love ice cream and hot chocolate," Trouble states.

"If you don't like it, call your little friend back, and she can make something else at her place. That way, I can get a decent night's sleep."

Everyone stares at me, mouth half-open, while I continue to eat.

"No. It's fine I just thought I was the only one who enjoyed hot chocolate with whipped cream and marshmallows. Plus if I was there, I wouldn't be enjoying this pleasant atmosphere you're providing along with the secretarial duties. Any message?" he asks cockily.

I roll my eyes at his attempt to defuse the situation. "Yeah, call a bitch back. Now Eat!" I command everyone.

Everyone does as they are told. Once I have finished, I leave the table and proceed to clean up and keep myself busy. I want to be on the road real quick. Everyone pitches in with the cleaning, so we got done and are on the road by 2 p.m. Sunshine and Storm drive down together while I throw the keys to Trouble and tell him to drive.

"Don't scratch my baby," I tell him.

Autumn got me the new Range Rover Sport for Christmas last year. He ignores me and shakes his head and smiles. I jump in the front as Auto and Darius get in the back.

"Girl, you know you're cute when you're mad, and sexy as hell. I should let you answer my phone more often because that pussy seems to get fatter too," he says as he gets in and turns the engine on. I can hear Darius agreeing with him from the back.

"Dawg you see what I'm working with. Most times I piss her off, just for the fun of it," Darius states.

They both laugh, and pound fists while me and Autumn look at each other and shake our heads in disbelief. I turn up the music in the car loud and drown out everyone. Autumn's s curled up in the back in a deep conversation.

I'm happy when we arrive home in Birmingham . We take the lift up, and the phone starts going off again when Trouble turns it on. I shake my head, and they all laugh. But I am not amused. It isn't that I care that other women are calling him; no, I couldn't care zero, but when it's disturbing my sleep believe me, I have concerns.

"You want to get it?" he asks, taking the piss out of my life, sniggering at my expense. But I just ignore his dumbass.

I enter the house and grab a tub of cookies and cream to soothe my soul and head to my bedroom and close the door behind. A knock at my door follows, and he enters with a smile and a lame-ass apology. But I just ignore him and continue to change my clothes; I make sure to walk around in just my underwear for at least 20 minutes. I call Storm to check that he went to the store and check that everything's going smoothly. Unfortunately, he is still there sorting things out. I call Clive to see if everything's going ok. Trouble is still standing in the room, gawking at me.

Once I have changed, I walk past him, and he sighs heavily, and he follows behind like a lost duck. I tell Autumn that I'm going in to check on Clive. She's so busy with Darius that I doubt she hears me. We take the lift down to the garage and jump in my baby Range. I drive us to the store with Destiny's Child, 'The Writings On The Wall,' album blaring out the speaker box while I sing to every tune. He sits in silence. See men hate the silent treatment even worse than women. I learned that from a teacher in school. I never understood how they could get so red when they used to talk to me, and I ignored them. I plan to drown him in silence for the rest of the day, maybe the entire week.

Autumn's Season
Birmingham Branch

~

Autumn

The past two weeks has been amazing and very profitable; we are able to pay the kids and their parents really well for each trip they take with us.

I go to visit my friend Peppa, and she looks amazing, all things considered. I can see why Darius wants her because she never looks broken or sad and miserable even though she is in a terrible place. We catch up, and she curses me out for dropping her, back in the day and even after she called and told me about my God baby Queenie. I visited Queenie once and have sent her money every year for her birthday and Christmas, but I guess if I was more involved in her life, I would have more than just a picture of when she was a baby and I held her for the first time.

Darius leaves early during the visit, so we have our gab fest. It's good seeing her again, it makes me realise how much I miss her, and how I need to stop seeing Darius. My girl has a couple weeks left to go in this trap hole, and she needs a friend, not someone moving in on her dick. I ask her about Darius, and it draws a tear to my eye when she says she is glad we are together again. Something inside makes me tell her that he is truly in love with her, and that as much as I enjoyed his company and head game, he's hers. I could never take her place or want to. The look in his eyes when he sees her as we enter the room is filled with nothing but pure love and awe. It's like he's home, he never looked at me like he stared at her. He looked at me with lust and hunger in his eyes, never love. I refuse to make the same mistake my mother made. I hug my friend and promise to send her some money and tell her I will visit my God baby before I leave for Jamaica.

I keep my promise to Peppa and send £200 to her prison account. I also find out that Storm sends her money every month. That surprises me, I'm not sure why he always had a soft spot for her.

It's the day of our Birmingham reopening, the news crew is outside waiting and the queue outside is getting larger. Thank God Trouble and Wint sorted out their differences because it kept her out of my business. Once I say a prayer for the day the shutters come up and the day begins. Sales are booming, and everything is running smoothly. The press do some coverage, and our photographer takes pictures of the event and records the production. The children enjoy it so much that we have to remind them to eat and take a break. The moms are a big help. There is one dad who is single raising his two girls all by himself here too. The women take him under their wings, and now he is an honoured member of the dream team. He now has sitters for life and people to call on if he ever needs it. I overhear the moms making plans for a barbeque and telling him that he has to come and bring the girls. I guess it takes a village to raise a child. The weekend ends as quickly as it began. Next week will be our last and final show.

Darius has been a great help; he's even helped me locate our father. I know Wint and Storm are going to be mad, but I have to meet him. He must want to meet us too, he could never be so cold. After meeting the two women the other day, it just confirmed what I have been feeling.

The week flew by, and we practise more that week than any other week. Wint makes sure everything is on point with the costumes. She even makes us summer dresses for the opening and Storm a shorts linen suit. I swear if he wasn't my brother, I would be on him like a fly on shit. That's how good my brother looks in his outfit. She even makes Trouble and Darius two T-shirts to wear on the day. I swear I'm always amazed by the things she can do. I'm always in awe of my sister.

On the day of the opening, the Manchester shop looks great, and everything is to our liking. We cut the colourful ribbon that is placed at the front of the shop doors to mark the opening and let everyone inside. This store has two floors so we have more room to play with. The day has a few ups and downs. A few reality stars come out, it's a pretty good day. There's a beauty salon next door, so Wint got all the moms a pampering treatment, as a bonus for all their hard work. At the end of the day, everyone is completely drained from all their hard work. I pay everyone again and send them home on the coach. It's finally over, time for this holiday. Winter and Storm stay in Manchester to micromanage the new store before we leave for the next couple of weeks.

I used that time to spend with Darius and research our father some more. Darius is a little upset that I haven't told Wint or Storm yet, but it is none of his business, plus I've told him in confidence, so he better keep his mouth shut.

We have two days before we leave for New York. So, we are spending every moment in each other's arms, and Trouble and Sunshine are keeping those two busy. Everything has fallen in place.

It's Tuesday night, and we are parked up outside a cottage-like home in a small village in Leicester. I take a deep breath inwards and listen to Darius complain for the umpteenth time about looking suspicious in a white neighbourhood, looking like we are casing the place to rob it. I tell him he's being ridiculous and to stop being so small-minded, he's starting to sound like Winter. We drive off and go to the Marriott hotel in the town centre. I am leaving in two days so I make sure that I overindulge in the man next to me because when I return from my trip away, we will no longer be together. I promise myself to make Darius free once I get on the aeroplane. But tonight, I plan on overdosing on him.

The next morning, I wake up with a purpose and a cause. I am on a mission. I am going to meet the sperm donor and confront him and demand he be part of our lives. I'm also going to say goodbye to my relationship with Darius and his big black dick, as Winter puts it, and heavenly tongue, even thinking about it makes me want to change my mind.

We get dressed and go downstairs for breakfast. We fill our stomachs and head out for the inevitable. We pull up outside the cottage again this time in broad daylight. It takes me a hot minute to pluck up the courage to go knock on his door. Darius stays in the car wanting no part of this. An elderly silver-haired woman with small greenish-brown eyes opens the door, she's a little meaty but who cares she's old and stumpy.

"May I help you?" she asks as I gasp for air to fill my lungs. I want to turn around and run, but my feet won't move.

"Hi, is your husband Jacob Edwards in? I'm from the university, and I would love to interview him for the uni paper as one of the professors who's changed lives," I tell her.

I don't know why I lied, but it just started pouring out, so I continue with it. She welcomes me into her home, and I follow her into the sitting room.

"I'll get my husband for you. Would you like something to drink sweetheart?"

She's kind and sweet so far. She leaves to go get her husband, my dad. I can hear them having a conversation about me.

"She's in the sitting room," she tells him, and I hear him reply.

"Ok. I'll wash up and come through now."

She returns as I am looking at the photos on display in their home. I recognise two of the chubby faces on the wall, they seem like a happy family.

"You have a beautiful family," I tell her when she comes back into the room.

"Thank you. What's your name, young lady? She asks me.

"Autumn," I reply.

"You look so familiar, but I just can't place it," she tells me.

"I get that a lot," I tell her.

"So, where's this young lady Doris?" I hear his voice much clearer as he enters the room and freezes in his stride.

"Catherine?" he murmurs.

"No, my name is Autumn, but that is my mother's name," I stretch my hands out for a handshake that never gets taken.

"I'm sorry I just had a flashback to a student I mentored in the past. You look just like her."

You mean I look like the woman whose heart you broke and walked out on. As he speaks those words, all the hurt and sadness comes over me, and I want to scream and shout.

"Doris, can you get us something to drink please. Go put the kettle on, thanks, sweetheart," he commands, and she leaves the room not before asking if I want something.

"Doesn't she have a pretty name, Jacob?"

"Hmm yes, dear very pretty. Ah, sweetheart the tea?"

"Oh, yes. I'll be right back," she tells him.

"You have to leave now. I told you already to never come back. I'm sorry, but I can't help you."

"First of all, you have never met me, that was my sister. Second, who told you I needed anything from you?" I ask boldly.

"So why are you here?"

"I just wanted to meet you and see if you wanted to possibly get to know me. Get to know us."

"Didn't your sister tell you; I don't want anything to do with that part of my life. I left it in the past. Now my wife is very sick, and I don't want you upsetting her. So, you have to leave and never come back here."

Is this man for real. I don't know why I expected more from him. I'm not sure what I want anymore, but it definitely is not this.

"You know what, don't worry about your precious little wife, I don't want to hurt a hair on her head, and for your information, we never needed you. We did just fine all by ourselves. We've achieved more than the average Joe, I'm sorry I ever graced your doorstep, it won't happen again."

I walk out and slam the door before the tears start flowing freely. I walk fast towards the car, and Darius is already outside leaning up against the car. He sees me coming with tears streaming down my cheeks. He opens his arms and embraces me without asking any questions. He holds me tight and tries comforting me. I can hear his jaw click with frustration.

"Let's go, please take me home." I plead.

"I'm sorry baby girl."

He releases me and opens the car door for me to get in. We drive in silence until we get to the apartment. I never tell him what the son of a bitch said. I just hop out, and he comes out to help with my luggage, but I tell him I am fine, I don't need his help and kiss him goodbye. I walk off without looking back until I reach the elevators. He just stands there with a sorrowful look on his face. He can see I am upset and need space, and that's one of the things I love about him. He watches as the door's close, and I know that it will be the last time I will be with the one that got away.

I ride the elevator up with tears falling down my face. When I get in Storm and Wint are sitting on the sofa laughing at something stupid on the TV. I quickly pass them and head for my room, without saying a word. How am I supposed to tell them that I made that man break my heart too? After they warned me. A few minutes later, I hear a knock on my door, and Winter enters, I seriously need to put a lock on the door like Storm did on his.

"So, what happened, where's Darius?"

"Nothing happened; Darius is fine, he's gone home."

"So why are you crying, call him back if you are missing him?" she tells me.

"I'm not. Please, could you just leave me alone?" I ask her.

"Oh, it's like that; I swear I'm going to kill him if he did something stupid," she mutters.

"Well, he didn't. So, drop it. I just want to be by myself, please Winter just drop it." I ask in a pleading manner.

"Fine but you better cheer up by tomorrow morning."

I feel awful lying to my sister like that, but she won't forgive me if she ever finds out. I stay in my room and cry myself to sleep. I'm supposed to be having a good time with Darius for the last time, instead I'm having a pity party for one.

They All Have To
Learn The Hard Way

〜

Winter

I can't take my sister in such a miserable mood, so I go out and buy ice cream for the night. We have already emptied the fridge in anticipation of our trip. While I am out, I try calling Darius, but all I get is voice mail. On my way back, he calls back, and I ask about Autumn, but he doesn't have anything useful to say.

All he says is, "She's going to need your support because she is going through some serious shit."

Now tell me what the fuck is that supposed to mean? Now I'm pissed. What the fuck happened with those two? I hate being in the dark, and I hate surprises. So, I call Trouble, he'll know.

"Hey, Trouble have you seen Darius yet?" I ask sweetly.

"No Sugar, you coming to see me later or should I come see you?"

This man is forever trying to wear out my pussy like I don't have a use for it.

"No, not right now, I'm hunting Auto."

"Oh, she won't be back yet, they are spending the day in Leicester."

I hang up the phone in anger because I know exactly what happened. That bitch just doesn't learn. I spin my car around and head for the motorway. I call Darius back, and he answers on the second ring.

"Send me the asshole's details now, I'm heading to Leicester and don't give me no bullshit!" I command, and a few minutes later, he sends me the address I need.

I press on the gas on the motorway and is there in 45 minutes. I park outside, trying to get my bearings before I kick down the door. I call Storm to let him know where I am and text Autumn to let her know to never speak to me again. Since we aren't enough for her, I can be nothing to her. As much as she hurt me, I still feel the need to hurt the person who hurt her. I knock on the door like I am the police and a young man come and stands in front of me looking me up and down in frustration then it quickly turns to sexual admiration.

"Is our father in?" I ask with a lot of attitude; he looks puzzled like his brain is just catching up with what I am saying.

So, I snap my finger at him, "hello, where's your old man? I have a few words for him."

"He's inside."

I push past him, nearly knocking him over and hear him shout for me to stop, but I am like a bull charging in. I can't stop. I am fuming. I hear voices coming from one of the rooms, so I head that way and barge in. The young man catches up with me and grabs my arm.

I yank it from him, "boy don't ever put your hands on me." I tell him through gritted teeth then enter the room.

It seems they are having a little family gathering, good. Jacobs's eyes meet mine immediately, and he knows what time it is. I see all the blood drain from his face as his jaw hits the ground.

"Listen here old man, the next time your unwanted seed turns up at your door and begs you to love them, have the decency to let them down gently or better yet, use a fucking condom. Then you won't have random children coming to your doorstep years later in search of their good for nothing father." I bark at him.

"Miss, who are you and why are you in my home again?" the elderly woman asks.

"I'm a third of the mistake that your dumb ass husband forgot to mention and failed to abort. We've never met, but I'm guessing you met my sister Autumn."

"What do you mean a third?" she scornfully asks, sneering at her husband while everyone else looks at me in dismay.

"As in three! Triplets." I tell the room.

"Is that true dad?" his son asks.

"It's time for you to leave young lady," he speaks up and addresses me.

"Oh no! you gave up that right to tell me what to do the day you gave my mother money to abort my ass. So, listen up; all of you! Don't come by my store again, don't you ever go near my sister or brother again, or I will burn this fucker to the ground with you in it. Got it. And that's my promise to you, Jacob Edwards."

"That's enough, now go," he shouts.

I'm not sure who the hell he thinks he is dealing with, but I'm the wrong one. I walk over to him and stand face to face with him.

"Remember all the promises you made her that you never kept. Well, let me reassure you of one thing. I keep all my promises, so if your son ever comes here looking for you and you say the wrong things believe me when I say you will burn alive where you stand. That's my promise to you, Jacob. I don't need you or any of these people up here, so you and yours stay away from My Family." I say and spit in his face and turn to leave.

As I walk off, his wife stops me and apologises for all the hurt I must be feeling.

"Lady you have no idea. Look I'm sorry for interrupting your day, but he hurt the one I love. I just needed him to know how his word affects those around me. You won't see me again, and I'll make sure that my family stays away from yours." I tell her and start walking away out of the door.

But she stops me again. "I'm sorry for the pain caused by my husband but please forgive him; he's not well and living on borrowed time. I will speak with my husband, and I'm sure we can sort this out," she pleads with me.

"You're taking this pretty well, for someone who just found out that their spouse cheated on them and has a bunch of babies all over," I comment.

"My dear, I am an old woman. I have no need for a grudge, he told me about your mother Catherine and the pregnancy and told me about the abortion. I thought that part of his world was closed. He confessed, so I forgave him, because I was pregnant with our fourth child Robbie, with no skills, no job and nowhere to go with my children. He assured me that it was taken care of and it wouldn't happen again, until today when your sister came to my front door, and he thought he saw your mother. That's when I figured it out. But I never knew there were three of you."

She tells me the story of how she forgave her cheating husband and his misfortune with bone marrow cancer which is slowly taking his life away. I can't say that I feel any remorse for him. I say my goodbyes to the sad deluded old woman who for some reason, feels the need for me to forgive her husband.

I get in my car, and sit there for a while, then start my engine, I hear a knock on the window, so I roll it down; it is the young man from inside.

"Here, give me a call. Maybe we can all get together and have a drink and get to know each other. I would love to meet the rest of you."

I lay him a side glance and take the card and roll my window up and drive away because I know I won't be using it anytime soon. Kissing my teeth, I just drive. I don't even realise I am crying until I notice the gas empty sign on my dash screen is blurry.

The rain starts pouring down outside, so I pull into the service station and get gas and a large hot chocolate. The weather always reflects how I am feeling, it always rains when I am in pain and crying, it is like God and mama are crying with me.

I text Storm telling him I am on my way home. I get back in my car and just sit there for a while. I fall asleep without realising it. A bright light from a truck parked in front me dazzles me awake, and I wake from my slumber. The ice cream from earlier melts into milkshake and the hot chocolate is cold. The rain has ceased, I turn the engine on and drink my now warm ice cream and open the window a little to let fresh air in the car. I drive home with a heavy heart.

Once I get home, I walk past everyone and go straight to my room. I notice Sunshine, Trouble, and Darius are here too. I ignore everyone. I don't want to speak with anyone. I am not in any mood to entertain company. Autumn comes knocking and I open my door after half-hour.

"Get the fuck out my room, and stay the fuck away from me, you understand, I have no sister, now leave." I say, walking over to the door and slamming it in her face.

Some would say I'm overreacting, but they don't feel how I feel. Storm comes in shortly after and closes the door behind him.

"If you decide to go father hunting too, I will have no brother either. It seems the apple doesn't fall far from the damn tree in this place. Everyone seems to want rejection from the same man who clearly doesn't want us, or isn't my word real or true for you guys," I say with tears streaming down my face.

"Which part of that he doesn't want us, doesn't she understand. He made that pretty clear from birth." I emphasise.

Storm walks over to where I am sitting and hugs me, holding me until my tears subside and I calm down. He doesn't say a word as he picks me up off the floor and lays me down and covers me with the blanket. He lays there while I lightly sob into my pillow. I am plagued by thoughts of the betrayal of my sister, and my mother who abandoned us when we needed her the most. I miss her so much it starts to hurt again, it's like she died all over again. I fall asleep again.

When I wake, Trouble is lying beside me, holding me tightly, it is 3 a.m. I still haven't packed yet. I get out of bed, clean up my en-suite bathroom and the bedroom and pack my suitcase ready for the morning. I wake him up because he's drooling all over my velvet. He smiles at me as he wakes.

"You're drooling," I tell him.

"Yeah, for you, but you won't give me the time," his phone vibrates again, and I just chuckle at the notion.

"Boy, it was fun while it lasted. Time to go home. Get up I need to change the covers," I say and take the sheets and blanket off the bed.

I walk off to the laundry room, and he jumps up and takes the basket from me and walks with me down the hall. I clean out the hamper of dirty clothes and sort them and place them in the washing machine. I have less than three hours to do this washing and drying, so everything has to be quickly washed. I turn to find Trouble standing in my personal space, he's always doing that, making me catch my breath.

"What's wrong with you, get out my way, I have things to do," I say.

"Tell me, what's going on with you?" he asks.

"Your phones buzzing again," I point out.

"If it's not my mother or sisters, then I don't care," he replies.

"Whatever. Excuse me," I say, moving him out the way with my arm.

"Got to talk to somebody sometime, Winter, and I just want you to know that when you come back, no matter what, I'll be here waiting for you" he states.

"Just not right now, right?" I point out.

"I never said that, don't put words in my mouth," he complains.

"Please don't, because when I'm away, I won't be waiting for you, or thinking about you. So, I suggest you forget me instantly. Starting now," I tell him.

I brush past him and head back to my room. I feel my legs go from underneath me as I am lifted off the ground with a smack to my ass that has me squealing like a pig.

"Put me down Trouble, I'm not playing with you."

He smacks me harder on the other ass cheek and tells me to be quiet.

"Storm. Get him to put me down!" I scream.

Storm comes running out his room half-naked and sees me over Troubles shoulder, they nod their heads in salute, and that's it. I swear I have no loyalty anymore from anyone. I could be in serious trouble. That boy just gave his nod of approval. He slams the door shut and slaps me again on the ass and places me on the floor. Once I feel the ground, I swing after his ass, but he grabs my arms tightly and tells me to calm down.

"What do you want, Trouble?" I ask impatiently.

He places both our hands over my heart. Dear Lord help him, which part of enjoying ourselves without any strings attached did he not understand?

"Look I can't give you that," I tell him.

"Why not?" his phone buzzes off the hook again. So I step closer to him and take it out of his back pocket and press to answer.

"Hello. May I ask who this is?"

He rolls his eyes and takes the phone from me, and cuts it off.

"That's why. I'm no one's second fiddle or side piece. Plus, your phone likes to interrupt my sleep," I tell him.

"That's an easy fix. I just get a new number, and everyone will be dropped."

"Don't do that on my account, because I'm not dropping anyone for you."

I can see the green-eyed monster forcing its way to the surface at the thought of me being with someone else.

"I've got to finish cleaning my room. Please go home."

He pushes me against the wall hard so that I hit my head and back. Oh, hell no.

"Oh shit, I'm sorry, I didn't mean to push so hard, but I need you to understand something," he tells me while holding me pinned to the wall.

I hit my head hard, and I can feel the throbbing in my head with a surge of pain coursing through me.

"Oh, I understand," I raise my knee and hit him straight in his groin.

He screams in agony. I reach for my bedside lamp and go to town on top of his head.

"Don't ever put your hand on me or any other woman."

He shakes his head and sees the huge figure I have in my hand and jumps out of the way. He runs over to me tackling me onto the bed. He grabs my arms and places them above my head and tells me to calm down, but I can see the dazed look in his eyes. His head's hurting from the hit I gave him.

"Get off me," I squirm underneath him.

"Calm down, WINTER. Shit!" he yells. "I said I was sorry, just listen, I would never raise my hands to you, I just didn't realise how hard I pushed. I'm sorry," he explains.

"Fine. Now get off of me."

"No. Listen."

I roll my eyes at him in frustration because the first chance I get I'm fucking him up with the first thing I get my hands on.

"Lady, you are the most difficult person to deal with next to my sister. Damn, you're hard-headed, and stubborn as fuck but I'm in love with you. The past few weeks have been the best weeks of my life," I am speechless for once, and I don't know what to say.

So, I do the next best thing, I tell him to get off me. I calm down instantly and walk to the bathroom and turn the water in the tub on and add my essential oils and bath soap. I seriously need a soak; I can't deal with this right now. I think. I get naked and walk back in the room, and Trouble sits on the bed hurting. I walk towards him and lift his chin to raise his head so his eyes can meet mine. I take his hand and caress my body with it to make a point.

"Please don't confuse infatuation for love. You love the way my body feels, the way I look, especially the way I fuck you, there's a difference."

He rises to his feet and takes off his clothes and stands in front of me naked. I have to say, he is impressive; a man built with all the right parts to get a girl weak at the knees.

"See your dick knows it; tell your heart not to confuse the two. I don't do love. Love is made to provide pain," I whisper sweetly in his ear.

He kisses me and lifts me off my feet again. I wrap my legs around him, and he walks with me and places my back against the wall and makes love to my mouth with his tongue while he holds me in place. My breathing becomes shallow as I savour his taste.

I pull his head away from me to speak, "The tub is about to overflow."

He takes one look at the tub, walks over to it with me still in his arms and turns the pipes off. Then he steps in and sits down with me. Now tell me this isn't some movie type shit. The water spills over the tub, I lean back, and he tells me to continue, I am confused as to what I am supposed to be continuing with, so I just sit there with a dumb look on my face.

"Continue with your bath. When you finish, I will wash your back and get you dressed. You'll do that while I talk and you listen. That means not one word from you until I finish what I have to say."

"Fine," I lather myself up, and with my flannel and Irish spring soap. I've always loved the way it smells, and it reminds me of mama.

He goes on and on about how he loves me and how he is going to prove it and how I make him feel. I really don't want to hear this bullshit because I know how I feel and how I'm still going to feel after his little speech. So, I let him finish. Then I get up, turn and let him wash my back. I must admit his hands feel good on my body. I am going to miss him, his sex, but sex is sex, and I am not going to let that change my mind.

When he finishes, I tell him I'll think about it. I know I won't, but he doesn't have to know that. We make love one last time, giving him another reason to hate me when I stop returning his calls.

Fasten Your
Seat Belts...

~∿~

Autumn

We drive to Birmingham International airport for our flight to New York; Darius pleads for me to reconsider and from what it seems like Trouble is bent out of shape over Winter. Sunshine and Storm are all loved up as usual, seriously why aren't they married yet, it's maddening. I am sad and miserable because of my actions. I search for answers. My sister isn't speaking to me, some family vacation this is going to be. But one way or another, I will get back in my sister's good graces. I know this is going to be a mission, but one I have to complete. Winter's the stubbornest of the three of us. I can't believe she said, 'she has no sister,' she is so dramatic sometimes.

We arrive at the airport on time, check in and say goodbye to the men. Winter quickly ascends the stairs out of sight. I hug Trouble and tell him to send Peppa my love. I hug Darius and kiss him goodbye as a tear falls down my cheek. I tell him to let Peppa know how he feels, and until he does that and sees where things go with her, we can never be together. I cannot, in all good conscience, continue on with him, knowing that he's in love with another girl. I'd be a fool to think I could replace her love with mine, especially when deep down, he can never love me the way he loves her.

I refuse to become Catherine Valentine. I say my goodbyes and go in search of my stubborn ass sister. Storm stays behind with Sunshine. Lord help the two of them. I never knew another woman who could make my brother happy. Their relationship is always complicated, they fuck around on each other and are still in love, I just don't get it. He takes care of her like he takes care of us.

I climb the escalator in search of my sister, to have a heart to heart with her, but she's nowhere in sight. I walk around the duty-free shop and pick up some stuff for grandma Bird, who I haven't spoken to in over a month or so, so I know I'm going to hear all about it. I'm going to have to call her once I'm seated. I make up a hamper for Winter filled with her favourite things, to say sorry.

When I get to the gate, she's sitting with an older gentleman laughing, I walk over, and she cuts her eye at me.

"Hello," I introduce myself to the gentleman.

She gets up and walks over to the Virgin VIP members waiting area, and the smoke screen door provides a barrier and a reflection of our relationship. I go after her, but she is too fast. I take up a seat at the terminal waiting area, waiting for her to come out, but she doesn't. Storm comes up just in time as they start to call for first-class passengers to board the flight. I take my seat and wait for her to appear on board. She passes on the other side.

"We need to talk," I say, but she continues to ignore me.

She is giving me the silent treatment. She walks to the other end of the aeroplane, and a couple come and take up refuge in her seat. She's swapped her seat with someone in coach. She would rather be cramped up for 7 hours than sit near me. Well fine, two can play at that game. Why is she so upset, she gets to do the, 'I told you so speech' I sigh heavily, and Storm comes and sits beside me.

"I miss her Storm, and she is stubborn as usual."

"She's hurt because you made her feel worthless like she's not enough."

"Of course, she matters; she's my best friend, my left lung, my everything. How did she come up with that?" I ask.

"You not only betrayed her, but you betrayed our mother also," he says as a matter of fact.   "That's stupid" I snap.

"Well that's how she feels, and you got to give her space and respect how she feels she'll come around."

I cry into my brother's arms since he's the only one who seems to care about my feelings. If Winter wants space, then fine. An hour into the flight Storm goes back to his seat and falls asleep. He's had a long day and morning and dealing with me, Sunshine and Winter is a hard task at that. Oh shit, I forgot to call grandma Bird. I need to set a reminder. I sneak into the coach to see if Winter's ok. She's asleep on some dude's arm with a neck cosy around her neck. I place the gift bag I bought for her with the card that simply says, "SORRY," and kiss her forehead. She moves slightly in her sleep, opening her eyes, staring at me, and I walk away back to my seat.

I visit the toilets before I head back to my seat and take two sleeping pills; I need to sleep the rest of the way. I am not going to make it without my sister, I hate flying. She's always the one to hold my hands throughout the flight and reassure me that everything's going to be ok because we have each other. If we die, we are going to see mom again. Without her, there's no point in this holiday. It's going to suck. I put my sleep guard on my eyes that states: 'do not disturb,' and let the pills do their job and take me to a peaceful slumber.

I am awakened by a steward telling me about food. I kiss my teeth and tell him not to bother me until we land. I take two more sleeping tablets and drift back off dreaming of good times between Wint and me. Then I jerk out of my nightmare of the sperm donor laughing at us in the rain as we land. Storm's taking our luggage down from the overhead compartment.

"I see you still want to be treated like a first-class passenger and get off with us," I hear him say over my shoulders.

I look behind to see Winter stood with her back to us. At least she's ignoring the both of us now and not just me. I get up as the stewardess opens the doors to the plane, we exit in an orderly fashion and go to claim our luggage. As we exit JFK Airport, a man is waiting to drive us to the hotel with a sign that states: Valentine family. I am still tired from the pills I've taken, so I'm drifting in and out of sleep. Storm sit's in between us, which suits me perfectly because I need a shoulder to lie on. He was always our buffer growing up. It seems nothing's changed in that department.

We are booked in at the Four Season Plaza Hotel. I can't wait to reach the suite because these sleeping pills are kicking my ass, I'm drowsy as fuck. The hotel suite is gorgeous. I find the nearest bed and slump down on it before anyone can claim it as theirs. When I wake, Winter has gone out, and Storm's Skyping with Sunshine. I have the worst headache. I go into the shower, and I think spend about an hour letting the water pressure take my stress away.

Dear Lord! Help Me With These Crazy Females.

Storm

Autumn comes in just after 1p.m., and she's bawling her eyes out. Alarm bells go off, she ignores Wint and me on the sofa and goes to her room. This tells me she wants to be left alone, so, I'm gonna give her space for a minute before I figure out whose neck I need to break.

"What's happened to her?" Wint asks.

"I don't know. But she looks terrible." I reply.

"This one needs a lot of ice cream, and we've got none in the fridge, I'm going to get some. See you in a sec."

I watch as Wint leaves, which is good because I gotta find out what's wrong with Autumn and its best not to have her around as she tends to blow the simplest things out of proportion. I knock on Autumn's door, but she tells me 'she's ok just tired,' like I'm stupid.

"Girl you better be dressed because I'm coming in. It's just me, Wint's gone for ice cream," I slowly open her door, and there she is lying on the bed under the covers bawling her eyes out.

"So, what happened? and don't tell me nothing."

She explains the whole thing to me, and I'm disappointed in her. Why did she have to go searching for that son of a bitch?

"I know you are upset, but you deserve what you got because we all warned you and you were too stubborn to listen."

I hold her close and tell her exactly what I think; that this is a stupid move for such a smart girl. I can't believe she did something so stupid. Now I'm going to have to deal with two miserable women on my damn holiday because when Winter finds out all hell will break loose. We all know how she feels about that man. 20 minutes later, Winter calls to tell me what I already know. Shit! I say a small prayer for myself because I'm going to need it to deal with this. After Wint's call, I need to stay stress-free, so I call my baby Sunshine. There's no answer, so I send her a quick message telling her to hurry up. Tonight's my last night with her before I leave. I still feel she should come with us, but she refuses to come, I'm still going to bring it up every second, like I have been doing for the past couple weeks. Sigh! She keeps turning me down and pushing me away.

I call the boys to tell them to come through. I'm going to need a buffer tonight with these two simpletons I call my sister's because I want to spend my night inside Sunshine, not keeping them apart. The fellas arrive first with some Remy, Henny and chasers, they read my mind. Trouble even brings a tub of Ice cream for Wint. If he keeps fucking with Wint, she gonna have him for dinner. I see what Wint is talking about with him and his damn phone forever going off, but if she doesn't care, neither will I. Well I do a little because I'm going to be the one cleaning up whatever mess he makes.

So, I ask for my own peace of mind. "Yow fam. What's going on with your phone? You a drug dealer or something?"

He laughs like I give him some form of joke, "Naah fam, the ladies, keep stressing me, no big deal," he answers.

No big deal. I square my jaw and straighten my back to show my seriousness. Shaking my head at his ignorance. I leave him at the mercy of Winter.

"Just make sure it doesn't hurt Winter's head because then we got a problem, you understand me?" I tell him making him know that if he fucks with my sister, we are going to have a problem bigger than he can imagine.

He and Darius are 2 years older than us, but I don't give a fuck, age don't have anything to do with it, if he fucks with her heart and makes her cry.

"Winter's head has no reason to hurt her, it's because of her that it's blowing up like that because since we hooked up, I haven't had time for anyone else or want to find the time. So, the ladies are feeling some type of way, I guess," he explains.

"Well, bro, God be with you, because I know my sister and she is not going to want to hear none of that bullshit you are dishing out."

We all laugh at what Trouble is trying to say because we all know Wint isn't the lovie dovie kind of girl.

"Yow, Dee, need you to go keep lil miss company, sh'se still a bit upset, and I need you Trouble to keep Wint away from Autumn. As a matter of fact, where is Winter?"

I check my phone and see I've receive a message from Wint saying she is ok, and she will be home soon. That's not good, how far's she had to go for ice cream? And where the hell is Sunshine? I try Sunshine's line again and still no answer. She knows she should always keep her phone on at all times plus carry her charger and an extra battery. She's the next one that's determined to drive me crazy. This is definitely going to be a stressful holiday. I've already purchased an open ticket for her in case she changes her mind. I hope she does because I'm going to miss her, till I drive myself crazy, worrying about her. I try once again and there's still no answer. I turn on the tracker that I placed on her cell phone. It says she is in the building. I let out a sigh of relief as she walks through the door. Other than my sisters, she's the only one with a key to all our flats. She apologises immediately as she enters the room. She can see the frustration on my face and the relief in my eyes that she is ok.

"Where's your phone?" I ask.

"Here. So stop stalking me. I can't wait for you to leave the damn country," she replies with a kiss on my lips.

"You say that now and then it's going to be, when are you coming back? Blah blah blah."

"You two sound like an old married couple" Trouble states.

"We are. She's my pain in the neck," I tell him, and she rolls her eyes at me, sits on my lap and hits me in the back of my head. I chuckle at her lame attempt to hurt me and kiss her on the cheek.

"So, where's Auto and Wint at? she asks.

"Wint's gone to get ice cream and Auto's in her room. Yow Dee go sort that out, please?" he gets up and moves towards Autumn's bedroom, and she lets him in, thank God.

I get up and go over to the kitchen and grab a few fast food menus, throw them at Trouble and tell him to order some food. I grab Sunshine off the couch and lead her to my room.

"Is that how it is, just gonna leave a brother, all by my lonesome self," Trouble grumbles.

"I was born with pussy around me bro, not dicks, Wint will be home soon, just order some food and chill. Holler, when it arrives, the money's on the kitchen counter," I jokingly reply.

I take Sunshine for a quick quickie and to help with packing the suitcases. She helps me match outfits up and I give her a treat to remember me by, while I'm away. I ask her again if she wants to come with us and she declines again. How am I supposed to protect her if she won't let me? For a while, I have been thinking of hiring a permanent bodyguard for her, but she refuses that too. She has a security detail that follows her, when I'm not around which she originally didn't know about. Boy when she found out she didn't speak to me for nearly four months. It was the worst four months ever. It's for her safety and my peace of mind when I'm not with her or can't get to her quick enough, but she doesn't want to understand. This time I just have to insist that she has one.

Trouble shouts at us announcing that the food is here. I'm not hungry for food, but I need to eat to maintain my strength and stamina, with this one. We go out and eat. Autumn finally emerges from her bedroom but there's still no Winter, I'm starting to get worried.

"Yo, call your girl to see where she is, she is not picking up my calls!" I command Trouble.

I am starting to worry because no matter what, we always pick up or let each other know our whereabouts. I can feel her pain from a mile away, and I can also feel Auto's anguish too. If something happens to her, I will never forgive Autumn.

"Stop staring at me and call your damn sister and make sure she's ok else imma wring your neck too," I shout at Autumn since this is her fault.

A migraine 's starting to form; I squeeze the bridge of my nose in frustration. These women in my life seriously want to see me in a madhouse.

Winter comes in just after 8 p.m. with tear stains down her cheek, and her eyes are puffy from crying. She doesn't acknowledge anyone in the room. Normally her presence dominates a room, but something's missing, she looks broken. She slams the door, and I can feel the pain in both my sisters' hearts. Autumn jumps up and runs after her. I can hear Winter screaming at her once she reaches the bedroom, I know something's about to go down, so I march over, but when I get to Wint's room the door is being slammed in Auto's face, and she goes to her room and slams her door too. Damn. Here comes that migraine.

I go in to check on my Wint, sugarplum. There she is balled up on the floor. I pick her up, place her on the bed and lay with her. I wait for her to stop sobbing so she can speak clearly because I can never understand what the hell she's saying. Given the circumstances, I understood the pain and betrayal she feels. I let her vent and wait for her to fall asleep before I leave her in peace. I check on Autumn, but Darius is taking care of her. So, I go back into the living area.

"She ok?" Trouble asks with a concerned look on his face.

"Yeah, she'll be fine, just some sibling rivalry. They'll soon be best friends again. She is sleeping so I'd give her a little space until she comes around." I explain to him.

"And how long will that be? You guys leave tomorrow, and I really have something to tell her?" he complains.

"Whenever she's ready, and that's not now. She's sleeping, so don't disturb her." I grab the ice cream Trouble brought for Winter and whisper in Sunshine's ear to follow me. We finish packing the suitcases and clean up our mess and lay in bed together.

"So, I need you to think something through for me and give me your answer when I get back, ok? Take time to consider it," I tell her.

"What is it?" she replies with a heavy sigh and a facial expression that states she couldn't care less about what I have to say and that I am annoying her.

"Fix your face and reel your neck back in. Listen, and yes, we are having that conversation," I tell her.

"Spit it out, Storm."

"We've been doing this thing on and off for years now. We've both had plenty of different partners in between, but I'm sick of that now. When I'm with other women, my mind is on you, and we walk around here like we're already married. I don't want to see you with anyone again, EVER. I mean that. I can't bear it. So, when I get back, it's me and you, straight up. No more last-minute hook-ups. You are my woman, and I've always been yours. If not, we need to go our separate ways. My heart can't take it anymore, my heart is the age of a seventy year-old man from all the torture you've put it through," I proclaim, and she giggles.

"Why, why are you laughing? I'm serious."

"You're cute when you're jealous, is this about Junior?" she asks amused.

Who the fuck is Junior? I think. "No. this is about us. And I mean what I said." I say with base in my voice, so she understands the seriousness of what I'm saying because if she disagrees, I don't think I will be returning. Nana Bird is too old to be by herself. My house is done so I can move in and still run things from there. She knows this because we've been talking about this for some time now.

"You say that, but me and you know you're not going nowhere. And if you ever put that thought in your head again, I'll slice it off. Does that answer your question? I love you as much as you love me, but I need space as well, so that's why we do this dance of ours. So, continue fucking who you want and when their pussy dries up, come home."

"You're not listening to me, Sunshine. I don't want to fuck anyone else just you for the rest of my life. I don't want you with anyone else either. Just think about it. I know your space and independence is important, so I'm giving you three months to decide. Space or me?" I tell her and kiss her on the forehead.

"One other thing while I'm away, whether you like it or not, I've got you security," I tell her because I need my sanity. Something in me tells me she needs it.

"**NO. YOU. ARE. NOT.** I'm serious Storm, don't you dare invade my privacy like that again and have me followed. I don't need it. If you do, you can have your answer from me right now." She complains.

"I'm not going to be here Sunshine, and your safety means everything to me, so you're getting one, end of story. Bitch all you want," I tell her not caring one bit.

"I can't believe you would do this to me, we've had this conversation before, and we agreed..." she complains.

"No, you agreed, I disagree, and it's done. I don't want to talk about what can't be changed anymore; my word is final on this matter!" I exclaim.

"Fine when does he or she start?"

"Last week," I quietly say under muffled breath.

"What. You've had a stranger watching me like a peeping Tom. Do you not see what's wrong with that picture?" she asks.

"No. And he hasn't been watching. He had a week to prove to me that he can do the job, so I gave him a trial run. He's ex-military, husband and father of two, and he's charging a pretty penny, so I needed to know you were in good hands. I had him checked out, he generally guards high profile clients. He agreed to manage this for me as a favour to a friend of mine."

"Your ass doesn't have any friends so who exactly are you talking about?"

"It doesn't matter, all you need to know is that you are safe and that's all I need to know. He is coming to meet you tomorrow at the airport."

"I hate you," she says without any feelings behind the statement.

"And I love you," I tell her and pull her close to me.

She seems distant, but it's for her own good and my peace of mind. I would die if anything happened to her while I'm away, and if I can afford to take care of her the right way, why shouldn't I?

I hear Wint scream out in a panic, so I dash off the bed to see what's up with her, but Trouble has her over his shoulder, they're having a lover's thing. I need to be in with Sunshine all night, so I close my door and lock it. I strip off the rest of my clothes and crawl between her legs, stripping her of her clothing.

I ease myself inside and roll on my back so she's on top and tell her, "you can either ride it or just chill and lay with me inside?" We lay together till we drift into sweet slumber.

Before I know it, it's time to get up. When we rise up, I flip her and put it on her one last time before I leave.

The drive to the airport is real short, we check in, and Wint and Auto go upstairs, leaving me and my baby behind. I introduce her to her new bodyguard, and they actually hit it off. A little too much. They get acquainted, and I lay down the rules one last time to both of them, making sure he understands the rules and regulations I've planted in his big head the past couple weeks. I kiss her goodbye and send them on their way. Then I go to find my girls.

The flight is long as hell. Auto's bugging out over Wint and Winter's being hard-headed, that girl actually swapped seats with somebody else and sits in coach. I see this is going to be a hard one to put back together; if all the king's horses and all the king's men can't do it, then there's no hope for me.

The Four Seasons never fails to disappoint. The joint suite is amazing. Auto is out of it by the time we get in. Wint goes down to the gym. I get on Skype with Sunshine, check on our family accounts and check the Stock market. I always make responsible buys and check out what the richest people on the market are doing to ensure that we don't get left behind. We may live a simple life, but our bank account is larger than life; our great grandkids will live lavish lives. We do simple shit and sponsor the needy anonymously so that we never get robbed or stay in the spotlight. Peaceful and quiet is the way we like it. Our grandmother taught us to be humble above all things. Say what you want about Simon Cowell, but that man dresses in the most expensive material but the simplest shit.

Winter comes to New York xoxo

~~~~~~~~~~~~~~~~~~~~~~~~~~~~~~~~~~~~~~~

Winter

I wake up on the plane to Auto kissing me on the forehead and giving me a gift. Am I supposed to forget her transgression. I am not Jesus Christ, I don't forgive that easy, she better come better than that.

The New York chill is in the air when we arrive, and there's an old guy standing outside with a sign with our surname on it. Storm thought of everything. Love that boy. Talking about love, I can't believe the shit Trouble threw in my lap before I left. What am I supposed to do with that? The dick is damn good, yes, but not that good that I lose all my senses and fall hopelessly in love. With all that's going on I wish I had gone straight to Jamaica; I would have been higher than a kite right now and stress-free from the bullshit with my sister.

Storm got us adjoining rooms. Hope he knows that he's sleeping with Autumn or on the couch I don't give a fuck. I need to get away from this. They have a state-of-the-art gym facility; I'm going to take advantage of it and book myself in for some of their treatments. I need to relax before I explode up here. I put my gym outfit on and head downstairs for my work out while Storm jumps on his Apple Mac and Autumn disappears into one of the rooms.

"I'm off to get my gym on," I tell him before heading out.

When I got downstairs, I book a few spa treatments with the concierge and continue my evening at the gym. They underestimate the gym because they have equipment I have never seen before and the pool and Jacuzzi are remarkable.

I get on the treadmill and run for an hour. I burn rubber; my legs are almost numb when I get off. I walk over to a vibrating machine that is supposed to tone you up. I follow the instructions on the diagram, damn it feels like my brain's about to jump out of my damn head. My nose tingles. I sit on it like the diagram says and 10 seconds in I jump and scream out and everyone stares at me in confusion. I'm sorry that shit should not be in a gym, that thing is a straight-up vibrator. I swear 2 seconds more, and I would have cum all over the gym. I can't do anything other than laugh at myself.

They have a sauna and steam room, so I give up on the gym and think I'll go get myself a good old fashion steam out. I change into my bathing suit. There are three others inside the steam room. The sauna's empty, but dry heat makes me unable to breathe, so I stick it out. There's a pretty young girl with two older gentlemen. I smile and take a seat in the middle and inhale deeply, filling my lungs, and releasing all my frustration. The guys are all watching me intently, I guess home girl notices and doesn't like it, from the vibe she's giving off. Two more of her friends come in and sit next to her, and then the whispering starts.

I smile at them, half-heartedly and the blonde one introduces herself first.

"H., you do know, these facilities are for paying guests only, staff are down the hall, right?"

Is this bitch for real I should slap some sense into her dumbass. But I learnt a long time ago the best way to deal with whites like her.

"Since you know the directions and rules, why are you here?"

"Excuse me, do you know who you are speaking to?" her friend asks.

"I don't care in the slightest. Now please shut up before you let out the ignorant black girl you seek out of me."

"What a racist thing to say," she says. "I'm one-part African Cherokee," the smart mouth dumbass says.

"So, that makes you what, stupid?" I ask astonished.

"That means I can have you fired," she says with a spoilt rich bitch grin.

"Go ahead and try."

I swear the devil sent these bitches to fuck with me, or the lord is testing me. If you are lord? Help them quickly because I'm about to fail this test and beat a bitch in this steam room. The devil is alive in these hoes. She scoffs and continues making her bitchy comments. The men get up and leave the room, I'm glad because I don't want any witnesses if I have to fuck a bitch up. Eventually, they give up because they start talking about some bachelor auction. They make sure to mention out loud the fact that entry is $1000 a plate and there's a $500 entry fee. They giggle and speak about their outfits for tonight. The punk bitches don't even know that that's pocket change for me. Well, I guess I'm going to have to teach these simple bitches a new class lesson on how not to judge this book by the colour of my natural beautiful skin.

"You guys better start acting right, before I fuck your daddy and you have to call me mommy," I wink at them and leave them, with their jaws on the floor and with a new mission on destroying their pink Barbie doll New York high life. I'm on some gossip girl shit with these bitches.

I hurry to the reception desk to enquire about this ball or banquet those chicken-heads are talking about. The hostess almost makes the same mistake as those bitches downstairs and judges before she knows who I am. That's the thing with black people nowadays, still under the master's whip. What! Because I'm black, I can't own shit, or because I'm black I have to be with an athlete to have money. She gives me a 'you won't fit in look.' But I 'm not trying to fit in when I want to stand out so perfectly.

"You sure you want to go there; it's going to be a bunch of rich white people faking it with each other while they bid on each other for their so-called causes," she tells me. She is a young pretty black woman; I am digging her pixie jet black sleek haircut.

"Then come with me. I'm only interested because I need to teach these dumb bitches a lesson or two," I explain to her and tell her about the women in the steam room.

"And where am I supposed to find $1000 from? My piggy banks barely got 25cents in it," she says as she laughs.

"Don't worry about that, that's simple, can you get the tickets or not?" I ask her.

"I'll make a few calls," I wait for her to call around and she finally manages to get through and get me a seat at a table.

"Make sure you get yourself a seat as well, I could use the company," I tell her. She smiles and nods her head.

She points to the girls from the steam room with her chin.

"Are those them?" she asks, covering up the mouthpiece of the telephone.

"Yeah. That's them," I wrinkle my nose at them.

"Send your daddies my regards, tell them I'll see them soon," I yell loud enough for them to hear. Me and the receptionist laugh and she hangs up the phone.

"Girl, you're too bad, you know their daddies?"

"No, don't even know their names," I laugh. "They are just rude as hell. Racist pink bitches."

"They really got to you, huh? Well, you got two seats for tonight," she says.

"Ok, Cool. Also you got a good hairdresser? I need my hair done," I ask.

"Yeah, I know just the person for you, he's ghetto as hell, but no one can beat his hair design," she states. Then adds, "now where am I going to get a dress at this hour of the evening on a budget?"

"What size are you, you look the same size as me?" I ask

"Size 8, why? You got something I can wear?"

"I got that, what time do you finish?"

"Now, I am just enjoying talking to your wild ass, plus I'm putting in an extra hour or two over time, but I can leave now, Cindy and Alfie are here."

"Ok Call your stylist and get him over here so he can do my hair, tell him I also need extensions," I tell her, "Imma, Maid in Manhattan this thing."

She mentions that she's not allowed to associate with guests, so we have to meet outside. I'm not about to go out in the cold ass air that New York's producing outside. So, I tell her that I'll hire her as an assistant for the night. She agrees, and we go upstairs to the room.

"Hey bro this is... what's your name again?" we're having such a good time I've forgotten to ask her name.

"It's Gabrielle," she replies.

"Hey Gabby," Storm says as he looks over his shoulder, acknowledges us and graces us with a warm smile.

"No. Not Gabby, Gabrielle," she retorts.

"Well, alright then," I giggle at her feistiness.

"I'm sorry, Miss Gabrielle,. I'm Storm, like the one we have outside," he says flirting with her.

"Oh, and by the way we are triplets, so you may see another one of me somewhere round here," I tell her.

"Wow, that's cool!" she exclaims.

"Let's go, introductions are over. Let's find something for you to wear. You called your people yet?" I ask as I lead the way to the room and unpack a bunch of dresses for her to choose from.

She chooses a silk red evening dress that blends well with her skin tone. She's a coco chocolate powder babe with a banging pair of tits, so the off the shoulder piece really works for her. It shows her neck and shoulders perfectly.

"Girl this dress is beautiful, I love it," she confesses.

"Thanks, it's yours," I never wear anything another chick is seen in first.

"Thank you so much, it's got to be expensive, who's the designer?"

"Me, I designed everything you see here."

She looks shocked like it's an impossible task.

"Go take a shower, the bathroom is over there, so I can catch you up on how tonight's going to play out."

While she's in the shower, her larger than life friend arrives. Gayer than him I have never met, and don't think I ever will meet again. Man has on a scarf and thigh-high boots. Lord gimme the case and take the pillow for this one. Heaven have mercy, please.

"Hi, I'm Shaundra," he extends his hand for me to take it.

I am still a little shocked but smile and shake his hand and tell him to set up over at the vanity table. Storm calls me out, and I close the bedroom door and follow him into the living room of the suite.

"What the hell is that?" he asks.

"I'm not sure, but it's going to fix my hair for the ball tonight," I say with a little giggle.

"What ball and why am I just hearing about it now?" he enquires.

"Oh. Yeah, Winter shall be going to the ball tonight, lil brother."

"I need more details Wint?" he crosses his arms and asks.

"These white bitches decided I am too poor to be in their presence, so I'm about to take over their city. I need to teach these chicks a Winter lesson." I tell him.

He squeezes the bridge of his nose in frustration. "This is too much, just don't get arrested. Keep out of trouble please for me."

"I won't get arrested, trouble, maybe," I wink at him and leave him standing there.

"No. **WINTER. NO TROUBLE FOR GOD'S SAKE,**" he shouts back to me. I close the door, and Gabrielle's out the shower talking to her little friend.

"So, my girl tells me you need my assistance to kick some hating ass bitches off their pedestal," he says as more of a statement than a question.

"Yeah, they're acting up, and I'm just the Bitch to do it too. You got the hair I asked for?"

He opens up a suitcase of hair like a mini kiosk stand makes me laugh inside, this is some comedy TV shit. This only appears on comedy shows.

"Told you my girl had it locked," Gabrielle states.

"Well, that's fine with me. I'm going for sophistication, class and elegance. Can you do that, in less than 2 hours?" I ask him because he looks a little too fabulous for my liking, but I know better than to judge.

"Sweetheart, if I can't turn you into a prettier version of you then it's free, and I don't do free baby. I don't even suck for free. You got my money?" he asks me with attitude and sass.

"Yeah, do a good job, and I'll tip you better than the last man you sucked. Let's get this show on the road, then."

He sews the longest extensions in my hair. They are tight as hell, but I bare it, he even adds a dark red underneath for power. I explain the run-down of what tonight's about to Gabrielle. Once Shaundra finishes sewing my hair, I go for a shower while he styles my home girl's hair. When I return, he styles my hair and helps me apply my make-up. I don't usually do eyelashes because they always itch my eyeballs, but I got to admit homeboy knows his stuff. I look drop-dead gorgeous.

"There," he declares, once he's finished with the finishing touches.

I love it. My hair's banging, to say on point's an understatement.

"I would fuck you too if pussy was my thing girl. I'm tempted to switch just for your fine ass" he jests.

"Well thank you, fairy Godmother. I love it, and my make-up looks flawless," I praise her/ him, fuck it I don't know. Gabrielle has cleaned up the room and hung up the dress I found for myself.

"Girl that dress is beautiful, and yours too Gabbs, they look like they are made for you," Shaundra tells her.

"I know right, Winter made them, isn't she fabulous" Gabrielle states.

"Girl you are talented, you just have to come by the shop and show these bitches how it's done. Beyonce and Rihanna who? Yes, yes, Winter is coming. I will definitely be looking out for your line girl. Now, pay me! That will be $1200. I did two services, I ain't cheap!"

I shake my head and pull out $1500 from my purse and hand it to him.

"Thank you for everything," I thank him.

"Damn if I knew you had it like that then I would have charged you more," he says jokingly.

I show him out of the room, and he gives me a hug and tells me to knock them dead.

"Call me with details, tomorrow I'm taking you out on the town," he says.

"No problem," I tell him fully knowing I have no intention of going anywhere.

"Listen, is he free?" he suggests over my shoulder at Storm.

"No. Bye," I say and close the door.

"Storm that man wants you, you better be careful, I hear these Yanks are ruthless," I laugh and walk back to my room, where Gabby's waiting patiently while topping up her lipstick.

"Thank you for taking me tonight," She says.

"It's no problem. Plus you're the one who's doing me a favour, remember. Just have fun, and if you see something, you want to bid on it. It's on me." I say as I step into my heart-shaped neckline, champagne velvet colour dress. I made this dress for Autumn, but it will have to do for tonight's festivities. I step into a pair of my clear six-inch stilettos and realise that Gabbs has no shoes.

"Where can we get a pair of sexy kick them down heels at this time?" I ask her.

"Macy's is still open, but we would have to get them on the way."

"Ok, call the driver and let's go. You did get a town car right because we can't pull up in a taxi?" I ask with a little bass in my voice.

"Yeah, the hotel has a car service, we can take one. Mr Johnson should start his shift now he sometimes takes me home, so I'm safe. I'll call him," while she places her call, I get my matching purse and tell her to follow me.

"Hey Storm, I need more cash, have you got any on you?" I ask.

"Yeah, but what happened to yours?" he questions.

"Already done."

"Use the card. Winter. I'm busy," he says brushing me off.

"Doing what? I'll make sure you are ok in the morning. Please," I say in that annoying tone he hates.

"Fine. Look in my bag in the room, and we are doing lunch tomorrow?" I kiss him and thank him, just in time for Gabbs to tell me that the car is downstairs.

"Gabrielle, please keep her out of trouble," he tells her on our way out.

"Don't worry, she's in good hands," she says, smiling.

"I hope so, what's the name of this place you are going, so I know where to find you?"

I write down the information for him and kiss him on the cheek and leave. Autumn comes in as I am about to leave. I cut my eyes, past her and take Gabrielle's hand and march off. The driver is waiting at the curbside. He is an elderly old man, a little chubby with a pleasant smile.

"Miss Jenkin, Miss Valentine, I will be your driver tonight," he says as he opens the door for us to enter.

"Thanks, Mr Johnson, we need to stop off at Macys first to get some shoes. Stop round the back. I'll use my key card, staff entrance is much faster," she tells him.

"You have two jobs?" I ask.

"Yes, one to pay the bills and one to save for my mortgage," she tells me.

We stop, and she goes and comes back as quickly as she left. Before she left, I gave her $500 to get the shoes.

Those shoes are cute, I approve.

"You know I ain't never had a man pay for so much for me in one night, without giving something in return. So, I hope your not on that gay shit cause I don't get down like that," she says out loud with conviction.

"Ahhh trust and believe you have nothing I want. Other than your company tonight. You have the information I need, and that's all. And that's your payment for tonight," I tell her straight.

"Ok then let's pop the champagne and do this," she chirps.

We pull up at a museum. Outside there's a red carpet and photographers snapping pictures continuously. It is a bit too much for me. But I have a point to prove so the show must go on.

Winter Wonderland

Winter

The driver comes around and opens the car door and tells us to have a good night. I thank him and tell him we will call when we are ready. Camera flashes go off in our faces, and I walk along and pose when necessary for the cameras. They have a lot of questions, but I just ignore them all and keep it moving until the right question comes my way.

"Tell us who you are and who you are wearing tonight?" a reporter asks.

I smile and reply, "Winter $easons." The reporter looks puzzled and writes my answer down.

Gabby comes and stands by my side after posing for the cameras, and we take photos together, she's asked the same question, and she replies elegantly.

"It's a new arrival from the Winter $easons collection."

I smile at her answer. I hear one of the reporters say, "that one is British, she is a bit short for a model."

"That's because I'm not."

I turn and make my way through the entrance, where everyone is gathering. I need a drink. There are a lot of white folks. I feel like a deer in the headlights, but the smile I plant on my face never leaves, fearless I tell myself; they bleed red just like you. Gabby comes over with two champagne flutes, and I take one from her and take a sip. I want to down the entire thing, but I have to remain classy for the rest of the night. We walk around, and she tells me about the people in the room, who's who, what they do and their family history and background. A very attractive white man in his fifties approaches us.

She nudges me and says, "here comes bait numeral Uno."

I smile and drink the rest of my champagne.

"Get me another one of these and see if you can find a bar and add something stronger," I order, and she leaves my side to fetch the drinks.

"I don't believe I've ever had the pleasure," the stranger says, smiling with his hand held out for me to take.

"I'm sure you have but never with me. Hi. I'm Winter, and you are?"

He seems amused and takes my hands and kisses the back. I take my hands back and wipe them on the back of my dress.

"My name is Alexander, Alexander McDonald, the fourth," he declares to me.

"So, tell me who are you a guest of tonight?" he asks. Before I can answer Gabby returns with drinks.

"Here you go Miss Winter, they have notified me that we will be seated soon. Is there anything else I can do for you?" she asks politely playing her part as my assistant.

"Thank you, that will be all," I tell her and turn to address him.

"As you can see, I'm escorted by no one. I'm simply here to enjoy my night."

I flirt with him a little till I see his bitch of a daughter eyeing us then I get a little hands-on with him. The look of shock and disgust that's plastered over her face is a Kodak moment for sure. She starts to bolt towards us, and I take my leave. My hands lingering on his body a little longer than normal and giggling at whatever dumb thing he's spitting, I'm not really paying attention. I leave as she gets close enough. I go to the restroom to freshen up, and Gabby follows closely behind.

"Girl, did you see her face?" I say. We laugh and reapply more lip-gloss and I run my hand through my hair for good measure.

"That's what she gets for fucking with a black woman," Gabby adds.

"Let's go piss some more people off," I say.

We find another wealthy man to toy with. A mommy's boy, he lives off his parents' name and money, and so did his spoiled daughters and son's. Apparently, they are all a disappointment, and if it wasn't for great-grandaddy's slave trade money from back in the day, they wouldn't have shit. Yet they still look down on the less fortunate like they are better than them. Well, tonight they're gonna meet the Miss Black Bitch. Moments like this make me regret this weave and straight hair, but fuck it, damage already done. I go and stand really close to him so that when he turns, he can bump into me, or I bump into him depending on how long I can wait.

While waiting for the next jerk, I spot a handsome black dude with a fade and neatly shaved facial hair. He's midnight black and sexy with it too. Damn, he's fine as hell. Our eyes make four; I have to look away, trying to stay focused on my task at hand, having fun while fucking with white folks like they've fucked with me all my life. This thing's taking too long, I step back into the gentleman behind me, and he turns around to notice me. I watch his face go from angry to pure hunger and lust. The devil in him clearly makes him forget about the ring that's firmly placed on his index finger.

"Oh. Sorry, I'm just a clutz sometimes. Let me get that for-" he says as he finally looks me in the eye.

"Not to worry it's an accident, I'm sure," I say like he's the one who bumped into me.

"Well, I'm glad we had this one otherwise I wouldn't have the pleasure of meeting you," he comments.

I smile and bite my bottom lip, for good sexual measure. He offers me his hand to shake, and I comply. He stares in my eyes until he's lost in them. An elderly woman clears her throat for our attention, and he turns and tries introducing me to the woman he was engaged in conversation with before our encounter. She was polite, and I can tell she thinks I am beneath her.

"You are a very beautiful young lady," she finally addresses me after inspecting me from head to toe.

"Thank you," I smile and reply, "that's a lovely brooch you're wearing." The thing is awful and needs to be melted down for scrap parts, but I can't find anything to compliment her ignorant old ass on.

"Thanks, it was a gift from my David. God rest his soul," she tells me. David must not have loved you that much, I think. I smile so I don't have to comment again.

"That was nice of him," I say since it seems a smile isn't enough for the old bag.

"So, who are your family dear?" The tone of voice she uses to ask the question tells me she thinks I am lost and should not be there.

"Sorry where's my manners. My name is Winter Valentine," I declare.

"I'm not familiar with your family," she says.

"Not to worry you will be, soon enough."

Our conversation is starting to get boring; I am not here for idle chit chat with old ladies who still feel they should own slaves. I cut the conversation and turn to address her, anything for mommy, son.

"And what's your name?" I ask and then remember that I didn't ask the miserable old bag her name.

"David, I was named after my father," he says proudly.

"How cute, are you a bachelor up for auction tonight?" I ask with mock amusement.

"No. I'm one of the committee members hosting. So, England? Where in London did you attend school?" he asks.

"I didn't. So, what's a girl gotta do to be seated next to you tonight?" I ask.

He smiles bashfully and is about to answer when mommy dearest clears her throat and interrupts our conversation, again.

"A little rum and garlic will get rid of that frog in your throat," I tell her and roll my eyes at her determination of keeping her son from me. She gasps.

"Well, David, I've taken up enough of your time. Enjoy your night."

Well, that's a bust. I leave them standing and move to find Gabby. I seriously can't stand to be in the old lady's presence a second more. Even if it fucked with her mentally, my mental state is in jeopardy. I find Gabby next to the bar, and when she sees me coming, she picks up a flute of champagne and hands it to me.

"Thanks, damn mommy dearest was a buzz kill; I just couldn't stay in her presence for one more second. I had to abort." I tell her, and she laughs and grabs a second flute for herself.

"Definitely they're keeping it in the family," I say and shake my head.

There is an announcement from an MC letting everyone know to take a seat. It is time for our meal. We are seated at one of the head tables near the stage. Alexander comes to sit by my side.

"Is this seat taken?" he asks, taking the seat anyway without waiting for the reply. He is quite endearing in a George Clooney sort of way. I smile and remain seated. Blonde princess comes over and sits next to him, tearing his attention away.

"Daddy, our seat is over there, why are we sitting here", she asks.

"Go sit with your friend sweetheart I'll be fine. Save daddy a dance later," he tells her.

He is quite sweet with her and gentle, like a real father is supposed to be. I can't help but feel a little jealous of their relationship. She smiles and kisses his cheek, gets up and leaves to go sit in her appointed seat, but not before giving me the evil eye. I finger wave bye to her with a menacing smile.

"So, tell me, Miss, sorry, what's your name again?" he asks with a lustful smile.

"Winter," I state.

"Unique. It's different. You're very beautiful, just like your name." Like I haven't heard that before.

"Did you go to boarding school in England or did you attend one of their universities?" he asks.

"Why does everyone assume I attended some dull boarding school in England because I have a British accent?" I am very irritated. I already fucked with his bitch of a daughter, so I am done playing nice.

"I assumed because of your accent," he smiles apologetically.

"So, if a black man knocks up one of your precious daughters. Just ship the problem away. Out of sight, out of mind, right. Don't want to taint the family blood, is that it? Or put a stain on your family's name." I say, staring him dead in the eye, to show my anger.

He stumbles over his words a little, "I- I -I'm sorry I didn't mean to offend you, I just assumed that's what happened, and you've returned back home. I am not racist; I employ a lot of Hispanics." He explains to me.

"And you think that makes you some kind of hero or saviour of the coloured folks because you pay them to do your gardening and clean your house and pool?" I shake my head in disgust.

I can see he feels a bit at a loss for words for the first time. With every word he utters, I give him a revelation and make him feel even smaller than his dick.

"Lately I've been thinking about retirement," I tell him with confidence. Waiters surround the room placing meals on the table in front of everyone.

"At such a young age, retirement is possible. What, did you win the lottery?" he asks with amusement in his voice.

"No. I just can." Realising that I am divulging more information than I'd like to, I cut the conversation off by focusing my attention on the scraps in front of me.

After dinner is served, I am still starving. All that money for scraps on a plate? I am pissed and hungry, not a good combination. Alexander is still trying to share small talk, but I keep shutting him down. The nerve of these people is starting to make me regret coming to this awful place. I can feel my stomach talking to me crying out for me to feed it. This must be how the starving children feel, that are always on those Red Cross commercials. The plates are cleared. They should have told us to eat before we came. I am starting to miss my sisters cooking.

"Miss Winter let me apologise again for my ignorance, I would like to make it up to you. Can I take you to lunch tomorrow, preferably breakfast?" he bravely asks.

I swear this man has some sort of Viking blood surging through his veins because he is brave as hell.

"I would like to get to know you more. I find you very fascinating," he pleads his case.

"How about you teach your daughter not to judge a person by their skin colour: and not to follow in her daddy's footsteps and make assumptions about a person. Then maybe, maybe I might be interested in having you for company. My time is precious; Mr Alexander and I doubt you can afford it. So, no."

He chuckles in bemusement and asks, 'if I am serious.' I must be losing my touch because he just isn't getting the message. After about five minutes I smile and tell him fine I'll think about it, even though clearly my face says otherwise.

An attractive woman approaches the microphone on the stage and announces that the auction is about to take place, so please forward with your paddle number board, if you would like to bid. The men all stay in the back as the women flock towards the stage front and centre.

I must admit a few of these young men are attractive in a Zach Efron kind of way. It's showtime. For every bid Miss Princess puts in, I double and win. Her face when I win the first bid, is actually priceless. I can't keep the grin off my face. Between Gabby and me we clean house. We win three of the prestigious upper- class sons of some of the richest men and women in New York. Next up is the sexy black African Nubian king I saw earlier. Gabby and I look at each other and smile.

"I wanna trade my bid in, I want that tonight," I laugh at her boldness.

Seems we are both thinking the same thing. I am about to let all the hungry bitches bid first; bidding starts at 500 dollars. I guess all these uppity bitches don't want daddy to know that they love black dick, because you can see all of their eyes lusting after him but there's no brave souls in here, except Gabby.

"Bitch, stop spending my money. He's mine." I nudge her in the side and whisper to her.

"3000 dollars," I shout, getting the room's attention.

"Do I hear 31 hundred?" the pretty young lady asks, and no one answers.

"Going once, going twice."

"35 hundred," little Miss Princess screams out of nowhere. I smirk and think she may have some Viking in her too after all.

"5 thousand," I challenge. I can see the anger boiling up inside her. See the highest bid of the night now is for this handsome all-round American Justin Bieber look-alike from the Donaldson family. I buy him. I'm not quite sure what I'm going to do with all these men yet. I have 48 hours of their time to do as I please.

"10 thousand," she screams. I smile and wink at the sexy stud on the stage.

"Sold," I state out loud and laugh at her dumb ass. She thinks I am an amateur at this game. She thinks she's won.

"Boss lady, why did you make her play you like that, she got our man," Gabby moans with disappointment.

I smile at her and tell her, "this ain't over, trust me." She's playing right into my hands. She just brought a black man who clearly has eyes for me.

"You've overdosed on too much confidence; how do you know he's feeling you like that?" she asks.

"If I haven't told you before, I am the centre of everyone's universe."

Miss Princess is over the moon with her conquest. Her daddy doesn't look too impressed, and the rest of the room full of old biddies doesn't seem pleased either. She's gone all in to win and forgot to protect the family name. It's time to gather my winnings for the night, but instead, I walk straight over to little Miss Princess to introduce myself. Gabby is hot on my heels.

"Congratulations, on escaping with the man of the night," I say, ignoring her completely as I speak while looking up at the gentleman before us. I slide in between them and introduce myself turning my back to her.

"Hi, my name is Winter, and you are?" I ask as our eyes lock on each other.

"Grateful," he says while rubbing his chin in contemplation. With the biggest smile, a person can have on their faces.

"So Grateful, it's nice to meet you," I reply.

"It's finally nice to meet you, Winter, I've been eyeing you all night, but old boy has all your attention."

"Oh, no that's nothing. He's trying but I'm not interested," I tell him with a wave of my hand, dismissing the possibility.

"So, what are you interested in?" he asks with a gleam in his eyes.

I eye him up and down and reply, "a lot. Like the name your mother gave you at birth?" he chuckles and replies, "Marcus, Marcus Davenport."

"Winter Valentine," I shake his hand, and he closes the gap between us. Oh my goodness he smells like heaven. I can spot Hugo Boss Bottled Night aftershave from a mile.

"I think we are being rude to Miss McDonald." he whispers close to my ear, grazing his lips against my ear, and I feel my entire body shudder with sexual heat.

My sex automatically perks up and stands to attention. He places a business card in my hand and thanks me again for the bid and tells me to give him a call.

I smile and quickly snap back to reality as he is about to walk away. "Wait a minute hold up, if you want to talk you can contact me, this doesn't work like that I'm a busy lady. Here's my card I await your call, Mr Davenport," I tell him.

He smiles, chuckles and tilts his head back. He takes Miss Princesses attention as he approaches her and the look, she gives me makes me thank God that looks can't kill because I would drop instantly. Gabby and I look at each other and laugh like we are thinking the same damn thing. Damn my stomach is growling.

"Let's go, I'm done messing with these people," I tell Gabby. As we walk to the exit,

Alexander approaches us with one last plea. Lord help him, please. This dude just doesn't give up.

"Gabby, can you let the driver know we are ready, please?" I ask.

"Yes, Miss Winter," she replies and opens the door to the entrance.

I smile at Alexander and thank him for the lovely entertainment and to be sure to send me all of the gentlemen's details to me via email. I give him my card and take a step to move off but he grabs my arm and stops me in my tracks I see a flash go off in the distance, but I ignore it.

"May I have my arm back please?"

He releases it, and I thank him, he comes in close and whispers in my ear, "you've cost me a lot of money tonight, I would like to ensure I get your time," he says seriously.

"My time is very valuable Alex, if you would like to see me or speak with me, please contact me on the number on the card I just gave you and schedule an appointment," I say in a stern tone.

"You are a confusing woman Miss Winter, and I like it. I would definitely like to get to know more about you," he says as he moves a stray hair from my face. Another light flashes from a distance.

"Google me, you'll find all the information you need," I tell him. The driver pulls up at our feet, and I say my final goodbye to this man. "Have a Goodnight Mr Alexander, " the driver comes out and opens the door for me to enter. I release a breath of relief I don't even know that I am holding, once I get in the car next to Gabby.

"Thanks for an unforgettable evening, Miss Winter. Really. The girls at the shop are going to have a field day when I tell them," she says.

I smile and tell her, it was my pleasure. I instruct the driver to drop Gabby home first and then me.

A Smile To Die For

Winter

Once Gabby is dropped off, I stretch my legs and relieve myself of my shoes, letting all my little piggies breathe.

"Mr Johnson?" I call out to the driver. "Is there someplace we can go to get something to eat? I'm starving."

He smiles and replies, "I know a little place not far from here." He has a gentle smile that can warm the heart of any woman and eyes green and mesmerising. If I had a grandfather, I imagine he would look like him. We pull up at a small quiet 24-hour diner. There are about five people inside, eating.

"Would you like to drive-through or are you eating in. Miss Winter?" he asks. His voice is very deep and raspy.

I smile at how rough, but gentle his tone is and reply, "If you wouldn't mind, I would like to eat in please."

He parks and comes around to open the door, but I have already beaten him to it.

"You're off the clock, relax. I can get my own door, and my name is Winter, not Miss Valentine. That's for those white folks' benefit, like I said you're off the clock, so let's eat. You hungry?" he gives me that warm smile again. We walk to the diner, and he opens the door for me to enter, and we chuckle at the conversation we just had.

"Ladies first," he tells me.

I don't know what it is, but I feel safe and relaxed in his presence. I find an empty booth, and we take a seat. There is an elderly woman, a little overweight, with an old tattered wig barely hanging on for life, cleaning tables and taking orders, with a younger man behind the counter chit chatting to a young woman. The elderly woman walks over to the table. I can see she is tired and overworked and clearly, she is too old to still be working in a place like this. She smiles at Mr Johnson as she approaches the booth, I can see that these two have history from the way they look at each other with pure love and wonder.

"Morning folks. What can I get you?" she asks politely.

"Hello, sweetheart. This is Miss Val... I mean Miss Winter, and she's visiting from the UK. Bring her one of your specials." He orders my meal, and normally things like that would bother me, but not tonight. She looks at me for approval.

"It's just Winter. Thank you." I tell her with a smile, to ease her nerves and the boldness of her husband. I've noticed the matching wedding bands on both of their fingers, and it warms my heart, to see that not all black men are the same as we are taught by the media and society.

"Why do you have your wife working these kinds of hours," I ask once she leaves the booth?

The smile that is placed across his face slowly disappears, and he lowers his head. His shoulders slump in a defeated disposition. I immediately feel terrible for asking such a question.

"I'm sorry, my mouth sometimes runs away with itself!"

He looks at me and reassures me not to worry about it. He explains that even though they have both passed retirement age, they both need their jobs.

This job is the only job with hours that pay and doesn't cause too much stress and hard work for his lovely wife.

He tells me about the drug addiction that claimed their only child, and how now they are left with four badass grandkids with no manners. They have to provide for them because they don't want them to be left out in the streets or get caught up in the system, thinking no one loves or cares for them. That brought a small tear to my eyes, as I remember the day my mother died of cancer and how my grandmother had to come and take care of us. I share my story with him of my mother and what's going on in my life. For the first time, I see and understood the pain grandma must have felt when mom died, and how she had to bear the burden of three children, she never really knew.

It's easy talking to Mr Johnson. He tells me how once he finishes work he comes and sits with his wife till the early hours in the morning, waiting for her to finish her shift so he can take her home so she doesn't feel alone. I ask who's taking care of the children, and he explains that they are old enough not to open the door or answer to anyone. We eat and laugh and talk all night. He tells me about his worries for his ungrateful granddaughter, who seems to be rebellious to everything, unwilling to help out and how she is heading down the same path as her mother. I tell him not to worry, everything will work out by the grace of God. I tell him we can wait till his wife finishes her shift before we leave, plus I don't like the look of the crowd that just came in.

He laughs and tells me that Ms Johnson can handle herself, that I should feel sorry for the crowd. I laugh, and we continue our conversation. It turns out to be an enjoyable ending to the night.

Mr and Mrs Johnson turn out to be better company than the rich and famous I was with earlier that evening. I have never had so much fun in the presence of strangers before. During our conversation, I figure out what I am going to let these so-called bachelors do for me. It is perfect. I just need to tell Storm beforehand because dear lord when he sees the bill, I racked up tonight. Once Mrs Johnson's shift's over, Mr Johnson drops me back to the Four Seasons. I say goodnight and tell him I will be in touch once I wake up and not to worry about his granddaughter. I tell him I will pray for her, but little does he know I have plans to put my footprint in her ass.

Alone In New York

Autumn

I'm disturbed by a bunch of noise coming from the adjoining room, where Winter is. My sister is something else. She has only been here for 5 minutes, and she found herself a replacement sister. I ignore the noise and focus on the darkness that's taking over me. I slept like a new-born baby. The bed's so comfortable I don't want to leave it for nothing. When I finally emerge, I find myself in total darkness. I feel a bit groggy. So, I go in search of water. I trip over the suitcases and catch my little toe on something I moan in agony and manoeuvre towards the door. I open the door, and the light blinds me. I wait for my eyesight to adjust and step into the seating area where Storm's on the laptop Skyping with Sunshine. I shake my head at him and go to the refrigerator and grab a bottle of water. I sit next to my brother and rest my head on his shoulders and down the entire bottle of water in one big gulp.

"Hey, Sleeping Beauty," he says as he kisses my forehead, I smile and continue to down my water. Who knew I was so thirsty?

"Where's Wint?" I ask with sadness in my voice at the mention of her name. The door rattles and in comes Winter, looking magnificent.

Her hair's different. She's wearing a beautiful gown. But mostly I notice her hair. Wow, she's changed her look. It's beautiful, but she's taking this, I have no sister thing a bit far. We've fought thousands of times, and she's never done anything this drastic.

"You changed your hair, are you fucking kidding me?" I yell at her. She gives me the evil eye and kisses her teeth.

"Please. Stop begging for a free argument," she replies and heads straight to her bedroom and slams the door.

The nerve of this bitch, we always did our hair the same. How are we gonna be us if she continues with this one-woman show like she is an only child? This chick is on one. I say goodnight to Storm and stump off to the room and bang again on the suitcase in the darkness, I switch the lights on as I groan in agony.

I take a look around and for the first time, notice how big the room is and how big the bed is, noticing someone's missing from the picture.

Normally I would share with Winter, and her flamboyant self would fill the room, leaving no space for anything else. I unpack the cases and finally check my phone. There's a message from Darius, I quickly reply, letting him know that I'm fine and to leave me alone until he's sorted things out with Peppa. I throw my phone on the bed and strip off my clothes and go for a shower. I need a soak, but I don't have any of my usual bath soaking salts and candles. So, a shower will have to do the trick. I step in and turn the water on letting the water cascade all over my body. Placing my hands on the wall for balance, I let the water massage my shoulders.

My world's turning upside down, and I can't help but feel a little ashamed and to blame. I have a right to know my father, don't I? I just wanted to know who I am, where I come from. They may have given up that part of them, but I feel like I am missing a piece of me, with mom not here to answer any of my questions, that only leaves him. How can one man be so cold to his own flesh and blood, I just can't understand it. He didn't even try to feel anything for us. I can feel the hatred he has for us, for our mom. Why did he hate us so much, what did we do to him? What did I do to him to deserve such a rejection? I would never forsake my own flesh and blood like that.

As the thought creeps into my head, I feel the betrayal of my actions towards my brother and sister and understand Winter's pain.

I have to make it up to them to show them how much I appreciate them. Climbing out the shower, I notice Winter's room lights are still on underneath the joining doors of the room. I wonder what she's doing. I want so badly to go in and find out, to crawl in bed next to her like we always do, when we don't have company. I seriously miss my sister; I've got to get my left lung back. The lights go out under the door, and I leave the bathroom with sadness in my heart. Not having my sister beside me feels like my heart is breaking; it hurts more than it did when mom died. I get dressed and go in search of something to eat. I check the fridge realising that it is empty plus it's only a hotel mini fridge what do I expect, a miracle? Do these two ever sleep I think as I go into the living space?

"When are you two gonna hurry up and tie the knot?" I shout to Storm and Sunshine.

He's still Skyping with her like he's a love-struck teenager. Ever since he met Sunshine, it's been that way with him, no one can compare to his Sunshine. He looks over his shoulder and grins. I swear, it's like he sabotages all his other relationships just so she can come and comfort him.

"When she stops playing mind games," he says.

I smile at the thought of them together.

"Sunshine stop playing with the boy and put him out of his misery," I shout in the direction of the laptop. I sit beside my brother to hear what Sunshine has to say, she was always my favourite of all his little flings and so-called fucked up relationships.

"In due time," she tells me. I laugh because that's always her answer when it comes to Storm. We tease him all the time with it.

"Well you know we're going to Jamaica, and those girls don't play, when it comes to foreign meat, especially one as fine as my brother. I'm just saying you better stop playing all these games before he gets stolen away."

"You tell her sis?" he chuckles, and she laughs slightly.

"Well I'm not worried, just bring him back in one piece and without any fancy diseases or acronyms." I laugh at her analogies. She has just as smart a mouth.

"Well, I'm off to bed," I tell them. I don't think I can eat anyway. I just remembered that I haven't eaten in two days.

I go back to my room and lay down and try to come up with a way to get back into Wint's good graces. I twist and turn for a good while thinking of all the shit that we've been through since mom's death and how we always come out on top, no matter what. All the fights we've had, and all the beat downs we've had to give idiots for disrespecting us or even looking at us sideways. Most of the time Wint starts shit, but she also finishes them. I don't think I can survive without my sister in my corner. Thank God I still have Storm. I don't know if I could continue living if both my brother and sister were fucking with me. I grab my phone and leave a bunch of instructions for my dancer and for the store managers. Thank God for technology, we hook up all the store surveillance so that we can get live feed on our laptops and phones at any time. So, I know exactly what's going on when we are not in. That reminds me I need to finish this proposal for Wint so she can get her clothes up and running in the major department stores here. What better time to do it since I can't sleep anyway? By the time I do all my research and finish up the proposal for at least three different department stores, the sun is beaming through the curtains. I grab the phone and dial for room service and order a platter of different breakfasts, I figure everyone's gonna be hungry. I send the proposal to Wint and to the department stores. I take the laptop to the seating area where I notice Storm has fallen asleep and Sunshine is still online in bed, sleeping, I shake my head at the stupidity of them both. I sit at the table and do some internet window shopping while I wait for breakfast to be delivered. The food is delivered just after 8 a.m. I thank the server. I lay everything out on the table, but for some reason, my appetite shifts, I am no longer hungry. I drink some of the hot chocolate that I ordered, because I can hear Nana Bird and mom, in the back of my head saying, 'drink a cup of tea, and buss the gas.' I chuckle at the memory of the sayings Jamaicans come up with. Which reminds me I need to call Nana Bird?

I leave the table and go into the bedroom to grab my phone and place a call to my grandmother. Jamaica is only an hour behind America, and I know she's up, that woman rises with the sun every day. After speaking to my grandmother ensuring she's ok and has everything she needs, I hang up, but it takes a while, boy she can talk for the queen. I decide I need to leave the room and explore the rest of the hotel and the city before I implode in this place.

I put my gym sweats on, grab my gym bag and head down to the hotel gym facilities, but the website doesn't do much justice for the actual thing. It has everything; including a dance studio, I guess that's where they do their classes. I go into the studio and plug the headphones from my iPod in my ear and close my eyes and just let loose and let my emotions flow through me. I feel a little better anytime I dance. I can always feel all the stress and angry release from me through dancing. I just kept my eyes shut and block out the entire world and dance until the soles of my feet hurt. I am sweating profusely, dripping from head to toe. When I open my eyes, I have an audience that I don't realise is forming. I smile, grab my trainers up and bow my head down and exit the room. They applaud, and I thank them with a smile and keep it moving towards the treadmill for my hour power run. I jump on and run for dear life.

Still listening to my music in my own mental space, I don't even notice the handsome man that jumped on the treadmill next to me. He's trying to say something to me, so I take one of my earpieces out to hear what he has to say.

"What did you say?" I ask.

"You were magnificent in there, it was beautiful to see such passion," he said, and I sigh because I am not in the mood for small talk.

"Thank you," I say and smile. I start to place my earpiece back into my ear and try to continue with my run.

"Where are you from?" is the last thing I hear before I firmly place the earpiece in my ear.

I sigh, "Not around here. Sorry no time for talking, I'm training," I tell him coldly.

I don't mean to be a bitch, but I just want to be left alone and just run from my troubles for a while. Once I finish, my thighs are on fire, and I can feel my muscles throbbing all over my body. I stretch before leaving the gym but not before the gentleman who's running beside me jumps off and follows me to the door. He gives me his number, and I leave with a smile. The hotel has a Jacuzzi, so I take full advantage of it. I get into my swimsuit and climb in for a soak. I place a towel over my eyes and let the water and music from my iPod take me away.

I start pruning, and I am starting to get sleepy, so I hop out half an hour later and get a shower trying to refresh myself and head back up to the room.

It is pretty quiet when I go back in. Storm is still sleeping on the sofa. I get dressed in my true religion jeans and tan chunky heels and white off the shoulder jeans top from the Winter-Spring collection. I fix my hair and apply my lip-gloss and shades. I wake Storm up and tell him to grab the bed and then grab a piece of the pancakes that they brought up earlier and leave for the day. Some retail therapy will definitely lift my spirits.

A Storms Coming
To New York

Storm

The women in my life need to learn to just get along. The hotel is remarkable; they have us in a two-bedroomed suite, which looks more like an apartment. We are on the top floor of the hotel, so the view is spectacular. Only one person is missing, Sunshine. Because of Autumn's betrayal, I'm out on the sofa. I can't trust them to be in the same room and not kill each other. So now I gotta play piggy in the middle with these two. I spent all night talking to Sunshine. When I wake up Wint is at the table shovelling food into her mouth, and my laptop is closed.

"Eerh. That's been there all morning that should be cold. That's just plain greedy."

She shrugs her shoulders and continues eating.

"Is your sister back?" I ask.

"You mean your sister, and no, not yet," she replies whilst still guzzling down the cold food.

I roll my eyes at her and grab my phone to call Autumn to check on her.

"Hey, stop eating that, imma order some fresh food."

"These damn people don't know nothin about no good food," Wint retorts.

I shake my head at my sister's foolish ways. I call Autumn, and she's on her way back, she's tearing a hole into our pockets.

Speaking of pockets. "What's this nonsense you went to last night? And why is there such a big ass bill for some organisation I've never heard of before?" I ask Wint.

She stops mid feed. With a stupid look on her face, "Don't worry about it, I got it," she replies.

"That doesn't answer my question Wint," I say, waiting on the answer that's surely going to send my blood pressure skyrocketing.

"Ok. I went out and enjoyed my hard-earned money while sponsoring some charitable cause. Don't give me any damn attitude. I don't question when you spend money so don't question me, I spent it, and that's that!"

I swear sometimes I wish she wasn't my sister, so I wouldn't have to take her shit.

"Just be careful, and use only cards, while we are here. Don't walk with money while you're out on your own. Ok, just be careful," I warn. "I'm going to take a shower, and when Auto comes back we can go get some real food, as you call it," I tell her.

"Don't think so; I plan on checking out this nightlife New York's famous for. Fret not little brother I have an escort,"

I squeeze the bridge of my nose, and I feel my frustration rise. "What you mean escort, who?" I quiz, needing more information. I can understand the fear and frustration a parent must feel because I swear, I have two small children on my hands.

"Our Driver Mr Johnson, if you need to go somewhere, just ask for him. I have reserved him just for us while we stay here. So, tell your sister," she says casually like it's the norm.

"Whatever I'm getting a headache, just let me know where you are, at all times please, I'm going to take a shower. You and your sister need to remember that this is a foreign land and we don't belong. So, if they kidnap your asses, I'm not paying the ransom."

I go to take my shower and freshen up. These girls are going to be the death of me. We are supposed to be spending family time together, and we have never been so far apart. Everyone seems to be doing their own thing and I'm stuck in between. I get dressed and splash on my cologne and tie up my lion mane. I emerge from the bedroom, and Wint has retreated back into her room. I call Autumn once again and instruct her to hurry up. I open up the laptop and read the daily report on Sunshine that I asked for from her security detail. I check the stock market like I do every day to ensure that we are still in the green on all our investments while looking for new ones. Just because I can afford a day off doesn't mean the bills don't need paying. I schedule a conference call between us and the financial advisor. I send Sunshine a message letting her know that I will catch up with her later. Autumn comes in with what seems like the whole of New York. I can guarantee that most of those bags are filled with shoes. Women.

"There you are. I'm starving, let's go."

She drops all her belongings on the sofa next to me and smiles, "Gimme a minute. I need the toilet" she replies.

"Fine just hurry up."

I get up and take all her stuff to the bedroom and just throw it in and close the door behind me. Out of sight, out of mind, I mutter. I grab a bottle of water from the mini-fridge and wait for my snail of a sister. Considering she doesn't like to wait; she loves having others wait for her. She comes back out and grabs a bottle of water too. We are ready to leave, so I knock on Wint's door to let her know that we are leaving. She says bye without opening the door, and then we go, leaving Wint behind. I miss the trio.

Auto links arms with me, and we ride the elevator down. She starts telling me about her day and how shopping here is amazing. It's good to see her smile once again. Since Wint stopped speaking to her, her darker greenish-blue eyes have dimmed a little. We exit the building. The New York air has a crisp breeze to it. The sun has fully gone down, and the lights are indeed bright. This is definitely the city that doesn't sleep. We walk for a while until we find a restaurant nearby to eat.

We sit down and eat and I really get to the real reason for visiting our father. She tells me how she was feeling, and I am shocked that she hid her turmoil so well. I had no idea she felt abandoned and alone. Even as the words come out of her mouth, I can't understand it, women are complex creatures. I ask her what she needs from me to make her not feel like this. But she simply just lets the tears from her eyes flow. And all I can do is hold her hand and squeeze. I want to comfort her and take away her pain. I hate seeing either of them in any sort of pain, that's why when it's their time of the month I generally make myself scarce. But what my sister needs, no one can give her, it's simply impossible, no amount of money can help her. She wants her mother, and she's no longer here. And with no father, I guess Wint and I aren't enough for her. I pity my sister. I hope she finds the peace and fulfilment she is seeking, soon. I need them both to get their shit together because if Sunshine will have me, I will be moving to Bristol once we return to England. We've never been apart like that, so this will indeed make her feel worse. Shit.

We finish our meal, chat and continue exploring the busy streets and nightlife of New York. I tell her about Sunshine and me and how she was being stubborn and that I am tired of these other women because when it's all said and done, they are not Sunshine. She approves of my decision to give Sunshine an ultimatum. I pull her close to me and wrap my arms around her and kiss her forehead. Maybe I need to show her more affection and love, letting her know that I love her too and she can count on me for anything. I tell her that anytime she ever feels like that or alone and abandoned, she should always come to me first. I will always be there for her till her last breath. Maybe she needs therapy. I'm going to have to look into that when we get back home. She nods her head yes and smiles. We stop to take pictures of our surroundings. The night is turning out pretty good, but I still feel like Wint is missing out. But there's no point in chasing after Wint, you have to let her come to you when she gets like this.

We catch a movie and eat Baskin Robbins for dessert. We buy some for Wint too. It is around 11p.m. by now, so we hit up a wine bar. I leave the ice cream behind the bar and sit and watch as Auto dances carefreely on the dance floor. She is a vision to see.

"Is she your lady?" an attractive young woman asks as she takes the seat next to me.

"No" I reply and smile my 100-watt smile at her.

"Ok, so does that mean I still have a chance, cause for a hot minute I thought she was, because you kept staring? Well, in fact all you men are staring in the same direction," she states, with a jealous tone.

"It happens all the time, when she dances. Sometimes I think she's doing some form of mating call when she dances," I tell her.

"I thought you didn't know her?" she quizzes. I turn and give her my full attention because I can hear the dangerous direction, she's about to head in.

"I didn't say I don't know her. I said she isn't my lady. She's my sister, so please be mindful of how you speak about her. I was taught never to disrespect a woman, but that can all change," I tell her and smile. "Now since you're here taking my attention away from my sister let me buy you a drink, what would you like?"

She looks at me like she is confused.

"You can try to disrespect, but believe you would get nowhere with me, I'm not easily offended. I'm used to dumbass men and you're all irrelevant. I'll have Martini Dry."

The waiter gets her the drink, and I order another, making it a double.

"I can see your trouble with a capital T," I tell her, and she smiles and knocks back the drink like a pro.

She gets up and says excuse me and walks away. I can't help watch her behind as she walks away. It is mesmerizing as hell; I watch as she sways her hips from side to side. The dress she wears hugs her body tightly. Something tells me to check my pockets because something's off with her. She looks over her shoulder and catches me staring at her behind and smiles and disappears into the crowd. I don't even get her name.

I down my double shot of Remy Martin to shake off the effect of that sweet ass that just left my side without a word. We leave the bar around 3 a.m all eyes have been on Autumn all night. I hail a cab and hold her close to me, so she won't fall. She drank a bit too much, but I think she needed to let loose and forget.

When we get back to the hotel, I place her in bed and knock on Wint's door to check on her. She's fast asleep. I grab a bottle of water from the fridge and jump on my laptop to call Sunshine but there's no answer. I try several times till I get frustrated. I get up to change my clothes then try again. But there's no answer again. I check in with her guard, and he assures me she's ok and in bed. So, I call it a night and watch a movie on Netflix until I fall asleep again on the sofa.

The next morning, I wake up with my bladder ready to burst. I quickly head to the bathroom for a piss. As I finish, I feel a sickly feeling come over me. I chalk it up to the liquor from last night. I brush my teeth since I am already there. Halfway through I hurl up yesterday's meal and liquor, I just can't stop. The girls come rushing in concerned.

"You ok, what's wrong?" they ask.

I reply, "nothing, just had too much to drink."

I get up from over the toilet bowl and brush my teeth again, but the smell and taste of the toothpaste's making me feel nauseous. I quickly rinse my mouth and shower. Hoping that this feeling will go away. Great, that's all I need on this vacation from hell.

Winter 101

⁓

Winter

After watching Storm throw up everything from his night out with Autumn, he seems fine, so I decide it's time to let him and the Judas of a sister in on what I have going on. We only have a few days left before Miami, and I want to ensure that I help the Johnson family out before I leave.

"Storm call your sister please, I got something for us to do," I ask him.

"Call her yourself, she's your sister too," he replies with an attitude. "You two are getting on my nerves, if you don't cut it out, I'm gonna tell Nana Bird," he complains.

I sigh and leave to knock on her bedroom door to get her attention. She comes out and takes up a seat next to Storm.

"So, remember the Gala Dinner I went to the first night I was here, well I brought three men to do my bidding."

"What the hell kind of gala did you go to?" Storm asks.

Autumn chimes in with, "freaky," I roll my eyes at her.

"Wint you buying dick now? Thought you were too fabulous for that," they both have a good laugh at my expense.

"No. It was a bachelor auction for charity, and I bought three of New York's finest young rich bachelors to take me wherever I want to go and do as I want, for 48 hours. They are available for me until I leave. I want to use them to help Mr Johnson and his family. They are struggling to take care of their grandchildren after their daughter died of a drug overdose. They are old and need help. It's the cutest, saddest story you ever heard, and it reminds me of us and how we needed help when mom died. So, we are going to help them,"

I get cut off by Autumn, "I thought we were on a family holiday not a save the world mission. " Just like her to turn down anything I want to do.

"Well it's no longer a family holiday since you stabbed us in the back with 30 pieces of silver, so shut up, you don't have to help if you don't want to. I'm just letting you all know where I'm at and why I won't be around for this so called family vacation. Before you ask Storm, I won't spend too much, and I'll follow your stupid rules." Storm just nods and gives his approval.

"So, what do you need me to do, how can I help?" Autumn asks.

"It's like you're going deaf as much as being a traitor," I say, walking off and she gets up and follows me.

I close the door behind me, and she comes in. "Bitch get over your self-righteous self, what I did had nothing to do with you, it was about me, not you. We may come as a 3 in 1 package, but I came out of the womb first, independently. I don't rely on you; you rely on me, so get over yourself." The nerve of this bitch.

"Autumn you're right you are the eldest, you were first, so continue doing you and I'll do me. Oh, and run up on me like that again and I will **Fuck You Up,** sister or not. Don't forget who the fuck you talking to," I say calmly.

"Seriously Wint, you need to get over this bullshit, it was never meant to hurt you, but solve my problems," she tells me.

"And now you have one less problem, now leave," I walk by her passing swiftly to head toward the door and Storm interjects and comes and stands in front of the door looking like a raging bull.

"Sit down," he barks. I kiss my teeth and roll my eyes at him, and tries to get past him, but he blocks me and gives me an evil look. "I said sit," he says even louder. I take a seat on the closest chair I see, and Autumn sits on the sofa.

"The two of you need to squash this now. We are the Valentines. The dynamic trio. Not two, not one but three, so both of you get over yourselves and make amends; before I don't deal with any of you. And just for putting the thought in my head along with this migraine, I'm telling grandma, see how you explain it to her. You're both acting like children. When did we become divided? Yes, Autumn was wrong for going behind our backs instead of talking to us. Still, it's done, get over it and Autumn never do anything so stupid again. If you ever feel like that again you have us to speak to, we can conquer anything together, and if you don't feel like that, then we all have a problem" he snaps. But he isn't done.

"Wint learn to forgive baby, she messed up, how long do you plan to punish her for, she's already hurting, and needs you at this moment" he pleads.

"Fuck that. She betrayed me, not only me she betrayed our mother, the woman who gave birth to her when the asshole she craves for, wishes she was never even born. My mother struggled and put her life on the line to bring us into this world and raise us right. If she prefers to be with another family than us, she can go ahead, '*oh wait he don't want you*' if we are not enough for her then fine, I'm not stopping her she can have her family, but she can't have both, it's them or us. And she made her choice; so, she can drop dead for all I care, now get out the way before I move your big ass."

I storm out of the room with tears in my eyes. I can see the tears and hurt in my sister's eyes and the revelation of what her actions mean to me. I can see Storm's frustration and anger. But at this moment I don't care. I am not ready to forgive her, she hurt me, and she's got to feel the pain she caused and the consequence of her actions. I get to the front desk, and prospect number one who's called Matthew is waiting patiently on me. He has a slight grin once he sees me. I'm guessing he is pleased with himself.

"Let's go. I got something for us to do, and don't fuck it up," I tell him and wave my hands at him. He opens the door for me to exit it. "Get us a taxi!"

He calls for one, and a taxi comes almost instantly. We jump in, and I give the driver the address of where we need to go. Matthew looks at me puzzled, and I almost forget that I haven't explained what I need from him today and tomorrow.

"Look, today all I need you to do is redecorate and do it with a smile; I'll get you lunch and tools, and you answer to Mr and Mrs Johnson, do as they say," I tell him and proceed to look out the window.

"I'm confused. I thought we were going to lunch; I am looking forward to spoiling you," he says with pride and confidence.

"I can afford to spoil myself, and you're here to do as I say because if you had any notion of fucking me today or any other day, get it out of your damn mind. It won't happen, there's nothing you can say or do to get me to even be interested in you. You want to spend your money on someone, then if you see someone struggling today give them the money," I inform him.

"Are you gay? Because that works for me too," I shake my head in disgust without answering him, and we ride in silence.

The taxi pulls up outside Mr Johnson's home, I pay the driver and thank him generously. I step out, and notice that the police are chasing a couple of youths down the street and a young lady is chasing behind them screaming at the top of her lungs.

"Run baby run, leave him alone."

I think what a crazy new hell hole this is. I recognise the young girl from photos that Ms Johnson showed me. It's his granddaughter. I quickly get back in the taxi and tell him to follow them; he looks at me like I am crazy.

"NOW, DRIVE!" The driver pulls off, and I can see that my guest is a little nervous.

"Don't worry, you won't get shot today," I smirk.

"Get in front of them please, I need to catch her," I say, pointing at the child chasing the cops who are chasing the young men. He does as I instruct, and I tell him to stop at the end of the block, I get out and jump in front of the young girl, and she tries to go round me.

"Move Bitch!" she yells. The girl has no clue. I grab her and slam her against the taxi door.

"Get in before I wring your scrawny little neck, out here acting like a damn fool," I sneer through my teeth.

"Bitch get the fuck off me before I-" she yelps.

"Before what?" I ask with a stern face, and my fist raised. She doubles her fist and brings it up to swing, but I'm quicker and lighter on my feet. I dodge the blow and drop her on her ass, with one push. "Now get your ass up and get in and stop embarrassing yourself and your family, I won't ask again," I tell her. She looks at me puzzled and confused.

"Or else what?" she says, looking around and feeling all eyes on her. I open the door wider, and she gets up and runs off in the direction we came. I shake my head and tell Matthew to get out of the taxi.

"Pay him," I order. He does so and then runs to catch up with me.

What sort of nonsense did I just witness? The young women of this day and age have no manners or self-respect for themselves, following all these damn video hoes they see on TV. Fucking stupid, no woman wants her own shit anymore instead, they want some foolish man to pay for them. I look at Matthew and smile. I can see that he's nervous and scared as hell because of the neighbourhood we are in. When we get back to Mr Johnson's front porch, everyone's outside looking at the young women who's called Kerry. She's still acting bad. That's until she sees me stepping towards her. Mr Johnson comes out and gives me a hug and shakes Matthews's hand.

"Let's go inside," he says.

I look around, Kerry is still standing there with her friends on the pavement mumbling and rubbing her hands together. I am not in the mood to play games with this little girl. She's too out of control, besides, I know how these young girls play, she and her friends may be planning to get back at me for the hit I gave her, so I step to her first.

"Get inside," I say.

"You're not my mother!" she yells.

"No, because if I was, your stupid ass wouldn't be out here acting like you have no damn pride or self-respect. Now get in before I knock you on your ass again."

She kisses her teeth and looks at her grandfather for some defence but receives none. I've already told Mr Johnson that I'm gonna knock some sense into his grandchildren before I leave, since they are so sacred of them and worried about child services. My ass is leaving real soon, so I don't give a damn. See me, I care zero. I hate seeing these young dumbass kids with no respect for their elders or parents, throwing tantrums in the middle of the street and running their mouth off. It's just plain disrespectful. They don't know how blessed they are to have a parent in their little lives looking out for them. I would give anything to have my mom here again. They just don't appreciate shit these days.

Mr Johnson is fed up with the young woman's behaviour and manners toward him and her younger siblings. She is supposed to be in school, but instead, she's hanging out with thugs and pimps. Young people nowadays have no damn sense. She creeps the steps slowly and goes inside, saying bye to her little friend.

Mr Johnson shows us around, and Mrs Johnson's in the kitchen preparing something that smells divine. Kerry goes to her room and slams the door; I shake my head. I apologise to Matthew for my behaviour and introduce him to Mr Johnson properly. I tell him what I want him to do. I ask Mr Johnson if he's sure he wants to stay and live around here. He assures me that this is the cheapest place to live, plus it's his home. I smile and tell him not to worry, by the time I'm done with this place, it will look like a castle.

"Matthew here is going to help tear everything up," Matthew looks at me with a sceptical look.

"I've rented a suite for you and your family while we work on the interior of the home," I tell him.

"I can't allow you to do that, it's too much," he argues.

"No, it's not. I want to help, and I got the help I need so let's get started." I leave them all to clear out what's left of the old retired furnishings and mixed up stuff that's in their home. How they've managed to survive this far is a miracle. Now this overgrown headache, called Kerry. Mrs Johnson shows me her room, and I go to work on it. I go to Kerry's bedroom with a screwdriver and drill and start removing the door hinges. She gets up and starts screaming all sorts of profanities at me.

"People with no manners and respect deserve no privacy." I tell her. I can see a bag of weed on her bed and a roll up in her hand.

''I see you have some more growing up to do so I have a few days to knock some sense into you. Since you don't want to go to school, you are going to get a job and help pay some bills in this house."

I shout for Matthew, and he comes, and I hand him the door. He is still a bit shaken up, but he keeps a smile on his face.

"Change your clothes, we're going to the salon. You look like you just got your ass handed to you," I tell her grinning to myself.

"I ain't going nowhere with you" she yells defensively.

Mr Johnson comes out of nowhere. "You are going anywhere she tells you to young lady," he tells her.

I smirk at her and she gets up and grabs a jeans jacket that's way too small for her and shows off her midriff. Her weave is barely hanging on to her head, and her hair could do with serious conditioning.

"You know for someone who looks like such a mess you shouldn't have so much attitude, especially when she's about to get a free hair-do."

"My man provides for me, I don't need you to do my hair because my man promises to get it done this weekend," she says with way too much attitude for me.

"Dumbass." I can't believe the stupidity that's coming out her mouth. We get outside, and her little friends are still hanging out the front. I step past all of them, and they all nod at her. One asks if she's ok and she tells them yeah.

I take her to Shaundra's hair salon in downtown New York. It's loud and busy when we get there.

"Look what the cat dragged in, if it isn't Cinderella herself," Shaundra greets me with a huge hug.

"Now ladies take note, this is perfection. My new friend Winter." He says with a bright smile, forgetting about the client at his station. All the ladies in the shop smile and greet me with a "hey."

"Afternoon ladies" I greet them and turn my attention back to Shaundra.

"I need your help again on that," I point at Kerry and move out of the way. Shaundra walks over to Kerry and looks her up and down and then looks back at me with a dazed look.

"Girl I got you. I'll be with y'all in a couple minutes, just let me get my customer finished then I'm all yours,"

"Thanks, hun, I'm gonna get our nails and feet done, so take your time," I tell him and take up a seat in front of one of the nail stations.

"Little girl, park your ass down in front of that lady, let her do your hands and feet," I tell Kerry.

Thank God the nail techs aren't as busy as the hairdresser. Shaundra tells one of the stylists to pull out the mess that is in Kerry's head while she gets her nails done. I give the nail tech specific instructions to give her a full treatment and just a simple paint job of cotton candy and white tips—none of that fancy colourful crap. Less is more when it comes to nails. Neat and sweet. Kerry rolls her eyes and kisses her teeth and keeps screwing up her face at everything I order.

"Little girl you need to be a little less ghetto and a lot more gracious." I'm going to show her how a lady is supposed to bring herself.

The ladies in the shop are talking about all sorts of topics from relationships to who's cheating on who to politics. It is a straight-up scene from the movie Barbershop. Kerry gets involved with the conversations, but I sit back and observe her and take in her views. She is even more naive than I thought. Did this little girl just say it's ok if he wants to cheat, just as long as she's got what she wants?

"And what exactly are you supposed to get. HIV, AIDS, PREGNANT?" I ask, and she shuts the hell up.

A hairdresser they call Smiles is just as dumb as her name. Agreeing with Kerry. "Not everyone has the means to survive out here, so you do what you got to do and put up with what you got to put up with."

I've heard enough. "No, she doesn't, and neither does any other woman. The problem with women is that we ask too much from a man instead of going out there and getting it for ourselves. I've earned everything I have from hard work. The problem is we don't help each other, we tear each other down. Your self -esteem is too low to comprehend owning anything for yourself. I bet your pay cheque goes towards your man's lifestyle instead of something constructive."

The entire shop stops and stares at me like I am crazy for saying what I am saying.

Another hairdresser Merry, walks towards me with her hot iron in her hand like she's about to do something but Shaundra put his hands out to stop her, "Huh, huh, you don't want none," Shaundra says, and I laugh.

"What you laughing at? You about to get your ass beat in here," she says.

"O, please, you were going to try. Besides you're only mad because I'm right. What you need to do is think about what I just said and see how you can fix it," I tell her.

"Well damn Gurl you got balls, running you pretty little British mouth like that." another hairstylist says.

"I just know right from wrong, and dumb from dumber. What can I say?" I answer.

Shaundra changes the subject as he calls Kerry to come sit in his chair. "Now baby, what would you like me to do to this head of mess?" he asks, screwing up his nose in horror.

"I want that new style Rihanna is rocking," she says with confidence.

"I say cut it all off. It looks all damaged anyway," I tell him.

"You are right about the damage and rot. It's hurting my feelings," he states, and I chuckle.

Kerry's upset and unhappy about my suggestion. Still, it's for her own good. She can't afford weave, yet she wanted the biggest hairstyle.

"Lady, learn to live within your means. Can you afford a $600 bundle of weave?" I ask her.

"No," she replies.

"Then how the hell are you going to get a Rihanna hairstyle on an empty pocket?" I ask tilting my head to emphasise my point.

Shaundra cuts it short and gives her a cute pixie cut that's easy to maintain.

"Plus, hook her up with the lashes you got me."

That seems to put a smile on her face. I pay the nail tech for her service.

"Damn Gurl, you got a black Amex, whose dick did you suck for that?" Merry asks loud enough for everyone to take notice and start their assumptions.

"I sucked on hard work and late nights for this," I tell them.

My phone rings, and its Storm calling. I answer, and he enquires about my whereabouts. I tell him, and he tells me he's on his way since he needs his hair braided. I sit and tell the ladies about my clothing line and breaking into the financial world. Diamond, the third stylist, asks me to explain it more because she has three kids and she heard that's how the white people get down. That's the thing I tell them; we should also do as they do. Get in where they get in. I explain to her it's not about being safe; it's about taking risks. Whatever the richest guy is buying, that's what she should invest in and try to invest half her next pay cheque in some form of medical or government shit. There is always going to be war, so invest that way. The white man is just as criminal as the black man, but he doesn't kill his own, he goes to another country and kills there instead and calls it justified and makes his money. Everyone's engaged until Storm walks in and steals their attention.

"Ladies. Good evening," he greets them as he walks over and gives me a hug and kiss.

"Gurl that's how you rolling?" Diamond asks.

"Ewe no! Ladies this is my brother Storm," I tell them. I guess my hair change makes me look different from my brother.

"Well hell, he can rain on me anytime," Simone another staff member says. She has been quiet the entire time I've been in the shop until now.

"Come sit here baby, I got you." Storm goes to sit in her chair since she has no clients, she asks him suggestively, ''what would you like?''

I shake my head and turn my back to them. All the ladies are staring and watching Storm in Simone's chair. I forget the effect he has on women sometimes. Once we are all finished up in the shop, I pay for their services and say bye to the ladies. I give Shaundra a hug before leaving and leave him with an extra tip. All the ladies say bye to Storm in unison. I chuckle as he flirts with the ladies in the shop, tipping his stylist a little too much. He even quietens young Kerry for the first time.

"Where to next?" he asks,

I reply, "shopping."

"So, introduce me to your friend," Storm says. She'd been so quiet that I had almost forgot about her.

"This is Kerry, she's Mr Johnson's eldest granddaughter. Kerry, this is Storm, my brother, so be nice," she smiles, and he places his arm around our shoulders, and we walk down the street to the train station.

"I like your hair, it's cute Ms Kerry, very sophisticated," he compliments.

She giggles like a schoolgirl. What happened to the loud foul mouth that I am accustomed to. We ride the train all the way to Manhattan. We treat Kerry to a new wardrobe, and I tell her to pick up clothing for her brother and sisters too. Storm leaves us to walk to the shopping area to get some things for himself.

I teach her how she should dress and put herself together, how to use her body for the right things. I teach her how to stand and how to walk with enough attitude to make a man want to know who she is but know within himself that she is out of his league. I give her a Winter 101 of being a bad to the bone, ghetto fabulous, untouchable chick who's to be feared by men and women. She watches as I deal with the men when they come my way.

A woman should be picky about everything. Within the first 2 seconds, you should know if a man is worth your time or not. Just because you're poor doesn't mean you should settle for less. Even if a man can afford to buy you the world, he should think twice before approaching you and have it in mind that you're still out of his league even if he can afford you. She gets shoes and handbags to match her outfits and the last Jordon's for her brother and sisters and Timberlands for them all. I make her see the importance of setting an example for her siblings, especially her sisters, who look to her for guidance.

She takes in everything I say and agrees to help her grandparents out more. I tell her if she doesn't, I will make her grandparents put her in the army so she can be blown to smithereens.

I keep in contact with Mr Johnson all day, and he tells me that the house is finally empty and it's time to release Matthew. When I speak to Matthew, he agrees to come back the next day as he's become fond of the couple and tells me how he's going to bring his friend to help out too. I thank him and apologise for my absence. He even offers Mrs Johnson a job since he's moving out of his family home and is in need of a chef. I'm guessing her home-cooked meal hit the spot. I thank him for the day and tell him Mr Johnson will drop him home. Today started out terrible but it is ending on a high.

While shopping, I approach one of the managers of Macy's and arrange an appointment for the next day as I haven't received a reply from any of the stores Autumn reached out to. Thank God it is a man in power. I take it upon myself to sort out my own interview.

"Make sure you get an outfit for tomorrow, we have an interview here tomorrow, so you better be on your best behaviour and dress the part," I tell Kerry.

Once we've finished our shopping, I take her to the fragrance department. I get her some new perfume and Fenty make up along with a new black leather watch and briefcase for work purposes and a gold watch for special occasions. She is really appreciative of everything. She keeps thanking me. Storm returns with a few bags of his own.

"You ready?" he asks us, and I look at Kerry for an answer. I look at her to see if she's learnt anything from our talk.

She straightens her back and smiles at him and says, "sure but I want to get one more thing."

I smile and feel proud of her, always keeping a man on his toes, they are always on your time, not the other way round even if they look like Storm.

"Lord it's a mini Winter. Life as we know it is over" he teases.

"What can I say, I'm a good teacher. Let's go, I'm starving" I tell him.

"How's all that going to fit in a taxi? Looks like you guys brought everything in the store," Storm remarks.

"We'll just get two taxis," I tell him.

We have the shop assistant help with all our shopping bags to the taxis. On our way down, I call Mr Johnson. I tell him that I will be meeting them at the hotel and to order whatever they need from room service.

But Mrs Johnson won't hear of it. She says that she'll make a home-cooked meal. I tell her to bring it to the hotel because I am starving. They get there before us due to New York Traffic. I thought London traffic was bad, but this is a whole different experience. I understand the use of trains in this city. Mr Johnson comes down to help with the bags.

"What have you done, this is too much, Ms Winter?" he says.

I wave him off and tell him not to worry. Let's just get these upstairs. I call for the bellhop and tell him to bring everything to their room and head upstairs. Kerry kept up with me. Her hairstyle and new clothes make her shine like the pretty young lady that she is. I taught her how to wear the clothes, not the other way around; not to make the clothes wear her. There is nothing worse than a woman who has to wear clothes to get attention. Confidence is everything. Once the elevator doors close, I tell her.

"Next thing you need to do is drop everyone in your social circle who is holding you back. That includes that good for nothing boyfriend who is controlling you with promises and an empty pocket." She laughs, I guess she finds it funny. But she agrees.

"No man is supposed to dictate your life. Anything he can get; you can get for yourself with diamonds on it. Never let a man own you." I school her, she tries to tell me otherwise about how he's in love with her, and he plans to take her out the ghetto.

I shake my head and ask, "how long is that going to take, or do you plan to start sucking dick to help with that dream or sell drugs too?" She goes silent as she thinks about the questions I am asking.

"Leave him alone, go to work and help your grandparents out with things around here. Help them get your younger siblings out of the fucked-up situation they are in. Your sisters are only twelve and five, and they need you to have your head on your shoulders and be strong. Today is a good day." I tell her.

Lord Help This Family

~

Autumn

The door knocks and wakes me out of my sleep. I didn't order anything, and Wint and Storm have a key. I can't think of anyone who would be knocking at the door. When I open the door, an old couple are standing there with three young children. What the fuck, is this?

The old man speaks first, "Hello, you must be Autumn. I'm Mr Johnson, and this is Mrs Johnson my wife, and these are our grandchildren. Kids say hello to Ms Valentine."

"Hello," they all say politely. I tilt my head slightly in annoyance still trying to figure out what the hell this has got to do with them all standing at my room door interrupting my sleep.

"Winter told us to come on over, she's on her way, may we come in?" he asks.

I am still a little sleepy and confused. I tell them, 'yes,' and the children run over to the sofa and take up residence. I escort the elderly woman to the kitchen since she is holding a pot of some kind.

"You can lay that there. Excuse me." I go to call Winter because she didn't tell me about this shit. No answer. Shit. What the hell am I supposed to do with these people?

"Young lady." Ms Johnson calls out, and I turn to give her my attention.

"Yes," I answer.

"Come help me set the table real quick," she says.

I take a deep breath and give her a hand. I turn the TV on for the children, and they ask if they can watch a movie, I tell them sure, just as long as they ask their grandparents permission.

"Your sister told us what happened to you and her, I'm not here to judge. You must have your reasons for your actions. So, what are they?"

Who the hell is this woman to be so damn inquisitive. I look at her like she is an alien or something, and that's exactly what she is to me, an alien.

"You can stand there and stare in my face, but the only thing you're going to notice is all these wrinkles. I'm just very fond of your sister. She's doing so much for my family."

I can't help but think she's only doing it to divert her attention from her real pain. I figure if Winter trusts her to tell her our business it is alright for me to talk to her. I tell her my side, and she comes around the table and gives me a hug and tells me it's going to be ok.

"Not to worry, she'll come around. She's just feeling hurt. She feels just as you do. The thing about pain, it never lasts long," she says and wipes the tear from my eye.

She reminds me of Nana Bird. Oh! Nana Bird, I know she must know by now. Little informer Storm would have told her by now. So, I have that to look forward to when I get to Jamaica. Mr Johnson leaves and goes down the stairs. Apparently, Wint needs help with her bags. Storm and Mr Johnson return before Wint. The men shake hands, and Mr Johnson gives his wife a hug, which makes me smile. They are a lovely couple. Storm goes over and introduces himself to the kids.

"You ok," he asks. I wrap my arms around him and tell him yeah.

"Look, Mrs Johnson cooked for us." I point at the table.

"Where's Wint?" I ask with curiosity.

"She's coming, she went to the Johnson's room, she'll be here soon." He tells me. A few minutes later, Winter and a pretty young woman come through the door.

"Good they're here, we can eat," Mrs Johnson states.

"What have you done to your hair?" she asks the young woman, who's called Kerry apparently and is the oldest granddaughter.

"You like it, grandma?" the young lady asks, and Mrs Johnson smiles and looks her granddaughter up and down with approval.

I see Wint put her touch on the young woman. She looks beautiful. We eat, I haven't had a good meal like that, that I didn't cook since the last time I saw Nana. When everyones finished, the children excuse themselves, and we all sit and talk for ages. Winter and Kerry take the kids out for ice cream, leaving Storm and me to entertain her guests. Mrs Johnson tells us all about Winter's plans and how she took the young lady's door off the hinges, something mom did to us when we got out of line and thought we were too big for our boots. I laugh at the thought; I knew she would turn out like our mother. I call room service and tell them to return the dishes once they are cleaned.

"It's time we left you to enjoy your night, thanks for having us," Mr Johnson gets up and says.

"Yes. Thanks again for your company. I enjoyed myself. Please come by the house tomorrow and help out, I would appreciate it." Mrs Johnson requests.

I promise her I will and escort them out. Mr Johnson tells me that he will pick Wint and the kids up because it's passed their bedtime, and I give him a hug and tell him to have a safe night. I am happy Wint's helping them. They are lovely people, but I still feel like doing some research on them. I grab the laptop and start to look. There's a story about their daughter laying out in a crack house, her body was found after a shoot- out, but it seems she was already dead. Poor people. I'm wide awake and in the mood for a night out. I ask Storm, but he isn't up for it. He is still feeling the effects of last night—lightweight. Damn, guess it's another early night in. I check in on the store, reviewing the video feed and the income for the week. We are doing well, especially the new store. Only three days left until Miami; I am not feeling this anymore.

The next day I get up and go down to the gym for my new routine exercise and dance session. The gentleman from before is there again. My sadness before hadn't allowed me to see him for who he is; a gorgeous specimen of a man with sandy blonde hair, big brown eyes, broad shoulders and a 100-kilo watt smile. This morning I notice because I am feeling much better about my day and the plans I have to spend with Mrs Johnson. He offers to take me to dinner. I accept, then I immediately regret my decision. I can't let Wint find out.

After my session in the gym, I go back upstairs and get dressed in the least expensive outfit I have. I knock on the Johnson's door at 7 a.m. ready to go to work. Mrs Johnson is trying to get the children ready for school, but apparently, they all want to wear their new outfits or some shit. The youngest girl comes over to me and asks for my help. I bend down to help her with her shoes and fix her hair, it needs a treatment. She is clingy towards me, last night playing with my hair and staring at me all the time.

"Where is your sister Kerry?" I ask her, and she tells me she is sleeping. I go in and knock on the door, and she curses at me. Oh hell, she got the wrong triplet. I go into the bathroom to find something to fill with water. I return and empty the contents on her.

"Get your ass up," I tell her.

''Bitch, what!" she yells.

Who the hell is she thinking she's talking to? I hear Mrs Johnson scream from down the hall for her to have some manners, but I am in no mood for the attitude of raging hormones and a bad attitude. I jump on the bed and grab a pillow and smack the hell out of her, clearly my sister is playing with this child, but I ain't, spare the rod spoils the child.

"Oh, you don't know me, don't ever make those words come out your mouth, especially if you can't defend it."

I hate a fast-talking child with no respect or manners. I always have to put a child in their place when they are acting up with their parents back home, I hate that shit. Her little sister laughs at her, and so do I.

"Go wash your ass you have to take the kids to school," I tell her.

"I can't today I have to follow Ms Winter to an appointment," she whines.

"Then you better get a move on because Winter doesn't like to be late. What do you think she is going to say if I tell her you haven't been helping out this morning?"

She immediately gets up then and gets dressed and puts her shoes on ready to leave the hotel.

"What kind of nastiness you on, go brush your nasty teeth." I look at her in disgust and disbelief.

"Have you all brushed your teeth?" I ask the rest of them because I can't believe this shit. Poor people must be so worn out that they don't have time to pay these kids the proper attention. They should be retired and enjoying their golden years instead of taking care of children.

"Inspection," I tell them, form a line in front."

They all line up like soldiers and one by one I inspect their mouth and hair and overall set up. I fix and brush their hair correctly. The little boy really needs a haircut, so I tell him that my brother will take him once he finishes school. He is so cute, he's only nine Omari is already a perfect gentleman. The baby of the bunch is a 5- year old girl called Surprise. I feel for her because she must have been missing her mama more and doesn't understand what is going on in the world. She just keeps sucking her thumb. The 12 -year-old seems to be the most helpful, she just needs guidance, and she looks worn out herself. You can tell they all have different fathers. But they are all good-looking children.

"Can you take me to school, please?" the little princess asks, and I smile. I can't say no.

"Ok, I will."

I turn and ask if they've had breakfast yet, and Mrs Johnson says no. I ask why and she just says they don't want to spend anymore of our money and they don't have the time, so they will have to just deal with it till lunchtime.

"Mrs Johnson, please stop that, these kids need a healthy meal before they go to school. Please don't let Winter know that they didn't eat, she has a thing about feeding people."

I call room service and have them bring some breakfast up for the kids. It arrives in 5 minutes,

"Now Mr Johnson, can you please bring the car around for the children to go to school."

"Thank you," he smiles and nods apologetically.

"No need to apologise, just make sure you are feeding them correctly. They will be finished in 15 minutes. I will ride along with them, and then we can come back and get Mrs Johnson."

"Okay, Ms Autumn," he says as he gulps down a glass of orange juice. The children eat, and I tell them to all go brush their teeth again. I tell Omari that he should always make sure he walks with breath mint cause the ladies don't like a man with bad breath. He smiles, giggles, and tells me his thing is always on point. I can't help but smile, at the little dude. I ruffle his hair and hand him a pack of Wrigley's Extra, and he runs off to brush his teeth again.

"Everyone ready?" I ask.

"Yes, Ms Autumn," they say.

"Ok. Let's go." I hurry them out of the door and stand in the doorway waiting for the Kerry who is still in the room doing God knows what.

"Wait here children." I walk to the room and open it to find out what is taking so long.

She is sulking in the room mumbling to herself, "yeah, kill me after you ride with us and take these kids to school," and in a split second, I change my mind because I don't want miserable ruining my day.

"Stay behind but get your ass up and go down the gym, your ass is sagging," I tell her, and she gasps.

I leave the hotel with the kids and Mr Johnson for the morning, we do a sing-along for the little girl, and she sings the loudest; she isn't bad for 5 years old, she's going to be a star one day. Omari, I think has a little crush on me. It is sweet. The 12- year- old doesn't say much, seems like she did the more for her siblings than Kerry, which is a shame. After we drop the older children to school, we have to drop little Surprise to school. She's a joy to have around. When we finally reach her school, the teacher comes out to speak to Mr Johnson about Surprise. I can hear her mention Social Services to him, and his head and shoulders hit the ground.

"Excuse me there's no need for that, I'm sorry for the trouble, I will make sure she gets what she needs," she looks at me with a quizzical look.

"And who are you?" she asks with a determined look.

"I'm her Aunt; I will be taking care of her from now on, please don't get the social involved in our lives. I've only just got back in town so my Father will have more help."

"This is the last warning. Surprise needs more care and attention and-"

I cut her off, "and she will be getting it from now on since I will be here. If you have any more concerns, please contact me. Here are my contact details please don't hesitate to call me if there are ever any concerns," I tell her.

"Well, we are concerned that she's not speaking, she just sucks on her thumb. The only time she makes a sound is when its sing- a - long-time," she tells me.

"Please I've only just arrived, so I'm getting in the groove of things, please just a few more weeks and you'll see," I tell her.

"Ok, but this is the final warning. If there's any more trouble I will have to contact Social Services," she says firmly.

"Thank you! Let's go, dad."

Once we get back in the car, I grill him about the problems the children have, and I have a stern warning for him.

"You must make sure they eat at least three times a day. I understand things and times are hard, and it's unfortunate for the situation you're in and that you're tired. Stop giving Kerry money to go buy things if she is using the money for herself. Don't ever send them to school without a meal even if it's just peanut butter or bread and butter," I tell him. "Please call us if you ever get stuck and need help."

I understand why Winter needs to help them. At this point, if she finds any more people to help, we are going to be broke as hell.

We arrive back to the hotel, and a young man is staring at me like he wants to eat me whole. What's he staring at I wonder. He walks over to us and says hello to Mr Johnson then turns to address me.

"I see you changed your hair, it looks nice," he says, licking his lips.

"No. I haven't, my name is Autumn, not Winter," I tell him and turn to walk away, the fact that he would be licking his lips at me like that in front of Mr Johnson puts me off instantly.

"I'm going to see if everyone's ready," I go upstairs to find Storm still eating breakfast. I turn to search for Winter, but she's already downstairs in the Johnson's suite. As I turn to leave Storm rushes to the toilet again.

"Stop drinking the water, it's causing you to vomit too much and drink bottled water."

Every morning he's been vomiting.

"I'm going downstairs, hurry up," I tell him as I leave the room.

He mutters something through vomiting. I go down the stairs and knock on the Johnson's door, and Mrs Johnson answers it. I enter and find Winter dressed for a corporate or something and her nasty apprentice is trying to imitate her.

"Check if she took a shower before you bring her to meet potential clients," I tell Wint, and she cuts her eye at me and spins around to look Kerry up and down.

"What is she talking about? And don't lie," she asks Kerry who seems a little scared.

"I almost left the hotel without brushing my teeth this morning," she explains.

"Almost," Winter snaps.

"Tell her how you had your grandparents doing everything in here instead of getting your ass up and helping out," I say as I take a seat. I know my sister, and she hates lazy people who want things for free.

"Is that true?" Wint asks Kerry.

"She told me to stay behind," she winces.

"But did you get up and help your grandmother?" Wint asks coldly.

"No, she was fine on her own."

"That's not the point, and how would you know. I see you've taken nothing in, just watch this space. Hurry up and let's go," Wint yells at her. She gives me the evil eye and continues to put herself together.

"Ungrateful," I mutter.

"Mrs Johnson, are you ready? The men are downstairs waiting for us," I can tell that she is still tired, and I feel sorry for her. "When are you back at work?" I ask.

"Tonight." Oh no, she needs to rest.

"I have an idea, how about you stay here and rest for today? We got this," I tell her.

"No, I'll be fine. I'm used to being on my feet, plus it's my house you're renovating."

"I won't take no for an answer, and I'm not renovating anything. Winter is. I want to take care of you today. So, get some rest and a massage or something. There's a steam room and Jacuzzi, just relax today. Please, for me." I plead with her. She finally agrees, and I leave her and go downstairs and order her a full relaxation package from the front desk. I spot Storm and Mr Johnson exiting the elevator, engrossed in conversation.

"You ready lil brother?" I ask, and he wraps his arm around my shoulders and kisses me on the forehead.

"Let's go," they all follow behind us. Mr Johnson comes around and opens the door for us all. It takes half an hour to get to the other side of the city and then another 20 minutes just to get to the house.

Matthew speaks up, "you British girls are truly feisty aren't you; nothing like the African American girls." I think he thinks that's a compliment.

"I never understood that context," I say to him.

"What context?" he asks.

"African American, they are not Africans; they are Americans they were born here, so why are they Africans?" I ask, and I can see his little brain go to work.

"I'm not sure, that's just the way things are," he replies.

"Maybe it's just a way of reminding black people that they are still unworthy or slaves in your simple white mind," shit now I'm starting to sound like Winter. He sits there with his mouth dropped open like he's catching flies.

"I- I- I- I've never thought of it like that. On behalf of my evil slave owner ancestors, I apologise."

"Well damn you might just survive the Valentine hard knocks, after all," I tell him and just sit back and stare out the window at the scenery.

There are a lot of bridges in this country. When we pull up to the Johnson's place, I can't believe that I am in a real ghetto of America. England's slums have nothing on this place. I can't believe they live here and don't know if I can stay here for long. I grab onto Storm's arm for dear life. He squeezes my hands and winks at me, letting me know that I am safe with him. Boss up woman if you can't handle this how you gonna handle Jamaica. I tell myself.

We climb the stairs of Mr Johnson's stoop and enter the home. It's empty, and paint pots and sheets are scattered all over, it's stripped bare, like a construction site. I take a tour of the space, boy does it need work. This is where Winter shines and excels no doubt she already has a plan in place to make this look like a palace. She should have become an interior designer, but no, she wants to design clothes. She's always had the eye for design, no matter the context. A few minutes later, a team arrive with materials to start constructing; however, this canvas is going to turn out. They begin working, and everyone helps out.

I call to ensure that Ms Johnson is resting. I pick up the children like I promised and take them to the salon and out for burgers. I enjoy my day with the kids. It amazes me how much children know and how their innocence always pulls at your heartstrings. It also makes me realise that I want a family of my own one day. I hope I'm as lucky as my mother and just have triplets. Have them all at once.

By the time we arrive back at the hotel, they are all worn out. I help put them to bed. Surprise wakes when I am about to leave and reaches out to me and squeezes my hands. I sit back on the bed and brush the stray hair from her face and tell her that I will be back in the morning to take her to school.

"Are you gonna be my new mommy?" she asks, surprising me and then put's the finger back in her mouth. She completely takes me by surprise; I see why they named her Surprise. My heart completely broke instantly for her.

"No baby, you already have a mommy who is looking out for you from heaven. I'll settle for being your auntie; ok; now go to sleep, I'll be here for you in the morning," I tell her and wait for her to fall asleep again, with that damn thumb in her mouth. While I sit there, my mind can't help but remember my own mother and grandmother.

Finally

―――――――― ❧ ――――――――

Winter

Finally, the home is finished; even Autumn comes out to help, and that chick hates hard labour. The inside of the Johnson's home is truly a cut out from an IKEA magazine. Shit, I'm proud of the work everyone did. Even Kerry and her lazy ass start helping out.

After the interview with the Macy's department Director, he agrees to give me a spot in the department store, and I give young Kerry her first job. I hire two other assistants to help her out and give her some responsibility. I watch as she takes charge, she loves being in charge. I teach her how to see things for what they are and how to appreciate her grandparents.

Instead of going to Miami with Storm and Autumn, I stay behind and tell them I will meet up with them at a later date as I need more time to ensure that everything runs smoothly but that I will be in Jamaica for Nana Bird's party. Kerry's come a long way, I had to beat the sense into her, but I think she gets it now. I order one of the new electronic tills that sends me every bit of information to make sure that she nor anyone else is stealing.

I show her how to merchandise and manage things around the station and how to rotate the clothing and when to purchase more orders. I buy her the latest iMac and iPhone, so we can always be connected, and she can help her siblings out with their homework. I get her to take some night classes to get her GED. (General Educational Development certification)

It's been 6 weeks since I first landed here, and I finally start forgetting about all the mess I left back home with my sister. Trouble won't stop blowing up my phone with his, 'I miss you and come back home soon.' I must admit I do miss him a little, well a lot. My mind keeps going back to him every time I go on a date or see a black man; I can't help but compare them to him. But he will never know that. I refuse to settle for a dream. Little Ms Surprise keeps asking for her Auntie Autumn, seems Autumn really made an impression on the sweet little girl.

The next step for Ms Kerry is to get her driving; my new manager should not be seen on a train. Mr Johnson tells me her birthday is coming up, so I plan on taking her car shopping since she's made significant improvements in her behaviour and social circle.

Nana Bird curses my ass out for not speaking to Autumn, which I knew she would, small price to pay. After a few weeks all by myself, I am starting to miss my family. The Johnsons make me feel welcome and a part of their family, but it isn't the same without my own spare parts. I just need some time apart from Autumn and her Judas mentality. I miss my brother, but he understands.

I don't let the Johnson's know, but I set up the accounts for the shop to contribute to their livelihood and wellbeing. Yes, we get a cut, but the majority goes to them. I set up savings for all the children so that when they turn eighteen they will have some form of income and I buy bonds and shares for them.

They will be notified when they're of age. So, they have that to look forward to and only they or I can cash it in and yes, we will be benefiting from it as well. Mama never raised no fools. Don't think I would be giving and not receiving anything. I learnt a long time ago that nothing is for free. Mrs Johnson quit her job at the diner and now works for Matthew and a couple of his friends. She is her own boss, and so she has more time for herself and her grandchildren.

Mr Johnson helps her with the catering, so the only person he takes orders from is his devoted and loving wife. Every day they sing our praise and thank God that we've come into their life when we did. She keeps saying that she kept praying for a miracle from God and he sent it in the form of me.

This always makes me smile. Autumn got little Surprise her own piano and got her lessons. This little girl can sing, she is going to be the next Beyoncé when she is older. Her older sister April seems to enjoy reading and writing; she says she wants to be a writer one day. Omari, on the other hand, just wants to be a lady's man. Typical pretty boy complex which reminds me of Storm back in the day. He would always be the first to jump to his sister or grandmother's rescue if anything bad ever came out of anyone's mouth about them and I respect that.

Tonight, I have a date with Marcus, I almost forgot about his sexy ass because he's taken so long to call me. He thought I was going to call him first. I usually like to take charge. The poor thing, doesn't know that I forgot all about him in a flash. OMG let me back up. That flash from in the distance at the Bachelor Auction Gala is a camera flashing and taking pictures of me. That creep, Alexander, put my face all over magazines and gossip blogs. The mystery woman who stole the night away. Now I don't usually pay attention to all that gossip but Kerry brought it to my attention. The girls at the salon have had a field day with that information.

Shaundra uses it as a ploy to get the paparazzi at the salon. He calls and tells them that the mystery woman is at the shop, all for some publicity. I left England where I am never in the limelight and keep to a quiet life, and on the first night here I am already in the papers with my name going through the mud. It makes good publicity for the clothing line, so my little section in Macy's is doing pretty good. I have to find a new salon, I can't trust Shaundra anymore. You can't use Winter Valentine for free, no way no how.

I fix my make-up and slip on my jumpsuit, thanking mama for the arse she gave me, and for the curves these bitches are killing themselves for. I am feeling myself. I look damn good, good enough to eat. I pucker up and kiss myself in the mirror as I hear the knock on the door, letting me know that my date is here. I give myself a once over one more time and am still pleased with myself. Get a Vex fare check, never leave home without it. Nana's number one rule when leaving the house.

Mr Johnson usually insists on driving me around since I've decided to stay a few more weeks, so I give him the night off tonight. I appreciate it. I open the door to find a very handsome man standing in the doorway, looking fresh to death.

"I hope you got your dancing shoes on," he says playfully.

"I can dance in anything. So where are we going?" I ask.

"I'm going to show you my New York," he replies with a smile that could melt ice. I follow, and we both head down in the elevator. "You look amazing," he compliments.

"Thank you," I reply and give him my kilowatt smile. We exit the elevator and head to the car park. He is driving an open body jeep. I climb in and notice that he doesn't open the door for me like Trouble or Mr Johnson. He drives to a club uptown. It is packed and popping off, everyone is enjoying themselves.

"Let's get caught up," I tell him and head for the bar, he follows behind. He shakes the bartender's hand, and they exchange words and he places an order. He doesn't ask me what I want to drink. Just for that, I'm going to be difficult. He gets a bottle of champagne. I think he thinks I'm impressed.

I shake my head and order a stronger drink, "a double shot of Remy with coke please," I order, and he looks at me and smiles a wicked smile like I am amusing to him.

We find a spot in the club, and I make sure to enjoy myself. I dance all night. After the bottle of champagne finishes, he orders Remy Martin's for the rest of the night. I start feeling a little too off-balance, so I go to the bar and get myself a bottle of water. The thing about my liver is it expunges alcohol real quick. When that club's over we go to another spot, apparently, it's the after-party spot, but I am starting to feel tired as hell. He holds me close and grinds on me all night.

"Do you know that every man in here, has his eyes on you tonight?" he whispers.

"Only tonight? I never noticed because my eyes are on you," I turn to face him and grind my hips closer on him.

A song by TLC comes through the speakers, so I sing along and work my hips to the beat. He holds me so tight that not even the Holy Ghost could pass through. I can feel that all eyes are on us. So, I close my eyes and perform like I am on a stage for the spectators. The track skips and moves on to the next track, and I can feel the buzz of the alcohol that refuses to leave my system. I am dripping with sweat and the baby oil that I applied before leaving the hotel makes me glisten even more. The more my feet hurt, the more I dance. At the end of the night, he carries me on his back, and we stroll down the street, laughing and acting like children. We stop off at a little food joint for something to eat; we are still all over each other. He quizzes me about the article on the social blogs and magazines. I explain, and he laughs. He has an infectious laugh. We talk and laugh till the sun comes up. I ride his back again to the car. I fall asleep on the drive back to the hotel; the early morning breeze knocks me out. Once parked in the car park, he tells me he's had a good night and enjoys my company and would love to do it again sometime. I tell him to make it soon because I will be leaving sooner than later. He looks upset about that idea, but I couldn't care less. I need to get out of this place. I missed out on Miami. I am not going to miss Nana Bird's birthday.

"So, when can I see you again, since you're leaving me so soon?" he asks.

"When would you like to see me?" I ask flirtatiously.

"How about dinner later?" he smiles and flutters his eyelashes like a schoolgirl.

"Sure. I would like that."

As sweet and cute as Marcus is and despite everything he's done, I can't help but compare him to Trouble. I get out of the car and walk to the elevators. This idiot doesn't even budge from his seat to walk me to the elevator. I shake my head and instantly miss Trouble's warm touch. I ride the lift to my suite and crash out on the sofa. I can't even be bothered to find the bed. An alarm wakes me from my intoxicated slumber. Storm is calling to nag me and ask when I am coming again, like he's done every day since he left. He threatens to come get me if I don't come soon.

I answer, "I'm sleeping, call you back," I say into the receiver and hang up. He rings back, and I ignore it, so he calls on Skype. He is starting to get on my nerves even though I miss his big head. I click the answer button on the laptop.

"Yes, what do you want?"

"Who, you hanging up the phone on little girl?" I hear my grandmother says in her thick Jamaican accent and I straighten up immediately.

"I'm sorry grandma, I thought it was Storm bugging me again," I tell her.

"So, you hang up on me. Likkle girl, what did I tell you about respecting each other? It's like mi never teach unno nothing, from you born," she says.

"I'm sorry grandma, won't happen again," I tell her.

"Make sure. Now. When are you coming to look for me? I don't like you over there by yourself. Enuh. Suppose something happens to you, eeh chile." I have to control my eyes from rolling in the back of my head.

"I'll be there soon, before your birthday I promise," I tell her.

"Listen, you bredda told me about the good deed you are doing for that family but hear this, get you backside here now, by the end of the week otherwise I'm coming to foreign for your likkle backside, you hear me?" she threatens.

"Yes grandma," I say and sigh.

"What do you, mek you a breath soh heavy every minute," she asks.

"I'm not breathing heavy grandma, I'm fine. I'll be there next week, I promise."

"Make sure or else. Bye baby." I can hear her ask how to turn off Skype. I love my grandmother, sometimes I think I get my attitude from her.

I get up and go for a shower and hit the bed naked as the day I was born. I turn my phone on silent before falling asleep. When I wake it is night again, I must have spent the entire day sleeping. I grab my cell phone and check the time, it is nearly 10 p.m.

I have several messages from all over the globe. Trouble's messages make me smile making me miss him, so I send him a quick reply telling him I'm missing him too. That should shut him up for a minute. Storm calls and texts. He's booked me on a flight for next week Thursday. I sigh heavily again and remember my grandmother asking about my breathing when I sighed, that makes me chuckle a little. I ignore him. He can wait till tomorrow; let him worry for a while. Marcus calls several times too. I call him back to apologise for messing up our date. He tells me that he is going to bring dinner to me since I can't make it out. I hang up and rush to the bathroom to freshen up and quickly clean up the little mess that's lying around the suite. Half an hour later he knocks on my door, with a bag with Styrofoam boxed food, a bottle of Remy Martin and a bottle of coke.

"If I never knew any better, I would say that you are trying to get me drunk Mr," I say coyly.

"Maybe, or maybe this is just for me," he says. I let him in, and we sit in front of the TV to eat. I order a movie starring Sandra Bullock. We talk and watch the movie cuddled up in each other's arms. But his touch isn't like Trouble's touch, nonetheless, he is comfortable.

After the movie, I order another, this time a Marvel movie, The Avengers. I enjoy the company he is bringing, but I still can't shake Trouble from my mind, especially since he keeps blowing up my phone. When I get back to England, I'm going to have to change my number. I catch Marcus staring at me and then he leans in for the kiss. His lips are soft and sweet, I brace myself for what is about to happen, but stupid Trouble's voice is in the back of my head fucking with my brain. Shit, when did I become this person? I don't fall for people. They fall for me. The dick cannot have been that good, I tell myself over and over. It's just a silly crush, it will pass. I keep having to remind myself so that I can enjoy this man on my sofa. His lips may be soft but they're not like Troubles. I break the kiss and smile. I get up and go to the refrigerator for a bottle of water because I need to get some space in-between us and cool the fuck down. Get it together bitch, he's sexy and fit as fuck what's your problem?

"Is everything alright?" he asks.

I pop my head out of the refrigerator to answer his question, "oh, yeah," I walk back over to him sipping from the bottle I just opened to quench whatever thirst I have that isn't Marcus. I climb on top of him and straddle him and place my lips on him, and he caresses my back with his bare hands. I can feel his fingers undoing my bra, and I almost flinch at the thought. Once he opens the back of my bra strap, exposing my breast under my white vest top. I hold onto the back of his head and moan in his mouth. He kisses me, sending surges through my entire body.

"That's it Trouble," I moan out a little too loud, and he stops and looks at me.

"Yes, you're in so much trouble," I kiss him deeply to send a different message other than the one my heart is trying to send me. Seems like he believes what I am selling because he gets into it. But when he gets the condom out and tries placing it on himself, I get up and ask him to leave. I just can't perform. I can't concentrate with this nagging feeling in the back of my head. He protests and says that we don't have to if I don't want to.

"I do want to but, I shouldn't."

He looks even more confused than I am at this moment.

"And why shouldn't you?" he asks.

"I don't know. This has never happened to me before. Trust me I always close the deal, but an annoying bird is stopping me," I tell him, not wanting to admit to him or myself that I am falling for a man who has more women than Hugh Heffner.

''Is it someone else? Because if it is you don't have to worry, I'll never tell as long as you never tell my wife either," well that sparks my interest immediately.

"What did you just say? Your wife?" I ask with astonishment.

"Yeah, my wife." He has the nerve to repeat that shit.

"Leave now, get the fuck out." He gets up and protests, singing me some fucked up story. I go to the door and open it for him to get the message, but he isn't budging, so I go for the punisher, since he isn't ready the punisher always gets them moving. I spin my bat in my wrist like a pro baseball player.

"I'm going to count to one and then start swinging, see if I can hit a home run." He quickly gets the message and leaves and I slam my door and shake my head and trail off to call Autumn.

I reach for my cell phone and call my sister; she answers on the fourth ring. It sounds like she is sleeping. When she answers I freeze realising what I am doing, I hang up in her ear. She calls back immediately. I answer and tell her never mind and hang up again in her ear. I miss my sister, but I'm still not ready to speak to her. Normally I would run to her with things like this, and we would laugh and eat ice cream in bed. I realise I am alone in New York, it's time for me to go be with my family. To pass the time, I call the annoying voice of my conscience Trouble. We talk until I fall asleep. I don't even know when he hangs up.

Mr Johnson comes over the next day, because he didn't hear from me yesterday, which is sweet. The last week has shown me how much I miss my family and how I truly feel about Trouble. I did enjoy our time together, and he is someone I can get to know better, but those women would have to go immediately, like yesterday. Mr Johnson is outside waiting to take me to work today as usual. He waits till I get myself together before dropping me to the store. Kerry is in and assisting customers. I am proud of her; she has really turned her life around.

"Let's have lunch today around 1p.m. ok," I tell her and she agrees without complaint.

I check in on my other venture back home and catch up on the accounts for the store. By the time I spin around, it is time for lunch. We leave to go out and one of the other ladies watches the store while we are out for lunch. We get hot dogs from a street vendor. I ask her to follow me to the car dealership. Once we get there, I ask her opinion on which car she likes, making her think it is for me. She chooses a BMW convertible, a girl after my own heart. We move onto the next dealership, and she chose a Mitsubishi Navigator and a Land Rover Navigator.

"So, which of the three do you think I should get?" I ask with a gleaming smile on my face. She is in two minds between the BMW and the Land Rover. She finally chooses the BMW; I tell her thanks for the help. I start the paperwork for the car and tell the dealer that I will be in contact for delivery, but I ain't getting no.

"I thought you were going to drive it out of the dealership today?" she enquires.

"No, I want to personalise it, make some changes to it, you know pimp it out a little," I tell her.

She agrees and sips on her cup drink. We go back to the shop for the rest of the day. During the afternoon, I contact the dealer with the address. I tell him of the finishing custom job I need doing on the vehicle. I change out the colour of the seating with lime green leather and black streams. I engrave her name in the headrest, get her up to date navigation and electronics, including Wi-Fi. I make sure it is safe for a young lady to be driving around in and tint the windows and order the matching sunglasses. I am about to make a young woman's day. But Mr Johnson and I have an agreement that she isn't allowed the keys until she gets her GED and her full drivers licence. Since I am not going to be here for her birthday, I get it early. What Nana Bird wants; Nana Bird gets? No questions asked.

Mr Alexander calls me, and I finally decide to put him out of his misery, since I won't be here for that long. It's something to pass the time. I decide to let him take me on a date he can't be any worse than that fool who thinks it's ok to cheat on his wife. He picks me up from the hotel in a stretch limo, with two single roses. I thank him as he opens the limo door for me. I've worn my deep purple chiffon top with a sexy tailor-made lilac pant to match and these cute new heels I got from a store called Nine West. I am on fire. I wear my hair naturally out with my curls wild and free. We sit in the limo for a while in silence, then he gives me a compliment about my hair.

"So, what have you been up to other than internet stalking me and constantly blowing up my phone like I ran away with your millions?" I ask.

"Well, after our brief encounter, it felt like I was going to implode if I didn't see you again. To be honest, since then I've spent most my days jerking off at the thought of you" he tells me. I sit there in shock with my mouth gaping open. Well, I'll be damned.

"With that in mind, what are your hopes from this little encounter?" I am more amused than anything. I am curious to see what would take place on our date. I thought I would have some fun tormenting this man. I smile at the thought of all the trouble I can get into, messing with him.

We pull up to a restaurant, and the limo driver gets out and opens the doors for us, and I thank him. Alexander sticks out his hand for me to take, and I take it letting him lead the way. We enter the restaurant in which there are several couples and families. The look and feel of the place is very intimate. He is a perfect gentleman. Who would have thought it Winter Autumn Valentine out on a date with a white man. I guess hell has frozen over after all, or the lord is coming. Something is about to happen.

"Tell me why are you so obsessed with me, Mr Alexander? I say sweetly. He chuckles and shakes his head.

"Why wouldn't I be obsessed with you? You're talented and beautiful, and apparently, you're going to fuck me and have my daughter call you mommy, I'm quite looking forward to that." I am shocked to hear my words repeated back to me. It just doesn't seem right coming from his mouth, but it does make me laugh.

"That tells me that you're close with your daughter or you're fucking one of her friends?" I state, and he gives me a bemused look.

"Well, you have a unique way of looking at things Ms Winter Valentine."

"I just see shit and know not to step in it."

"Did you just call me fickle matter?" he asks.

I laugh. "Sir, I'm here for the free food."

"Here I am thinking it was for my company."

"No. It's free food," I tell him while eating the piece of bread from the breadbasket. He looks crushed.

"Are you always this crude with your dates?" he asks, and I look at him. I take a moment to understand his words. I straighten up in my seat and decide I am being rude, and I need to actually try.

"I'm sorry, that was rude," I apologise. There is a moment of silence. The waiter comes over and takes our order, and he orders a bottle of wine for the table. I'm not much of a wine person, but tonight I'm going to learn to love it.

Once the waiter leaves to fetch our order, I ask, "so, what else did your search tell you about me?" curious to know what he thinks he knows about me.

"Only what you want the world to know," he replies with a slight smile.

"And what's that?" I ask playfully.

"Let's see. You're a third of triplets, you and your family own a small boutique business chain in England. You went to college, but not a university. Your family has made a name in the stock trading game, putting the rest of us to shame, but only slightly," he says confidently. I think he's offended, finally.

"ONLY SLIGHTLY," I remark a little offended also, with one eyebrow raised.

"Yes, slightly. Your brother has been making a lot of noise all over the trading world and is yet to be seen."

"We're more like the morning dew, fresh and clean, just right for your lungs. We leave just as quick, as we appear, and I would like it to remain that way," I tell him, and he chuckles.

"Well, I would love to meet him and ask him how he does it."

"Why not just ask me?" I tell him. The waiter brings our meal, I've ordered the chicken dish of the night. His choice of wine is exceptionally good with this chicken.

"Ok, how does he do it?"

"Simple. None of your business. What else did you hear or find?" I enquire.

"Let's see. You're beautiful and very talented."

"The internet told you that?" I ask.

"No, that's what I know. Well when you're not insulting me and, I must say I think you're a little racist."

I smile at his words.

"Maybe," I shrug and say.

"Are you serious?" he asks, surprised at my response.

"What, white people aren't the only one who can be racist, it's racist to think that," I tell him.

He laughs and takes a sip of his wine and digs into his meal.

The night goes on smoothly, and he asks a lot more questions about how me and my family made our money but gets no answers. I swear he sounds more and more like the police. I want to know about who is who in New York, and who I can contact for details on the business scene and fashion scene. Too bad his daughter is such a bitch because she would be the one, I should be having this conversation with. At the end of the night, he returns me to the hotel, and I say good night. He takes my hands as he walks me to the hotel's rotating doors and tells me he enjoyed my company. I must say I did enjoy his company too. I thank him for a lovely evening.

"Well, thank you for a lovely evening," I say and take a step towards the door.

He grabs my arm, and I turn to look at him. I look at the spot that he holds me and then back in his eyes.

"You're not going to invite me up?"

"No," I say simply.

He chuckles "So when can I see you again?" he asks.

"Who said that I want to see you again?" I reply.

He looks at me quizzically and then smiles.

"Thanks again for a lovely evening. Call me," I tell him and walk into the hotel swaying my hips just for his benefit.

I get in and call Mr Johnson to let him know that I am back in the hotel. Mr Johnson has me call him, every time I leave the hotel and return, ever since Storm left. In the last few weeks, he's been more of a father to me than the sperm donor.

The car dealership call me on Wednesday to inform me that the car is ready, so I give them a delivery address and pay the balance on the car. I tell them to have it parked outside Kerry's house by 10 a.m. Thursday morning. My flight is 1 p.m. and I can't miss it. I sleep at the Johnson's, in Queens, New York that night because it is closer to the airport and I want to see her little face lighten up.

Thursday morning, I am woken up bright and early by Nana Bird letting me know that I shouldn't miss my flight. The children are up and rushing around as usual, but now Kerry is taking charge and roping them in. I get a shower and get dressed in my white shorts and matching t-shirt, and blue converse—Ready for my flight. We eat breakfast. The Johnson's, all take the day off to take me to the airport, which is sweet. I'm going to miss them all, but this just means that I will be back. I'm going to miss my weekly shopping and Mani-Pedi with young April and the cheekiness of Omari, and his Gentleman way. So far, the best little boyfriend I've had since I got here. Little Surprise is still hanging on for dear life to that thumb of hers and is always calling me Autumn.

I get the call that the car will be arriving in 5 minutes. I anxiously wait for the doorbell to ring and when it does, I meet Mr Johnson's eyes. He smiles that smile that captures my heartstrings every time. If I ever had a dad or grandfather I imagine he would be like him.

"Kerry get the door, please?" Mrs Johnson asks.

"Yes, Mam," she politely replies. She clicks the intercom and answers the door.

"I have a package for a Kerry Silverman," the gentleman says.

"Ok, I'll be out in a second," she turns and tells us all that it is for her and she'll be right back.

As she leaves through the door, we usher all the children out of the house, following behind Kerry. The car has a huge bow on it. Blood red, wheels gleaming, it's just perfect for her. I am happy with the result. Kerry's eyes widen with surprise, and she jumps up and down, causing a big scene for passers-by. Neighbours come out to see what the commotion is; she keeps jumping up and down screaming; you would think she'd won the lottery. She runs back up the front steps and gives me a big hug thanking me, with tears in her eyes. She is so excited she nearly knocks everyone out. The kids run up to the car to touch and get a closer look.

"Look, Kerry, it has your name on the seat," April states.

"What, shut up, you lying?" she screams again reaching a new pitch. She runs down and opens the door wide, searching and pressing every button in the car.

"You think she likes it?" I ask rhetorically. With a chuckle, I make my way down the steps and over to the car. I jump in the passenger seat and tell everyone to get in.

"Once round the block," I say and hand her the keys.

She squeals again and grabs the keys and turns the engine on.

"Seatbelt," I state.

"Get in," she tells her family, the children all get in, but her grandparents stay behind. We pull off and 'You the boss' by Rick Ross, and Nicki Minaj booms out the stereo, this is one of my requests from the dealership. We all sing along with the windows down.

"Keep your eyes on the road, remember your families in the back," I tell her.

We go around the block about three times and then pull up in front of the house. Once out of the car, I snatch the keys and tell her the rules of the car. What she needs to do to maintain the car and to be able to own it permanently and until then her grandfather will be holding on to the keys. She squeals and hugs me again. I thought she was going to protest and moan, but she agrees and thanks me again, and promises to make me proud. She thanks me for changing her and her family's life, with tears in her eyes.

It is time to head to the airport, so we all pile into the minivan and head out. Once at the airport, I check in and say my goodbyes, and we all cry. Surprise gives me a message for Autumn, I get a kiss from smooth-talking Omari, and I encourage April to continue to write. I give Kerry my last warning, and she cries and nods her head continuously.

"Take care of each other, don't worry Christmas will be here soon, so you'll see me again, we family now," I tell them. I kiss them all goodbye one last time. Who knew I could be this emotional about strangers?

Out Of Many One Family!

Storm

Shit, I can't turn around down here without walking into someone claiming to be my cousin. For broke people, they seem to be spitting these kids out left and right. I love and hate Jamaica all in the same breath. That's one of the reasons I make sure I don't sleep down in the ghetto with Nana Bird. I made sure I built my manor on the hills so I can get a peaceful night sleep. Nana Bird won't leave Kingston for nothing.

I fixed the dilapidated house she calls home and fenced it, and the woman had the nerve to call it a prison and demand it be taken down. Nana Bird's house had a couple spare bedrooms that she had built on because just like Winter, she always tries to save everyone. We make a significant contribution to the local nursery school, known as the basic school. Plus, every day Nana cooks for the elderly people so they can get something to eat, this woman never stops. Well, I hired other people to assist her. They should call her 'feed the nation.' My grandmother is one of the oldest residents in the community and well respected by the local thugs, mainly because she feeds and takes care of their badass kids.

When we used to visit as kids, we never ran out of people to have fun with, there are always children in the yard. Autumn and Winter haven't been back in a long time, but I make it my duty to come see my grandmother at least two to three times a year to check up on her. Since she never liked to travel, once we were old enough to take care of ourselves she moved back to Jamaica, back in her old two bedroomed shack as I used to call it. Now the shack looks like a mansion smack bang in the middle of the ghetto. Now that's ghetto. Noise 24/7. One thing with Jamaica it's always on the move. I ask her all the time to let me move her out just in case one of these idiots decides to bite the hands that feed them, but she always refuses saying we're her only earthly riches. I never understood that concept but what Nana Bird wants Nana Bird gets. My manor is finally complete after how many years of hard labour. I plan to retire here one day. Hopefully Sunshine will come with me.

I can't believe I'm still feeling sick. I can't seem to shake the nauseating feeling. All the doctors I visit seem to think its stress related. Nana Bird seems to think that I got someone pregnant, with her silly old Jamaican superstition. I kiss my grandmother and Autumn on the cheek before leaving to fetch Winter from the airport. I'm still vexed about her ditching us to stay in New York and then to make matters worse Autumn wanted to leave Miami early. I swear this holiday ended before we even left England. If the doctors are right, I'm going to need a holiday to get over this holiday. Get away from the crazy women in my life. Other than what they think is stress, the doctors say I'm healthy as an Ox and I would have to agree.

Sunshine has been dodging all my calls, the past couple of weeks. She's always tired as hell. Her security detail tells me she's resting a lot and Junior seems to be always popping up, lucky for him he's gay. Other than her safety, the security detail is excellent at getting information on any men who come around. She went to the doctors the other day again. She locked the guard out of the room. Apparently, she went to the sexual health clinic, since she hasn't told me to go to the doctor; I'm assuming we are good.

The drive to the airport takes 45 minutes due to traffic. Jamaican transportation gives me jokes all the time, there's always people hanging out the bus barely hanging in there, music pumping. It takes skill to drive like that. I'm sure the front of a car is only supposed to hold two passengers; no not in Jamaica that shit can hold six people. Shaking my head and laughing at the sight of the Jamaican public transport system, I speed down the highway to get to the airport. Blue flashing lights along with a siren catch my attention, letting me know to pull over. For fuck sake, not now. I pull over to the side of the road, ready for my interrogation. Hopefully, this won't take long. Two officers walk along both sides of the car, I place my hands on the wheel, waiting for instruction.

"What's the problem officer," I ask through gritted teeth and frustration.

"Licence and registration pretty boy and step outta the vehicle," the fat chubby fucker tells me.

I flip down my visor and hand him my details. He takes it, while the other comes around to stand next to his partner.

"Both hands on the car," he yells.

I do what I am told, and the younger officer proceeds to pat me down. "Where you heading?" he asks.

"The airport," I reply.

"You travelling? Open the trunk," he instructs.

"No, picking up my sister" I reply.

"Yow, wasn't you telling me about Birdie grand pickney," the fat one says to his partner.

"Yeah a wah?" the younger slimmer one replies.

"See one yah," he tells him nodding in my direction.

"It's your lucky day, your granny is my people, and for him granny too," he tells me. I am still confused about what that means for me at this point.

"Yes, Miss Bird is my grandmother, so what of it?" I am curious about how I can use this information and be on my way quickly.

"Means you a family, it is granny too."

"Oh sweet, how come we never met before," I ask. I mean, I met every other so-called family around the place near and far.

"I grew up in the country, just move to town you zi me. So weh you say you going again, mek we give you an escort, and make dem idiot yah kill off dem self," young blood says.

"The airport, I'll follow behind you," I tell him, and he hands back my documents

"Pay the man a thing for his service. Nothing's free here family or not, his family has to eat too," he says. He has an eastern Jamaican accent, sounding more like someone from Liverpool.

At this point, I just want to get to the airport. I am already late, and I don't need to hear Winter's mouth about it. I give him $3000 Jamaican dollars and jump in my Navigator. They get back in their car and lead the way. I get to the airport, and Winter is surrounded by horny dogs eating out the palm of her hands.

"I see you wasted no time with your shenanigans," I smile and hug my sister.

"What else was I supposed to do for entertainment since you took so long?" She hugs me back and looks over my shoulder with a puzzled look in her eyes.

"Ah baby boy do you know the police were following you?" she asks with a whisper.

"Oh yeah they escorted me down here, apparently he family," I tell her and point out our new-found cousin. They walk over to us, and the men scatter.

"This is Winter, my sister, are we cool?" for some reason, I don't know if we are supposed to trust him or not, but either way my eye and guard is now wide open.

I introduce everyone and take her luggage and throw it in the back.

"Winter what the hell you got in these dead bodies?" I ask sarcastically. She waves me off and hops her ass up in the front seat after greeting this so-called cousin. She invites him round for dinner, and he agrees. We leave the airport, and they escort us halfway before going about their business.

"So, you done with this bullshit you got with Autumn?" I ask out boldly, and she simply kisses her teeth and rolls her eyes like that is an answer.

"Wint I need you to squash this shit. The doctor says you guys are stressing me out, and I need a vacation. Shit, I'm on vacation and still need a vacation," I point out.

She ignores me and sits looking out the window like I am invisible or just plain white noise to her.

"So, what have you been up to since you been here?" she asks, ignoring me and changing the subject.

I shake my head at her and decide to ignore her dumb ass too. I pull in at the nearest patty shop to get her favourite cheese and beef patty and coco bread sandwich with grape soda.

"So where are you staying at the manor or at Nana Birds?" I ask so I know what my plans are for the night.

"You know Nana ain't gonna let me stay up there, plus I can't take her complaining every day."

I laugh because I am going through that exact same thing now. Most nights I sleep at her house instead of the million-dollar house I've just built. Just to get her to stop complaining.

"So, how's preparation going for Nana's birthday party?"

"Ok so far. All the church folks are helping out with cooking, and they're gonna get everything prepared while we take her to the restaurant for a meal. For an 80- year- old woman she is pretty strong," I tell her as we pull up at the house. Nana is still sitting outside on the veranda on her chair.

Winter jumps out the car, runs over to her grandmother, kneels down in front of her and gives her a hug and kisses her all over her face. It is a happy sight to see.

"I missed you," I hear her tell Nana followed by an, "Ouch, what's that for?" Nana slaps Winter, and I can't help but laugh as I get all her bags out of the Navigator.

"For leaving your family. Who told you that you could stay in America for so long, don't you live anywhere?"

Winter looks at Nan and at me like she is crazy.

"Look at me cross-eyed again and see if I don't poke them out for you," Nana says, and Winter pushes up her lip and hugs Nana again and smiles at her grandmother.

"I'm sorry Nana, won't happen again." Wint apologises with sincerity in her voice.

"I miss you though, my granddaughter,"

Wint smiles even bigger.

"You ok though right grandma?" she asks.

"Mi a turn eighty and still can knock you out, so I'm more than good," she laughs and hugs her granddaughter.

My grandmother has her ways, but you can't help but love her, regardless. I leave the ladies outside to catch up while I put all of Winter's load in the house. Once I make my third trip, I get fed up and leave the last case on the veranda for Wint to take in.

"So, grandma, what are we doing tonight?" I ask her the same question every night, knowing the answer.

"Just going sit yah soh and wait for the good Lord to send for me," I smile and go to get her medication. Every time I'm here, I make sure she takes them on time like clockwork. I sit with her till she falls asleep or gives up and goes inside to bed. It never takes long either, I can set my time by that woman.

"Well that won't be tonight," I tell her as I hand her the glass of water and her pills.

"Do you see your sister, she hasn't come home all day," she says.

"She's across the road, you want me to get her?" I ask as Wint sits in the chair next to my grandmother and rolls her eyes. I get up and go to fetch Autumn.

"That boy breed somebody gyal. He thinks it's a joke, he hasn't stopped vomiting and sleeps like a pregnant woman," I hear her tell Winter and they both laugh. I leave them and go across the way to fetch my pain in the ass.

"Grandma wants you," I address her when I get close enough to her. The local men are all out smoking, drinking and reasoning, as they call it. Autumn excuses herself and walks over to the house.

"Soon forward, just gotta lock up," I tell them and follow behind Auto.

"Likkle gyal come yah, come sidung," my grandmother tells her.

"I'm good," there is only a seat next to Wint, so she isn't about to do that.

"Me say fi sidung you deaf?" she snaps, and Autumn kisses her teeth and sits next to Winter and Winter scooches over.

I already know what's coming. Grandma's about to put her foot down. So, I take my seat for the show that's about to take place.

"Likkle gyal what did you just do, a nuh cut you cut your yiye after me, come let me juke dem out for you since you nuh have no use fi dem inna you head. Sidung and listen to me before mi get di strap."

My grandmother is the boss I love her, so much her spirit is something to be preserved at all cost.

"You two are fighting like likkle pickney. Bout unno nah chat to each other, mi nuh care a wah happen, but unno better fix it, before I die, because mi can hear the Lord calling me home, but mi a gawn ignore him mi nuh ready yet," she tells them.

"Nan stop with all your negative morbid speech, you are not dying, and if she doesn't want to try and understand or speak to me then that's fine by me," Autumn says.

"A who you raise your voice pon woman, your draws getting too big, it seems. Weh me say. I say to chat to you sista and sort out unno petty squabble cause me nuh want it in here. You a family; bredda and sista, what did I teach unno. hmm?"

"Family first, nuh matter what." They both state, mockingly and I chuckle.

"Weh you a laugh fah, you just as bad making them a war lacka dis."

"I tried grandma, but neither one will listen they're stubborn," I tell her.

"The three a unno listen to me. You only have each other, no one else. That me teach unno, learn to forgive family, the three of unno is mi pride and joy next to the almighty. My lifeline, if you're not strong, how am I supposed to be strong, I'm not going to live forever, you know, so kiss and makeup. Have you heard what I said? Oh." she says sternly.

"Yes, Nan." They both say and hold their heads down in shame. It is funny seeing them quiet for once. Especially Winter.

"Autumn go get you, granny, some of the lemonade inna d fridge?" she asks as Autumn goes to fetch the drink; I have to ask about the police officer that I encountered today.

"Hey Nana, I met an officer today, said he was your grandson too. I didn't know mom had brothers and sisters?"

"Yeah your uncle's pickney. Him live a country with your grandfather's side of people." She tells me, all casual like it's the norm.

"Ok. I never knew that Uncle Patrick was our real uncle, thought he was like the rest of the family we seem to have around here," I state.

"No Patrick a mi bwoy. Him never good so I send his backside to country else I woulda charge for murder. Him vex when you madda got to go foreign, jealous bad. I sometimes go down there to see him, you know mek sure him alright and ting put him pickney dem through school. But that big head boy of his turn police. He is staying with me likkle. God knows where he is now. He called and told me him a stay with his friend; must one gyal. Keep him from you woman that's all I can tell you," she informs me. She tells me the story of our family in the country and the gentleman I met today is indeed our real family.

"Well I met him today. Had to pay him three grand just to continue on my journey. He said he will be coming for dinner tonight, so hopefully we get to spend some time."

"Rajah a good boy head on his body. Him just needs guidance; you know. But keep your eyes open still. I can see his daddy in him. Go call them boy over soh fi dem dinner, mi a get hungry now," she tells me.

The only woman I need him to stay away from is thousands of miles away, mad at me, so I couldn't care less about that. I get up to go call the men over for dinner; I swear this house is a soup kitchen or the salvation army.

"Oh, hell no, why all these people here?" Winter asks, coming out of the house.

"Nan seems to want to feed the nation every day," I tell her.

"Well they better come up with some form of change, nothing for free. Nan is this what your spending your money on, where's theirs, Nana?" she asks my grandmother.

"Likkle girl stop the noise and share out yours before they start playing up in the pot," she tells Winter.

Autumn got the same answer when she first arrived; I already know how she is and I'm used to it. My grandmother's house is where the needy and hungry come when they are in need.

"Wait, Jerome, you go last. I heard you say that nasty gyal down the road a mingle, so wait last, till my grand pickney dem take their share. Share out some fi Rajah you hear Starm," my grandmother demands.

I love the way she pronounces my name with an A instead of an O. It makes me giggle all the time until I'm in trouble. That is then it's a curse.

"Ok, Nan."

Everyone forms a line. Winter grabs her suitcase, pushes her nose up and goes into the house.

After dinner, the boys and I do our rounds to the local elderly and moms in the area that Nan tells us to visit who are having trouble and need our assistance. Once I get back, I sit next to her till she is starting to fall asleep, 7 p.m. like clockwork. I help her to her bedroom and kiss her goodnight and close her door. I go to sit back out on the veranda with the boys. When I walk back out, they are all talking about some party up the road.

"You rolling dawg?" they ask. It amazes me how no one has money to feed themselves but have money to party every single night. Jamaica is simply backwards.

"Who's on duty tonight?" I ask.

At all times, I require two men to be guarding my grandmother's house. Non-negotiable its part of the job description. This is what they get paid for, and I don't want to hear any bullshit. If they want to party, they can party on their own fucking time. I like to get what I pay for. They seem to be doing it shift by shift when it's party time, but I don't care just as long as my family is safe at all times. They give me the rundown of the night, and I am satisfied.

"Maybe, the girls may wanna go" I state.

"Yeah Autumn says she's rolling," Skippy says with a little too much enthusiasm.

"Cool, I'll see what I'm doing; if my lady decides to speak to me, then it's a no, no."

"See Rachelle a come yah, we a leggo. Watch your 6," Skinny whispers.

"Mash up you ting dawg," Turner says and turns to walk away. The men leave to take up their posts and do what they do best.

"Yeah, later I'll call you," I tell them.

I am well known in the community since I put most of these people's kids through school and Nana feeds them. I pay most of them to guard my grandmother while I'm away, and now my sisters, for their safety. I became the leader of the community a while back. So, I generally don't have much issue with people around here because most people know not to fuck with me. But I trust no man. With the amount of family around to be responsible for plus the livelihood of these people, I have a lot on my shoulders. I make sure everyone knows the rules of living in this area.

Since being here, I've already had to sort out three domestics and two idiots arguing over a machine. Now they all know better, since no one's allowed that kind of machinery in the area. The only people allowed to have one are my four closest generals and myself. They aren't allowed to even walk with it too much because their pistols are legal and waving it around isn't something I condone. I can take them from them as easy as I got it for them. I don't condone domestic abuse in my community, men need to learn to appreciate their women, they never understood my logic. When they feel like they don't need to follow my rules, they get a visit from me, and they get a taste of what it feels like to hit a defenceless person, they feel what it feels like to feel weak and helpless. I already have an agreement with the leader of the next community and am on a peace treaty. If anyone from either side decides to interrupt that, then they will disappear permanently. The safety of the community is my number one priority if someone dies in my community. It must be from a disease or accident. This is why no one ever knows when I'm coming or going. They don't even know that I have a house out here. As far as their concerned, I rest my head right here.

The next sexy headache, Rachelle is a girl I smash whenever I come to Jamaica, except for when I bring Sunshine along, and she knows the rules about Sunshine. Never mention her name or refer to her period. I help her out now and then, make sure she's good. It's been real hard not sleeping with her, since her body is firm and full with all the right assets. She is one of the only girls who don't have any children in the area. I have been taking her to dinners and to every party that seems to be popping off. I brought her a bunch of clothes and shoes from New York since Sunshine helped me pack my luggage when I was leaving England. With the ultimatum I gave her, I think it's only fair that I stay focused only on her, but Rachelle is making it hard as hell and I mean really hard. I avoid sleeping at her house, I don't think I would be able to control myself.

"Let me check Nana's good before we go," I tell her.

"Weh we a go?" she asks in a thick west Kingston accent and I smile at her with a mischief in my heart.

I love Sunshine, but she has been acting funny for the past few weeks since I left. I think she's punishing me for the security detail I placed on her. It's been more than 6 weeks, and she is avoiding me. We never usually go a day without talking no matter where we are in the world. I'm starting to think she's fucking the security detail because he can't seem to give me any fucking information either. I have been sick since I left England and she doesn't even care. I text her, and I get no reply for days. After the first week in New York, she's been distant. She's got my mind going one hundred and ten, constantly; and here is this sexy ass woman willing and waiting and I keep treating her like second-hand goods. I know she's fed up with my bullshit because normally her freaky ass would have me balls deep in every part of her and this trip she gets nothing more than a peck on the cheek and a grope here and there in the clubs.

If Sunshine's not willing to commit, then why am I here holding out, when I could be enjoying my holiday? I'm starting to feel like a sucker in love by myself. I grab my overnight bag because tonight I'm going to empty all my frustration on poor Rachelle. She's been begging for it. Who am I to deny her what she's been asking for? I've already taken her to the clinic to have her checked out, our routine procedure whenever I'm here before we can get down. I make sure I'm stocked up on the morning after pill because ain't no babies coming in this equation.

Welcome to Jam-Dung

Autumn

Winter arrives today, and I thought she would have at least lightened up a little, but the bitch can hold a grudge. I offer to pick her up, but Storm declines saying it would be better if he does it alone. When she comes out the Range, I am about to go say hi, but the bitch gives me the evils like I am her worst enemy. Well, fine, since I'm her worst enemy, that's fine with me.

During Nana's little speech, I am dying of laughter on the inside, I think she thinks that we are still teenagers or 5-year-olds the way she is threatening to whoop our asses. I love my grandmother, but she can barely move around for too long to be threatening anyone anymore. I'm actually contemplating staying out here with her since she's gone up in age. Plus, she's talking about dying and shit, and I'm starting to believe her. Saying she's ready to meet her maker and dumb shit like that. Who the fuck talks like that? I mean the woman even has a resting spot picked out and shit like that. She's more tired lately; I regret not coming to spend more time with her like Storm does. He's out here every year with her. Bless his little cotton socks.

The eye candy isn't all that bad out here either, and their accent is super sexy, sending chills down my spine everytime they open their mouth and the children all seem so cute with it. I have been teaching some of the local kids some new dance moves since a few have seen me dancing in the back and decided to follow; more seem to turn up every day. So, I do it as my daily routine for exercise.

I love the parties out here. They are so full of energy, and everyone seems to be enjoying themselves and not just watching each other. There are a few good dancers out here, they seem to take dancing as a sport out here. I love the whole culture, why mama left I will never understand. It is beautiful here. There's a party for every single night out here, no matter which part of the island I am at.

The rivers are mystical; they have so many different theories for stupid shit that clearly back in the day the elders made up to entertain the children because they had no TV or radio. I always look at them like they are the dimmest people on earth, but they just let it flow over their heads like it doesn't matter. As the phrase foreigners like to use, 'no problem Môn,' I hate it when they do that, it's the most irritating thing in the world. I mean I was born in England. I have a Jamaican mother, and that's all I know, and you don't see me speaking like a complete twat.

My life seems to be falling apart. I seem to be making all the wrong decisions in life. Nana's eightieth birthday is coming up. The kids are doing a dance for her, my way of showing my appreciation. I see why she came back home after we were old enough to be by ourselves and Storm's obsession with the island. Since Wint wants to be a pain in the ass and it's my fault she's feeling hurt, I think I'm going to make the first move and try and resolve the friction between us. I miss my sister,

I have so much to tell her. She usually would have great advice about Darius and have the cure for me.

"Yow, Storm what are you doing tonight?" he looks up at me and tells me to shhh, he is doing his routine checks on Nana. "Sorry, so what are you doing?" I ask with a whisper.

"I was going to Rach's, then probably that party up the road, Sup?" he replies.

"Well I want ice cream, so grab your little friend, and I'm going to get Wint, and we can go Devon House," I tell him.

"Not tonight, I wanna spend some time with Rach," he tells me.

"Nope, you are taking us to Devon house, besides, it won't take long. I got a plan."

"A plan for what? he asks.

"You'll see," I giggle and run off in the direction of the bedrooms.

I knock on my grandmother's door and let myself in and give her a kiss goodnight. I promise her I will work on things with Wint. Then, I go in search of Wint. She is in the north part of the house, sorting herself out. I lean in the doorway, and she looks up at me with a blank stare, and I just stand and admire everything about my sister.

"Get ready, Storm's taking us for ice cream at a garden ice cream parlour, in the city," I tell her and walk away before she can decline.

I go to my room to get myself together. I am ready in half an hour and when I come out everyone is waiting for me in the car. As I thought, Rachelle is sitting up front and Wint's in the back. Traffic's moving pretty good, and we get there in 20 minutes. Parking is a little trᴜckier. I discovered this place the other day when a guy from Canada tried taking me on a date. He was cute, but dull in every sense of the word. I think the night sky is beautiful, there are so many stars in the sky you can't help but look up at them. I know Storm will know it since hᴇ comes here so often, he knows the place like the back of his hands. We hop out and make our way to the ice cream parlour because it's coming up to closing time, and the queue only seems to be getting longer.

As usual, Rach is all over Storm like an infection, which makes me sᴜck. There's something about the girl I just can't stand, and from the way Wint's face seems to be screwing up every time she opens her mouth, I know she doesn't like her either, but I don't know enough to get rid of her yet. I don't entertain the women in the area because they all want something. I have no patience for them, it's always, 'beg you dis nuh,' 'left that widd me nuh,' 'when you aggo weh?' Seriously don't they think I own it because I like my stuff, that's why I buy it. For broke ass bitches Jamaicans have the worst, I don't give a fuck attitude about them, they could have just licked your ass, they still feel they are better than you and have the upper hand. Something my mother used to call Tallawah. She used to curse us out saying we too Tallawah. I never really got it until now. Because I'm a get straight to the fucking point kind of bitch, while I'm beating the crap outta you with a smile, I stay in my lane and just hang with the men. That seems to be causing some trouble, but because Birdie is my grandmother, they all know better than to open their mouth. Everyone seems to respect Storm, he's some sort of icon to these people.

We buy extra-large ice creams and go walking in the garden. There seems to be a lot of lovers out tonight, and me and Wint keep eyeing each other laughing at the ones who think they are being caught. I keep trying to make small talk with Wint but she's more stubborn than before.

"Come on Wint, what I got to do for you to forgive me? I said I was sorry," I stop directly in front of her and look her straight in the eye. Hence, she has no choice but to address me.

"That's the point you shouldn't have to apologise, and no you have not apologised, I warned you about him, but no, you chose them over us. I ain't Jesus, so I don't have to forgive you," she snaps loudly with venom in her tone.

"Wint, I am sorry, this had nothing to do with you or Storm," I point out.

"That's the point; you didn't care how we would feel, or what effect this may have on us, as usual, it's all about Autumn, and I want my daddy bullshit. Well guess what, your daddy doesn't want you. I mean you're a self- made millionaire businesswoman making more than most people, and he still doesn't want you, but you want his old ignorant ass?" she rants.

I just stand there and listen as tears fall down my cheek as every word hits home and my ice cream melts in its pot and around my fingers. I can see she feels the same.

"Winter I'm sorry, but I never meant to betray you, that was never my intention. I want my sister back, please," I beg.

"We all want what we can't have, plain and simple. You always choose others before us then we have to pick up the broken pieces, but not this time. You wanted a new family here you go; you can have them." she says and takes out a card from her purse and hands it to me, as the tears fall down her face, she storms off.

I take off strolling behind with my tear-stained face and heartache from the awful truth my sister just flung on me. I catch up with them all by the Navigator. Winter has already planted herself in the front seat, while Storm and his current situation are squeezing on each other.

"Get a room!" I bark at them with frustration.

He brushes me off, and I jump in the driver's seat. I sit and contemplate the revelation I've just had. Am I a selfish sister? Do I only think of myself when it comes to my family? I miss my mother even more. I've never thought about my actions towards my family before. I know I can count on them for everything, and I hope they know the same about me. There's nothing I won't do for my siblings, no questions asked.

"Yow, I'm ready, stop messing around and get in," I shout at Storm, who is feeling all up on this chick, that I still can't figure out.

From what grandma says, she seems to be all grounded when Storm's in town, but as soon as he leaves, she's whoring it out. She thinks my grandmother doesn't hear about her exploits, but Nana Bird hears everything. She's the town information guide as far as I can see. I drive through Half Way Tree to get to Duhaney Park Estate, where my grandmother lives. It takes about 20 minutes to get home, but my mind is on Winter's words. They seem to be eating away at my soul. I never knew that's how my siblings see me or think. I have to make some changes; I park up outside Nana's house.

The usual men are placed up outside, holding up the walls on the corner, and the females are under the tree and light post gossiping as usual. Wint is the first one out of the car; I sit back and dig the card out of my bag that she gave me in the park. It's a business card of a business called Gardeners' Elite. The owner is Jacob Junior. I stick the card back in my purse and exit the car leaving Storm and his new flame to their privacy. I ain't in the mood for a party, I have a lot to meditate on and to figure out how I am going to get my family back together in one piece.

Red, Green and Gold

―――――――――― ❧ ――――――――――

Winter

I see why my brother visits this island so often; I've forgotten how sweet it is to be here. I used to enjoy myself when we visited with our grandmother back in the day. The entire place and things that seemed so huge when I was a kid seem so small, even the routes to places seem shorter. Mama always said I had an active imagination.

I wake this morning with the sound of the damn cockerel making so much damn noise I am tempted to kill it and have it for breakfast for ruining my sleep again. I already know that I'm heading up to Storms house soon, so that I can live all civilised. I don't have to commit murder, to a chicken or Autumn for annoying the hell out of me. I mean does she really think ice cream would make me forgive her, for her sins or her lame-ass apology. I am not Jesus. I don't have to forgive so quickly.

Jamaicans move fast, even though the people seem to be so laid back, they all seem to be 'jamming Môn.' How about that? Nana seems to be spending all her money on feeding these hungry ass neighbours and the starving nation. The amount of food she cooks on a regular basis ain't no joke. Oh no, her allowance will be cut immediately. She needs to stop feeding these people and let them go find a damn job and put food on their own table, instead of just relying on her to provide for their hungry asses.

Since I have been here; I have been partying all night and sleeping all day. I get fucked up every night. Every party we go to they all seem to know Storm and gather around him. Autumn is always in the middle with the dancers enjoying herself, and I must admit it is nice seeing her enjoying herself naturally. Being carefree brings me back to when we were younger, and it was just us. Every now and then I catch her staring at me like a deer caught in headlights. It's Nana Bird's birthday in a few days, and she is helping the kids prepare a dance routine to say thank you for all she's done for them. It seems my grandmother is loved by everyone in the community. She has over a dozen visitors every day, checking in on her. Even the local church sisters come by and pray with her, even though that woman wouldn't put her foot in a church. She's always saying that she refuses to mix and mingle with the heathens and that she doesn't want to get caught up when God comes for his earth and she accidentally gets mistaken for the hypocrites. My grandmother is something else and has always got something to say about everything.

I generally emerge from my bedroom around 3 p.m. Today something tells me to get my ass up and go outside. Even though I want to sleep, and the sun is at its peak, I can't shake the feeling that something is about to happen. I get up and brush my teeth and wash my face and head to the veranda. Storm slept at his house last night, so I grab my phone, but as I'm about to dial his number ,that's him calling. That triplet psychic ability comes in handy sometimes.

"Hey baby boy, I was just about to call you," I say, smiling into the phone.

"Ok, so you're ok. I'm trying to get Autumn, where she at? I'm getting that I need to fuck up somebody vibe," he tells me removing the joy from me.

"Me too, but I don't see her," I tell him and turn to my grandmother and ask her for my sister.

She tells me she sent her to the shop.

"Storm let me call you back I'm going check something out," I tell him.

"I'm on my way," he tells me and hangs up.

When we get that bad feeling, that means a greater storm than Katrina is coming and when Storm's mad, World War 1 or 11 ain't got nothing on him. I quickly drag on my all-stars and grab a two by four that is sitting by the gate and head out. No doubt Autumn is in some form of damn trouble. Here I go again having to stick my neck out for this bitch, and these Jamaican bitches don't play. By the time I get to the store, she is nowhere to be found. My active imagination starts to do 360 degrees, my head is spinning, and all sorts of thoughts start going through my mind. Everything she's done doesn't seem to matter at that moment I just need to know she's ok.

"Hey, have you seen my sister, little boy?"

"She looks just like me." I ask another one of the local kids, and he tells me she went down the road, so I speed off down in the direction he points, while praying to God for mercy for her. I can hear a commotion from the direction the child has told me, so I pick up speed. As I get closer, people are surrounding a group of girls. I spot Autumn's curls through the crowd. I sneak through behind the crowd, out of sight, until I get a good grasp of the situation. Autumn seems to be arguing with a group of ladies. She is clearly outnumbered, but she seems calm as a cucumber. See the thing about Autumn is she can go from a prissy woman to a ghetto girl quicker than a crackhead, could make a dick disappear. My palm's itching to smack a bitch for disrespecting my sister the way these bitches are going on.

"I don't have time for you immature children, who can't keep a dick, so you are trying to blame the next chick?" I hear Autumn say but she knows better than to turn her back on these bitches.

It seems they're mistaking Autumn for me; I'm finding it amusing until these bitches start getting closer and closer to her face.

"Hey gyal who you a call pickney, next time I see you with Biggie, I'm going to beat out your raas," this loud, mouthy girl says pointing her finger in Autumn's face.

That's my cue because she's getting way too close for my taste.

"I guess that makes me Faith Evans or Lil Kim," I interrupt, pointing my weapon of choice in her face causing her to back up a little.

"So what, because your sista is here, weh unno feel like? No wonder Rachelle hasn't stopped nyam out you," one of her little rats' chimes in.

I am becoming more and more irritated at the sound of their voices, and I'm starting to see red.

"Bitch I will fold you like paper, back the fuck up," I tell her. She is skinny as hell, with too much mouth.

"And mi will empty you like a bokkle," she replies snarkily.

"The way your man emptied me like a cold Red Stripe last night. He was nibbling on the end of my pussy-lips like a starving animal. So, what the fuck you going to do?" I ask, waiting for the bitch to get froggy.

"A second ago, you had nothing but mouth, but guess what you fucked with the wrong one, bitch. I don't like all this talking and cursing bullshit so if you're not going to do shit, we out of here," I stand my ground and Autumn stands by my side. We step backwards.

"Bloodclaat, Mercy you ago mek dem British gyal du you so? Box dung a gyal, afta dem gyal yah a nuh, nuh baddi," one of her flunkies speaks up boosting her which prompts Autumn to speak up.

"Why don't you hit her yourself? I dare you, leap bitch!"

The young woman is the bravest of them all, she comes at Autumn, but Autumn is quick on the draw, and sees the slap that is about to hit her and steps back. Timing that shit perfect as she throws a solid punch that connects squarely to the girls left temple. She stumbles backwards trying to catch her balance, but Autumn just keeps going, the second hit echoes through the crowd. Me I swing first, fuck that wait for a bitch to hit first. I swing my piece of wood and hit the bitch that is attacking Auto in the back of the leg, bringing her to her knees and then swing it around connecting with the bitch called Mercy's jaw. I raise my leg and give her a forward kick straight to her stomach, sending her flying into the crowd. I feel a kick to my leg, I turn with my bat in both hands and swing with all my might connecting it with whoever the fuck hit me, I swear I hit six with that one because all I see is blood, as the girls drops to the ground. Another one is about to hit Autumn in the back, I make a quick step and stomp the shit out of her, still holding onto my bat. Mercy finally comes at me with a hit from behind; a punch to the back of the head which only enrages me even more. I grab her by the hair and go to town, but she is loose with her wild windmill jabs, which opens her dumbass up to more blows. I give her an uppercut like Storm taught me. She lands on her ass, and I land a firm stomp to her stomach.

I guess the locals get tired because a bunch of men come to their rescue. I scan around for Autumn and see a dude is about to push her over. I wriggle out of the grip of the three men who are holding onto me and as he pushes her away from the bat, that is now on the ground. I grab it and plant a firm hit to his back.

"Get the fuck away from her!" I yell.

It is the idiot all these girls are getting an ass whooping over. He turns and sees me, and I guess he sees red because he grabs me around my throat. With that I drop the bat, choking, I have to use both my palms and hit him on both sides of his head. Autumn comes up behind him, and I'm not even sure when she gets a hold of the bat but she goes to town on him, blow after blow. The more people try to pull us off, the more I get enraged and want more. It seems like a force of nature takes over and takes control of us. It takes at least ten men to haul us away from the scene into a home that isn't familiar. All I know, they fucked with the wrong British girls. The other girls seem to still want more, but some of the locals are warning them off while me and Autumn just stand side by side, praying for them to release us.

Well I am anyway. They thought they could try us because we remain simple and quiet, they thought wrong. I hear Storm's voice through the crowd. I hear someone telling him where we are, and he pushes past everyone.

"You're bleeding," he points out, I don't even notice. I see the anger boil over in him, this is about to get even worse. Shit! Shit! Shit!

"I'm good, it's a scratch," I tell him, trying to reassure him, because as bad as I want to beat the DNA out of those bitches and that dickhead, no one needs Storm's rage.

"Auto, what the fuck happened?" he asks with rage in his eyes and voice.

"They started it, this bitch mistook me for Winter and decided to warn me off from her man, but she got her ass handed to her," Autumn tells him. Shit, she could have just said anything but that.

"Who's her man?" he asks with more rage.

"The idiot bleeding over there. Me and Wint had to beat his dumbass too because he tried to choke Wint," she tells him.

I want to strangle her, 'stop talking' I think.

"Let's go," Storm walks out of the house, and we follow suit, and in slow motion, just like the incident that just took place I see my brother draw a gun from behind his back and fire two rounds into the air. The sound makes my entire body shake.

Everyone scatters but before Biggie can move Storm shouts, "Bitch don't move."

"Sorry boss, sorry," this punk already starts apologising.

As Storm gets closer, Storm points the pistol at his temple. I am dazed as fuck at this point as to what is going to happen to this fool because Storm's temper is a whole other adventure.

"Why did you have to say all that?" I whisper to Autumn, but she just shrugs.

"Apologise!" he demands.

The dude cries and inhales with his bottom lip trembling like a child in trouble.

"Don't let me repeat myself, man, I hate that shit, now apologise, before I let her put one in you and turn your lights off," Storm spits out through clenched teeth.

I dare not speak. The unfortunate thing pisses himself.

"I'm sorry" he spits out between cries.

"Learn to control your bitches, control your home, and let them know that Birdie's grandchildren are off-limits, **MY FAMILY ARE. OFF. LIMITS!**" He screams to everyone in the surrounding area who is listening and peeking out.

I look around and notice that only Storm's little crew stand around and a few residents. Biggie is nodding his head frantically at Storms demand.

"Got it." he spits.

I even get it, with all that fury surging through him. I swear I see the devil in him. I make a mental note to speak to my brother about a few things.

"Get in the car," he instructs us, and we do as we are told. I mean, who am I to disobey him?

Clean Up Crew

~~

Storm

I hate that feeling of my sisters in trouble, and I am nowhere to do anything about it. I speed down the road swerving through traffic to get to my destination. The built-up tension is killing me, my chest is tight, and I need release, I know something foul is happening.

When I get outside my grandmother's house, I hear someone shouting for my grandmother to come quick, saying that my sisters are up the road arguing. My grandmother is seventy-nine, what the fuck is she gonna do? I look across the road at the fuck ups that I pay to protect my family, and they all look at me with a frightened look on their faces. I'll have to deal with them later. When are these people going to understand that I'm not to be fucked with? Because I haven't bodied anyone in a very long time, they think I'm soft. I pull my gun from its secret compartment in the house. I summon the idiots, and they all know what time it is.

Just to prove a point I ask, "Where are my sisters?"

No one seems to have an answer; looking at each other sheepishly.

"Get in," I yell.

As I drive to my destination, everyone seems to be like Michael Jackson speechless.

"What the fuck do I pay you guys for? If anything happens to them, people are going to get hurt," I state as I pull up outside the commotion.

I slowly move through the crowd listening to the crowd recite things, but my sisters are nowhere to be found, I try calling but there's no answer I am becoming impatient. I shout out for Winter, with all the commotion and talking they are definitely here. A young general tells me where to find them. I find them in a house, with several men surrounding them. Autumn has a satisfied grin on her face. I tell people she's evil as fuck because like a psycho she enjoys fucking people up. They are both bleeding. Winter seems happy to see me. After what I hear from Autumn, she comes out of her trance. She sends me into a psychotic rage. Never ever touch my family; rule number one.

I fire two off in the air and everyone scatters and clears the way except for one dude, the rival gang leader across the other side of the city. All day the only thing these idiots seem to have done is find the idiot named Biggie in the distance. He is placed up across the street; I march over to deal with him.

"Get out my sight," he scurries away, like the flea he is.

I go back to the house where I find my sisters and pay the owner for their hospitality and thank them. I ask Skinny where the ladies that were involved in the fight with my sister live. I find each home. It seems my sisters did a number on them; they are all messed up. I speak with them, make them all aware of the position that they put themselves in and how stupid they were to fuck with my family. I warn them to never let it happen again, else I won't be so generous with their lives. If they value it, they will stay clear of my family and me at all costs.

I call them a taxi and tell them all to get in, and they comply. I tell Turner to go with them, pay for the medical bills and keep me updated. I am starting to get irritated all over again with this asshole girl problem. I hate spending unnecessary money.

I know the repercussions of threatening a man in Jamaica. I know what has to be done to Biggie, especially since the girls beat his ass and everyone saw him piss himself. I hate making these kinds of decisions, but he showed the ultimate disrespect by putting his hands on my sisters. He is from the other side of the community, so I know I'll have to make some form of a visit to their leader to discuss what's about to go down. We have mutual respect, and since his dumb ass community member fucked with mine, they have to pay. Once everyone is dealt with, it is time to take my queens back home. They can deal with Nana Bird; I ain't in the mood for that kind of noise right now.

"What the fuck wrong with you two, always in some shit?" I ask my two pain in the ass beauties.

"Hey, they attacked us, plus I had a lot of frustration to release so hey, who better to take it out on than some bitches who think they can?" Autumn speaks up.

"Wint? What the hell, you use to fuck that imbecile up?" I ask.

"Me? That was Autumn, she went to town on his ass. As he released my neck, I just kicked the shit out of him."

I shake my head and laugh as my sisters recall the mess that just went down. I take them to Tasty's patty for something to eat before returning back to Nana's house. I listen to their tale and laugh at the outcome. It is hard to stay mad at my queens, especially since they are laughing and talking to each other again.

"Well, you all better come up with something to tell Nana Bird. Winter you sure you ok? There's blood on your head,"

"I'm good, it's not mine I only got an aching pain. That Mercy connected to my head. I swear Auto is some form of Ninja the way she dodged those punches," she laughs.

I give them wet wipes to clean themselves up before they get out of the car to go face judgement. As they exit, I can hear Nana Bird ranting and raving, cursing them. I jump out of my ride and head over to the rest of the clique. I kneel down, letting them all know to do the same. They all hold their heads in shame except Skinny. He looks me dead square in the eye.

"So, who's going to explain why my sisters were in a fight and why that poor soul is going to have to lose his life?"

No one speaks as I look around the circle.

"What's the number one fucking rule?" I ask in a low growling tone of frustration, **"WHAT'S... THE... FUCKING. NUMBER ONE. BLOODCLAAT. RULE?"** I slow down the question since they don't understand.

Skippy's voice finally opens up. "Protect your family at all costs, boss," he declares.

"Ok, since you all failed to do one simple task, your only task, every man gets a pay cut. Somebody better take care of that idiot because I don't want a man to feel like he wants vengeance or even think of anything stupid. Because of your negligence and stupidity, a man's about to lose his life. You guys better pay for his funeral since this is your fault. How did you let both of them slip your sight, in the same fucking minute? I mean she had a fucking two by four in her hand. How did you miss that?" I ask, frustrated.

"Sorry boss I'll make it right" Turner speaks.

"See that shit get right, tonight. My grandmother's birthday is at the end of the week. No witnesses. Make sure you get this done right, or it will be me killing one of you. Oh, and please have the sense not to use your own shit. I got you those legally, so don't let that shit trace back to your dumbass."

They all remain silent as I get up and leave them to contemplate the instructions, I've given them. I don't care, all I know, if I see that nigga still breathing after today, more than one body will be bagged. I like to get what I pay for when I pay for it. With all the shit I've been going through, the stress of this family seems like it's choking the life out of me. These people around here seem to forget who the fuck they messing with and what I'm capable of doing and it's time I remind them. I walk up the steps of my grandmother's front porch.

"Everybody come outta mi yard," she orders.

See what the girls don't know is that Nana Bird is a gangster in her own right. Back in the day, she was a warmonger, the best. She ran with the best of them. Our grandfather was one of the baddest men around, we have a legacy. Everyone clears out of the yard and the men take up posts around the yard.

"Wah happen up the road?" she asks.

"Don't worry about it Nana, everything's sorted," I reassure her.

"That's not what I asked you, I say what happened? And don't tell me nuttun," she says calmly.

I explain the situation leaving out the gory details.

"You take me for an idiot, I may be old, but I'm no fool. Think I nuh know what you deal with round yah. Mi see everything that gawn in yah, and hear everything, so before I ask a question, I already know the answer. Mi know you see your sister neck and I know you a man that nah go mek dhat go unpunished cas mi know you. You're my grand-pickney, so I know vengeance inna your blood. Think I don't know what you come for. Just watch yourself hear mi don't do anything that ago put you inna problem?"

"Like I said it's taken care of like you taught me Nana," I tell her.

"Gyal thing nuh matter to me, I teach my grandbabies well, they can beat up anything, I like how they can defend themselves. Just like you, madda."

My grandmother is to be feared when she gets philosophical and family orientated. I never knew mama was like that, though. Growing up, I never heard her curse or get in any arguments. The only reason my grandmother sent my mother away was because the war between her, and some hot head was becoming heavy, and she didn't want her to get caught up. She told me a story of back in the day. Schooled me on the streets of Jamaica and how these people are and who to trust. From my first trip out here, she has been schooling me and showing me the running of her operation quietly. See there's a reason for everything this old woman does. She never ceases to amaze me. She's old now and out of the game so to speak but I make sure that our family name still reigns strong through the streets of this little city. I never get my hands dirty, but these dumbasses are making my palm itch for their blood. Grandma is one of the original old people still living in the area, and the only old woman I know who has a shotgun by her side for a walking stick. When we were younger, it was a machete, always sharp as hell.

"Help me up, time for my programmes," she says.

I comply and do as I am asked. I help her to her chair inside and come back out to try this chick on her phone again. Sunshine is driving me fucking crazy. My daily report last night said that she revisited the doctor yesterday. She's fine, she's been sleeping a lot lately too, her iron levels are low or some shit, according to the report; and that asshole friend of hers is spending too much time around her. I still don't believe that gay shit. Again, she ignores my call. FUCK! I gave her a decision to make, so I guess she made her choice. Sex with Rachelle just isn't cutting it anymore, her shit just isn't holding up, I feel sick after every fuck. Her shit just isn't the same, like she's been beat the fuck out, so I'm gonna have to let that go. On to the next one, so to speak. I'm gonna stop calling Sunshine's ass too if she doesn't get back to me by the end of today.

The Two Most Important People In Life Are The People At The Beginning and The Person At The End.

⁓

Autumn

I can't believe that all it took for my sister to be by my side was for me to defend her, the way she did all my life. We laugh about that fight over and over. Those bitches never saw us coming. Not sure why Jamaicans feel like because we're British we weak, well we showed them. I bet they won't make that mistake again. I'm glad I have my sister back in my life, and I'm not about to make anything or anyone take that away from me again. We are close again doing everything together, the way we are supposed to.

Today we are going to Dunn's River Falls, one of Jamaica's favourite tourist attractions. Just the three of us like we planned all along, we finally have some family fun. I get caught up with everything that happened in New York with her. That bachelor party she went to sounded like a hit. My sister always finds herself in the strangest predicaments. She tells me about my little suck finger baby Surprise who by the way keeps calling me every day before and after school and most of the time she doesn't even speak. I'm not sure why she glued to me like that. I mean, I look just like Winter, and she never clung to her like that. I speak to Nana Bird about it, and she just says that's how kids are; sometimes they see what we don't see. She says that she sees me as her mother and no one should tell the child otherwise, but sure that's not healthy, she needs therapy. She curses my ass out about therapy and tells me to do what my heart is telling me to do, but what the hell is that supposed to mean. This woman is too cryptic for my liking. She speaks with Surprise many times, and that's the advice she has for me.

My day is becoming a great memory to cherish. We climb the falls, and even though the signs say not to carve on the rocks, we still carve our names in every rock we can. It's a great day out. We shop and do the tourist thing. We buy a bunch of stuff from the stores and take pictures. I watch as heads turn for all of us. The people out here are bold as fuck. Men and women alike, every time we start to enjoy ourselves; another one comes along and tries their luck. But today it's family day out, so everyone gets dismissed.

We book into our hotel around 5 p.m. and change for dinner at a seaside fish restaurant. We get dressed and meet up outside the hotel. Me and Winter wear the same outfit like we used to when we were kids, well like we always do. After all, she is my left lung, my heartbeat, my happiness is because of having her in my life. I wish this could last a lifetime, but I know the end is coming. We drive down the coastline to the seaside restaurant all lit up with LED lights and the music of soulful reggae pours out of the restaurants. We choose one called *#3*, it's only fitting. We chuckle as we speak and pick the restaurant without even speaking. We sit and order every seafood dish on the menu, crabs, lobster, steamed fish, something called conk, mussels, clams – everything, we want to try all of it. We eat, drink and talk into the late hours, it is like old times again. I am stuffed, and I can feel niggeritiss taking over. I can see it taking over them too. We drive back to the hotel with plans to meet up at around 2 a.m. once we've all had some rest from all this food and river water. We kiss our baby brother and tell him 'see you later.' I am glad to be sharing a room again with Winter. We collapse on the bed beside each other in laughter.

"I'm glad we are friends again, I missed you," I tell her.

"Me too. Just next time you have a stupid urge like that again, promise me you'll come talk to me first please?" she begs.

"I promise. Won't happen again."

"And I promise to listen to how you feel about that side of things," she says yawning.

I turn and kiss my sister on the cheek, and she smiles at me and tells me she loves me and always will.

"And I have your back no matter what?" she laughs, and it is a magical sound. She falls asleep, and I watch her sleep. I doze off into a peaceful, sleepy abyss.

I wake up to my phone singing, Winter turns in her sleep, and I quickly reach for it so I can cut the noise off. I search the call to see who's calling and it is none other than Surprise. I swear this child's name suits her well, always surprising everyone.

"Hey baby, what's up, why are you up at this hour shouldn't you be sleeping?" I whisper into the phone. I can hear her crying and mumbling into the phone. I can't understand what she's saying. So, I get up and go into the bathroom, so I don't disturb Wint.

"Ok, baby, what's happened?" I ask her.

"When are you coming back? I had the bad dream again," she explains.

She's having recurring nightmares about her mom's death. She found her mom dead on the living room floor when she was just three, and she's had nightmares ever since. I feel awful for her. I'm not sure why she only seems to talk when I'm talking to her or when I'm around. According to her grandmother, they've tried everything. I don't know what to do about her. She's become a real concern for me.

"Sweetheart, where's your grandparents?" I ask.

"They sleeping."

"Ok, remember I told you when your sacred what you should do?" I ask.

"Yeah."

"Well, you wanna try that?" I ask.

"Ok, but can you stay on the phone till I fall asleep again please?" she politely asks.

This is becoming a recurring thing between us. I stroll back in with the phone to my ear and Wint is awake, and I mouth Surprise to her, and she smiles at me. Once I hear slight snores and am content that she's asleep, I hang up my phone.

"What are you gonna do about her?" Wint asks.

"I don't know, she's going through the same shit I went through when mama died, but it's worse for her because she's only five. She shouldn't be going through that shit. I don't know how to help her other than just be there for her when she calls, I swear she must be running that phone bill skyrocket."

"That's all you can do, it's not like you can have her with you 24/7" she replies, and I look at my sister because I just had a light bulb moment.

"Whatever it is think before you do, I know that look. You about to do or say something stupid," Wint accuses me.

I am thinking something stupid or possibly brilliant. I could adopt Surprise. When I am with her, we are inseparable, and it is like she is mine. It broke my heart to leave her behind, it was like I was leaving a part of me behind. I miss her everyday just as much as I miss my sister or my mother. I sit in contemplation and Wint gets up and goes to the bathroom. I sit on the bed and think about the dumb idea I am having. Wint comes back in the room with a toothbrush in her mouth, speaking in between brushing her teeth.

"Get up. Let's start getting ready. Tomorrow you can tell me about whatever you're thinking about," she tells me.

I jump out of my trance and go and grab my toothbrush and follow suit in getting glammed up.

Storm knocks on the door, at 2 a.m. right on time. Between him and Nana Bird, I swear that's how people set their clocks. Always on time, they don't know anything about black people timing. Wint lets him in, and he complains about timing as usual, and we do our little we don't know time dance.

"You two better wear more than a piece of cloth when you are with me. None of that skimpy shit." He shouts at us in the bathroom.

"Oh, shalaap, we will be out in a minute," I tell him.

15 minutes later we both exit in leopard print twin suits that hug every curve of our bodies.

"Let's go," I say like we'd waited for him all night, and Winter laughs as he shakes his head.

One Cannot Predict What Lies Ahead, So Why Worry About What's Past

Winter

We dance all night long at the strip club. At first, I am apprehensive about going to a strip club, but apparently, it's one of the best clubs in the city. Go figure. I dance with Autumn all night till my feet ache. We actually enjoy ourselves once we get in on the action with the ladies, we paid them. They dance like it is raining dollar signs up in there. It is an amazing night, we watch a midget fuck a pretty young thing that almost makes me sick, but I can't pry my eyes away from what is happening on the stage.

Storm gets ill again from whatever disease he has. I am starting to worry about him, he seems to be sick every other day. My mind is now running away with me because now I am thinking cancer, just like mama, cancer is going to take my brother from me, my protector, my king, my all. But he is determined to have fun, even if it kills him. So, I keep one eye on him and the other on the show these perverts are giving me. I know you may think it's a bit weird brothers and sisters together in a strip club, but like I said we are more than brothers and sisters, we are best friends.

I meet a dude called Trey from Canada on a bachelor party holiday type shit and we hang for a minute. With all the liquor surging through me and my pussy throbbing to the sound of the beat, I am willing and in need, especially since I need to get Trouble out of my head and pussy. I need someone to get the job done. Even in a drunken state, I am still thinking about that fool. I can't believe it. I grab his hands and follow him to his limo that he had parked out front. I tell Autumn I'll be right back; she knows what time it is, she shakes her head and mouths the word WHORE, and I wink at her and smile. Even through all this heat and tension, my mind is still on Trouble.

Oh, just shut up, maybe if you just concentrate on sucking this pussy, instead of asking a bunch of stupid ass questions then I would be finished. I think.

"Does it feel good?" Trey asks again for the umpteenth time.

"Oh, my goodness! Get up now! Look, no more questions," I say.

Trey gives me a side glance filled with confusion and he goes back to work on my sweet spot, but I can't seem to enjoy him. The musical tone from my phone catches both our attention. Saved by the bell.

"Hello," it's my saviour online; she always knows when I need rescuing, "Thank God," I answer the phone.

"What?" Trey asks, looking up at me from between my legs.

"I said I have to go."

He is confused. As I push him off me, exit the car and pull my dress down. I turn to address him:

"The next time a woman decides to give you her greatness shut up and just do the job. Stop asking so many damn questions."

With that, I leave. Poor thing looks baffled like it's the first time a woman ever told him that his game is whack. Seriously if you're going to do something, do it right the first time otherwise don't do it all. I mean women should stop telling men these lies about they are the best because they want whatever little cash they have in their pockets. A car horn blows outside alerting me to sexy, damn this girl is impatient, you would think she has somewhere important to be. I quickly hurry to the Rover. Storm has passed out in the back snoring lightly. I shake my head at the sight of him and smile as I hop in the front seat with my bestie.

"Child you need to learn patience," I tell her once I get in the front seat.

"So how was it?" she enquires.

"Lame," I reply and kiss my teeth, and she laughs at my anguish. "It's not even funny. Idiot just kept asking me a ton of questions, like I'm on who wants to be a millionaire, I'm already a millionaire I don't need that shit," I tell her.

She laughs at me and tells me that's what I get for hooking up with strangers.

"You need to live a little," I tell her as I sulk in my seat while she drives. I open the window to let the fresh sea-salted air take away my misery.

I swear this so-called holiday is going to entitle my black ass to another because it sucks and ain't no one can take care of a girl's needs. I'm happy that Auto and I are on speaking terms because since that's happened, we've been having mad fun, doing different shit every day. She has a bunch of kids following her around like sick puppies. It's so cute, and she's got her dance class. Storm seems to be having nothing but bad luck because he's forever throwing up and dozing off. Nana says he's knocked someone up, which reminds me I need to call Sunshine and ask what's up. I'm praying she is pregnant because the other alternative is, he's sick just like mama. And when the fuck did my brother become Al Capone? I mean what I saw the other day was something else, he had those niggas shaking in their boots, I can't believe it. I am glad he was on my side because I was shaking for them too. I'm glad I changed my number since I got here because Trouble would be blowing up my phone constantly with his lovie dovie bullshit. Since he stopped calling, I seem to miss him more and can't seem to get him off my mind. The drive home is soothing, damn I'm tired and in need of my bed. We arrive at the hotel and carry Storm to our room; I don't trust him all alone, since he keeps throwing up and shit. We are driving back tomorrow, and I need to make sure he's up for it, because I don't know the roads like he does.

When we get back to Nana's, she is sitting in the same spot, we left her. I swear that woman is going to die in that spot. I exit the vehicle and wave at the locals, I see a new face, but he shifts too quickly, so I don't recognise who it is.

"Hey Nana, you sat there all this time?" I tease, but she just ignores me, like I don't exist.

I swear that's where we all get that temper and attitude from because ain't nobody else can make you feel like shit without speaking like she can. I walk over to her and greet her in the correct way I know she wants.

"Good evening grandma, how was your day?" I ask and bend over and kiss her on the cheek.

"Much better now, you're back. Come go dung a pharmacy for me?" she asks.

I nod my head and go to put my bags in the room. I swear I'm gonna be like this old woman when I'm her age. I can't help but laugh at the thought. I see Mr Henderson outside, crossing the street. He always cracks me up, he has all the best stories about mom. I take the prescription paper from Nana and head out to say Hi to Mr Henderson.

"Hey Mr Henderson, how are you doing today?" I ask.

"Hello! Mi say, man, every time I see one a unno pickney, me see unno maddha," he replies, with a strong thick Jamaican accent.

Mr Errol Henderson is one of the family's oldest friends. He lives across the road from my grandmother. He's always got a big head spliff hanging from his mouth and grinding out another. Today is no different; he is grinding more of the island's greatest plant known by many names. The scent is potent, the strongest I ever smelt. It always reminds me of the first time I came to Jamaica, and I sat behind the family house with my cousins and smoked. I coughed so much my chest hurt, for two days. My cousins laughed so hard they started coughing. I absolutely love the smell, which alone can get me high. The stuff back home can never compare.

"I'll take that as a compliment," I tell him.

"Yeah man, you madda was a pretty woman," he tells him with an innocent smile.

"So, which one is you, pretty Gurl?" he asks in his very best English accent, I think.

"I'm Winter, my sister is spending her time in the outdoor shower," I tell him.

"Oh! We call that the shower, just the shower, we already know seh it outside, you nuh affi tell wei!" he says mockingly, and I giggle.

"Daddy? Evening! Mommy called you," the new face comes out from the side road saying.

He is wearing cut off leg jeans shorts with a white Puma t-shirt and matching sandals on his feet. I search his features, and they are familiar. He is pretty handsome. His body is thick and firm. I know these men out here don't go to the gym regular, so whatever he's doing I thank God for it and my sight. Skin smooth like buttermilk, tall, eyes deep brown, with lashes thick with a bushy brow. He definitely can make the cut.

"Winta you member mi son Parker?" Mr Henderson asks, interrupting my examination of the man before me.

Of course, I remember him. He was all over Autumn back in the day and much skinner and scrawnier. The last time I saw him he was rude too.

"Not really. Hi how you doing?" I ask and our eyes meet once again.

"Mi good man, I remember you and your sister," he tells me.

"If your granny neva send weh Catchrine, she woulda be fi you sister too," his dad retorts and takes us all by surprise.

"Well, I'm glad that never happened because she looks sweet doe daddy," he says, causing me to blush a little.

"Bwoy Sugar and honey sweet. Mi nuh juss say she could be you sister you a come talk bout sweet. A wah de rawtid?" he asks his son.

I can't help but laugh at Mr Henderson and his son. I guess Rasta nuh mix up inna bangaarang, strictly Ital. He's funny as hell. The day we had that fight he brought me Guinness and rolled me a fat joint and told me I was a don, he wished I was his daughter, it was a proud moment. I felt blessed and appreciated. He taught me how to smoke the correct way, I felt like a boy learning the right of passage or some shit. He is super cool; I can hear his wife calling him.

He gets up and leaves, "Mi aggo see weh she wanted and mek unno young people talk," he tells us.

I stand there blushing with a stupefied look on my face. Parker stares at me with an intense look.

"So, you don't remember me, huh? I remember you though."

Did I just hear correctly. He speaks perfect English. A little American but perfect, nonetheless. I stare at him with a confused look.

"Where did that come from?" I ask with a higher pitch than I'd like. I clear my throat.

"Where did what come from?" he asks with the sexy accent.

"This accent?" I say interrupting.

He smiles a devilish smile, and I swear I see a little twinkle in his eyes.

"I live in Atlanta, but whenever I come home, my parents keep asking me to repeat myself, and it gets annoying. I hate repeating myself. And anyway, you didn't answer my question?" he replies with a challenge in his eyes.

"And how long have you been doing that for?" I ask, trying to ignore the pressure of the silky wet feeling between my legs.

The corner of his mouth curves in a wicked grin. I swear his eyes are sparkling from the glare of the sun.

"Winter!" I hear my grandmother shout from her spot.

"I'm going now Nana!" I shout back to her.

"Hurry up, man, before me dead in yah," she yells back.

I sigh. I wish she would stop calling down death on herself.

"Follow me to the Pharmacy?" I ask the devilishly handsome man staring at me. I can't get over how he's changed drastically, wait till Autumn sees him she's going to die.

We walk to the pharmacy and back, catching up with each other. I give my grandmother her medicine and the fruits I bought for her from a street vendor. They are these sweet plum kind of fruit with a seed full of spikes called June plum, all I know is I love them. I don't care if it digs out the inside of my mouth. I especially love them with salt and black pepper. I get myself a coconut water from an actual coconut, the real deal. I drink one or two every day just for fun. The vendor makes sure he has mine set aside freezing waiting ready for me every day as requested. I could live on just that alone. Parker holds my bags as we walk back home together. After I hand the things to my Nana and get a lecture about doing things on my time, I go back outside and chill with Parker for the rest of the day. We catch up on the last 12 years since the last time I saw him. I still never admit to remembering him. He is cool like his dad; we laugh and joke all day. We end up in the local bar, drinking and talking. It is a different kind of day, and for once, my mind doesn't think of Trouble, not once.

The Love Of A Child
Is All We Need!
~

Autumn

"**G**randma, who's Winter talking to?" I ask, curious as to who the sexy specimen my sister is drooling over is.

"Errol's pickney from 'Merica, he came yesterday. Dah gyal there nuh hear enuh, look from when I send har to do sinting," she grumbles and shouts out Wint's name.

I am ready to go to the back to do my usual yoga and dance session. I know the children will be here in a bit. But first, I want my grandmothers' advice.

"Nana, when mama died, and you had to come to take care of us. How did that make you feel?" I ask her, and she gives me a puzzled look.

"What kind of question is that? Who else is going to look after unno? Unno as much mines as much as your madda. Unno a fi mi and mi never did argo make no government look after unno." she tells me sternly, I already know my grandmother loves us, but I want to know how she knew it was for her.

"So, you didn't feel obligated or anything? Or like we were a burden?"

"Wah kind of a burden, yeah unno did bad nuh raas, but you were pickney, you nuh know better, but unno did a me flesh and blood. Coming like me right breast, the right one wouldn't look good without the left one. The decision is easy. Why are you asking me about all a dis?" she asks.

"I just got off the phone again with little Surprise, remember her? I let you speak with her on the phone. I mean I'd only known her for a week and a half, and she's grown fond of me, a little obsessively. She calls every day crying asking when I am coming back. She lost her mom, and I think she thinks I will replace her mom," I explain to her.

She puts her hand on mine and cuts me off mid-sentence. "Baby, listen to your grandmother, if I never give you any good advice before, please tek heed to what I aggo say to you and open up your ears and listen good."

I giggle and agree to listen to what she has to say.

"That little girl seem very much like you and yours when your mother died. I know how you feel about this likkle baby, she's grown on you, and you're falling in love with her. If you think you can take her life into your hands and do a great job like I did with you, don't hesitate. I neva regret taking you in or loving unno like I push you outta meself. Love doesn't see colour or faces; it only sees the true nature of a person's heart. So what if she wants you to be her mother, the question is are you up for the job? I see how all these likkle pickney gravitate to you. They trust you and depend on you when you leave, dem aggo bex bad. If you love that little girl like I know you do, go sort something out. You hear me, don't hesitate, to be honest, the two of you need each other, I can see that. I never understand young people. Unno quickly fall in love with idiot boys but when real love comes unno push it weh and dig bare hole in it and try to fix it when it nuh bruk."

My grandmother gives me a lot to think about. Her birthday is in 2 days, and I can't wait for her to see what the kids have done for her. I get up and kiss her and tell her I love her. I walk to the back of the house to the dance stage that I had the boys build for me. I sit down under the tree, for quiet meditation. I should get Wint, her stubborn ass needs to come and join me because I know she's going to be complaining about her weight later with her forever stuffing her fat face. 10 minutes later, and I finish my stretches. I close my eyes and do my 20 minutes dance exercise, ready for when these kids come rolling up in here.

I open my eyes to find the most beautiful creature standing before me with what looks like appreciation on his face. He licks his perfectly shaped pink rose lips, which sends the sweetest feeling down south. I stand still with a wide-eyed expression on my face and my heart pounding, staring at the perfect round silky caramel toned, curly-haired being. Inhaling deeply trying to regain my breathing without this stranger noticing how erratic and in awe I am. In-between trying to regulate my racing heartbeat I manage to ask,

"Excuse me, can I help you?"

"Continue, I was enjoying the performance along with the view," he says in his strong Jamaican accent.

My entire body goes on full alert at the sight and sound of the movement of his lips.

"What can I do for you, Sir?" I ask with a slight tremble in my voice. I can't believe this; I've never met someone who can take my breath away in an instant. Get it together, Autumn.

"Is Ms Birdie in?"

Why is he wasting my time. Although I don't mind. My grandmother hasn't moved from her spot yet, and he has to pass her before getting to the back. I lean my head to the left and inhale deeply before I answer him.

"No, can I take a message?" I say

He smiles a wide grin showing off his pearly whites.

"No, I'll catch her later."

Does he think he is being smart or something? Sometimes I swear my grandmother is some sort of dealer the amount of people that come through here every day.

"So, what's your name pretty lady?" he asks.

I watch the curve of his lips move in motion with his words. I swear I learnt to lip read instantly because I don't hear a word that comes out of his mouth only see the motion and grooves his mouth makes.

"Pretty Lady," I reply, hoping he will take a hint and leave because I am losing all my senses around him, and I don't care for it. Plus, those hypnotic brown eyes are undressing me a bit too much.

He chuckles at my reply. "Ok, well, my name is Moses, people call me Prophet."

Oh that voice.

"Well they call me Pretty Lady, so if that's all I'll let my grandmother know that you dropped by Mr Prophet."

His eyes narrow, and then he smiles, "You are too gorgeous to be arrogant and miserable."

What the fuck I'm not miserable? I clear my throat and answer him. "I call it confidence. Besides, I don't like being sneaked up on or spied on."

He stares at me a moment, his eyes do a once over again of my body, making me feel vulnerable and excited all at once.

"Look me and mi dawgs dem a keep a party up di road, All white, woulda love fi see you pretty face deh, deh," he asks, but it sounds more like a demand.

"I'll think about it," I reply confidently.

"Don't think about it, just come, mi wah see you again tonight."

This nigga just can't take no for an answer and why should he. I want to dip him in honey and chocolate and have my way with him. Lord, now I'm thinking like Wint.

"Mek sure you come, matter a fact mi a come fi you bout one, how dhat sound?" he asks with a cocky grin plastered on his face.

"See you at two, Mr I don't know the meaning of no," I reply with a shy smile then turn and walk past him real close because I want to inhale his scent. I have to leave because if I stand there one more second talking; the tension building up would surely show.

I hear the gate shut, so I go back outside. I run the routine with my little people, I cut class early today because they are already on point. I got to say these girls' rhythm out here on point they pick things up quicker than the dancers back home. I love it.

I have Surprise on my mind, and I've promised to call her back once I finish class. I call the Johnson's and have a chat about all the calls Surprise is making. They are aware since she keeps nagging them about when I will be back. They are very concerned with her behaviour and obsession with me. So, I offer a solution, and they agree. I know I need to talk to Storm and Winter about this one, but it's something that I need to do, to soothe something that's been nagging at my soul and heartstring ever since I met her.

Remembering what I promised Winter, I go to her first and tell her my plans, and she smiles and tells me she knew I would do something like that, and that she approves of my decision. I tell her about tonight, and she agrees to come along with me. I go back in and pack an overnight bag and sort things out. I go to Storm's room to search for him and let him in on my little plan, but he is in a deep sleep. He'll be awake soon because we have plans to take Nana Bird to dinner, plus tonight's the night nana will be spending her first night at his place. We are trying to get her out of this place and move her in at his place, it's so much nicer and quieter. Much more peaceful. But she complains about dying alone up there by herself, she's driving everyone nuts with all this dying talk. My grandmother is the strongest person I know, and I'm not ready for her to leave this God-forsaken Earth yet. So, if that means my black ass has to stay here and take care of her, then so be. I can't believe Winter is still over there talking to Parker. She looks so smitten with him, and I remember when we were younger, she couldn't stand his ass. Always drooling over me like I am cake.

I jump in my new favourite new pastime, the outdoor shower. I especially love it when it rains; it's like showering under God's blessings, being cleansed by the Lord himself. I could live under this shower. Once I get out, I'd get dressed in my canary yellow pants suit, with gold accessories. I bunch up my hair and bring it forward, so it drops on my forehead and pull a strand down on each side. I leave and go to get Nana ready. It seems like I'm the only one who remembers about this meal. I grab my phone standing on the veranda and dial Winter, and she turns around, staring at me and answers.

"Dinner with Nana. Remember? Leave that boy alone and come on," I tell her.

"Ok, I'm coming, two minutes."

"Hurry up please, anyway he probably thinks you're me so leave that boy alone," I tease.

"Shut up!" she yells across the road, and I laugh at her.

I go inside to wake Storm because it's time he got up; this boy seems to be sleeping for England. Wint's right; we need to keep an eye on him closely, cancer will not have him. When both his kidneys failed when we were kids, me and Wint gave him one of ours each so he has two and we both have one, but it was worth it to have him in our lives and we will do anything to keep him here. I knock on his door and let myself in. He's laid out in front of the fan snoring like a pig. He must be drained because that's the only time he sleeps like this. I jump on the bed, jerking it and he wakes up startled and grabs for his gun which is under his pillow. This is the second time I have seen him with a gun, looking all crazy eyes.

"I won't even ask. Get up, it's time to go for dinner," I tell him and leave him with a strange look in his eyes.

What have they turned my brother into? I remember him coming back from one of his trips here and then enrolling all three of us into classes in how to handle a gun. We never questioned it, and now I'm thinking maybe we should have. I go out to help my grandmother up out of her chair. I choose something cute for her to wear for our meal. I sit outside, waiting for everyone to sort themselves out for the night.

I, on the other hand, am in total contemplation over little Surprise and what will be best for her. I call her and make sure she's doing ok. She always puts a smile on my face. She sings me a little song and tells me how she did in school. She also tells me that the teacher has been asking about her Auntie Autumn, so I make a mental note to contact the school and find out why she is questioning the child. Mama always told us if teachers or police ask you anything tell them to contact your lawyer or her, so I plan on telling her the same. Nosy little bitch questioning a 5- year- old. I hang up with Surprise and grab my laptop.

I want to check out things back home. I've been leaving that up to Storm lately. It seems he's having a stressful time because he keeps complaining that he's stressed out by us. We all know who the cause of his stress is, he only gets miserable when Sunshine and he are having their little lovers quarrel. I check on the spend account first for all stores including the new spot Winter acquired in New York. It seems the turnover is doing really well. Ms Kerry seems to be managing things well. But damn Wint spent a tonne while she was in New York. Why the hell did she buy a car? I need to remind Storm to give up that home in Manchester, and I'm sure we don't need the apartment in London since we have no plans on moving there. Either that, or rent it for a profit because with all this spending this quarter alone, I know we put a dent in our finances.

I check our stock options, and they seem to be climbing which is always a positive for us. Going into stocks and bonds is the smartest idea Storm ever had. He took a quick course on the subject and started building our financial portfolio when he was fifteen. He brought some stocks that went through the roof. We make more money than we can count zeros. This nigga's been lucky three times with that shit, now. I swear he must have some insider trading secrets because thanks to him, we never have to worry about anything. When we ask him how he did it, he always says the same thing. Mama told him in a dream. I can hear my grandmother calling for me, so I close the laptop and go to attend to her. As I enter my grandmother's room, Storm is coming out of the bathroom.

"Hurry up," I tell him, and he just ignores me. "Yeah Nana, how can I help?" I ask her.

"Pass that over deh soh, inna dha blue bag deh?" she asks, but I can't see any blue bags, I approach the area she is pointing to, but I still can't see what she's talking about.

"Nana, I don't see any blue bag," I tell her.

"See the bag deh mi a look pon?" I look at her with a side glance.

"You mean this?" I ask, picking up a small clear pouch.

"Yes," she replies.

There is something wrong with Jamaicans'. Mama used to do the same thing to us, send us for something with the wrong description and expect us to figure out that shit for ourselves, calling it common sense. I swear they are all born with capital sense; since we have to have all the common sense to figure out whatever they want from us.

"Nana, this is not a blue bag," I tell her and shake my head.

I hand her the item. She opens it and takes out her pearl necklace and earrings. I help her put them on. She's a breath of fresh air, my Nana, she's the kindest person next to Winter I know, and beautiful too, I see where we get our distinct features from.

"Them pickney ready?" she asks as I stand staring at her with a smile and heart full with joy.

"I'm not sure, I'll check," I tell her and leave the room to check on the whereabouts of my siblings.

Storm's taming his lion's mane, and Wint's dragging on her jeans. I report back to my grandmother, letting her know we will be leaving in 15 minutes. She tells me to help her to her chair and to close all the windows and turn off the AC and grab her overnight bag. She will be staying at Storm's until her birthday in 2 days, and I can't wait. Miss Harrison let the cat out the bag, a smart mouth church sister who can't keep it shut, told her about the surprise party, but we still want her to relax and not do a thing. The best way is for her to leave, so she can't bully anyone around and tell us how to throw her a party, or better yet not to throw a party is her new favourite.

Finally, everyone's ready, we can leave. Teach me to be on time again, with a family like mine. We hit up Usain Bolt's Restaurant uptown, Kingston Tracks and Records. It is quiet and intimate with all the low lights and lovers in the place. I love the table décor. It has different board games painted on it. I think it is very clever. We order and talk about everything, and as usual, Nana gives us the most jokes. She speaks of mom, and we listen intently. Her stories about mom always seem to grab our undivided attention. She tells us about her days as a young woman, Nana was a boss. A bad bitch. She also tells us that her actions from the past made her the way she is, now she is making up for lost time. She feeds those who need it and shelters the homeless. These chips Usain's serving in here are the best with this sauce. I mean, I need more to take home with me. I place an order to go.

On our way out I tell Storm that I will be leaving tomorrow, and I'll be back in time for Nana's party, and he agrees with my decision. He kisses me and tells me good luck. But tonight, I'm looking forward to this all-white party, and since Nana's staying at Storm's he's going to have to stay with her. We drop him off at his house first and make our way back to Nana's house. We get back around 10:30 p.m. I tell Wint about Mr Moses, and she tells me all about Parker. She invited him to roll with us. We even decide to play our switch on them, to see if they notice and tell us apart. We're both excited about the upcoming party tonight. To be honest, I can't wait to see my Prophet again, especially since I haven't connected with anyone since Darius. It's about time I find a new interest.

We find the perfect white outfits that complement our curves and individual shapes. I set my alarm for 12:30 a.m. We sit around and talk and laugh about all the wild schemes we've come up with over the years. We even call Ms Kerry on Skype and catch up on what's happening with her since Wint left.

Not Even The Wife
At Home With The Teeny Tiny Can Do It Like Me.

Winter

Today is a great day, I mean even Autumn met someone who she wants to devour. I can't wait to meet him the way she is talking about him and Parker is absolutely mesmerizing. We talk all day and drink in the local bar until we make our way back to the house. Our weekly dinner date with our grandmother is one I look forward to every week. As I sit here with my sister enjoying each other's company again, I reflect on the stories of my beloved mother. I miss her with the mention of her name. Or every time I look in the mirror or at Autumn. We look so much like our mother. That's why it is so hard for me to forgive her for the sin she committed because it's like our mother was returning back to the asshole who gave up on her for his so-called real family. She's always told us never to play second in anyone's life, so why she would want that from a father who never cared for us is still baffling.

Auto's alarm alerts us to the time, letting us know that it's time to start getting ready. I am beginning to feel sleepy, but the thought of seeing Parker again, gives me the motivation needed to get myself together. I quickly call him, letting him know that I am getting ready so he can start getting ready too. I wake him from his slumber. We talk while we get dressed, and Autumn mocks us.

"Wear something just for me," he tells me.

"Like what?" I ask.

"Something to make everyone jealous of me because I have you on my arm," he says.

"That could be anything because it won't matter, they still gonna be jealous," I tell him.

"I was born as a triple threat. I was born with the Boom, Bang, Kahpow!" I tell him and Auto and I laugh.

"You're hilarious, you know that" he states.

"I know" I smile and blush at the simple compliment.

"So, what are you going to wear to make the ladies envy me, more than they do already?" I ask in a flirtatious tone.

"You sure they not just scared of you, the way you knocking people out with bats like you're a baseball player," he chuckles.

I am not impressed, to be honest, I want to forget that day. It isn't my proudest moment even though it was a good day because it brought my sister and me back together. We hear a knock at the door, and chatter outside. I cover up and go to answer the door, I check the security cameras first before opening up because it's the middle of the night. I'm not expecting anyone, and the only person I am expecting is on the other end of the phone getting dressed.

"Hey someone's at the door, hold up," I tell him.

"Ok, I'm going to jump in the shower I'll be over in about 20 minutes," he tells me, and I am disappointed he's hanging up. "Sure, you don't want to come wash my back," he asks before I hang up and my smile returns.

"Get dressed, see you in a bit," I say then hang up the phone.

I see a familiar face on the security system and one I don't recognise. I open the door to address the two gentlemen on my doorstep.

"Hey Skinny, Storms not here," I cut to the chase because I have nothing for neither of these two.

"I know, I saw him come in and thought I'll check out wah gwarn you zimme. But a good youth still. A him keep the little party up the road, unno ago tonight," he tells me.

"Oh, ok," the stranger is sexy as hell though in his all white. I mean he looks bad to the one but more like one of those gangsters you see on TV, who's the bad guy, but you can't help but fall in love with him anyway. I'm digging his style and his whole stance. I can't help but slightly bite on my bottom lip.

"Hey, Pretty Lady. Are you ready?" he asks, and I look at him with a confused look before I realise, he thinks I am Autumn. Damn, he failed already, but they only met today, so I'm going to give him a second chance.

"I'm sorry baby, wrong one. Don't worry, we get that a lot, just don't do it again. I'll get her for you," I tell him and excuse myself and close the door behind me and go in to fetch Autumn.

"Your man is at the door and OMG I want to eat him up, he is fire. Now does he have a twin?" I joke.

"Already? I told him two. What's he doing here so early?"

We both run to the security camera and spy on him standing outside. I throw my towel at her and tell her to wrap it around her to go talk to him. She does and I follow behind her because I want another peek at the walking sex in the flesh. I stand behind the door, making faces and sexual motions at Auto; she tries to keep a straight face but fails terribly. I listen to them flirt with each other. He leaves with a promise to return, but she declines and tells him she'll just meet him there. She closes the door, and I can't hold in the laughter.

"I want the details on that one. For once in your life Autumn double strap that nigga up and ride it into the sunrise and then come give me every single detail."

"No. there's something wrong with you, you know that," she says.

"I am who I am; besides he's already into you. So, I can't get a touch, so I'm counting on you, to fuck the shit out of that island sweetness, show him what we are made of," I tell her.

"What are we made of huh, exactly what is it that we are made of," she asks.

"Girl you are Autumn, turn that gangster into a bitch, like autumn changes summer into its bitch. Changing the leaves on a tree from green to red or orange. It's what autumn does? You make changes."

She laughs, "Parker was right, you're hilarious," she says.

"Well, you better do something, and get yourself some of the island's best products."

I put my shorts on and thigh-high gold gator boots with the gun heels. I swear these are my favourite heels of all time; I had them specially made for Auto and me. Tonight, we are out to kill it, so it's only fitting we wear them. She wears her white shorts with a matching halter neck top. It shows her perfect midsection. I envy my sisters body. I mean we are built the same, but she has the flare about her that's undeniable. The only thing different about us is our matching tattoos. She has my name and vice versa. I have Storm and Autumn inked under my left breast, with a cute little rose and heart. My phone alerts me to a call from Parker saying he's outside. I am pretty excited; I feel like a child on a Sunday when the ice cream truck comes around. I sashay to the door and grab the handle and fling it open. He stands at the door in his straight white fitted jeans and a white vest top with a gold Versace belt and a simple link gold chain and bracelet to match. He looks like a well-groomed Will Smith.

"So how did I do? You think they're gonna be jealous," he asks with a smirk on his face.

"If they not, I am," I tell him.

"And why are you jealous?"

"I want to be the one to be plastered all over you, instead of those clothes," I flirt with him.

"Well that can be arranged," he replies, pulling me closer to him. I lose my balance a little, but he holds me up tightly. Autumn comes out, alerting us that we aren't alone.

"Fuck later, it is time to party, and you are not leaving me tonight. Let's go," she informs us. I giggle at my sister; she is so rude.

"Hey Parker, good to see you grew into them teeth and I see you put some muscles on them scrawny bones of yours," she spits.

"And I see you haven't changed at all, still looking beautiful and sexy as ever," he compliments.

"Clearly I have because you no longer hunting me, you caught yourself a cold Winter," she says, and I open my eyes wide.

"Shut up and close up and leave him alone," I tell her and walk towards the car,grabbing Parker's hand.

"When we were children, I did childish things, and now I'm grown, I can handle intense, harsh weather, not so easily sick. So, the winter weather doesn't bother me. I don't have to settle for autumn weather only." He retorts.

"Hmmm, we'll see. Just take care of my Winter," she tells him with a stern look.

What's her problem? She closes the gate behind us, and jumps in the passenger seat, Skinny and Turner are standing outside waiting for us. They seem to be our shadow as of late. Skinny has a thing for Auto, so we just indulge him. Everyone crams in the Navigator. I sit on

Parker's lap, which I can't complain about, his legs are perfectly toned and muscular, and I can feel his third leg making an appearance. The drive to the party is fairly quick.

I swear I love Jamaica there's always a party around every corner or just over the other town. I'm going to make this my second home away from home. We park up. Skinny walks in front, and Turner seems to be lingering in the back. Parker's glued to my side as we walk into the party.

I spot one of the dumb bitches that we scrapped with, but I've already decided she's irrelevant and couldn't care less because her looks can't hurt me at all. I guess Autumn saw her too because she turns to look at me and nod her head. We smile at each other. I take up a spot by a wall, and everyone comes up by me. They are playing some rocking old school classic RnB, and I start grinding on Parker. In unison, he grabs my waist and pulls me in closer, and we rock the night away. Autumn takes up post in front of me swaying to the rhythm of the music; as usual, she has all the attention of the crowd when she dances. Her little friend comes over and drops off a bottle of Henny and a bucket of ice. I already like him. I mean he doesn't say a word just drops it at our feet and leaves which is a little rude, he best not fuck with her tonight. I don't care who he thinks he is. She turns and looks at me, and I answer her unspoken question with a shrug of the shoulders.

I call for Skinny's attention and ask him about the dude that just put the drinks down next to us, and he gives me the update on him. Apparently, he is a boss from across the way. The area leader for the bitches we just fucked up last week.

My next question then is, "Why the fuck we here?"

He tells me not to worry, he's cool he isn't really into all this battling shit he's all about the peace, but he has a high body count. He hasn't sent any threat or spoken up about that shit. But I'm on high alert. I also know Auto's feeling a little hurt about the move he just made. I ease off Parker and step forward and place my arm around her waist and tell her that I'm thirsty. She smiles because I know my sister, isn't going to drink that shit he just dropped at her feet like a fucking butler. I hold her hand and we stroll swaying our hips in unison over to the bar and wait patiently for our turn. We can feel the entire party's eyes on our asses. It's something we always do when we want to prove a point to niggas and bitches alike. Pretty boy comes over like a true boss as we knew he would and leans on the bar in front of us.

"Something me can get for you pretty ladies, other than a dance?" he says, trying to be cute.

Autumn squeezes my hand, and I squeeze back because the aura he's giving off is sending mixed fucking signals to my body too and I know she feels it.

"No, thank you. We are just waiting to be served," she speaks up, and he just smiles at her. Even his smile is a turn on.

"Well I can serve you, what would you like?"

"Fine, a bottle of Remy or Henny, and six Boom and a bottle of white rum... aaaaaaah, and six Magnum," she replies, and his eyebrows raise.

"Unno love fi drink, what happen to the drink me just gi unno?" he asks.

"Oh, was that for us? Didn't know. No one told me," she retorts she's on fire today.

"No not fi us, for you," he replies.

"And exactly how am I supposed to know that it was for me? You didn't say a word," she says.

"I told you, you too pretty to be so arrogant, but you sexy nuh fuck widd it," he tells her.

"Excuse me I would like to place my order now please," she says and turns to face the bartender, and he laughs at her attitude. One of the bartenders comes over to serve Autumn.

"Move from yah soh. You see me a talk and come a pose," he turns to the bartender, and he moves quickly.

"Fine, I'm sorry I was busy, neva wah disrespect, I will bring you your order," he tells her and strokes her face.

Yow, I swear my sister should have been called frozen because that girl doesn't even crack a smile or anything, absolutely no emotion. But she's squeezing the hell outta my damn hand.

"So, you going introduce me to you family?" he asks with a smile from God himself.

"This is Sexy lady," she tells him, and I can't help but laugh, what the hell's that.

"Oh, so Pretty Lady and Sexy Lady. Alright, I like it," he says.

"Yeah," she says and raises her left eyebrow.

"Hello, Sexy lady, mi name Prophet."

"I know who you are, my question is, what do you want from us?" I ask sceptical of him.

"Weh you mean?"

"I mean, I know who you are, and you know who we are, and as a leader, if you are looking for some retaliation, let us know now. I saw you and those girls we busted up, and you've never come by the house before; so, what do you want?" I ask with a stern look and tone, and Auto looks at me with a surprised look in her eye.

"No, big man nuh get involved in a gyal thing. Plus, I'm kind of scared of you chicks I tried pulling you off that dude, and unno nearly mash up my raas, no worry you self, mi and you bredda and grandmother have an understanding. No baddi round here caah touch unno again, so you accept my apology?" he asks.

"Didn't know you were apologising," Auto tells him.

"Well I am. Especially to you since I want to get to know the only woman who evva lick me and get weh wid it," he smirks.

"What do you want, some kind of payback?" Auto asks.

"No, just get to know you better, like I say I like what I see. And I want to know more. So, can I get a dance, or you plan fi vex wid me fi di ole night?" he asks.

"Haven't made up my mind yet. Let's go," she tells him and grabs my arm and walks off swaying her ass that sexy way we do.

He stands at the bar, watching her ass move from side to side as he shakes his head and smiles.

"Do you trust him?" I ask her.

"Not sure yet, but I think he's too damn charming for my liking," she says.

"I know that he was getting to you because he was getting to me and he wasn't even talking to me," I tell her.

I spot our so-called cousin, the officer, and I go to say hey and introduce him to Autumn. I ask him where the hell he is, he just tells me, working. I bring him over to the rest of the clique. He pounds fists with everyone, and I give him a drink.

"A soh unno a roll family?" he asks.

"Yep, that's how we do it every day, if you came round more often you would know. So, you are coming to Nana Bird's party, or you going to be M.I.A again?"

He laughs and tells me, yeah, but I just give him a fake laugh.

"Well let's party, and we can get to know each other tomorrow, and you better come by. I know Storm can do with some male company from the family side."

"Yeah man, I promise" he replies.

I get back to grinding on delicious Parker.

God Bless A Woman Who Can Hold Her Own

Autumn

I know there's something wrong with this man, why does he have to be the leader of an area. Fuck. He seems sincere with his words. I don't even remember him from the other day, then again, I kind of blacked out during the fight. I just know anyone who doesn't look like me is going to get knocked down. He keeps staring at me from the corner of his eye, I guess I can now see how busy he is, and everyone keeps stopping him to talk or pound fists. I can see he has a lot of respect around here. He brings me the order I made. This time he addresses me and plants his feet permanently in front me blocking my vision of the crowd. A smile spreads across his face, as he talks about how he won't move till I forgive him. Skinny keeps screwing up his face as usual when I dance or speak with other men, but I don't do skinny men who follow behind my brother. Every now and then he'll have to go deal with something or other, but he returns and takes up his place behind me. He doesn't really dance much, but I guess that's just him, but I don't mind. Because I am a one-woman show when it comes to dancing anyway.

In the early hours, the party picks up, and all dancers march out to the middle and do their thing, including me. I do a ballerina spin, and the DJ stops the track and wipes the sweat from his forehead and screams and pulls up and tells me to do that again. One thing I see that I can't wait to learn is this girl's waistline which does the vibration whine, which is amazing. Winter is still crushed up with Parker. This song comes on, and a young dude who is dancing with everyone comes up to me and picks me up. I grab him around the neck, ready to do the damn thing, but then he suddenly puts me down and when I look behind me at what he is staring at my eyes connect with Prophet. I shake my head and think coward. I walk off to the house that everyone seems to be using to go to the bathroom. Before going, I grab Wint because it's time to swap and see what these idiots are really about. Since he wants to block my show.

I switch tops with her and pull my hair out of the bun I'd placed in earlier. I reapply my lipstick and she does hers. I give her the extra lollipop I had, and we head back out to see who will notice. I go to Parker, and she goes to the Prophet. I stand in front of Parker, and he grabs me from behind, and I grind on him like Wint has been doing. Damn his shit is rock hard. Parker keeps talking some nasty shit in my ear, and I can't help but laugh at his dumb ass. I see Wint's enjoying her little session with Moses and I am getting jealous of them.

"You're quiet," Parker states.

"Am I? I'm just enjoying myself, trying to enjoy our time," I tell him in a low whisper.

"Oh, so why are you hanging with me instead of over there dancing with your own? You've hardly spent any time with yours but you over here with me," he says.

"What do you mean?" I ask.

"Well, I know you are not Winter," to my surprise. I guess Wint made an impression on him after all, after just a couple hours. I wonder how Wints is doing.

"Busted. What gave it away?" I ask because I need to know.

"Well your movement differs to your sister, and plus you smell different. Plus that beauty mark you two share is on the opposite side. I noticed that from my earlier years of being obsessed with you. Unfortunately, Autumn doesn't do it for me like Winter does." he tells me, and I smile and kiss him on the cheek.

I leave him holding up the wall and go over to my Prophet and place my arm on him and ask Wint, "You done groping on my sexy beast?"

He turns on and pushes his face closer to mine and pecks me on the lips and asks, "You done play games?" he grins.

I smile and tell Wint to bounce. Henny and Magnum are working and sending entirely wrong signals down south. I need to remember to stop with the Magnums because it fucks a sister up.

"Oh yeah, he passed too," I tell my sister, and she squeals.

My sister is like a child sometimes. I wrap my hands around his neck and rest my head on his shoulders and grind on him the entire morning.

These people sure do know how to party till the sun comes up, and they're talking about the party just getting started. I have less than 38 hours to do what I have to do and get back in time for Nana's birthday party. I can't wait till she sees my present for her. I sway with my Prophet till the sun comes up. I am getting tired, and my feet are throbbing from the pressure I have put them under. I release him and peck him on the cheeks and tell him goodbye. He holds me in place and tells me he will walk with me to the house. I smile and agree. I tell everyone that I am ready, and they all nod in approval. Everyone goes to the car, but I decide to walk with Prophet. Wint jumps on Parker's back, and he carries her off to the Navigator. I'm happy for my sister.

"I'll be there in a sec," I tell her, and she just smiles and asks if I am ok. I tell her yeah and warn her to go straight home, and she sticks her tongue out at me, and I repeat the action towards her.

"I will walk with you," Skinny offers.

"No, she good, mi will mek sure she reach round," Prophet tells him.

"No disrespect boss, but I just follow orders you zimme?" he replies. STORM I scream in my head.

We walk in silence for a while, but my heels are killing my feet, so I stop and take them off. "Don't judge." I look up at Prophet and tell him.

He just laughs at my pain and replies, "Never. So weh you a do later?"

"Getting on a flight in four hours," I tell him.

"You a leff me already?" he looks at me with a slight sadness.

"Ah, why are you gonna miss me?" I stand up with my heels in hand and I wish I had my sandals on. The road surface in Jamaica is not good. He just shakes his head because he can see my discomfort.

"Well I was hoping to get to know you a little more, thought we had a little more time," he tells me.

"Well you have four hours, what do you want to know?" I

ask. "Everything" he states.

"Everything, like what?" I ask.

He tells me to hop on his back. I decline so he scoops me up and I squeal in surprise, "Put me down, put me down!" Damn he is strong.

"You ago come pon mi back?" he asks.

"Yeah, yeah just put me down," I do as I am told and hand Skinny my heels and he shakes his head in disapproval. But I don't need his approval.

"Pretty Lady, oddah than that, weh you madda call you?" he asks.

"Autumn and she doesn't call me anymore. She's dead." I tell him.

"She gave you a pretty name to suit a pretty lady. Sorry to hear about your madda," he tells me.

"It's ok. I got my family," I tell him.

"How old are you?" he asks.

"Twenty-five, and you?"

"Me thirty, do you have to leave?" he whines.

"Yeah. Already booked my flight. Don't worry, you'll see me again soon. Why do you want to get to know me?" I quiz him.

"Why not?" We get to the house, and I can see Winter and Parker still chilling in the Navigator, I wave passed them and go inside. I invite Prophet in and tell Skinny to go home.

"Storm will be here in a little while, Autumn, so mi will just hang out yah soh till he comes," Skinny tells us.

"Whatever," I tell him and drag Prophet into the house, and he follows me into the bedroom.

"I need to get myself ready, I'm already packed, just got to shower and get dressed before my brother comes," I tell him.

"No problem, so when you come back a yard?" he asks curiously.

"Tomorrow," I tell him, and he smiles.

"So, a wah kind of trip that?" he asks.

"A little business and pleasure," I walk to the bathroom to take my clothes off, and he follows.

"What are you doing?" I ask. I am puzzled for a second.

"Mi caah wait," he replies and plants a wet kiss on me. My brain is saying no, but my body takes over and says fuck it.

He pulls me out of the bathroom back into the bedroom. I straddle him, and I can feel a gush falling from between my legs. He smiles and kisses me deeply. Before I know it both our clothes are on a pile on the floor. Pulling a condom from his pocket, he places it over his length. For the first time, I see what he is working with. Dear Lord, help me this morning, I think. That shit is thick and long, a deadly combination for a black man. I am starting to regret my decision to let him fuck me. Every muscle in my body freezes and twitches with excitement. I am here already, no turning back now; since my pussy won't calm the fuck down, I can feel it flooding between my legs from just the feel of his touch. He fiddles with my delicate flesh again; I moan with sheer delight as the familiar feeling from earlier runs down my spine. He guides me onto his shaft, slowly gliding me down. I close my eyes tight and hold on for dear life. He tells me to open my eyes and relax, reassuring me that he would never hurt me. So, I relax and grind on him, using the muscles in my pussy to massage his dick. As I move up and down in circles on him, I can feel the world disappearing and turning to heavenly bliss. The earth shatters between us, and I hear him call for God.

"Don't scream for God, he can't hear you," I moan in his ear, as I tighten the grip I have on his dick and squeeze the life out of it.

I am on such a high from the liquor I grind on that boy like I am going for gold. He squeezes me tight, and I can feel my leg shake, and I go into a daze. I can feel something take over me, I can't explain it, but he's making me weak. I come with a different rush of uncontrollable energy and I swear I hear something pop inside. But I just keep going. From the way he's moving his hips I know he's on the verge too. So I grip him tighter with my muscles and move up and down his length massaging the tip every chance I get. The last move I make is squeezing the head of his manhood with my womanhood and playing with his balls sending him over the edge. Winter taught me that little trick, she calls it squeezing the bitch out a man. We both stare at each other and laugh at the explosion that just went down between us. I climb off him and drag him to the shower, and as we quickly shower. He asks a bunch more questions. Then we get dressed, as we are heading outside, Storm is coming in.

"What the fuck are you doing in my house?" Storm asks rudely.

"He's with me, so be nice," I tell him and peck him on the cheek. But he isn't trying to hear what I'm saying.

"Big man, we'll talk later, yow I'm ready, you're going to be late." I can feel the tension between the men. I hate when he gets all big brother on us.

"Here, I'm ready" I give him my bag, and he leads the way to the Navigator. I see my grandmother has already taken up her spot on her chair.

"Good morning Nana," I tell her and kneel down beside her.

"Good morning Mama Bird, how are you doing?" Prophet asks.

"Mawning. Never know you did deh," she replies in disgust.

"I just followed your granddaughter home, mek sure she get home safely," he tells her.

"Awh that's nice," she replies with caution.

"Nana I got to go; I will be back tomorrow, yeah. I just got some business to sort in the country, ok, I'll be back," I tell her and kiss her cheek, and she says bye.

I go to say bye to Winter and leave. Prophet comes with us. Just the three of us driving to the airport sends a slight chill down my spine and not the good kind. So, on the journey to Norman Manley airport, I ask the question because clearly there's an elephant in the room.

"So, what's going on with you two?"

Storm looks at me through the mirror at the back and replies, "Nothing for you to worry about, just go do you and get back in time," he tells me.

"Should I be worried, because last night you told me you and my brother are cool?" I turn and address the man I am sitting next to.

Looking freshly fucked and happy, he lifts my chin and pecks me on the lips and tells me that it will be ok. He tells me that he took a chance and stepped over a mark he shouldn't have crossed. But he can't help himself since the first time he saw me. He's so sweet.

"Make it right with my brother otherwise we can't be together when I get back. I won't leave my brother hanging," I tell him and then whisper in his ear, "No matter how big your dick is," he laughs and tells me not to worry.

"We good Storm? Please don't be mad at me, I just got my sis back I don't want to lose my brother in the same instance."

He looks at me and tells me that will never happen. He parks up outside the airport, and he gets out and opens the door for me, and I get out. Prophet follows and grabs my bag, and I go in, to check-in while Storm goes to park the Nav. The queue isn't that long since it's a charter flight. I check in with an hour left. Storm comes in as I'm talking to the check-in girl and starts flirting with her. It's like she's

336 | S B R I N A

forgotten that she has a job to do. Even her colleague gets in on the action. Only my brother can be talking to one chick and get three without trying. I check in and call the Johnson's to let them know that I am on my way as planned. I give them the arrival time once more, and Mr Johnson assures me he will be there to greet me. I turn to my handsome devil, who it seems, won't be for much longer, if Storm continues.

With just half an hour to go, I figure it's time to go. I kiss my brother and tell him to be nice, and he reassures me that everything will be ok. He kisses me and tells me to hurry up and get back. I turn to Prophet and tell him to behave and go easy on my brother. He kisses me passionately and says goodbye and I disappear around the corner.

A trip to New York again, for my new Achilles Heel. I am starving, so I stop at one of the food vendors upstairs and get myself 2 boxes of patties for the kids, and I get 2 singles for myself with a D&G black grape soda. They call for my flight, and I go through to my seat in First Class. I sleep the entire way to JFK. I am still tired when we land, I can't wait until I get in and get some sleep before I have to pick up my little miss. I get to my check out point in departure, and the sassy American is giving me hassle about only being in the country for one day. I explain that I am only here to pick someone up and she isn't satisfied with my answer, so she takes me to a private room for a search. I am pissed, but who am I going to complain to. She does her little search of me and my luggage, and when she's satisfied with her interrogation, she lets me go. I am glad to get out of there. I know I'm going to be hassled again tomorrow. As soon as I see Mr and Mrs Johnson, I forget a little about the ordeal I just had to deal with. I hug the couple, and we drive to their home. I barely have any time to sleep because it's already after 3 p.m. I have so much to sort before I can even lay my head to rest. I call home to let them know that I am fine. I tell them what happened to me at the airport and I tell Storm to sort something out just in case I get into the same problem tomorrow.

We pick up my princess first, and she squeals just like Wint when she sees me. She runs up to me and squeezes me for dear life. I am happy too. I pick her up and kiss her face all over.

"I told you I'd be back for you."

She puts her arms around my neck and hugs me. I put her down and tell her I need to speak with her teacher. I go in and sit with the principal, and we talk about Surprise and her progress, and I tell her my plans to have her with me permanently. She asks if I am financially stable and all the usual mumbo jumbo. I also make her know not to question a baby about anything without her lawyer present. That's how financially stable I am. I write her a cheque for the school fund and tell her goodbye. Money is a language everybody understands no matter what country they come from. I come back out, and Surprise's face lights up again, but she still has the thumb in her mouth.

"We're gonna have to do something about that thumb of yours," I tell her.

I go for the rest of the babies, and they all run to give me a hug, it's a happy moment. We all go to see Kerry at work, even though she's so glad to see me, she thinks I am Winter at first. She shows me what she's up to and introduces me to the rest of the team. I make her clock out and take them all out to eat.

It's already after 7 p.m. when we finally get back to the Johnson's home, I'm beat, but everyone wants to show me what they are up to.

Surprise has been drawing nothing but pictures of her and me. Our flight leaves in the early hours of the morning, so I put her to bed, shower and go to lay with her so she can fall asleep and I can finally get some rest since we have to leave at 4 a.m. in the morning. It seems time waits for no man because I'm up at 3 a.m. waking my girl up and getting her ready. I tell her it's time for us to leave. I tell her to go say bye to her siblings, and she hugs everyone; her grandmother cries and hugs her while kissing her all over. I remind her that she'll be back soon, but we have to leave. Mr Johnson drops us off, and we say goodbye. They have a whole lot of questions, but I'm prepared with a letter signed by her legal guardian and a lawyer, giving me permission to take her out of the country. We get on the plane, and she's so excited. She's awake the entire journey looking at the clouds, she watches the in-flight movies while I sleep.

We land, and we are questioned by another bunch of rent-a-cops. Luckily, Storm contacts somebody and gets us through quickly. Once released, I stop off in the bathroom and get my princess dressed for her debut performance. I put her pretty silver sequin dress on with a white bow at the back. It has small little butterflies sticking out of it, with some cute silver shoes. She looks amazing. I put my matching dress on. It's white with a silver bow and cute silver Valentino heels to match. Unfortunately, we land in Montego Bay, so the journey's long as hell. She complains about the heat, so Storm turns on the air con for her. She sits up front with Uncle Storm and they sing together while I catch up on sleep. We stop for something to eat, and Storm spoils her buying her fruit from every damn vendor he passes making the journey even much longer.

"How's the party going?" I ask curiously about what's going on at home. It seems everything's in place, and Nana's bossing people around as usual. My phone buzzes with a text message from Darius. I am in no mood to deal with his, come back to me, please. The conversation goes like this:

Darius: *Hey, Sweetcheeks.*

Autumn: *What's up Dee?*

Darius: *You tell me, you don't call, don't text, can't hear from my baby. She on some save the dick for the next chick crap.*

Darius: *I mean, I already know what I got with you, and you want me to go be with your friend. I just can't understand it.*

Autumn: *Okay, we've had this conversation before, we can't be together because I refuse to be second place in any man's life, no matter how good his dick is.*

Darius: *So, you think my dick good?*

I can see where this is leading, Lord knows how I feel about the man and his thunder dick. I want so badly to be his and his only, but I can't shake the feeling of him and Peppa out of mind. There's nothing I want more than to make this man mine and mine only, but I know better, there will always be her between. Especially when she's released and where there is Trouble there is Peppa and Darius.

Autumn: *Your head game too but that's still not going to make me see things clearly.*

Darius: *Can't be that good if you're refusing to have any more of it.*

Autumn: Darius, it's clear to me and the world that your head over heels with my Peppa. Why would I play piggy in the middle with that, makes no sense? I know, and you know that your heart belongs to her.

Darius: No, I don't know. You are the only one who keeps talking all that shit in my ear. I've always been honest with you Autumn, I have never lied to you, you're the one who broke up with me, it was up to me we would have been married and had a family long ago. Yes, I had a crush on Peppa when we were kids. I'm a grown-ass man now Autumn, and even then, I never disrespected you in the slightest, never treated you less than you deserve. I never put a soul above you or gave you a reason to feel second to none. You're the one who got in your head that me and she got something going on. Like I told you, yes, I care for her and yes, I take care of my Godson because that's what I'm supposed to do, I like spending time with the little man. And I make no apologies for that. His daddy is a punk, and I'm not going to let him suffer because of it. Most of the time, little dudes with me and Trouble. So, I don't see the big deal.

Autumn: The big deal is that you are already playing happy families and still drooling over my best friend. Whether you made a move on her or not, your desire to have her has not gone away after all these years. When you see me you just want to fuck, when you see her you want to protect, consume, love and everything in between and I want that for myself. You see me, your dick gets hard, you see her, and the sun comes out for you. Trust me there's a difference.

Darius: If you haven't noticed, I love my dick, and anything my dick loves is always good for me.

Autumn: My point is NO we can't be together until you get Peppa out of your system. She would be an issue in our relationship, sometimes you have to let things go and see if it comes back.

Darius: Lol, dumb girl, you broke up with me and came back into my life like a bulldozer knocking shit down like a force of nature and I'm still trying to prove to you that we meant to be.

Autumn: Tell me if Peppa told you she wanted to fuck you or have your babies you wouldn't take her up on that.

Darius: Lady, what is wrong with you?

Autumn: Answer the question.

Darius: First of all, if I'm with you I won't need to fuck or have babies with anyone but you. You never had to worry about me in that way, wtf.

Autumn: Answer the question, Darius.

Darius: No, she would have no chance. Why would I fuck her when I could be with you?

Autumn: Now you just said you would never lie to me, be honest.

Darius: Autumn breeze, I'm a one-woman man when it comes to you, always have and always will be. I don't know what else to say to get you to gimme the chance to prove to you that I'm yours for 100%

Autumn: Do you still go to see her?

Darius: Yes, What? Do you want me to stop?

Autumn: NO.

Darius: *Then what?*

Autumn: *Do me a favour, say hi to my best friend and just tell her how you feel about her. I found someone for me out here. Peppa is the one for you, not me, you'll be doing yourself a big favour. Bye Darius.*

Darius: *Why the fuck you didn't say that in the first place instead of talking all that shit, I should be with Peppa bullcrap. Enjoy your new dick. Bye Autumn.*

When we get there, we can barely park. The place is rammed with people having fun, Nana has everyone out dancing and enjoying themselves. Storm leaves us in the car to go get little miss a microphone. Winter is wearing a mini version of my outfit, still, under Parker's spell, I see. Nana Bird is sitting on the throne that we rented for her. It's dressed in a champagne and gold colour cloth and painted gold. Fit for a queen. They bring the cake out filled with sparklers. That's our cue to make our entrance. Storm returns with the microphone and tells everyone to be quiet and hands it to Surprise and tells her to start singing. Everyone becomes quiet and settles down, I bend down and I tell her everything's ok . Just do it like we practised, and she takes the thumb out of her mouth and starts singing. Storm picks her up and walks her over to Nana while she's singing Happy Birthday to her, it's beautiful. Nana's so happy, I hug her, kiss her and tell her Happy Birthday. She tells me she's proud of my decision.

I Came; I Saw; I Conquered.

~~~

Storm

My phone seems to be blowing up every second, but it's never the call I want. It's either these incompetent dumb ass niggas or Rachelle. She's been going crazy since I cut her ass off. She made the mistake with what comes out of her mouth about my family and Sunshine. That's when I stopped answering questions and simply dip and leave her standing because she's going to make me do something, I told myself I would never do. I've been feeling a little better lately since I stopped fucking with this chick and since my sisters' stop acting crazy and pulled their shit together. I haven't called Sunshine in 3 weeks. After I stopped calling, she seems to start being interested. I am tired of her mind fucks and heartbreak. She sends a text letting me know she's ok and she needs to speak with me, but I ignore her just like she has been doing with me for the past 8 weeks. I still get daily updates from her security detail.

Today is my grandmother's eightieth birthday, and I am determined to have a great time for her. Everyone comes out to celebrate with my grandmother; we have jerk men, jerking chicken and pork for everyone and a local cook, cooking up something fierce. The music's been playing since 10 a.m. this morning. It's going to be an event to remember. People from near and far come out for her. The children are enjoying the small amusement rides that I acquired for the day and the bouncy castle, cotton candy, juice slush machine, popcorn and ice cream. There is a raffle for the children and then one for the adults. We give away household appliances such as a TV, mixer, stereo, and a 30- thousand- dollar shopping trip to Mega Mart. We make Nana hand out all the prizes. She's so happy; she wears the gift I got her from Tiffany's. It is a simple necklace with a canary yellow diamond. She curses me out for spending so much on a necklace but gives me a kiss anyway.

We have a poetry reading from the kids, and some even sing for her. But she's happiest when little Surprise surprises her with her Happy Birthday song just before we cut the 3- tier cake Winter had made. Only Winter would order a wedding cake and call it a birthday cake. When little Surprise sings for her, she knows exactly who's singing and gives her a huge hug and tells her thank you. She is well and truly surprised by that because she thought Autumn was in Montego bay on a business trip.

"This is my present for you Nana," the little baby tells her.

She replies. "And it's the best gift I will get all day,"

Surprise sticks by her side and helps her hand gifts out and blow out her candles. Autumn and her dancers do their performance, and everyone erupts in applause and cheers. Everything's going well. Wint has made a suit for her to wear and she looks like an angel. Wint's made an outfit for her and Auto too, but it's even cuter when they dress poor baby Surprise in the same outfit, now all four look similar. Today she's the centre of everyone's attention. We cater to her every need and make her feel special. Local singers sing and DJ their hearts out. Even our so-called cousin shows up and wishes her a Happy Birthday.

What the hell is she doing here? Now I told her ass to stay the hell away from me, is my first thought when I see Rachelle? This girl is starting to piss me off. Rachelle walks over to me and asks if I missed her. Did she hit her head?

"No, now leave me alone," I tell her and put my cup to my mouth and take a sip. She tries to touch my arm, but I pull away from her, "Don't touch me."

"Why are you treating mi soh a true you know seh mi love you doh," she states, am I supposed to be moved by her?

"Hear mi a say, move from in front a me. There are only four women I have ever loved in my life, and you were never one of them. So, move before mi haffi move you!" I speak angrily, and Winter senses my anger from across and flies over, and Autumn is hot on her tail.

"A bet mi flop you suck pussy show STARM."

I lean off the car and stand straight up to address her threat but before I can Winter head buts her and Autumn grabs her by the hair and is about to go to town on her, but I don't want to disturb my grandmother's birthday or upset her any more than needed. So, I tell them to let her go. Prophet dashes over once he notices the commotion, and I ask him to remove her before I release my sister on her.

"Ladies what have I told you about fighting?" I ask my 'knuckleheads kickass and ask questions later sisters.'

"Whatever, she doesn't get to disrespect you like that and get away with it," Autumn says.

"You know how long I've wanted to do that, but you were playing?" Winter chimes in.

I shake my head, "suppose you broke her nose, that's a hospital bill and possibly more unnecessary attention to our lives. Just think before you act, please. You two can't keep fighting everyone who pisses you off, you got a baby over there watching you!" I tell them.

"Well, you go tell Nana why I just had to head butt your walking Aids test. I need a pain killer," Wint says.

My two pains walk off giggling to themselves, and the crowd goes back to enjoying themselves. I go over to my grandmother and apologise for the disturbance. She smacks me on the hand and tells me to go get my phone. It's Sunshine trying to Skype me, but I ain't interested in her bullshit right now. I already plan to leave her behind. I plan to end the guard's contract and pay them in full. I send her to voicemail and place the phone beside my grandmother. I kiss her forehead and go back into the crowd.

I find Autumn and her new boo. I still don't know how I feel about her dealing with him. Especially since I just put him on the payroll. He wants peace and is about joining the community together. I'm all for peace in the community as long as my grandmother is safe. And since I can't find a lieutenant worthy of the post and I can trust him and his people, when it comes to certain things I find it is in both our best interests, so I make him my second. After my warrior princesses fought, we met and came to an agreement. We have been talking for the past 2 years but never really come to an agreement, but now a peace treaty is called to order, and I've sent out the same command to the local men. Some have issues with it, but I care zero because they all know the score of disobeying the rules. I have taken a backseat for too long with these men. They are getting complacent, so I show them what will happen if they disobey my orders with Biggie's display of consequence.

"Autumn, remember that you have a responsibility now and that you need to set an example" I point at little Surprise. I leave her with that mental realisation.

Little Surprise comes to get me for my grandmother, and I hold her small little hands and manoeuvre through the crowd. But the crowd is too engrossed in their own thing that it's seems that they have no recollection of the children around them. I pick her up and put her above my head with her thumb still in her mouth. I go over to the DJ booth and make an announcement telling all the adults to be aware of the children and tell the parents to keep their children close by. I don't want any accidents happening because I won't be happy if a child gets hurt. I make my way to my grandmother to see what she needs. She has the brightest smile on her face; I can't help but smile too. I take Surprise off my neck and put her down, and she goes to sit on my grandmothers' lap.

"Hey, Nana what's up you ok?" I ask.

"Yes baby, I just got the greatest news, mi did a tell you," she says.

"What are you talking about Nana?" I ask incredulously.

"I answered your phone, it never stops ringing. Sunshine, me mek she tell you. Gwan inna de house," I take the phone from her. The thought of Sunshine leaves a large lump forming in my throat. Nana finally figured out Skype.

Sunshine's face looks a little chubbier but still pretty. I go inside and lock the door for privacy. I walk to the back of the house to my room and close the door, trying to lock out the noise as much as I can. I sit on the bed and stare at the phone. I cut it off by accident and sit there, contemplating if I should call back. I don't want to be drawn back into Sunshine. I want to be free from her since she clearly will never want to be with me properly. I call her back on the laptop so I can see her properly when I tell her I ain't coming back home. She answers on the first ring. I see tears falling down her face, and my heart sinks.

"Does this mean you don't love me anymore?" she asks.

"No. just means I'm tired of fighting a losing battle."

"Who said you were losing? You are my best friend, and you know I love you," she cries.

"Yeah, but not in love with me, right?" I ask, with a straight face trying not to be affected by the tears streaming down her face.

"Don't say that. Who told you that?" she sniffles.

"Why are you crying? This is what you wanted, to be independent and left alone. I'm tired of loving you at a distance Monique. I want you for my wife to make you a part of my life permanently, but that's not something you want. So, I'm giving you what you wanted," I tell her straight faced.

"But I need you. I miss you; we miss you," she says.

"You don't need me, and you've proven that. I won't bother you anymore. Goodbye, my Sunshine," it shatters my heart to say these words to her.

"But I do love you, Storm, I am in love with you," she cries out.

"Sunshine, why are you doing this, what do you want, I've given you everything you wanted, why are you making it so hard and on this day of all days. It's my grandmother's birthday. Now I won't let you ruin my mood. Goodbye."

"I'm pregnant, and they are yours!" she screams out as I'm about to close the laptop down. I open the laptop instantly.

"What are you talking about, Sunshine? I know you, you're always on that damn pill," I say with a surprised look on my face.

"I'm pregnant," she repeats. I sit on the bed trying to put my thoughts together, "I found out just after you left, but the doctor said they weren't gonna make it, so I didn't see the point in making you come back if they weren't going to be here when you got here," she says interrupting my train of thought.

"That was not your choice to make Monique. I've been here sick as fuck and throwing up every morning, noon and night and it is because you're pregnant!" I shout.

"Don't be mad at me, please. I need you; our babies need you," she says through snot and tears.

"I am mad Sunshine. I should have been there for you, but you denied me that. Denied me of my child."

"I didn't know that they would survive this long, the doctors were concerned because their heartbeat was so weak, and I am constantly bleeding. I didn't want to worry you," she tries to explain. I sit and stare at the screen for at least 5 minutes before I have anything else to say.

"Have you thought about the question I asked you before I left?" I ask her.

"Yes, I already knew the answer before you left. I was just letting you get everything you needed out of your system before you made that commitment," she says.

"Lady. I love you. Which part of that don't you get? What the hell do I need to get out of my system? You are my damn system since the very first second I met your annoying stubborn ass," I snap at her, and she jumps. "Why do you gotta make everything so hard, Sunshine?"

"I'm sorry. Just stop yelling at me." she squeaks.

"I'm not yelling. Look at me. I'm happy. I'm coming home," I tell her.

"No, you don't have to do that, just come back next month like planned," she says.

"This isn't a debate. I'll be on the next flight out." I cut her off and drop the laptop on the bed and go back outside. I kiss my grandmother, and she holds my face and tells me that she is very proud of me and that my mother would have been proud too.

"See, now I can't die, yet I need to meet my grandbabies."

"Wait. Babies, she said babies?"

"Yes, baby twins, she never told you?" she asks.

"Yeah but I never acknowledged it because I was furious with her. Nana, I'm sorry, but I'm going to have to cut my trip short. I have to go to her."

I hug my grandmother again and go to find my sisters to give them the good news. I find them in the crowd dancing with Surprise in a circle. I smile and join in. I pick Surprise up and kiss her and tell her that she has brought me so much luck.

"Ladies. It's official, you're going to be aunties," I say, and they look at me with a smile.

"Wait who's pregnant, because if it's that bitch, we need a DNA test now," Winter says, and I laugh because I'm not sure which bitch she's referring to.

"No, it's Sunshine she's having my babies, twins." They both scream and jump all over me and hug me tightly. I release them and tell them that I'm leaving on the next flight because she's having some difficulties.

"We gotta celebrate tonight. I'm so happy for you, baby boy," Autumn tells me.

"I guess Nana was right, that's why you were so sick, huh?" Wint points out.

"I guess so, I gotta go make the arrangements," I tell them before I walk away smiling from ear to ear.

I get the number I need and call the airport and find out that the only direct flight is leaving on Monday. I am determined to be with

Sunshine and my unborn children. I ask the assistant to find me a connecting flight, no matter the cost or destination. They find one via Chicago with a five-hour stopover. I tell her to save the seat, and I make the payment. I pack everything I need including the 25- carat diamond blue Tanzanian engagement ring I bought for her from Tiffany's and put it in my jacket pocket. My flight is tomorrow from Montego Bay, so I have to drive down tonight after I put my grandmother to bed for the last time this year.

I call a quick meeting with all the men and tell them that I'll be gone, so their number one priority is the safety of my family and I don't want to have to return and crack skulls. I give the order to make sure that this peace plan goes ahead and they all nod their head. I keep Prophet behind for a one on one.

"If anything happens to my sister, there will be a 2- million- pound bounty on your head and I'm not talking Jamaican dollars. You will die a slow, painful death, understood. If she even gets a scratch, that's on your ass." He laughs and tells me not to worry. "I don't know why you are laughing, just make sure all we talked about comes to pass. These niggas aren't going to like it, so expect a little rebellion." He sees the seriousness within my eyes and straightens up quickly.

"Nuh worry about a thing, your family is in good hands," he replies. And I just pound his fist and leave him standing.

I don't want to leave them, but they will be there only for a few more weeks, and then they will be back with me safely. After the party ends and everyone leaves, the men help break down everything. I take my grandmother to bed and kiss her good night one last time. I promise to send her a ticket once the babies are born. The girls join me in my room, still hyped up about the good news. Everyone has a permanent smile planted on their faces. I'm overjoyed about Sunshine. I tell them about my plans to make Sunshine my wife, and that just makes them squeal even louder, waking pretty little Surprise.

Autumn goes to comfort her and me, and Wint just look at each other. "I hope she knows what she's doing," Wint says.

"Me too," I tell her.

She tells me about her little Trouble situation, and I tell her people can change if she'll let them and not everyone is her father. Sometimes she needs to let someone in and stop playing around.

"You can have your holiday adventure, but you know that you are going to have to face him sooner or later," I inform her.

"Make that later because you are not going to tell him I'm coming home. I'm not ready to settle down like you. Beside you saw how his phone kept going off when we were together," she reminds me, bringing a chuckle to my lips.

"That's true too, but he also said it was going off because he hasn't been paying them hens no attention since he hooked up with your wonderful ass."

"I don't know. I want to trust him, but something's telling me not too, it's too soon. I don't know, maybe I'm just being paranoid," she declares and I give her a daah look.

"Maybe. You know I got your back no matter what," I tell her and give her a hug. Autumn comes back and sits on the bed.

"Don't I get one of those?" she asks and we both turn and jump on her squashing her, as she tries to get from under us. We laugh and get off her.

"So big sis, what are you going to do about the young princess in there?" I ask.

"I was wrestling with the idea of having her around permanently; she fits right in at home with me, and I have to admit I missed her as much as she missed me. So, this is a trial run for me to see if I can handle it." she explains.

"You're thinking of adopting her, she already has a loving family," Wint points out.

"I know, but I just can't shake the feeling that I'm supposed to do this, for her and for me," she tells us sincerely.

"The two of you are going to be the death of me. Ok if that's what you want to do, I'm here for you anything you need, just let me know and I will do my best to make it happen" I tell her.

"You are not encouraging her, are you?" Wint asks.

"No, I'm giving her my support and praying it's what's right for her. If it makes them both happy, who are we to stand in front of their happiness?" I point out to Wint.

"Please Wint I need your support and approval on this one before I make any decision" Autumn begs.

"I support you; Auto just make sure it's what you want. She's not a purse you can return when she doesn't work out," Wint tells her.

"I know" she replies simply.

"Why's everyone trying to have babies around here?" Wint asks no one in particular. I laugh at her and tell her to grow up.

"So what time is your flight baby boy?" Autumn asks.

"Tomorrow morning, from Montego Bay, I'm driving down tonight," I tell them, and they both give me their puppy dog sad eyes.

"Which reminds me, do not, and I repeat do not take any of your conquests or side pieces to my manor. Don't even mention it and bring all my keys back with you" I tell them both.

"Oh, please we already know," they chime.

''And Autumn when you leave give your little man my Navigator keys. But until then nobody gets my baby. I'll take a taxi down tonight," I tell them.

"I'll drive you down baby boy, what time do you want to leave?" Autumn asks.

"I wanted to leave tonight, but sleep is drawing my eyelids so it would be good if you could drive me, that way I could go as soon as Nana wakes in the morning," I suggest.

"Good, I'll drive you down, and that will give me a chance to take my little miss to climb the falls like we did. You coming, Wint?"

"Yeah, why not. I do love the falls plus I get to see if our names are still there," Wint says excitedly.

I call Sunshine back on Skype and her and the girls talk most of the night. I can't get a word in they are talking about shopping already. Apparently, I have no say. I fall asleep before everyone, and when I wake, everyone is lying next to me. I go outside, and Nana is already up with the sun and sitting in her chair.

"Morning Nana. Have you eaten yet?"

"No, baby. What time are you leaving?" she asks.

"After I get you something to eat," I tell her.

"Don't worry about me, just go take care of your business and get back. I miss you when you are not here."

That makes me a little sad for leaving her. I never stay away from her for more than 6 months; I am always out here with her. She is my queen, my leader, my soul.

"You could come stay with us if you want, you don't have to stay here by yourself," I remind her.

"I'm never by myself boy, now go, your future awaits."

I kiss her and go to find her something to eat and wake my two annoyances. Little Princess Surprise comes out of her room, rubbing her eyes and sticks that thumb of hers right in her smelly little mouth, I shake my head and offer her something to eat.

"Why are you up at this hour young lady?"

"The birdies was making too much noise," she tells me.

"Yeah, they do that a lot around here, go brush your teeth and come get something to eat," I tell her and smile at her.

I wake up Autumn and tell her that Surprise is awake and it's almost time for me to go. She gets up and goes to Surprise and sorts herself out. Once I feed Nana, I jump in the shower for the quickest shower I've ever had. We all jump in the Navigator, and head to the other end of the island, for the airport. It's a 3 and a half-hour drive non-stop. The women leave me once I check in because I am late and have to rush and run immediately all the way to the gate for departure. The stop-over is the worst. Damn Chicago weather ain't no joke, I'm colder than a motherfucker. I meet a team of figure skaters on the flight, and they are all firm and slender, but my mind is strictly on my ray of Sunshine. I can't wait to be in her arms once again.

I get into Birmingham Airport, and my baby is waiting for me. I spot her before she ever sees me. I approach her with caution, but once she sees me, she hurries into my arms and kisses me passionately. I can't hide the joy I find in her. I get down on one knee and ask the question I've been dying to ask since the day I first met her in the middle of the street at the carnival. People stop and look on. She smiles and tears fill her eyes as she cries and says yes. I place the diamond on her finger and lift her off her feet with a kiss. Everyone claps and congratulates us.

Finally, life begins...

Epilogue
Storm & Sunshine Saga
LOVE AND WAR

~∿~

Sunshine

I have been waiting for the day, when the greatest love I've ever known figures out that I never wanted just a casual relationship with him, I wanted forever, forever and ten thousand tomorrows with him. I'll never forget the day he asked me to marry him 5 June, the perfect day in the year, next to my birthday and his and soon to be next to the date of our bundles of joy. The doctor says that I need bed rest with the amount of bleeding I've been through. All because of the damage that was done on the most horrific night of my life, the night I was raped.

Storm's number was the only one I could remember off the top of my head, and even though it'd been over a year and a half since we'd seen each other last; I was praying that he hadn't changed his number. By the grace of God, he came running in a heartbeat and never left my side since, even when I scream, shout and call him all the horrible names under the sun. He remains by my side, even if it's sometimes from a distance. That's how I know that he will always be there, no matter what for our new family, he will be there. And I can't wait to be Mrs Storm Valentine. I dare a bitch or bastard try and come between us with their petty fuckery. It's been over a month since he's been back and as usual, he's a perfect gentleman. I couldn't ask for anything more.

Even though he's smothering me most of the time and I have to get mad bat crazy for petty stupidness for him to give me some space and let me just breathe. I love my man, but sometimes I need to fart without him being there to inhale it. I love everything about him, even his obsessions because I learned to deal with his dumbass a long time ago, so it's expected, and I just wave his ass off now. After all, I'm learning not to swear so much because I'm about to become a mother. But if I have to, then I have to. Fuck it. There's only so much a bitch can take. Storm's everything a woman could ever want in a man, financial stability, security, and a man to fight for us. He has proven that time and time again. All women want is a man to prove to us that they were wrong and die trying to show that they will protect us and never hurt us, a man who needs our trust, a man who holds our emotions dearly and is delicate in all he does for us; a man who will take over, take charge and take care of us mind, body, soul and wallet, complete utter devotion. He wants to get married once his sister's return, but that ain't happening no way I am getting married, looking like an overstuff beached whale. It's just not happening. He's just going to have to wait. He's waited this long sure he can wait one more year.

As I lay here watching his bare chest move up and down, moving to his perfect rhythm, I have to give thanks and praise for the man that god sent to love me unconditionally. Examining his features carefully, I make a mental note of all his unique features imagining what our children will look like. Will they have his long thick eyelashes, his long bushy deep brown hair that turns a bit ginger in the summer, will they have his cute button nose with small freckles surrounding it. I want twin boys but anything I get I will love just as much. I brush the stray hair from his beautiful face, he's been talking about cutting his hair, but I'm in love with his lion's mane, so he's not allowed. I would have nothing to grab hold of when he puts it on me really good if he gets rid of it. In the past, I told him I need space because his love is so all-consuming and full-on, it takes over, and I lose myself in him; lose who I am. If you knew Storm, you know his confidence and presence sucks everything away from you. Sometimes I can't breathe, can't think, can't function because he's in the room, and when the rest of his siblings are around too, there's no room for anyone else's personality. You can't help but fall in love with him, with all his faults, especially those come fuck me silvery greenish, blueish eyes. Everything about him is perfect. Shifting in his sleep, he opens his eyes and turns and smiles at me. I love the fact that even if he turns his back in his sleep, he has to make sure he has one hand on me, holding me at all times.

"You ok?" He asks this question a million and one times a day, it gets annoying, but now I just ignore at least a thousand of them.

"Yeah. Just admiring the way you sleep."

"Well you supposed to be sleeping too, you need to rest. You heard what the doctor said."

"Well tell the doctor to calm these butterflies in my stomach."

He leans and kisses my small bump, and I smile at the touch.

"What can I do to put you to bed?"

I give him a knowing smile as I roll on top and straddle him and a thousand-watt smile caresses his face. He is definitely awake now at the thought of being inside me.

"Yeah, just be gentle," he licks his lips and says, "it's your show, I'm just following the leader," in a cocky but sweet way.

I can't help but bite my bottom lip as I felt his erection grow from beneath me instantly. I always love the way he's always ready for me no matter what, where, when or how, I can always count on him to stand to attention for me, like I was a commanding officer. He is a petty officer at my beck and call. I take hold of his manhood and massage it to full strength and place it at the entrance of my pink lotus flower and ease myself down his shaft. I can never go all the way down with him; I swear he's the true definition of a mandingo. As I clench all the muscles of my vaginal wall and make tiny circles with my hips, I lean in for him to devour my mouth with his sugar-lips. Boy, the man has the sweetest lips you will ever taste. With every kiss, tremors shoot up and down my spine and direct their way to my groin. The feel of his hands all over my body always sends me in a daze of complete sensual bliss. Being with him is like living on cloud 55, yes 55! He was utterly intoxicating.

I feel a gush of something unfamiliar run down my mid-section, it all feels different, I've been soaking wet before, but this time it is different. A shooting pain follows. I feel like my entire womb is falling out. I grab on tight to him, screaming out of pure agony. I feel like someone stabbed me several times down south. He sees the terrified look in my eyes because his motion became stiff, and a look of panic takes over his expression. I grab hold of my stomach and fuse over in pure distress.

"What's wrong?" he asks in a scared tone. We both look down, and there is nothing but blood covering both of us. It is like a scene from a horror movie. I have never seen anything like it or seen him move so fast.

About The Author
Sbrina

~

S brina, a mother of two sons was born in Jamaica and came to England when she was eleven years of age. She entered a reading competition organised by her local library and won, this is when her love of writing began.

   Follow **Sbrina_book** on Instagram

www.marciampublishing.com

Printed in Poland
by Amazon Fulfillment
Poland Sp. z o.o., Wrocław